92 Park Street · Adams, MA 01220
phone · 413 743-8345

** DID I READ THIS ALREADY? **

Place your initials or unique symbol in a square as a reminder to you that you have read this title.

R. WJF				

The
Last Summer
at Chelsea Beach

Center Point
Large Print

Also by Pam Jenoff and available from
Center Point Large Print:

The Ambassador's Daughter
The Winter Guest

**This Large Print Book carries the
Seal of Approval of N.A.V.H.**

The Last Summer at Chelsea Beach

Pam Jenoff

CENTER POINT LARGE PRINT
THORNDIKE, MAINE

35.

ISBN: 978-1-62899-696-8

Library of Congress Cataloging-in-Publication Data

Jenoff, Pam.
The last summer at Chelsea Beach / Pam Jenoff. —
Center Point Large Print edition.
pages cm
Summary: "In a story of heartbreak, hope, and second chances, a
young woman sets out to face the past and carve a new future for
herself in the midst of World War II"—Provided by publisher.
ISBN 978-1-62899-696-8 (library binding : alk. paper)
1. Large type books. I. Title.
PS3610.E562L37 2015
813'.6—dc23
                                                          2015021115

For my own brother, Jay.

Prologue

New Jersey
August 1944

I sense home before I can see it. Five miles out, the wet salt air enters my mouth and fills my lungs, and the cries of the gulls rise harshly to meet me. But it isn't until I round the final curve and the wide expanse of murky brown water springs into view that the lump in my chest grows and my eyes begin to burn.

"Damn you," I say aloud as I pull to the side of the road. "God damn you to hell."

Absecon Bay remains unmoved. Its calmness seems hypocrisy.

I shift Uncle Meyer's Buick into gear once more; the engine revs weakly. It is midafternoon and the sun glistens high above the water, the air late-summer warm. The smell of fresh lemon polish rises from the dashboard, mingling with the sea air and lingering cigar smoke. A station wagon passes in the opposite direction, laden with beach chairs and a barbecue grill. Despite the war, some things have not changed: the flight of the summer renters, dusting the sand off their sticky-fingered children and returning to normal life as Labor Day nears, is still the earliest sign of fall. Along the

Black Horse Pike on my way down the shore, the prices of peaches and cherries and other summer produce, plentiful even while other food is in short supply, have been slashed, preparing to give way to apples and gourds. Hand-painted signs tout end-of-season corn. Some of the drive-up stands that did a brisk business in hot dogs and root-beer floats all season have already closed.

I pull onto the road, passing signs that exhort me to watch the coast vigilantly for German ships and to buy war bonds. As I guide the car along the edge of the bay, high sea reeds rise from the marshes, obscuring my view of the water. Exhaling, I focus on the casual tangle of shops ahead. Everything had seemed so much bigger in my mind's eye. Now the houses, with their blackout curtains and flags, are miniature, like the ones Uncle Meyer built alongside his model railroad. The whole place could use a good coat of paint.

I begin to climb the gentle arc of the bridge. A narrow strip of water lined with docks and small boats comes into view. I startle, accidentally slamming on the brake and scarcely hearing the car horn that blares behind me.

I wipe my damp palms against my cotton skirt, which has become wrinkled during the drive. Then I press my foot against the accelerator and continue south, clenching the steering wheel, knuckles white. "Knock it off," I mutter aloud through gritted teeth, "or you'll never make it."

Which, as I think about it, does not seem like a half-bad idea.

Just before the Esso station marked with rationing notices, I take a right turn and then another. Then I turn left onto Sunset Avenue. The block which holds such weight in my memories is nothing more than a half dozen or so houses parallel to the bay, built decades earlier, their clapboard fronts scarred, like the lined face of an old woman, from the storms they have weathered. As I drive past each house, I rattle off mentally the people who had lived there: at the fourth house, kindly Mrs. Henderson, known as Aunt Molly to the kids, Joe and Louise Steiner at the fifth. Many of the neighbors are undoubtedly the same—except for the sixth house, which has been vacant since the day the Connallys drove out of my life forever.

I stare straight ahead, trying to focus on the road. But it is no use—even in broad daylight, I see the nightmare that I have lived so many times in my sleep: I am standing on a narrow, deserted strip of the boardwalk, looking out at the vast green-gray ocean. I watch as the tide comes in and the water level grows continually higher. A black wave rises like an enormous hand to twenty feet or more. The wall of water crashes down from above, knocking me to the ground and enveloping me completely. I fight, unable to stand or breathe, as the water fills my lungs and swallows me whole.

Suddenly my vision clears, the image gone as quickly as it came. I tell myself that it isn't real, that the past will not return. Why be afraid when there is nothing left to lose? But it is no use.

My nightmares have returned again, the surest sign that I am home.

PART ONE

One

Washington, DC
November 1943

I did not fight the umbrella which blew inside out as I stepped from the streetcar. Instead, I clung tighter to my nearly soaked cloche to hold it in place against the icy rain that slanted sideways across Pennsylvania Avenue. Navigating the slick pavement carefully, I swam through the mid-afternoon crowd, mostly women and a few men too old or broken for service, who were waiting in line at the Red Cross canteen truck for coffee, or making their way between government buildings and the makeshift tent offices that lined the Mall.

Brushing the raindrops from my overcoat, I slid under the awning that shielded the security booth outside the Department of State Building, pausing to fumble for my press pass. The guard eyed me incredulously as he scrutinized my credentials. Ignoring him, I gazed up at the White House, pale against the stormy gray clouds. Something moved on the roof above, the swivel of an anti-aircraft gun pointed upward. My heart skipped. Washington was a city occupied not just by the thousands who had come here to work, but by the army that defended it as though the

Germans might at any moment descend from the sky.

Lowering my eyes, I caught a wistful glimpse of my disheveled reflection in the window of the guard booth. I'd left the rooming house in good form to a sky that, if not sunny, had certainly not suggested this downpour. Arriving at the *Post*, I expected a day like most I'd had these past few months, typing stories from shorthand notes on a Remington at a desk barely wide enough to hold it, pressed close to a dozen other girls. I didn't mind; I needed work and I was grateful that my high school secretarial course had qualified me for it. Though it would have paid a few dollars more, I had dreaded the prospect of working as one of the government girls at the War Department. I couldn't bear to endlessly type letters telling families that their sons were not coming home, seeing Charlie's face in each of them.

During my first few months at the news bureau, the work had been quiet and predictable. But one afternoon nearly two weeks ago, a man with his sleeves rolled up had opened the door to the steno pool. "Italian?" he bellowed. A cloud of cigarette smoke appeared before him as he exhaled, making him seem a gray-haired dragon. The room fell silent. Chip Steeves, managing editor of the *Washington Post*, never came into the typing room. "My secretary is out and I need someone to call a translator." Impulsively, I raised my hand. Then I looked around. I was the only one and I started to lower it.

But Mr. Steeves was already weaving his way through the desks, descending upon me. "You can find me someone to translate Italian?" He spoke through the cigar stub clenched between his teeth.

"No." I looked at him squarely. "I can do it myself."

He eyed me for several seconds, his face a scowl. "Well, come on," he barked impatiently, as though I, and not he, had hesitated. I could feel the eyes of the other typists on me as I walked from the room.

"Montforte, isn't it?" he asked, surprising me as we entered his office. The desk was covered in piles of papers, the floor littered with dirty coffee cups.

"Yes." I cleared my throat. "Addie, that is Adelia."

He didn't introduce himself; he didn't need to. Chip Steeves was legendary as journalist and terror. "You're the girl who caught that mistake in the U-boat story." I straightened slightly. My job was only to type articles, not proofread them. I had seen an error in one of the stories, though, a date that I knew from my own reading was wrong. I had pointed it out to Mr. Steeves's secretary, who oversaw the typists. But I did not know that the message had been passed on—or that I had received credit. "That was good work. You speak Italian?"

"Yes. I was born in Trieste." Being foreign-born was not something that one announced loudly these days, and I'd worked hard to remove all trace of an accent. This might be the first time it was an asset.

He thrust out a pen as if he might hit me with it, and I fought the urge to cower. "Well, translate this, Adelia Montforte." I took the paper he offered and moved an overflowing ashtray from the nearest chair, then perched on it and scrawled the translation hurriedly. It was a cable about a skirmish that had taken place near Salerno, brief but with a few military terms I wasn't quite sure I'd gotten right.

When I finished, I handed it back to Mr. Steeves, who scanned the page. "This is good."

"I could do better with more time," I offered.

"Couldn't we all? But you don't botch the feel of it, like the real translators do."

After that, Mr. Steeves sent more translation work my way through his secretary. But he had not reappeared himself—until this morning. "Montforte," he hollered as he stuck his head into the steno pool, causing me to jump. I'd leapt up and grabbed my pen and pad, assuming it was another translation job. But when I started for the door of his office, he waved me away. "Be at the State Department this afternoon at three."

I stared at him blankly. "Me? But why?" He tossed me a press pass and disappeared into his office.

The guard handed back my pass now, along with a visitor's badge, which I pinned to the collar of my blouse. I stepped uncertainly into the massive lobby of the State Building, marveling at the high chandelier, better suited to a ballroom. But before I could take it all in, Mr. Steeves appeared, grabbing me by the arm. He led me unceremoniously past a marble staircase, down a corridor and into a room with a long oak conference table. "The deputy secretary has called a meeting with the press to talk about our coverage of our allies, making sure it doesn't hurt the war effort, that sort of thing."

"I don't understand. Isn't there something you need me to translate?"

He shook his head. "Nah, kid. My cub reporter's been called up so I need someone to help me cover the meeting. You were the best one for the job."

"The best one? I'm a typist. I can't possibly cover a story."

"Just take one of the chairs against the wall and take notes. And don't say anything," he instructed, then disappeared into a group of uniformed men clustered in the corner.

I took off my overcoat and folded it in the lap of my navy blue skirt, noticing as I sat down a run in my nylons. Then I tried to smooth the wrinkles from my pleated-front blouse. I was the only woman in the room, except for the one setting out coffee cups. The war might have brought women to work, Rosie the Riveter and all that, but in high-level Washington meetings like this, the seats at the table were still reserved for the men.

The door opened and a man I recognized from the papers as Undersecretary of State Edward Stettinius came in. "Be seated," he said, as the others came to the table. "I've only got a few minutes so I'll be brief. I've called you here to ask for your help in talking to the American people about the war." He launched into a discussion of a new initiative by the Office of War Information to work with the press on the way it would communicate information about the fighting.

I scribbled furiously. Though I frequently typed the shorthand notes of others, I had seldom taken dictation and I feared I would not be able to keep up with Secretary Stettinius's rapid English. But as I listened, I became absorbed by what he was saying. The relationship between newspapers and government had always seemed adversarial, one seeking information and the other holding it back. But he was speaking now of ways they could work together. "I'm happy to take your questions," he concluded a few minutes later.

A correspondent from the *Washington Star*

whom I did not recognize raised his hand, then spoke without waiting. "It sounds good on the surface—but isn't it something of a conflict of interest?" I had been wondering the same thing: Could the newspapers still maintain their independence and integrity while working with the government?

Secretary Stettinius offered a vague explanation of how it would all work without compromising the independence of the press.

"Surely you aren't suggesting we show you our stories before they go to press?" another reporter pressed. "That would be censorship."

"No, of course not," Secretary Stettinius replied, looking tugging at his collar. "We simply want to be a resource." Across the room, Mr. Steeves folded his arms, unconvinced. "My deputy will be in touch with each of you individually to discuss specifics," Secretary Stettinius promised, cutting the questions short. He rose, signaling that the meeting was over.

As the newsmen stood and chatted among themselves, I tried to catch Mr. Steeves's eye, but he was engrossed in conversation with a foreign correspondent. I made my way toward the door of the too-stuffy room, uncertain whether to wait for him or return to the bureau.

As I neared the massive foyer, a door across the hallway opened, letting loose a low din of chatter from another meeting. I started past. "Then we are agreed," a voice broke through the others, unexpectedly familiar. I stopped mid-step. "We'll meet again when we have the plans drawn up."

Charlie! My head swiveled in the direction from which the voice had come. It couldn't be. I craned my neck, trying once more to hear the voice. I had imagined him so many times since coming here, seen him in every uniformed soldier on the street corners. But I'd never heard his voice.

I stepped toward the door of the other room, not caring that I had no business being there as I scanned the crowd. "Oh!" I cried so loudly that a man in front of me turned to stare. I brought my hand to my mouth as Charlie's broad shoulders appeared above the others. Joy surged through me, making my head light. It really was him. But how? There was no reason on earth for him to be in Washington. He was meant to be off training somewhere or deployed, not standing in front of me, tall and glorious. Had he come for me? No, there was simply no way he could have known I was here—which was exactly how I had wanted it.

Anxiety rose, eclipsing my happiness, and the walls of the immense room seemed to grow close. I started to duck away, the idea of facing Charlie unfathomable. But even as I took a step toward the door, I turned back, drawn to him. He looked different to be sure, aged by all that had happened, with lines in places I hadn't remembered and a permanent sadness about the eyes.

His brown hair was cut short and it was thinner, too, without the thick, rich curls he had once had. He was still beautiful, though. My breath caught. That did not, could not, change what had happened. I had to leave. Now.

I stepped back toward the corridor, my ankle turning inward and causing me to stumble. As I struggled not to fall, I dropped my notebook, which clattered against the marble. Heads turned in my direction, seeming more annoyed than concerned. As the others resumed their conversations, Charlie stepped from the group and moved toward me in the hall, his face breaking. "Addie?" His tone was disbelieving. I froze, unable to move or speak as he drew close. He reached out, as if to touch me, but his hand foundered midair before falling to his side again. He leaned in to kiss my cheek and his familiar scent made the room wobble. I struggled not to turn and meet his lips with my own. "Addie." There it was in that single word, that voice which cut right through and connected with my insides as it had since the first time I heard it. "What are you doing here?" He didn't know any of it—that I had left Philadelphia, or how I had come to be here. Because he had gone first.

"I'm working for the *Post*." I watched his face for any sign of disbelief. But Charlie had never doubted me. "I never expected you to be in Washington," I added.

His face flinched slightly as though he had been slapped. "You aren't pleased to see me."

"Of course I am. It's just that I thought you were training." My words came out too quickly, piling on top of one another.

He fumbled with the hat, neatly folded in his hands. "I was, for almost a year. But now I'm here for some extra briefings." There was a strange undercurrent to his voice. A year had slipped through our fingers. How was that possible? Once it had seemed unthinkable to keep breathing without Charlie, but somehow the clock had kept ticking. I tried to imagine his days in between, all of the things he had done and seen since we'd last laid eyes on one another. But my mind was blank.

"Your hair," he blurted. I raised my hand to my temple, wincing at how tousled I was from the rain. "It's short." It was the bob, so different than last time he had seen me. "I mean, I like it." I couldn't tell if he was just being kind.

"How's your family?"

"Holding up as well as can be expected." He shrugged, helpless but not indifferent. "My folks are in Florida. Mom has thrown herself into the women's auxiliary." It sounded so much like Mrs. Connally that I had to smile. "Dad's Dad." Guilt at having left them flickered across his face. "It tore them apart, you know." Yes, I knew only too well. The Connallys lived in a place where their grief would always be as raw as the day it all happened, no matter how much time passed or how far away they moved. "They're together, but in a separate kind of a way. They know now," he added, and I wanted to ask if he meant about the army, or what had been between us, or both.

The question stuck in my throat. "And the boys?" I asked instead.

"Jack, well, he works at a plant in Port Richmond. He's taking night classes at Temple, though." Jack had been the real brain of the boys—he might have gone to an Ivy League school and practiced medicine as he once dreamed, but for money and circumstance. "He hasn't been called up yet, thank God. Mom couldn't bear to lose another son."

I swallowed. "And Liam?"

Charlie stared hard at the floor. "I'm not sure." But surely his parents knew about Liam's whereabouts, and whether or not he was okay. Or had they cut ties with him as well? My stomach tugged. I still hated Liam for what he had done, yet I could not help but worry.

Charlie and I watched one another, not speaking. We had talked about everyone, of course, except the one name we could not say. "How long will you be in town?" I asked, not sure what answer I was hoping to hear.

Before Charlie could reply, voices came from the conference room behind him. He looked over his shoulder. "There's another meeting. I'm going to have to go." A knife ripped through me at the idea that he might leave again just as quickly as he had appeared. "Addie, I want to talk to you. Meet me tonight?" he said suddenly. "The Old Ebbitt Grill at seven." So he did not want our chance reunion to end either.

I peered at him, trying to read the meaning behind his words. Were we merely two old friends, trying to catch up? No, it was still there, that hungry, yearning look in his eyes I had first seen the night on the dock. He wanted to pick up once more and return to that moment when we had stood on the edge of the world, gazing down at everything that lay before us. He wanted to make things whole again.

Something licked at my insides then, familiar like a forgotten dream: hope. Even after everything that had happened, Charlie still reached a place in me that made me believe things could be good again.

But something held me back. "I don't know." I was suddenly angry. Did he really think we could put all of those broken pieces back together and not see the cracks? Doubt thundered beneath my feet like a freight train and the ground began to sway. I had managed to make my way back from the place that nearly killed me and stand despite it all. I could not afford to let him in and risk going there again.

"Please, Addie. I'll wait for you." There was a

desperation about him I had only seen once before in my life. Before I could answer, the men spilled forth from the conference room, enveloping Charlie, and we were separated by a sea of suits and uniforms giving off the odor of cologne and cigarette smoke. I had not had the chance to answer.

Our eyes met and locked, his making a silent plea before he slipped from sight.

Two

Philadelphia
June 1941
Two years earlier

I struggled to stand in the crush of unwashed bodies that surged forward from the ship on all sides. Then I squeezed my way to the side of the dock, pressing back against a rotted wood railing that I hoped would hold. I lifted myself to the tips of my toes in Mamma's too-large shoes, struggling to see above the ocean of heads around me. Shoulders pushed close, blocking my view. I hoisted myself onto the rail, grasping it tightly so as not to fall, and scanned the sea of travelers. I wished that I might see the familiar face of one of the girls from steerage (not that they had been so friendly). But I recognized no one from the massive ocean liner, even after traveling on it for seven wretched, seasick days.

The travelers moved in small clumps, couples and families of three or four. Across the wharf, a woman flew into the arms of a man waiting for her, reunited. Everyone was carrying things, boxes and bags and children. But I was alone, my hands empty. Worry mixed with the hunger that had been gnawing at my stomach, growing to a burn. In her haste, Mamma had not given me so much as an address for my aunt and uncle who were supposed to take me in. What would I do if no one came for me?

Think. I inhaled, then took in the scene again, framing it and trying to find the right angle to make sense of the situation. Back home I might have snapped a photo with the old camera Papa had given me. But here I was overwhelmed by the chaos, great swirls of strangers moving in all directions, colliding with one another. A dog trotted along the edge of the dock, sniffing at garbage. Even a stray seemed to somehow know where it was going.

Looking around the smelly, crowded harbor, my spirits sank. Lucky, I'd heard a woman remark days earlier as the Italian coastline had faded from view. Heads around her had bobbed in agreement: we were fortunate to be away from the violence that had worsened ominously against the Jews in recent months. But as the ship pulled from the Stazione Maritima, I did not feel lucky, but alone. My parents were still there—and I wanted to go back.

"You!" a male voice barked, and I turned with a flicker of hope. Perhaps my uncle had found me after all. But it was one of the burly stevedores who had herded us from the boat. "Down!" I scrambled from the railing, trying to fade into the crowd. The travelers had moved forward, though, dwindling and leaving me exposed like a broken shell on the beach at low tide. "Keep moving." It had been like this the whole of the trip, deckhands shouting orders to the lower-class passengers, not bothering to maintain a pretense of courtesy. "Someone here to get you?" the man pressed.

I processed his English slowly. Good question. What if the message had not gotten through and no one was coming for me? Perhaps they would let me go back, I thought with fleeting joy. But after all of the struggle to get me out of Italy, Mamma would think that a failure.

It was only a week ago that I had been reading in our two-story apartment just off the Via del Monte, snug in the bedroom that I had shared with Nonna before she passed two years earlier, when Mamma came running in, breathless. "We have to go." Downstairs, Papa was throwing papers into the fire that never burned in summer, with an energy I thought he no longer possessed. "Come!" Mamma ordered, urging me down to the street, and lifted me onto the handles of her bike.

"Where are we going?"

My mother did not answer, but pedaled fiercely through the darkened streets. It was after curfew and I feared the police might stop us. We neared the harbor, drawing close to the docks where too many people were crowding onto a rickety ship. Mamma stopped, climbed off and pulled me from the bike, breathing heavily. Perspiration glistened on her forehead and cheeks. "You have to go first."

I stared at her in disbelief. "Where?"

"America." She handed me a satchel heavy with coins, and a ticket and papers, though real or forged I could not say.

She could not possibly be serious. I reached for her, panicking. "I can't go alone!" The sight of the dark water behind the ship filled me with terror.

"There's no other way. You'll be fine. You're strong." Mamma had never coddled me, forcing me to find my own way from our apartment through the city to market from a young age and do almost everything for myself. It was as if she had known and somehow been planning for this.

"Why now?"

"These documents." She gestured. "That ship. You'll have to transfer in Gibralter, but there's no telling when we might get another chance." But her voice was evasive, and remembering Papa burning the papers, I knew it was something more. I would be leaving them behind in danger.

"Papa and I will follow." I knew it was a lie. Papa was too weak to travel. She urged me forward onto the rotten-smelling dock, finding gaps in the crowd that I could not see and making her own with shoulders and elbows where none existed. Her hair fanned out around her, a lioness with her cub.

We neared the front of the crowd and Mamma pushed toward a uniformed man and handed him a fistful of bills, saying a few words I could not hear. She turned back. "Come." We reached the edge where the dock met the ship and my toe caught in the gap. Mamma grabbed my arm hard to keep me from stumbling. "Stay out of sight as much as you can." Her fingers bit into my skin. "Talk to no one. I will send word to Papa's brother." She took her mizpah necklace, with its half-heart pendant made of gold that she had always worn, from around her neck, and fastened it on mine. My father had given it to her years earlier, keeping his half in his breast pocket, close to his own heart. She did not kiss me, but pressed me tightly to her once, firm and hard. Then she released me and, before I could follow, dis-appeared into the crowd.

"Hey!" The stevedore's voice came again. My vision cleared. Impatient now, he gestured with his thick hand in the direction of the large building ahead. "You gotta go in there. Police come for the kids who've got no one to claim them." There was a quiet thud in my chest, as I carefully pieced together his words. What did the police do with those kids?

I ran my tongue over the chipped spot on my front tooth as I glanced back over my shoulder at the ship. Once dirty and confining, now it seemed a refuge. But I did not have money for a meal, much less a return ticket. "You can't go back, only forward." The man stood with arms folded, blocking the way behind me, and I had no choice but to move in the direction of the building.

Inside the high-ceilinged arrivals hall, bodies pressed together, making the air warm and thick. Conversations in different languages, German, Yiddish, Italian, rose and clashed around me. I hung back from the queue that shuffled forward, trying to figure out what to do. In an alcove to the right, a few of the other kids from the ship sat forlornly on a wood bench. A policeman lorded over them in the doorway. Nothing good was going to happen to that lot and I didn't want to join them. But I was not about to go up to immigration and announce that I was alone.

I saw a sign for the ladies' room at the far side of the terminal and made my way toward it. Pressing inside through the wall of stench, I grimaced at my reflection in the cracked mirror. On the boat I had tried to cow my thick dark hair back into braids, as Nonna had done each morning. But pieces stuck out in all directions. The scratch on my cheek had just begun to heal. I pushed my way to the basin where women jostled at the sink like pigs at a trough. Reaching my hands into the fray, I managed to get a few drops of water. I desperately wanted to drink it, but didn't dare. Instead, I used it to smooth my hair and wipe a smudge from my forehead.

Back in the main hall, the crowds from the ship had thinned. I walked to a newspaper stand in the corner, pretending to be interested in the headlines. Ten minutes passed. "You buying?" the man behind the kiosk asked. I moved away, feeling exposed in the vast, emptying arrivals hall. If I stood here any longer, the policeman who took the kids was going to notice. In the short queue which remained ahead, a family with several children was nearing the immigration desk. I moved close to them, hoping to slip through with them.

But as the family stepped past the desk, a hand caught my shoulder, stopping me.

"Papers?" I drew myself up to my full four feet eight inches, then handed my passport to the man in a dark blue cap and jacket whose eyes darted back and forth as he scanned the paper in front of him. An open pack of Lucky Strikes peeked out of his breast pocket. I held my breath, praying that the papers were good, and that the money my mother had given the ship's purser was enough to have my name added to the manifest. The waiting room on the far side of the immigration desk, where cleared arrivals met their hosts, stood just feet but oceans away.

The man looked up beneath bushy brows. "Who's sponsoring you?" I shook my head at the unfamiliar word. "You have family here?" he asked more slowly.

"My aunt and uncle. They're expecting me." My accent sounded thicker than when I had practiced speaking English with Mamma back home.

"Where are they?" I faltered. "Children have to be collected." He made me sound like luggage. I bristled at the notion of still being called a child at almost seventeen, then decided not to complain. He gestured toward the guarded side room with the kids. "Otherwise you'll have to go to the Home until your relatives can collect you."

"Home?" I repeated, picking out the word I recognized.

"It's a place for kids who have no one."

My stomach tightened. "My uncle, he is . . . sick," I said, spinning the lie as it came out. "They couldn't came."

"Come," he corrected. "You have a letter?"

"It blew away." I gestured with my hand, then fought not to blink as he stared at me. "On the boat."

He took off his cap and scratched his head. "I'd like to help you. But we can't just let kids go loose in the city." Now he sounded like a zoo-keeper. My heart sank as he raised his hand to wave over the policeman who was guarding the children.

Over the edge of the immigration desk, I spotted a grainy family photograph. "You have children?"

The man hesitated, unaccustomed to others asking the questions. Then he lowered his hand. "Four. A girl and three boys."

"Your daughter is beautiful. How old?"

His face softened a bit. "Mary's six."

The officer rubbed his right temple with thick fingers. Behind him, the clock struck five. "Joe, we're headed to O'Shea's," another man called from behind him.

"My aunt and uncle lived close to here," I said, not stopping to correct my grammar as I sensed a crack in his resolve. "I will bring my aunt back tomorrow to sign for me? Please."

The man hesitated. "What's their address?"

"2256 South Fifth," I replied, making up the numbers and hoping they sounded right.

"I could lose my job for this."

"You won't. I'll come back." The man stamped my passport. I took it and hurried past him. I scanned the waiting room, but did not see anyone who might have been my aunt and uncle. Not daring to linger in case the immigration officer changed his mind, I scurried through the station and stepped out into the light.

On the far side of the door, I stopped again and scratched at the back of my head, hoping I had not picked up nits. The street in front of the Port of Philadelphia was packed thick with buses and taxis and black sedans, choking the already thick summer air with exhaust. An enormous American flag flapped in the breeze above. At the corner, a hot-dog cart gave off a savory smell. My mouth watered. Food had run out in steerage almost two days before we docked. I had not eaten, except for the scrap of bread an upper deck passenger had carelessly tossed below in waste. I moved closer to the cart, eyeing the soft pretzels stacked high on the edge. I could take one without anyone noticing.

No, I was not going to start my life here by stealing. Better hungry than a thief. I turned from the cart, focusing on the street in front of me. I had made it through immigration, but I still had no idea where I was going.

"Adelia?" a voice called behind me. I froze. They were going to stop me from leaving after all. But this time the voice was female and it had spoken—not barked—my name. I turned. A sturdy woman in a flowered dress and thick brown shoes was walking toward me, a thin, stooped man at her side. My shoulders slumped with relief. So Mamma had been able to send word after all.

A look of something—disapproval perhaps—

passed over the woman's face as she neared. She leaned in to kiss my cheek, flinching at the travel smell I could not help. "I'm your aunt Bess. This is your uncle," she added, gesturing toward the gray-haired man in horn-rimmed glasses who stood behind her. I tried to stand straighter. I wanted them to like me, to be glad they had taken me in.

"Meyer," he offered, switching his cigar to his other hand so he could shake mine. I strained to hear his voice, one step above a whisper. There was something familiar around his dark, almond-shaped eyes that made him an older, less handsome version of Papa. Homesickness washed over me.

"I'm so sorry we were late. There was construction on the road and then we had the wrong dock," Aunt Bess said, sounding harried. I struggled to keep up with her rapid-fire English, catching only a fraction of what she said. "I suppose we have to clear you through customs." She pointed to the building.

"I already did." As if on cue, I saw the immigration officer who had let me go walking from the terminal, jacket thrown over his shoulder. He turned, a wave of recognition crossing his face as I gestured toward my aunt and uncle. I had been telling the truth after all. He raised his hand, wishing me good luck with a kind of salute before rounding the corner.

"But how did you manage that? Oh, never mind," Aunt Bess added before I could share my tale. She took me by the arm. "Oy, you're all bones." The comment stung. Before I'd left Trieste I'd been developing, with new curves that made my clothes fit differently. But all that seemed to melt away during the days of hunger on the ship and now my elbows and knees stuck out like a scarecrow's.

"You must be hungry," Uncle Meyer offered more kindly.

"A little," I lied, nearly swooning at the mention of food. My eyes traveled once more toward the stack of pretzels on the hot-dog cart.

But Aunt Bess opened her purse and fished out a bagel wrapped in tissue. She dusted off a bit of lint that had stuck to the corner and handed it to me. "Thank you," I managed, trying to mask my disappointment as I bit into the stale, crusty bread. I gulped the first mouthful, then forced myself to slow down as my stomach roiled.

"You don't have bags?" I shook my head. "We'll have to get you some things," Aunt Bess said, as though it had only just occurred to her. I followed them to a black car at the corner. "We're headed to the shore. That is, the beach. Atlantic City. We take a place there in the summer. It's nothing fancy, just a few rooms in a boardinghouse. But we thought the sea air might do you good." Aunt Bess spoke quickly, using too many English

36

words that I did not know. "Do you understand?"

She must have noticed my confusion. I tended to wear my emotions on my face—a habit I'd been trying to break. "*Si*. I mean yes."

"You'll like that, *nu*?" Uncle Meyer asked, his whisper kind. I did not answer. How could I explain that, even though I'd been raised in coastal Trieste, the ocean was in fact the one thing I hated most?

A tear escaped from my right eye then and trickled down my cheek. "Oh, dear," Aunt Bess said, mistaking my sadness for gratitude and hugging me awkwardly. I let myself be folded into her stiff, unfamiliar arms and took a step into the life that was waiting for me.

Three

Hearing the screen door slam behind me, I shielded my eyes and peered up at the slope-roofed beach duplex where we occupied the second floor. Aunt Bess labored down the rickety wood steps, straw purse tucked under her arm. Though it was not yet midmorning, the sticky July heat had already caused damp spots to form at the armpits of her dress. "I'm headed to Margie's." Aunt Bess's routine was always the same, the only question if it was canasta at Margie's or mah-jongg at Flo's. "Do you want to come?"

I considered saying yes, just to see her reaction. "No, thank you." Aunt Bess's shoulders dropped slightly with relief. She hesitated in that way she always did, not quite sure what to do with a teenage girl whom she'd only just inherited less than a month earlier. Things were especially awkward during the week. Uncle Meyer traveled in the Buick, selling pots and pans and other household items to the housewives of Elkins Park and Cheltenham and other neighborhoods northeast of Center City. Until he returned Friday afternoons, it was just Aunt Bess and me. "There are some leftover *prakas*—I mean cabbage rolls —in the icebox for lunch." Aunt Bess's family had come from Pinsk some thirty years earlier, fleeing the pogroms. She regarded herself as American, but little bits of the old country seeped through, like a white slip peeking out beneath the hem of her dress. Sometimes I felt as if I were an embarrassment to her, the immigrant niece a reminder of the world from which she'd tried so hard to distance herself. "There's cheese for sandwiches and some potato salad," she continued, as if rattling off a grocery list. She was forever trying to feed me. "I'll be back this afternoon."

I watched as Aunt Bess padded, dingy white sandals scraping, down to the corner of Monmouth Avenue. She was not an unkind woman; she simply did not know how to do this, like a muscle stiff from lack of use. I did not dare to ask if she ever wanted kids of her own.

I was supposed to be grateful, I knew, from the looks and not-too-low whispers of Aunt Bess's friends. Grateful to her and Uncle Meyer for the clothes that were new, but not quite the right size, and for the secondhand books that were a few years too young for me. Grateful that they had taken me in, even though they really hadn't had a choice. And I was grateful, but I wished they might just once ask me what I wanted, or even let me choose for myself.

When Aunt Bess had disappeared from sight, I climbed the steps of the duplex and went inside for some calamine lotion. We had two rooms, if you counted the screened sundeck with the daybed that made me an easy target for the mosquitos as I slept, plus kitchen privileges down below. I rubbed the lotion into my legs, avoiding the scrape on my left knee. Then I straightened, licking the salt from my lips and peering out across the horizon where greenish bay water met overcast gray sky.

My hand wrapped reflexively around the mizpah pendant, fingers feeling the engraved Hebrew: *May the Lord keep watch between you and me when we are away from each other,* or so Mamma had told me once when I was little and had asked about the charm around her neck. Hebrew was nonexistent in our home, and the item's value to Mamma was sentimental, not religious. I had not taken it off since Mamma fastened it around my neck that night she put me on the ship. I pictured the other half in my father's pocket, close to his heart. Sadness seemed to seep from the cool metal through my fingers as I thought of them and what might have happened in the weeks since I left. Had their lives had gone on much the same without me?

The sound of a car engine interrupted my thoughts. I looked down through the screen window, surprised. Our street was narrow and not a major thruway; vehicles this time of day other than the milkman and garbage truck were scarce. A boxy black station wagon lumbered into view, with suitcases strapped to the roof that looked ready to topple off at any moment.

The car stopped just past the duplex. I stood up, curious. The sprawling house next door with its wraparound porch had been vacant since we'd arrived three weeks earlier. Aunt Bess had sniffed at its dilapidated state, but I liked the empty place—I played under the eaves and even found a rabbit's nest there. There had been signs in recent days that someone was working on it, though: a whiff of fresh paint coming from a suddenly open window, a pile of fresh lumber on the back porch. Once I thought I glimpsed a man through one of the windows, but when I moved closer to peer inside, he was gone.

But there was no mistaking the arrival now. A woman got out of the driver's seat. She was pretty, with pale skin and strawberry-blond hair I would have loved for my own, and a smattering of freckles that said she'd better keep out of the sun if she didn't want more. Behind her, several brown-haired boys spilled out of the car and raced toward the house, shouting and laughing. At first it seemed that there were too many to count. A little one, not more than ten or so, scampered ahead. He was followed by two boys about my age. They looked nearly the same, except one wore thick glasses. I'd heard of identical twins, but these were the first I'd actually seen. A dog bounded from the car, barking noisily at their feet.

Finally an older boy unfolded himself from the front passenger seat. He had long legs and wide shoulders, hair in a neat side part but that still curled at the edges. My stomach flipped, like the time Papa had taken me on a roller coaster at the carnival.

A family moving in. I waited for a father to appear, but the woman and the boys began unloading things and carrying them to the house. The oldest boy lifted a case from the roof of the car, his muscles flexing under his T-shirt. One of the twins hung back, head low, until his mother went to him and said something, cajoling a smile. They laughed at a joke I could not hear.

When the boys had finished unloading the boxes, they disappeared into the house. I looked down at the street, which seemed emptier than it had before they'd come. Then the screen door to the house next door banged open and the boys appeared once more. They jostled like puppies as they pushed outside. One of the twins carried a football, which the boys began tossing among them on the thin strip of grass that separated our two houses.

I watched the scene play out below, wanting to go down and join them. I stepped forward, starting toward the door that led downstairs. Then I stopped. But I kept watching, fascinated. The hair of the oldest boy seemed to glow gold in the morning sun. He didn't so much run as fly, feet barely touching the ground. He leapt for the ball and his shirt pulled free, revealing a bit of mid-section. I inhaled sharply at the unfamiliar sight.

"Hey!" a voice called out. It took a second to realize that it was directed at me. The youngest boy had his head tilted upward toward the porch, hand raised to shield his eyes from the sun. I stepped back from the window, but it was too late. He waved his brothers over. "A kid."

The others stopped playing and gathered to peer up at me. "A girl," the oldest brother corrected. "Don't be shy," he coaxed in a voice too rich and hypnotic to resist. "Come down and join us. We won't bite."

"We might," the twin without the glasses taunted. I hung back. Then, curious and struck by the kindness of the oldest boy's eyes, I opened the door and started down the steps.

"I'm Jack," the twin with glasses said when I'd reached the bottom. He held out his hand. Closer I could see that he had a fuller face than his brother, splashed with freckles. Long lashes blinked behind the thick lenses.

I opened my mouth but no sound came out. "Adelia," I croaked finally, wishing my accent was not so obvious.

The leaner twin cocked his head. "She must be the greenhorn from Italy that Dad mentioned." How did they know about me? I blinked, caught off guard by the rudeness of his tone. My cheeks reddened and I started to turn. Coming downstairs had been a mistake.

"Don't mind Liam," said the oldest boy, his voice low and resonant. I stared up, not answering. He was even more handsome up close, with hazel eyes and a wide smile. Bright sunlight seemed to cast a halo of gold around him. "I'm Charlie." My breath caught. I brushed my hair from my face, trying to think of something to say that would impress him, make him take notice. He cupped his hand on the head of the youngest boy standing beside him. "And this is Robbie."

I smiled down at Robbie, who had wide, round cheeks that seemed to cushion his eyes, and front teeth still a bit too big. He stood very straight, trying to look taller in a way that I recognized from doing it myself. "Nice to meet you," I said solemnly.

"Adelia," Charlie said, as if trying my name on for size. Hearing him say it, my insides warmed. "That's a mouthful. Is it okay if we call you Addie?"

I nodded, liking the short, easy sound. "*Si*. I mean, yes." I blushed. My knowledge of English was not awful. Mamma had insisted that I learn other languages since I was a child. I had read as much as I could since coming here, mostly *Ladies' Home Journal* and the other women's magazines Aunt Bess loved. And I had listened to the radio programs, too. But I had not had much opportunity to practice speaking and when I was nervous it all seemed to fade away.

"Come meet our mother." Before I could reply, Charlie strode across the lawn, covering it in about two steps. The others followed. "Mom!" The red-haired woman emerged from the house, wiping her hands on the apron that covered her light blue shirtwaist dress. "This is Addie. She's staying next door."

The woman smiled with a kindness that said she had heard about me. "Hello! We've been summer neighbors of your aunt and uncle for years, though we usually get here a good deal earlier. I'm Doris Connally."

"Where did you come from?" Robbie inter-jected.

"From Trieste, in Italy. On a boat."

"All by yourself?" he asked. I nodded, standing straighter.

"Well, that's something," Mrs. Connally said, her voice full of admiration. "I normally wouldn't even make the trip down to the shore by myself, but my husband had to work and the boys wanted to be here for the fireworks on the Fourth."

"Who lives there with you?" Robbie resumed his interrogation, pointing up to the screened porch where I had stood minutes earlier.

"Just my aunt and my uncle."

"No brothers or sisters? Any pets?" I shook my head twice, trying to keep up with his questions. "Boy, you'll sure be glad to have us around!" His brothers chuckled.

Robbie turned to his mother. "Can we keep her?"

"Robbie, she isn't a puppy. But I do hope you'll join us often," she added.

"Because we really need more kids," Liam said wryly. His words stung. But he did not sound as though he was trying to be mean, just truthful.

The yellow dog I'd seen earlier bounded down the porch steps and stopped at Liam's feet. "This is Beau," he added, face softening.

"Jack and Liam must be about your age," Mrs. Connally remarked.

"I'm sixteen." I heard my accent again, the way my voice did not sound like theirs.

"I'm taller," said Liam improbably.

"Okay," I conceded, because it seemed to matter to him a great deal.

"Would you like to join us for lunch?" Mrs. Connally offered. "I haven't much 'til we get to Casel's, just sandwiches."

I still could not get over the way Americans spoke so casually of food—something I would never again take for granted. "I wouldn't want to impose."

Mrs. Connally smiled. "Hardly. With these boys, I'm already cooking for an army. Come on, everyone. Let's eat."

Charlie lifted Robbie across his shoulders like a sack of potatoes and started for the door with the twins at his heels. Inside, the house was airy and cool. There were little touches, like the carved oak bannister and wide windows, that said the house had been built for someone to live in year-round, and not merely as a vacation home.

As we passed through the living room, I paused to admire a chess set which sat already unpacked on a low table. "It's lovely," I said, fingering one of the carved wooden rooks.

"Do you play?" Charlie asked with new interest.

I tried to calm the fluttering in my stomach. "I did. My father taught me." In recent years when he had become broken and withdrawn, it was my one way to still connect to him. Papa had no one to play with him now. I imagined the chessboard sitting unused by the fireplace in our apartment in Trieste. It had been my dearest possession—the one thing I might have brought with me, had I known I was going.

I followed Charlie through the open boxes that littered the floor to the freshly scrubbed kitchen smelling of lemons. Mrs. Connally unpacked a basket of meats and cheeses and began slicing thick white bread. My stomach rumbled embarrassingly. Even after several weeks here, every meal felt as though it might be my last.

The boys whooped and hollered their way to the kitchen table, its enamel top scratched from years of use. Charlie plunked Robbie down in his chair before grabbing Liam and Jack under each arm and pretending to bang their heads together.

"Boys!" Mrs. Connally admonished, but her tone was good-natured, as if the chaos was normal. She turned to me. "Why don't you sit here next to me where these little rascals can't bother you."

"Thank you." I slid into the chair Mrs. Connally indicated, then looked hopefully at the empty seat next to mine. But Charlie dropped down between the twins on the other side of the table.

Mrs. Connally passed me a plate of sliced tomato. "We just bought these at a farmer's stand on the way into town." The piece I took was warm. Biting into it, I was taken back to sun-soaked holiday afternoons at the cottage outside Trieste, filling our baskets with tomatoes off the vine for Nonna to make her thick sauce.

Mrs. Connally handed around the platter of sandwiches and glasses of milk. The kitchen turned quiet as the boys attacked their lunches. Each of them ate differently. Charlie wolfed his meal down in great bites, barely pausing between mouthfuls to breathe or speak. Jack was meticulous, as if auditioning for a part. Liam sat back and nibbled disinterestedly, while Robbie played with his food just shy of irritating his mother. I ate carefully, taking care not to leave crumbs.

From where I sat at the kitchen table, I could see that the house was a bit down-at-heels, the paint peeling and woodwork worn. "It's been in my family for generations," Mrs. Connally said, seeming to notice. "It's a lot to keep up, but I couldn't bear to sell it."

"We live in South Philadelphia back home," Jack offered between bites.

"We do, too, I think. Fifth and Porter," I said, repeating the location I'd heard from Aunt Bess.

"That's the Jewish neighborhood," Liam observed.

"Liam, mind your manners," his mother cautioned.

"Is it true that Jews don't believe in Jesus?"

Robbie asked. I nodded. His eyes widened with disbelief. "We're Catholic."

"Sort of," Charlie corrected. "Dad is, and we go to church sometimes. But Mom is a Quaker."

"What's that?"

"It's just a different kind of church," Mrs. Connally replied. "And we Quakers are pacifists, which means we don't believe in fighting or war." Still not fully understanding, I made a note to look up the words later.

"Is that why you don't want America to help stop Germany?" Charlie asked his mother. His voice was rich and resonant. "Because you're a pacifist?"

"Partly, I suppose. Mostly it's because I have four sons." My heart sank. I had heard such talk at the drugstore and among Aunt Bess's friends. Back in Italy, I'd just assumed that the Americans would come and help stop the Germans, that it was only a matter of time. How could they not? But here people spoke of the war as though it were unreal, a book or movie, or simply someone else's problem.

"We live about ten blocks from you," Jack said. I turned to him, grateful for the return to an easier subject.

"You'll attend high school in the fall?" Mrs. Connally asked me.

"Ugh, only Mom would ruin a perfectly good lunch with the *S* word." Liam ducked as his

49

mother swiped at him playfully, then tried to wipe mustard from the corner of his mouth.

"At South Philadelphia High School, I think."

"It's called Southern," Liam corrected disdainfully.

"Us, too," Jack chimed in. "Charlie's gonna be quarterback of the football team."

Charlie shrugged and waved his hand. "We don't know that yet."

"Naw, unless Tommy Thompson decides to stroll down from Eagles' practice and try out, I think you're in like Flynn." I smiled, trying to look as if I understood.

When the food was gone, I stood to help Mrs. Connally clear the plates, then returned to the table. She passed each of us a miniature Hershey's bar. I stared in disbelief. Aunt Bess's idea of a treat were the cookies she'd brought from the kosher bakery in the city, dry even before they had gone stale. I had not had chocolate since coming to America. "Thank you." I tore off the paper and popped the whole thing in my mouth. Sugar rushed through me, heating my blood.

"You kids go on back outside while I clean up and unpack a bit more." The boys pushed back their chairs from the table and started for the door.

Outside, Robbie held a baseball bat he had pulled from one of the boxes. "Wanna play?"

"She's a girl," Liam sneered derisively.

I bristled. What was his problem? "Sure." In

50

truth I'd never played before, but I wasn't about to admit it to him. The bat I took from Robbie felt strange and cumbersome in my hands.

"Here." Charlie walked over and adjusted my hands, his fingers pressing warm on my own. Jack threw the ball in my direction, soft and slow. I swung and then released, putting all of my weight behind the movement as the bat made contact with the ball. It sailed high into the yard on the far side of the Connally house and there was a sudden crash, followed by the sound of shattering glass.

I dropped the bat. Everyone froze. "Uh-oh," Robbie said. His jaw dropped.

A man came around the fence angrily holding the ball. "Who broke my car window?"

I hesitated, trembling. "I did," a voice behind me said. I turned, surprised to see Liam stepping forward before I could speak.

Mrs. Connally burst through the door. "Liam, how could you? I've warned you boys about playing ball by the houses." She reached into the pocket of her dress as she walked toward the man. "Mr. Steiner, I'm so sorry," she said, handing him some dollar bills. "This should cover it." The man took the money and walked off with a harrumph. Mrs. Connally turned back to Liam, hands on hips. "You are grounded and no allowance until you earn back what I just gave Mr. Steiner." She stormed back into the house.

I turned to Liam. "You took the blame for me."

He shrugged. "People expect me to get in trouble. No one would believe it was a girl who hit that far anyway."

I opened my mouth to issue a retort and then thought better of it. "Thank you." But he just stomped off around the side of the house.

I walked to the door of the Connally house and knocked softly. "Ma'am?"

Mrs. Connally knelt over a box, unpacking clothes. "Come in, dear."

"It was me who hit the ball and broke the window." Mrs. Connally looked up, surprised. "Liam was just protecting me."

Mrs. Connally straightened. "Why didn't you say anything?"

I looked away. "I know I should have. I'm sorry. But I is, I mean was, was afraid."

"Afraid of what?"

I swallowed. "That they would send me back." Something had changed in the past few weeks, I realized. Though I desperately missed my parents and wished they would join me here, a growing part of me wanted to stay in America—today, having met the Connallys, more than ever.

"To Europe? Oh, honey." Mrs. Connally opened her arms and I stepped into them, inhaling the cinnamon smell. "That won't happen. This is your home now."

I relaxed slightly, secretly relieved—and a bit

guilty for feeling that way. A moment later, I pulled away. "I should let my aunt know where I am." Really, Aunt Bess would not be back for hours, but I didn't want to overstay my welcome.

"Well, hurry back." I tilted my head, not understanding. "You'll go to the beach with us."

I faltered. I'd managed to avoid the beach since coming here. Aunt Bess had offered to take me once, but I'd made excuses and, though puzzled, she hadn't pressed. I could not tell Mrs. Connally about my fear of the water, which seemed silly even to me—and I did not want them to go and leave me behind. "I'll be right back." I hurried next door to the boardinghouse, finding the polka-dot bathing suit Aunt Bess had bought me, with the Gimbels tags still on it.

When I walked downstairs a few minutes later, the Connallys had assembled in front of their house, buckets and other beach toys in hand. I stopped, suddenly self-conscious of my new suit. When Aunt Bess had given it to me, I'd loved the bright pink color and ruffles. Now I was embarrassed at how it clung in some places and gapped in others.

"Wait for me," Robbie called, struggling to keep up with his brothers' long strides as we started down the block. Charlie reached down and scooped up Robbie, then hoisted him to his shoulders.

I studied the boys out of the corner of my eye

as we walked. Liam looked more like Charlie than his own twin. With the same almond-shaped eyes and angular jawline, he was almost a copy of his older brother. He was much slighter, though, and his skin was a paler shade. They stood opposite one another like sun and moon. Charlie's movements were sure and deft and he seemed to hover above his brothers, guiding their movements, steering Jack around a pothole so he didn't trip, then putting out an arm to stop Robbie before he stepped into the street. The other boys fell in behind him like geese following in formation. I was drawn closer, longing to walk beneath his protective wing and be one of them.

We soon reached the boardwalk that separated the road from the beach, wide planks forming a neat pattern with a railing that overlooked the sea. Just to the north loomed the Chelsea and other grand hotels. As we climbed the worn plank steps, I could hear waves crashing hard on the other side, so different from the calm Adriatic I'd known as a child. I froze, nauseous. I'd had the nightmares for as long as I could remember, of dark waters rising and pulling me under. The week on the ship, feeling the water rolling beneath, had been nearly unbearable. But this was worse, because even though I had never been to this beach, the spot where we now stood looked exactly like the nightmare I'd had for a lifetime.

Charlie set Robbie down. Robbie scampered

onto the sand, racing to a dune that lay just below. He began to climb it. But as he neared the top, he wobbled. A look of sheer terror crossed his face as he lost his footing and began to tumble. "Robbie!" his mother cried with alarm.

Charlie raced up from behind me. In two swift strides, he reached the bottom of the dune and extended his arms, catching Robbie neatly in midair. "You need to be more careful," Charlie scolded as he set Robbie down. "I'm not always going to be here to save you." But the protective note in his voice suggested otherwise.

I hung back as the boys ran ahead down the wide beach, which was dotted with other groups of bathers, women in stylish swimsuits reading magazines and families with small children digging for sand crabs and splashing in the surf. To everyone else, the beach was a happy, relaxed place.

"Are you all right?" Mrs. Connally asked, noticing my distress. She adjusted the wide brim of her straw hat, then took my arm. "Come, let's set up." I followed her to the spot where the boys had cast down their things, and helped spread out the blanket. I tried not to stare as Charlie pulled off his shirt, revealing a broad torso and muscular shoulders. His eyes traveled in the direction of a girl a few years older than me, sunning herself in a suit with a cut-out midriff. My heart sank; I could never hope to fill out a swimsuit like that.

"Are you coming?" Charlie asked as he started toward the water. I shook my head. "I'll take you," he offered, softer now, seeming to sense my fear. How I wanted to trust him! I almost felt as if I could.

Then a wave rose behind him and thundered down. Panic gripped me once more. "You go on." I stretched out in what I hoped would be a glamorous position on the blanket. A biplane buzzed overhead, advertising the diving horse show at Steel Pier.

Jack settled down beside me on the blanket and pulled a book from his mother's bag. *The Red Badge of Courage*; I'd never heard of it. "Summer reading assignment," he said, noticing me looking.

"Oh." I didn't know if I was meant to be reading something over the summer. "I'm worried," I confessed.

"About school? Don't be. I'm sure the other kids are going to like you a lot." Jack smiled so brightly I almost believed him.

"It's the schoolwork. I'm mostly nervous about the writing."

"Why don't I help you? Tutoring, they call it."

Robbie peered over Jack's shoulder. "Whatcha doing? Homework in summer. Aack!" He ran away.

"It's the beach, for goodness' sake!" Liam protested as he followed Robbie to the surf.

"Buddy system!" Mrs. Connally called after

them. Her eyes darted back and forth attentively, never leaving the water.

"Don't worry, I've got them," Charlie called from the water's edge. He dove in without hesitation, then swam out to meet his brothers, his stroke as smooth and confident as a lifeguard.

"Come on, Addie!" Robbie cried, his voice drowned out by the crashing of a wave. I watched longingly, wanting for once to take part in the fun, instead of simply standing on the sidelines watching.

But I couldn't. Instead, I took some of the lotion Mrs. Connally offered. Sand from my fingers mixed with it as I rubbed it into my arms. I inhaled deeply, gazing northward down the beach where the boardwalk bustled in front of the Claridge Hotel and Convention Hall. Haze swirled around the top of the roller coasters and other amusements on the piers that jutted out into sea. The air was salty but curiously sweet, a bit of taffy or caramel corn drifting in from the piers.

A few minutes later Jack closed his book and went to join his brothers in the water. I lay back, squirming against some sand which had worked its way into the bottom of my bathing suit. I closed my eyes and let the sun lull me into a semi-nap. My parents appeared in my mind. We had been happy once like the Connallys. I saw Mamma and Papa dancing around the kitchen, the three of us and Nonna enjoying long leisurely meals of fish and cheese and bread out on our balcony in summertime. When I was ten, I had asked if it was the lunches that were making Mamma's belly round. She just laughed. She and I spent long days strolling the city, wading in the fountains and pointing out interesting things until it was time for Papa to come home.

Only one day he didn't. At first Mamma tried to be cheerful. "He's just gone to see friends," she reassured. But a night passed, then another, and then she forgot to maintain her pretense of calm. She left me with Nonna and did not return by morning. I tried to pray in the darkness at night for their safe return. Please, I said over and over again, because I did not know any other words. It seemed to work, because two days later Mamma came back. She was pale and drawn—and still alone. She took to her bed. Nonna ran for the doctor.

A few days later, Mamma emerged, but her stomach no longer swelled as much. "Is Papa still with friends?" I asked.

Mamma shook her head. "No," she replied bluntly, not bothering to cushion the truth. "He's been arrested." My heart froze. I'd seen a man once, taken from the street by the police. People whispered that he would not come back. I prayed more, adding more *please*s until I was saying the word a thousand times each night before finally falling asleep.

Papa did return a week later, walking through

the door as unexpectedly as he had disappeared. He looked the same, right down to the same clothes, now dirty and creased. He'd even managed to keep the mizpah heart and not have it taken. But he fell into a chair with a wince that suggested he was hurting on the inside, and a haunted look in his eyes that did not go away. He did not return to his work after that but wrote from home, welcoming in the occasional visitor. Instead it was Mamma who took to the streets, leafleting and attending meetings and protests against the Fascist regime, calling for elections.

I jumped as a drop of cold water hit my back and the vision evaporated. I rolled over. Liam stood over me, a mischievous grin in his eye. He had come up from the water's edge, shaking droplets of water from his hair like a wet dog.

"Why, Addie," he drawled. "You haven't even gotten wet. You're missing all of the fun."

"I'm fine," I protested, but he reached down and picked me up. I tried to pull away but his wiry grip was surprisingly strong.

"Liam Scott Connally, don't you dare!" his mother began to admonish, but it was too late. Her voice faded as Liam carried me toward the water. "Please put me down," I begged, flailing. But he stared straight ahead, not listening. The boy who just hours earlier had protected me from a neighbor's wrath over a broken window was now my tormentor.

I closed my eyes, knowing what was coming next. The waves thundered in my ears, a sound I had heard thousands of times in my nightmares. Water splashed around Liam's ankles as they reached the surf, kicking up the icy spray against my bare skin. Then he let me go. I screamed as cold darkness enveloped me. I reached wildly for the bottom, trying without success to find my footing. A powerful wave slammed into me from behind, tossing me like a ball until I could no long figure out which way was up. I flailed my arms, panicking. Water filled my nose and mouth, salt where air should have been.

Suddenly I was lifted to the surface. "Hey." Charlie's strong arms encircled me, holding me close as I coughed the water from my burning lungs. "It's okay. I've got you." He had reached me in a few long strokes. "Easy." His voice was soothing. He raised me higher as a wave lifted them so it would not break on me. "I've got you." I did not answer, but leaned my head against the wetness of his chest, still trying to catch my breath.

A second later Jack reached us. "Addie, are you okay?"

"That was so cool," Robbie exclaimed, dog-paddling up from behind. He and Jack followed Charlie as he carried me to shore.

Charlie neared the beach blanket and set me down gently. Mrs. Connally wrapped a towel around me. "Liam, how could you?" she demanded. "Addie, are you all right, dear?"

"It was a joke," Liam replied defensively.

"You idiot," Charlie swore. Liam's face crumpled and he slumped forward, as though he had been punched in the stomach. Clearly his older brother's opinion meant everything.

I nodded and assured Mrs. Connally I was fine. A man carrying a white ice cooler on his back walked down the beach calling out, "Ice cream!" Mrs. Connally fished in her bag for coins. "Come with me, boys," she said, standing. Robbie and Jack started after her. Liam hung back, watching Charlie, as if wanting to make what he had done all right. But Charlie did not look away from me, until finally Liam followed the others reluctantly.

Charlie put a hand on my shoulder and slid closer. "You want to talk about it?"

My trembling eased slightly. "There's nothing to tell." I fought the urge to put my head on his shoulder. Though I'd only just met Charlie, he seemed to have a way of making everything okay —even the beach.

"But Trieste is on the coast, isn't it? You've lived by the water your whole life. You can't swim at all?"

"I don't know," I confessed, pulling the towel closer around me. "I can't even breathe when I get near the ocean."

"I could try to help you."

"No, thanks."

"You're not ready. I understand." I wanted to tell him I never would be. "I hope you'll come to the beach with us anyway. 'Cause I promise," he added, shooting a murderous look down the beach toward Liam, "that what happened today will never happen again."

Four

I was losing the battle to stay awake in civics class as Mrs. Lowenstein droned on about wartime production in Britain. I blinked against heavy eyelids, but the polka dots of her dress seemed to blend together, making my vision swim. Normally I enjoyed the class, which purported to be about the past two centuries of history, but in fact focused unabashedly on the war in Europe. But Mrs. Lowenstein's monotone recitation of facts about steel manufacturing today hardly seemed relevant.

The rest of summer had passed much like that first day with the Connallys, afternoons on the beach with the boys and trips to the boardwalk in the evening. But then the days began to shorten and we only had a bit of time on our Schwinn bikes after dinner before the sun dropped low to the bay. There was a tiny release in the humidity, like air leaking from a balloon.

One day I spied Aunt Bess taking out a large box. "What are you doing?"

"Packing. It's only a week until we return to the city and we have to register you for school." Life at the shore was all that I had known here. I had almost forgotten about Philadelphia.

"What grade will I be in?"

Aunt Bess looked confused. "I suppose they'll have to test you."

"Will I need to bring my own school supplies? How will I get there?" I piled my questions on top of one another, realizing from her expression that she did not know the answer. She had not done this before either.

She paused to set down the pile of shirts she'd been packing, then swiped at her brow. "I suppose," she said, "we will have to figure out all of this together."

"I don't want to go," I had burst out to Jack as he helped me through Steinbeck's *Of Mice and Men* on the porch of his family's beach house that evening.

"We're not that far from you in the city," Jack offered. "We might even have classes together." But I was not consoled—it was not the same as being next door, hearing their laughter through the open window as I fell asleep.

I waited until a few days after we returned to the city to ask. "I want to go see the Connallys." We had just finished supper at Aunt Bess and

Uncle Meyer's house on Porter Street in the small dining room sandwiched in between the parlor in front and kitchen in back. The row house was so narrow I could almost touch both sides with my arms outstretched.

We'd moved into the parlor after eating, sitting three across on the flowered, slip-covered sofa, facing the fireplace we never used. Aunt Bess may have tried to seem American outside, but the house was filled with tarnished framed photos of grandparents and other relatives from the old country and the Shabbes candlesticks and Kiddush cup sat on the mantel.

Aunt Bess was reading *Home Chat* magazine while Uncle Meyer smoked his cigar and listened studiously to the news on the radio. I had waited until after the weather report to bring up the Connallys. Uncle Meyer followed the forecasts and their accuracy as studiously as though he was embarking on a great sea voyage. Even Aunt Bess, who spoke at him constantly, did not talk during the weather. But I had to ask quickly; after the news, Uncle Meyer would retreat to the basement, where he'd constructed an elaborate model railroad, complete with farms and a town, stretching nearly the length of the parlor above. I wondered if he wished I'd been a boy so he might have someone to share it with.

"I have their address," I added hopefully.

"You can't go," Aunt Bess replied distractedly,

bending to smooth the area rug which was a bit frayed at the edges. "It's practically across town."

I had looked at a street map and knew this wasn't true. "It's no farther than walking to school. I can do it." It was the first time since coming here that I had spoken up for something I wanted and it felt good.

"The Irish neighborhood is dangerous," Aunt Bess replied.

"Why?" I pressed. I did not want to be rude to my aunt and uncle, who had done so much for me, but I could not leave it alone.

"They don't like Jews," she replied bluntly. So she had not been speaking of crime, but of the hatred of Jews that existed here as surely as it had back home in Italy.

"But the Connallys aren't like that." She shook her head, unconvinced. My heart sank. "Uncle Meyer?" He lowered the newspaper, blinking with surprise at being included in the conversation. Normally it was Aunt Bess who did all the talking. My uncle could not be more different from Papa, who was a decade younger and so fiery—or had been, at least, before his arrest. "Do you think I can go?"

My uncle adjusted one of the two pens that always protruded from his shirt pocket, then glanced over at Aunt Bess before answering. "It's different here," he said, his voice stilted.

"This isn't like at the shore. The goyim and the Jews . . . people are separate."

"Why?"

He took off his glasses and rubbed at a speck of dirt, fumbling for an answer. "That's just the way it is. There are lots of nice kids right here on the block. You should be with your own kind, especially now." He stopped awkwardly. He was talking, of course, of the things that were going on in Europe. The Germans had continued their march across the continent, seeming to occupy another country each week. Hitler hated the Jews, was banning them from schools and professions and even the streetcars. There were stories of arrests. And Italy had allied itself with Germany, which meant things were worse now, too, in Trieste. My stomach tightened. My parents had been persecuted for their political activity—they were hardly religious at all. But Hitler would not see it that way—a Jew was a Jew.

"About that . . ." I licked my lips, changing to the other subject I'd been wanting to ask them about. "I heard on the radio about a program offering visas for some refugees. Maybe my mother and father would qualify."

My aunt and uncle exchanged a look. "Getting visas for your parents isn't the problem," Uncle Meyer said gently. My spirits lifted. "We offered to arrange it a long time ago. They want to stay in Trieste and keep doing their work." Uncle

Meyer's voice was even scratchier than usual. He had left Italy when he was fifteen and made his way here alone. His skin was a shade more olive than most here, but beyond that did not have the slightest accent or trace of the old country. He had not looked back. He still cared for his brother, though, and it pained him that he could not bring my father to safety.

"Oh." I looked away. All this time I'd assumed that Mamma and Papa could not come, and that they would follow when their papers were ready, like Mamma had said. But the truth was that their work mattered more than I did. It always had.

"When all of the fighting is over, I'm sure they'll come." Aunt Bess spoke as though the war was wrapping up. She had not seen, though, the things I had before leaving, the way people over there were stocking up supplies and digging hiding spots ahead of the armies rolling in.

I swiped at my stinging eyes, then stood and walked upstairs to my room. It was tiny, no more than a large closet that could just hold a twin bed and dresser. But Aunt Bess prepared it the way she thought a girl my age would like, with pink flowered sheets and curtains. She and Uncle Meyer were trying their best, but it wasn't the same as my own family.

I reached for the photograph of my mother and father, which sat in a frame on the corner of the dresser. When we'd come to Philadelphia from the beach, I'd been surprised to see this photo of my parents by the seaside on the mantel above the fireplace. "They sent it right after they were married," Aunt Bess had told me. "Why don't you put it in your room?" I ran my finger over the image. They looked so young and carefree.

So my parents wanted to stay in Italy—or had anyway, the last time we'd been able to reach them. I wrote to them each week, but so far there had been no reply. "Overseas post is so unreliable," Uncle Meyer offered, to try to explain the lack of a response. I was not consoled. Things might have worsened for them and they could be trying desperately to leave.

I set down the photo. There was a section of newspaper from yesterday's *Bulletin* on the top of the dresser as well. I picked it up, along with the dictionary beside it. I'd been working through the paper at Jack's suggestion as a way to improve my English. But the story, about refugees displaced by fighting in France, just made my heart ache worse. In my memories, my childhood in Trieste was idyllic. That was gone now, though, and the reality, of war and violence and suffering, leapt off the pages at me. What was life like for Mamma and Papa now?

The doorbell rang and I looked up from the paper. Visitors were constant on Porter Street, neighboring women dropping by to borrow a cup of sugar or share the latest bit of gossip, and men from the tiny shul on the corner of Porter Street needing Uncle Meyer for the minyan, the ten men required to pray on Shabbes. "Good evening, sir." Joy surged through me as Charlie's rich, familiar voice flowed up the stairwell. I dropped the dictionary and leapt up, then smoothed my hair, hoping the smell of Uncle Meyer's cigar did not linger about me.

"I was just in the area," I heard Charlie explain. It was, of course, a lie. He had no cause to be in our neighborhood, far from his own home. It was as if he'd heard me calling out for him. "And I thought . . ." He stopped midsentence as he saw me at the top of the stairs. I had seen him just days earlier at the beach, but here, dressed more formally in chinos and a collared shirt with his hair held in place by a bit of pomade, he seemed somehow older—and even more handsome. "Hi, Addie. Would you like to come over for ice cream?"

Trying to contain my excitement, I turned to my aunt. "May I?"

"I don't know." She looked at Uncle Meyer uncertainly, hesitant to be rude to Charlie by saying no outright. "It's so far, and she doesn't know the neighborhood." Her voice was heavy with concern. My heart sank. They were going to say no.

"I will walk her there and back personally, sir,"

Charlie said, voice solemn and low. There was something about him that could be trusted.

Uncle Meyer relented. "Fine, but have her home by eight."

"Don't overstay your welcome," my aunt cautioned in a low voice, and I wondered if she was just talking about the Connallys or if I had somehow been a burden here, too. I tried to stay neat and out of the way, not cause extra work or expense.

Charlie held the door and I hurried past before my aunt and uncle could change their minds. Outside, it was still warm and neighbors sat on their porches or marble steps, smoking and watching the children play handball in the street. They stared curiously as we made our way down the block. Everyone knew about the immigrant girl from Italy who had come this summer to live here—but who was this goy walking with her?

Charlie seemed not to notice, whistling a bit as we reached the corner, passing the barbershop where Uncle Meyer and the other men played cards. I glanced at Charlie out of the corner of my eye, trying not to stare. "Mom thought you might like to come over."

"Oh." I'd wanted it to be his idea.

"But I offered to be the one to come get you." My spirits lifted again, riding the endless roller coaster I'd boarded the day I'd spied the Connallys across the rooming house yard.

I followed him northeast and the streets grew wide and unfamiliar. The Irish neighborhood ran close to the shipyard and soot-covered dock-workers made their way home, empty lunch tins in hand. "Careful." Charlie grabbed my arm to guide me around a pothole at the curb. I shivered at the contact. Then the sidewalk grew even and he let go of my arm once more. Finally he stopped at a corner house with bright yellow curtains and a small garden of flowers beside the front step. "This is it."

But the lights of the house in front of us were darkened. Perhaps the others had gone out. I followed Charlie inside uncertainly. Did he mean for us to be alone? "Surprise!" Lights flickered on and the Connallys stood around their dining room table, a cake before them aglow with candles.

"Got her," Charlie said, sounding as if he'd gone to the grocery store for milk.

"Addie!" Robbie cried, running to me and wrapping himself around my waist.

I was too surprised to respond. Robbie had asked me once at the shore when my birthday was, but I hadn't thought anyone else had heard, or might remember. As they sang to me, a chorus of smiling faces, illuminated by candlelight, my mind whirled. September 9, my seventeenth birthday, was still three days away and Aunt Bess had mentioned something vaguely about going out to dinner on Sunday to celebrate.

But I hadn't expected this. Mrs. Connally served the cake. It was just big enough to hold the candles that had been crammed on top, and there was a tiny slice for each of us when it was cut up, none leftover for seconds. It was homemade, though, right down to the wobbly writing that said Robbie had helped. I had not had a real cake since Nonna made one for my twelfth birthday in Trieste. After she was gone Mamma had been too busy with her causes to manage more than tiramisu from the café down the street. And Aunt Bess, for all of her good intentions, could not bake and relied on store-bought Entenmann's. This was the most delicious thing I had ever tasted.

Scraping the icing from my plate, I looked around. The Connallys' house seemed a smaller replica of their place at the beach: casual furniture, piles of paper and toys stacked haphazardly. A grand piano occupied one corner of the room.

When we finished the cake, Mr. Connally handed me a box with a bow. "Happy birthday, Addie."

I'd finally met Mr. Connally a few days after the rest of the family had arrived at the shore. The boys and I had come home from the beach to find a man stepping from the car in a crisp white shirt, short-sleeved and a bit wrinkled from the trip. The boys flocked to him, calling out excitedly, and he lifted Robbie high up in the air.

Mrs. Connally had returned to the house early and as she greeted him in a ruffled pink cap-sleeved dress there was a warmth between her and her husband that reminded me of my parents in earlier days. I'd stood back, an outsider as their circle was now complete. But Mr. Connally welcomed me just as readily as the rest of the family. A large man, reminiscent of a grizzly bear, he seemed to be always smiling. The mustache above his mouth was yellowed from the pipe his wife would not let him smoke in the house.

"You didn't have to get me anything." I opened the box and inside sat a chess set. I lifted it out. Though it was not an exact replica, the pieces were iron just like the ones back home in Trieste.

Mr. Connally cleared his throat. "I saw you admiring ours several times, and I remembered you mentioning something like this."

"It's perfect." They had thought, really thought about what I wanted. My eyes stung with happy tears.

"Help me with the dishes, Addie?" Mrs. Connally asked, and I followed her to the kitchen, pleased to be of use.

After we cleaned up, we all settled in to listen to Abbott and Costello on the radio. Mrs. Connally sat on a long sofa, Robbie and Jack on one side, Mr. Connally on the end.

Liam hung at the edge of the room, seeming uncomfortable in his own house. I started toward him, wanting to draw him in. "Game of chess?" He had a smart, analytical way of looking at the world and something told me he would be good at it.

"Nah, I've got plans. Happy birthday, Ad." He slipped from the house, leaving an emptiness in the otherwise perfect night.

"Come sit." Mrs. Connally patted the small triangular wedge of sofa beside her. I looked uncertainly toward Charlie, wishing there was room for him too. But he had already dropped comfortably to the rug. I slipped in close to Mrs. Connally on one side, my leg pressing against Jack's on the other. Beau ambled into the room and nestled on my feet.

And just like that, I was home.

What was it the Connallys liked about me? I wondered now as I recalled that special night nearly six weeks earlier. They already had enough kids, as Liam once pointed out. How strange that in this family that was already so full there seemed to be a place waiting for me. Over the summer I had become something different to each of them: the daughter that Mrs. Connally never had, a friend to Jack, and the one who would listen to Robbie when the others were all too busy. But what was I to Charlie exactly: a little sister, or something else?

A loud siren blared unexpectedly, cutting through Mrs. Lowenstein's lesson. I sat bolt upright, suddenly wide-awake. Boys and girls looked around, uncertain how to react to the unfamiliar sound, more shrill than the fire alarm. "This is an air raid drill. Under your desks, everyone," Mrs. Lowenstein instructed calmly. "Put your heads beneath a book." The others obeyed slowly, joking and talking as they went. But I scrambled under my desk, trembling.

Mrs. Lowenstein ("Roberta" I'd heard another teacher call her once) crouched down and put her hand on my shoulder. "It's only a drill." America was not at war; we were only practicing. But the fact that the drills like we had back home had begun here seemed to signal something ominous. The siren droned on relentlessly. The hard linoleum floor pressed unpleasantly against my knees. The exercise seemed futile—if bombs actually came, a desk would not protect me. A minute later the siren ended and there was a beep signaling the all clear. We climbed out.

Mrs. Lowenstein smiled reassuringly at me as I took my seat. "With respect to shipbuilding . . ." she continued, resuming her lecture.

I jumped when the bell rang ten minutes later, but this time it was just signaling that class was over. "Have a nice weekend," Mrs. Lowenstein called over the din of chatter and desks slamming. I gathered my books and walked down the hall, which was covered in student-made Halloween decorations and smelled from a mixture of Clorox disinfectant and leftover lunches. I put my books in my locker and grabbed my coat and lunch bag, then closed the door again and leaned against it. The sharp knob cut into my back as I pressed against the wall to escape the surge of students, laughing and talking as they jostled roughly past between classes. I drew my cardigan more tightly around myself like armor. I still could not get used to the size and chaos of Southern High.

I looked longingly in the direction of the tunnel. Southern was in fact two schools, one for the boys and one for girls, and our homeroom, cafeteria and gym were separate. But they were connected by an enclosed walkway so kids could take classes together on either side.

When there was a gap in the crowd, I started for the cafeteria. I eyed the swarming lunchroom warily from the doorway. The girls seemed to camp in clusters, Italians in the far right corner, Irish on the far side of the room, as if trying to recreate the divisions of the local neighborhoods. A few of the girls from Porter and Ritner Streets sat at the first long table in a tight circle. Aunt Bess tried to help me fit in, buying me the popular plaid wool skirts and sturdy saddle shoes, so unlike the loose, flowing dresses and sandals I'd worn most of the year back home. "Maybe you could invite a friend over after school," she'd suggested more than once—as if it were that simple. My olive skin was still darker than the others, my accent undeniable. The girls from the Jewish neighborhood, who had grown up together, had no room for a foreigner.

I carried my lunch box toward a nearly empty table on the far edge of the room. At the end a little girl with skin even darker than mine sat by herself, staring straight ahead, chewing purposefully. "Coloreds," Liam called the small group of black kids at Southern. They, too, kept to their own group—except for this girl, who was alone like me.

"Mind if I sit?" The girl shrugged. "I'm Addie."

"I'm Rhonda. You talk funny." The girl's tone was matter-of-fact. "Where you come from?"

"Italy. I moved here a few months ago, but we were at the shore for the summer."

A harsh laugh came from two tables over. A few of the Irish girls were looking at Rhonda and me, making jokes.

Rhonda finished her lunch and stood, casting the remnants of her lunch in a trash can. "See you." I watched her go, wondering what Aunt Bess's reaction would be if Rhonda was the friend I invited over. Not wanting to remain at the table alone, I took the rest of my sandwich and folded it back in the wax paper. I still could not get used to the amount of waste—or take for granted that there would be food tomorrow.

My science class was in the boys' school so I started down the tunnel. Unsupervised, the long, dim corridor was the one place boys and girls could meet and I averted my eyes from the couples that loitered close to one another against the walls, necking. I didn't know much about sex, other than what I'd gleaned from a few books and whispers in the girls' bathroom. But I sure saw some things here.

I glimpsed Liam at the far end of the tunnel. Seeing just one Connally boy was always strange, like a game piece that had been separated from the rest of the chessboard. My eyes caught his and I started toward him, hoping we might talk before class; I didn't even mind if he teased me. But Liam had become more aloof since returning from the beach, not just from me but from his brothers. I saw him hanging on the shadowy out-skirts at the edge of the playground with kids who smoked and more often than not had only one parent at home —a place he didn't belong.

As I neared the boys' school, Charlie appeared from behind the open door of a locker. Happiness flooded me as it always did when I saw him. But it quickly disappeared. Looking up at him adoringly from beneath his arm was Stephanie Weidman, a blonde senior who led the cheer-leading squad. Her hair was neatly rolled and pinned back and the cuffs of a crisp white blouse peeked out beneath her pink cashmere sweater.

I should not have been surprised. It had not taken me long to figure out that Charlie was very popular with the girls. "Why are you giggling?" I'd demanded of the girl at the locker next to mine the very first day when he'd passed by. I would not have anyone make fun of him.

"He's Charlie Connally," the girl explained, her voice hollow with awe. "The quarterback."

At the shore he had just been Charlie. Here, though, he was larger than life, the "bee's knees," one of the girls called him. Crowds seemed to part as he passed and girls looked at him in a way that I had not understood before. Even those who didn't like football and didn't understand the game, including myself, sat in the stands, shivering, with their hands around a paper cup of metallic-tasting cocoa just to see Charlie in all his glory.

I started to duck away now but Charlie's head swiveled in my direction and he started over, leaving Stephanie standing alone. There was a hushed silence in the tunnel around us, then whispers and stares as the school's star quarterback walked over to talk to the small, foreign girl who nobody knew. "Hi, Addie." Charlie smiled brightly, as though we were at the beach and it was just the two of us. He wore his varsity letter sweater, black with the red *S*. He'd grown taller since summer and wore his hair in a neat combback with pomade, not loose and curly as it had been at the beach.

Behind him I noticed Liam watching our

exchange, eyes longing. He always seemed so separate from the rest of us, in a way he just didn't have to be. *Join us,* I pleaded silently. If I went to him, he just might. But my feet remained planted, not wanting to give up this one moment with Charlie.

Charlie turned to Stephanie, who had come up behind him. "Do you know Addie?" Of course not. Girls like her would never even see me—nor would Charlie if it hadn't been for the shore. "Addie's like family," he said. The words, intended with kindness, stung. Not family—*like* family. There was always that one step separating me from them. Stephanie sniffed, unimpressed, and turned and walked down the hall. Charlie looked after her, as if he wanted to follow.

But he did not.

Warmth surged through me. I loved him. Loved. I had realized it late one afternoon near summer's end as I watched the boys play in the lot between beach houses, sunlight streaming down. I knew he did not feel the same, but the very idea seemed to change things. It wasn't just his image—he was smart and sure and he had a way of making everything safe and all right when he was in the room. I had begun to dream about him, too. The previous night I dreamed that he had pulled me from the water, rescuing me as he had last summer. In my fantasy, though, he did not set me down, but held me, bringing his lips to mine. I'd woken up breathless, my skin damp.

I had other dreams too, not the kind that came unbidden at night but the film that ran all day in my head: What if Charlie really saw me? We could go steady, be a couple. I imagined myself on his arm. No, it wasn't that he didn't quite think of me as family that I minded. I wanted him to think of me as something more.

He looked over his shoulder, then lowered his voice. "I saw you with that colored girl before in the cafeteria." I was flooded with confusion. I always looked for Charlie, but I hadn't known he'd noticed me as well.

"Rhonda?" He shrugged, as though her name was unimportant. "What about it?"

"It's just that colored and whites, they keep to themselves here."

"Why?" I demanded. He blinked. Charlie was not used to being challenged.

"I don't know," he said, revealing a crevice of doubt that he could not show as the oldest always trying to protect the others.

"You play football with some of the colored boys, don't you?"

"That's different." He glanced uneasily over his shoulder. "Maybe we should discuss it at home."

"Whose home?" I liked Charlie, and the last thing I wanted to do was fight. But I couldn't let it go. "Because if what you are saying is true, then perhaps the Jews and the Irish, they should keep to themselves too."

I was right and he knew it. But he clenched his jaw, as though admitting he was wrong would somehow be a weakness or flaw. Charlie saw the world in terms of black and white. "It isn't that simple."

We stood facing one another squarely. He was clearly surprised that I'd stood up to him in a way that few people had. But he would not back down either. There was a light in his eyes, a respect that I hadn't before seen.

"Anyway . . ." Charlie cleared his throat, retreating. His eyes softened, holding mine. "I'm glad to see you." My stomach flipped. Had he somehow guessed the truth about how I felt?

From across the hallway, I heard a snicker, unmistakably aimed in my direction. My face flushed. The fact that I did not fit in here, it was always bubbling beneath the surface with my accent, my slightly darker skin. Kids simply could not imagine why the Connally boys, especially Charlie, wanted to be friends with me. Charlie did not seem to hear it or notice—things like that were below his line of sight. My anger grew. "They're laughing at us." This, coupled with the girls laughing at Rhonda and me in the cafeteria, was too much to take. I started down the hall.

"Addie," Charlie cautioned, wanting me to just leave it alone for the sake of peace. But I had never been able to look away from unfairness.

My mind reeled back to one of the first mornings on the ship when I had awoken to find the chain which perpetually hung around my neck, holding the mizpah, gone. Across the narrow galley, I saw an older girl palming it casually.

"Give it back," I'd demanded. When the girl ignored me, I lunged for it. I was on the ground then, pinned under the larger girl, nails gouging like fire at my cheeks. With all my might, I lifted my knee and pushed the girl off of me, grabbing the necklace that had skittered across the deck. I put it back on, defying the other girl to try to take it again.

I hadn't been able to leave it alone then, and I couldn't now. I approached the boy who had laughed at us. "Something funny?"

His eyes widened, unaccustomed to being called out for his bullying. "Why don't you go back where you came from?"

As I opened my mouth to answer, the bell rang. "Come on," another boy said, urging him outside. I started toward class. But as I neared the end of the tunnel there was a clamoring outside, and I saw Liam crossing the playground with swift, long strides toward the boy whom I'd confronted minutes earlier. I opened the door in time to hear the other kid say, ". . . Jew lover?" Liam drew back his arm. I heard a sickening crunch, flesh splitting, as Liam's fist connected with the boy's face. "Liam!" I cried, running toward him. He had a quick temper, an Irish temper, his mother had called it. He was forever getting into arguments. This was the first actual fight I had seen him in, though. The last thing he needed was further trouble.

But Liam was on top of the boy who lay on the ground now, both hands around the boy's neck. "Apologize," he commanded. The boy gurgled helplessly, blood trickling from his nose.

"Liam, he can't apologize if he can't breathe." I tugged at his shoulder. "Let him up."

Teachers and lunch aides surged forward, pulling Liam and the other boy apart. Charlie rushed up beside us. "What were you thinking?" he admonished.

The principal, Mr. Owens, crossed the school-yard. "I should expel you!"

Charlie stepped forward quickly. "Respectfully, Mr. Owens, that isn't necessary. I will take him home right now myself."

The principal paused, then acquiesced. "Fine." Charlie was a student leader, someone he trusted. He wagged a finger in Liam's direction. "But next time, you're outta here."

"Dad's going to wallop you." Charlie scowled once the principal and other teachers were out of earshot. My heart ached that Liam would be punished simply for sticking up for me—again. I wanted to run after him and explain to his parents.

"And now I'm going to be late for class." Liam's face fell. He could handle expulsion or whatever punishment his folks might hand out. It was Charlie's disapproval that was too much to bear.

"But he was only trying to stick up for me," I began.

"I don't need your help," Liam cut me off tersely. He did not care about punishment, or what the other kids thought of him—except for Charlie.

"Come on." Charlie started to lead Liam from the schoolyard, then turned back. "Addie?"

My heart lifted as it did every time he said my name, wondering if maybe this time he would mean it differently. Was he finally noticing?

I spun back hopefully. "Yes?"

"Will you stop by the science lab and tell Mrs. Ferguson I'm going to be late?"

They set off across the parking lot, leaving me behind. "Sure." I turned away, dejected. How could I possibly have thought he would say something more?

Five

I had always been able to sense change, like the way Nonna's leg used to ache before a storm. My neck would tighten and stay tense for days. My appetite would fade to nonexistent and I'd grow tired, sleeping long, restless nights that were full of vivid dreams, even darker and stranger than usual. I'd awaken more exhausted than I'd ever gone to sleep, as though I had traveled great distances in my dreams.

I'd been that way for more than a week now and I yawned as I stood in my wool coat on the porch, which was still damp from the night's rain. I hadn't seen the boys since school on Friday. I still went to the Connallys' most nights during the week. Charlie (or Jack, during football season when Charlie had practice) would call for me after dinner and then bring me home. My aunt and uncle had stopped fighting me about visiting the Connallys, as long as my homework was done.

They insisted, though, that I stay home on Shabbes. Back in Trieste, my family had been secular, attending the large synagogue in our neighborhood only on high holidays. But here the block quieted Friday nights and Saturdays, the men making their way to shul and the women keeping the children busy without putting on the radio. It was always a long, sluggish day in the tiny house, and I filled it as well as I could, doing my assignments for school and writing letters to my parents.

"They haven't written back," I fretted the day before at lunch.

"The mail is disrupted," Aunt Bess said, speaking authoritatively, though she could not possibly have known for sure. "I'm sure they're fine."

"But what if they aren't?" I'd pressed. They could be trying to get word out, or even want to leave now, and we would have no way of knowing. My question hung unanswered in the air.

It was Sunday now and I could leave the house. But there was no sign of Charlie. Perhaps he had forgotten about me. Did I dare to find my way to the Connallys' on my own? "I'm going out," I called inside to Aunt Bess, who was getting ready for her Hadassah meeting. Then I closed the door before she could stop me. Pulling on my stocking cap and gloves, I hurried down the steps and ran, past the drugstore and the shoe-shine boy at the corner until my feet hurt beneath the stiffness of my Mary Janes and my blouse grew damp, finding my own way for the first time.

The sun shone down brightly on the worn pavement. But a breeze, sharp for early December, cut across the street. I walked south, past shops on the bottom floor of buildings, shoe stores and a dry cleaner's. I turned east toward Pennsport, the Irish neighborhood where the Connallys lived. Soon the streets began to change, like an unmarked border crossing between countries. Breathless, I slowed to a walk. Though Christmas was nearly three weeks away, almost every house sparkled with lights, one brighter than the next. I passed a tavern, noisy through its open door even before lunchtime. Older, noisy boys played stickball on a corner lot. My skin prickled as I recalled Uncle Meyer's admonition months earlier about the dangers of this strange neighborhood. Perhaps coming alone had been a mistake.

But soon I reached the Connallys' and knocked. No one answered. The house was usually bustling with activity, so it had not occurred to me that no one would be home. I considered leaving. Instead, I turned the doorknob and stepped inside the house, looking around the empty living room uncertainly. "Hello?" I called out. "Mrs. Connally?" I eyed the piano in the corner, as I had so many times on my past visits. I made my way toward it, taking off my coat and then stroking the keyboard. It was a grand piano, so much bigger than the creaky old upright we'd had wedged into the dining room back in Trieste. I sat and played now, a simple piece that Papa had taught me back before his arrest when he still played. The notes rose above me like bubbles.

Hearing the door, I stopped abruptly. Mrs. Connally walked in and removed her coat, revealing her cornflower-blue dress. "Addie!" she said, taking off her hat. "I wasn't expecting you."

I stood hurriedly. "I'm so sorry, I shouldn't have come in."

"Not at all." She waved away my concern. "We were at church for the O'Neill baby's baptism and there was lunch and the boys stayed to help

with the nativity. They should be home soon."
Church. The Connallys went so infrequently and
so it had not occurred to me that was where they
might have been. But now the word seemed to
magnify the differences between the Connallys
and myself, which were otherwise so easy to
forget. "Do you like it?" Mrs. Connally asked,
gesturing to the piano. "I had hoped one of the
boys would take it up, but none of them did—
they can't sit still long enough."

"I'm sorry I didn't ask first."

Mrs. Connally waved her hand. "Don't be. It
does my heart good to hear it make music again.
You should come play it whenever you want, and
I hope that will be often. I'm going to change out
of my good clothes. Why don't you play something else for me?"

I sat and began to play again, "Torna a
Surriento," a song that Papa knew could always
get my mother to smile. Once I had struggled with
the notes, but now my fingers seemed to move of
their own will, as if he was here, leading me. I
finished the piece, the last notes echoing through
the house.

There was a noise behind me and I looked up,
expecting Mrs. Connally. But Charlie stood
watching me from the doorway, more handsome
than ever in his navy church suit. How long had
he been there? Our eyes met. Several seconds
passed, my throat too dry to speak.

He took a step toward the piano bench. "Hey." Something seemed to shift with that single word, in the quiet space between us. At school, he was larger than life. But here it was just the two of us away from the eyes and remarks of the other kids. Despite my fantasies of being his girl, this was the part I really wanted, the two of us alone, away from our families and the world.

"That was just beautiful, Addie," Mrs. Connally said as she appeared on the stairwell. Then she stopped. "Charlie, I thought you were helping with your father."

He tore his gaze from me, then cleared his throat. "I was, but I ran into Coach and he said there's a scout from Georgetown coming tomorrow. I want to get in some extra practice." Though football season had ended weeks earlier, Charlie continued to work on his game with a few of the fellows, hoping to catch the eye of one of the colleges.

"Georgetown? That's great, honey, but . . ." Conflict washed across Mrs. Connally's face. I suspected they couldn't afford a school like that. "Maybe somewhere closer."

"There are scholarships, Mom." I knew Charlie had never even contemplated forgoing college for a job at the factory as his father had, or even applying to a lesser school. He had always known he was meant for something great. "I've gotta go." He disappeared upstairs.

A minute later Jack walked in with Robbie in tow. "Dad's still at church finishing up," he told his mother. "Hi, Ad."

I followed them to the kitchen. "Addie, the boys had sandwiches at church. Have you eaten?" I nodded, thinking of the leftover gefilte fish and reheated soup from Shabbes that was a Sunday staple at my aunt and uncle's. She pulled a carton from the icebox. "Chocolate or vanilla?"

"Both!" Robbie interjected.

"Not too much. I'm putting in the roast and dinner is at four." Mrs. Connally handed me a bowl.

"Thank you." I broke off a bit with my spoon. Ice cream here was harder than Nonna's creamy gelato. It almost needed to be cut.

"I spilled!" Robbie wailed as his ice-cream bowl tipped, sending a creamy pool onto the linoleum.

Jack quickly set the bowl straight and scooped some of his own into it, evening things out as he so often did. "Want some help with the science homework after this?" he asked me.

"Sure," I said, grateful for the excuse for having come over later.

"Can I help, too?" Robbie asked eagerly.

Jack knelt by his brother. "How 'bout you give us a little while, and then maybe we can all play dominoes?"

"Marbles," Robbie sniffed.

"All right, but no cheating," Jack teased.

But Robbie's face was serious. "I'm going to beat you, fair and square."

"Why don't you let the dog out first?" Mrs. Connally suggested to Robbie.

He leapt up, whistling for Beau. "Come on, boy."

When he was out of earshot, Mrs. Connally turned to Jack. "Have you seen your brother?"

"Which one?"

"Haha, wise guy. Where's Liam?"

Jack shrugged. "I'm not his babysitter." But worry creased his face. Though Liam hadn't been in any more trouble since the fight in school nearly two months earlier, he was more withdrawn and absent than ever.

"Jackie," his mother pressed. "Where is he?"

"I don't know. He was hanging out with some of the fellas." He did not sound as though he was talking about the kids from church.

Mrs. Connally cringed. "I told him to come home right after you were finished."

"I know. I reminded him. He told me to mind my own business." I followed Jack up the stairs. Through an open door, I could see where Robbie had constructed a giant city out of his blocks, using cardboard boxes when he ran out. He loved to build and Jack loved to read, and Charlie loved football—but what did Liam love? Perhaps it was the lack of a passion that stirred him to trouble.

"I'm worried about Liam," Jack confided when we reached the room he and his twin shared.

"You should be. He's gone from school more often than he's there and those kids he hangs out with are awful. We have to do something."

"Like what?"

I searched for an answer. Liam wouldn't listen to us. Telling the Connallys and getting him in further trouble would only make things worse. "I'll be right back."

I raced downstairs and outside after Charlie, who had changed into his practice jersey and was climbing on his bike, shoulder pads slung over the handlebars. He turned and my breath caught, as it always did when he was near. "What is it, Ad?" he asked. "I've got to practice." But his eyes were soft, his voice warm. What would he do if I kissed him right now?

"I'm worried about Liam." He cocked his head, not following. How could he not have noticed? "He's missing school a lot."

"He's always been a wild kid, Addie. He just loves to give Mom and Dad the business."

"But it's different now. He could be drinking." Though I had not seen Liam with beer or liquor, I knew from conversations I'd overheard at school that some of the wilder kids drank. "Or worse."

"It's a phase. He'll get over it."

"What if he doesn't?" I pressed.

Charlie's brow wrinkled fleetingly. "I'll talk to him, I promise. But right now I've got to get to practice." He rose up on the pedals and started forward. "Don't worry," he called over his shoulder as he pedaled away, his voice fading in the wind. Longing tugged at my stomach. If only he would see what was going on with Liam. If only he would see me.

I started back through the living room toward the stairs. "Addie," Robbie called in a stage whisper, though no one else was around to see or hear. His head stuck out from a doorway beneath the stairs. He'd first shown me his secret hiding place in early fall, waving me in from the dining room during one of my visits while the others were busy debating the Lend-Lease Act to a small door that I had always assumed was a broom closet. I lowered my head and peered inside. "Come in," he'd urged. The tiny space with its low ceiling was barely big enough for the two of us, but he had decorated it with photos and pictures he had done at school and put two pillows on the floor. I'd squeezed onto one of them. "My hideaway." I understood. The house was so overrun, two boys to a bedroom, noise in every corner. This was the one place he could call his own. "No one else knows," he'd whispered. Though quite sure his mother did, I nodded solemnly, flattered that I was the one with whom he had shared his secret.

I hesitated as he waved me in now; Jack was waiting for me upstairs to finish homework. But I slid into the closet and Robbie curled up under the crook of my arm in a way he surely would not do for much longer.

"Look," he said, pointing to the sloped ceiling of the closet. He'd stretched black paper across it and in white he'd sketched the stars, trying to replicate the constellations. "I don't have them quite right," he fretted. I imagined how he'd worked on the design, biting his lip with grim concentration as he tried to get the positioning of the stars just right.

"You should ask Liam." Last summer at the beach, Liam was forever pointing out the different patterns of stars visible in the night sky. His eyes would light up as he explained a particular constellation; it was the closest I'd seen him to taking an interest in something.

"He's never around anymore." Robbie's words were a refrain of my earlier conversations with Jack and Charlie. Even at eleven, Robbie could see the change in his brother. My anger toward Liam rose: couldn't he see that Robbie looked up to him, and needed him in the same way that he needed Charlie? "Charlie's always practicing, and you and Jack are busy with homework." Robbie's voice was dangerously close to a whine now. "I'm bored."

"Wait here." I walked to the living room and picked up the chess set that the Connallys had given me. I'd left it here for the occasional game with Jack, since neither my aunt nor uncle played.

Robbie's eyes widened as I lowered the chess set into his hideaway. "Dad says I'm too young."

"Not at all. I started playing when I was seven." I held up the first piece. "This is the pawn and it moves a single space straight ahead, but diagonally . . ."

From outside the closet there came a clattering. At first, I thought it was Jack, coming to see where I had gone. But Mr. Connally's voice, low and urgent, rose from the entranceway. "What on earth?" I unfolded myself from the closet, meeting Jack as he came down the stairs. We found Mr. Connally in the kitchen with his wife. His usually jovial expression was dark as a storm and he did not greet me. A rock formed in my stomach. "What's happened?"

Grim-faced, he turned on the radio: "The Japanese have attacked Pearl Harbor, Hawaii, by air . . . The attack also was made on all military and naval activities on the principal island of Oahu . . ."

"America will enter the war for sure now," Jack said.

My heart lifted: surely the United States would declare war on the Germans, too. But Mrs. Connally was gripping the counter, knuckles white. "What's wrong?" I asked, forgetting not to be forward. "Don't you want the Americans to help? I know that the Quakers don't believe in fighting but surely now that it's for good reason . . ."

"It's not that," Mrs. Connally replied quietly.

"Then what?"

"Our boys are too young," Mr. Connally soothed, reading her unspoken thought. "And it will be over quickly."

"Yes, of course."

Charlie ran in breathless, still wearing shoulder pads under his practice jersey. "The Japs bombed . . ." He stopped, realizing we had already heard. We stood huddled for several minutes, listening to the reports of the devastation in Hawaii, ships destroyed, casualties possibly in the thousands. I had seen the edges of war in Italy, homes burned and shop windows smashed, people arrested. But the scope of the damage described on the radio was simply unfathomable.

Charlie cleared his throat. "Will you go down to the enlistment center with me tomorrow, Dad?" he asked. His mother's face seemed to fold with horror, as though her worst nightmare had come true.

"You'll be eighteen soon," his father said grudgingly. "I suppose you'll need to register."

Charlie shook his head. "Not just register. I want to join up." My heart stopped. Charlie could not go to war.

"Charlie, no. You need to finish school. You may not even get drafted."

"You don't understand. I want to go now." His eyes burned bright with an idealism that made me love him even more. "There's a chance to make a difference and really help."

Liam slammed through the door. "Mom, I was just . . ." Then, seeing us gathered, he stopped short. "What gives?"

"The Japanese attacked our base in Hawaii," Mrs. Connally said. "And your brother wants to enlist." She did not have to say which one.

Liam rolled his eyes. "Figures."

"There's no need to enlist. The war won't last long," Mrs. Connally said. This was the first time I had seen the Connallys disagree. As much as I wanted to be part of their family, I felt like an intruder listening in.

"Exactly. I want to go now, while I can help." As the debate went back and forth like a ping-pong match, I watched Liam. He was looking at Charlie, rapt, his face a strange mix of adoration and resentment.

"But what about college?" his mother persisted. "You were just talking about a football scholarship." Charlie bit his lip, trying to reconcile his dreams.

"It's out of the question, Charlie," Mr. Connally added firmly.

"But this is my decision."

"What if you just registered for now?" Liam spoke up unexpectedly, before his parents could respond. All heads turned in his direction. Usually it was Jack that made peace. "I mean, that way as soon as you graduate you can go."

"I don't want to wait to enlist," Charlie replied sharply.

"And we don't want you to go at all," his father shot back. His suggestion rejected by both sides, Liam slunk from the room.

Mrs. Connally turned toward me, Jack and Robbie. "Kids, would you excuse us, please?"

As we left the kitchen, I saw Robbie eyeing his hideaway, wanting to escape. The family quarrels were perhaps hardest on him. I put my arm around him. "Come on." At the front door, I looked back at the stair closet, wondering if it would be useful as a bomb shelter. Uneasily, I shooed the thought away and followed Jack out onto the porch. Clouds had formed, turning the air cold and blustery. I scanned the street. Where had Liam gone? I wanted to find him and tell him I thought his suggestion had been a fine one, but he was nowhere to be seen. Pigeons huddled on the rooftops across the street. Jack pulled a pack of Juicy Fruit from his pocket and offered both of us a stick. I unwrapped it and popped it in my mouth, the syrupy sweetness a contrast to the somber mood. "Why is your mom so against the war?"

He shrugged. "She doesn't believe it solves anything."

Anger rose within me. It was so easy to sit here thousands of miles away and say that. "Is your dad a pacifist, too?"

"Injured," Jack replied. "The army won't take him." I was puzzled. Mr. Connally looked just fine to me. "He had such a hard time during the Depression," Jack added. I didn't understand what that had to do with being able to fight.

Before I could ask further about their father, the door to the house opened and Charlie walked out, slamming it behind him.

"Charlie, I . . ." I began, searching for the words. I wanted America to go to war. But not him. "Please wait." But he walked straight past and stormed off, not seeing me, leaving me feeling small and cold.

Six

The smell of marsh grass baked in the late-August sun rose from the ground as I walked down the steps from our rooms at the beach house, brushing at some sand that lingered on my knee. A faint breeze, cooler than the day before, threatened to lift the hem of my pale yellow sundress, then set it down with a swirl.

I ran my fingers over the shell bracelet which Robbie had won for me from a boardwalk ring toss a few weeks earlier. It was hard to believe summer had come and gone again. We had arrived just before the Fourth of July, a day after the Connallys. Here there was no rushing home across the city after dinner, or worrying about the long walk between neighborhoods. Instead we had fallen back into our familiar routine of leisurely days on the beach and jitney rides up to the boardwalk some evenings. It was as if we had never left.

But everything was not the same. The country had been at war for more than eight months now. Life had changed in a thousand small ways, from the blackout curtains that lined the windows to the things like white sugar and sometimes butter that we were all meant to do without for the war effort.

One day, just after the war had broken out, my name was called over the intercom when I was in Mrs. Lowenstein's class, asking me to come to the principal's office. This had never happened before and I hurried down the linoleum corridor, trying to figure out what I had done wrong. I was surprised to find my aunt and uncle waiting for me. They seldom ventured beyond the neighborhood. "We need you to come with us," Aunt Bess said. They were both wearing their best clothes and their expressions were somber.

My apprehension rose. "Is it my parents? Have you had word?" Uncle Meyer shook his head and I followed them as we boarded the trolley downtown. Immigration and Naturalization, read a sign over the door of the office building at Fifth and Market to which Uncle Meyer led us.

Despite my uncle's denial, hope flickered in me for a second: perhaps my parents were coming after all and we needed to get them visas. I turned to Aunt Bess questioningly. "Your citizenship paperwork came through," she said. Annoyance rose in me. They had not asked if I wanted to be American; they had just presumed and filed the application without asking me. For a minute, I considered refusing. "It will make things easier," Aunt Bess added. Easier for whom?

We sat in a waiting room with a dozen other people where a clock ticked above a water fountain. Finally, my name was called and we walked into an office. Would I have to take a test like I'd heard about in civics class? But the bald man behind the desk just asked me to repeat after him words I did not quite hear over the buzz in my ears, something about defending the Constitution. "Congratulations." He handed me a certificate with coarse dry hands. Was that it? My heart sank a bit as I passed the paper to Aunt Bess, who folded it neatly and tucked it in her purse.

"That was wonderful," Aunt Bess said, hugging me as though I had won an award, though I had in fact done nothing at all. "Wonderful." I was not so sure. More and more lately, I had wanted to be like the Connallys and others here in America. I even dreamed in English, a transition that had happened so subtly I couldn't say when. But now a small piece of me slipped away permanently, widening the gulf between me and my parents and the world I had left behind.

After leaving the immigration office, we went for a late lunch at Famous Deli and ate our corned-beef sandwiches silently. "Now that I'm not an Italian citizen anymore . . ." I began.

"Shhh," Aunt Bess said, sneaking quick glances in both directions. I understood then the rush to naturalize me. With war raging overseas, people were growing more suspicious of foreigners here by the day. It was important to simply fit in, especially for a girl from Italy, which had declared war on America just days after Germany. Even on Porter Street, the chatter between porches that had mostly been Yiddish had become almost all English.

"I'm American now," I'd told the Connallys when I'd visited them afterward.

"Congratulations!" Jack exclaimed brightly.

"Great," Liam, on a rare evening home, remarked wryly. "You're just like everyone else." His words echoed my own misgivings. It was as if the part of me he'd admired—the part that was different—was gone.

The shore had changed, too—Atlantic City and the surrounding towns seemed to have been swallowed by the war. Fresh-faced young men in crisp new uniforms were everywhere and Convention Hall had been taken over as a training center. "Camp Boardwalk," they called it. In the morning, troops marched and drilled in neat lines before scores of onlookers. Though bathers still took to the beaches, they scanned the horizon as if a German U-boat might appear at any second.

"Maybe we shouldn't go to the shore this summer," Mrs. Connally had fretted in early spring. Hearing that, my heart sank. The long summer days at the shore without the Connallys were unthinkable.

"The Germans won't attack the coast," her husband replied gently. He spoke with confidence, certain the war could not possibly reach America. But I had thought that once in Italy, too. Now newspaper stories ran pictures of fighting in the cities and villages, ordinary people arrested. My parents were smart, I told myself. They would have left and gone into hiding if things got too bad. It did little to ease my fears.

Thankfully the Connallys had come. I crossed the yard and Beau bounded out around the side of the wrapped porch in greeting. I knocked, not waiting for a response before opening the door. Though it was dinnertime, the smell of bacon and eggs filled the air. Boxes were strewn across the floor, much as they had been the day I'd met them. But this time they were packing to leave. At the base of the stairwell stood a small trunk. A lump formed in my throat at the bag that would go with Charlie when I would not.

They were all gathered in the kitchen, Robbie and the twins picking at the dishes their mother was cooking before she could swat their hands away. A radio played on the counter, President Roosevelt talking about how each American could help the war effort. "Addie, we've got eggs!" Robbie exclaimed, excited about the dinner he once might have scoffed at. I ruffled his hair, noting Mrs. Connally's pained expression over his head. With rationing it was hard to get enough food for four growing boys, and even the ordinary things had become occasional treats.

Charlie sat at the table with his father, sharing sections of the newspaper. He wore a white T-shirt and his hair was still damp from his post-beach shower. Though I had seen him just an hour earlier, my stomach jumped.

Charlie looked up and his eyes seemed to hold mine just a beat longer than usual. "Hello, Addie," he said. Did I imagine the odd twinge to his voice? There were moments, just a few, where I wondered if he might like me as well. Like back in the city last winter, when I had gone with all of the boys to see *The Wizard of Oz* downtown at the Stanley. About three-quarters of the way through the movie, right about when Dorothy tried to go home in a hot-air balloon, something brushed my hand in the darkness and I lifted it, thinking it was a fly. Charlie's fingers hovered just above mine, then settled on them lightly. I wondered if it was intentional, but he stared intently at the movie, seeming not to notice. I did not breathe for fear of interrupting the moment. A few minutes later the lights came on and he stood, leaving me confused. As we made our way down the street to Horn & Hardart for hot cocoa, I searched his face for an explanation. But his expression was impassive and conversation ordinary, so ordinary I might have imagined it.

Things like that made me think that maybe he could like me, too. Why not? He was only a year and a bit older. But then he would retreat into his world of senior friends and dances and football, and I knew he would never feel the same way about me. He had spoken to me less recently, too, avoiding my eyes in a way reminiscent of Liam. I had wondered more than once if he was angry, though about what I could not fathom.

"Sit, sit," Mrs. Connally urged, setting a plate before me. Guilt nagged at me as I inhaled the savory bacon smell. My aunt and uncle kept kosher at home. They didn't ask what I ate at school or with the Connallys, but I felt fairly sure they hadn't contemplated anything so *trayf*. My stomach grumbled. What they didn't know wouldn't hurt them. I took a bite.

"We're going to the boardwalk while Mom and Dad pack up," Jack offered. He'd gone a bit pimply around the chin, an awkward phase that the other boys seemed to have been spared.

"I promised Robbie one last carousel ride."

"Two," Robbie corrected.

"Want to come?"

"Sure." I wanted to buy a box of saltwater taffy to bring back for Rhonda. We'd become friends in a way. I didn't see her outside of school —she had a gaggle of five younger brothers and sisters to babysit and I was busy with the Connallys. But we sat together at lunch every day and partnering up for relay races in gym. The other girls had either grown tired of mocking us or simply stopped noticing.

I took a sip of the juice Mrs. Connally had set before me, secretly studying Charlie as I ate. He was reading about a particularly difficult campaign that the army was waging in North Africa.

"I should be there," he burst out, slamming his hand onto the table with uncharacteristic frustration. He had gone to register for the draft, waiting more than two hours in the line that snaked around Federal Street. He had not enlisted, though, in accordance with his parents' wishes.

"Next year when I join the army—" Jack began. Gentle Jack was not a fighter, but he would do anything he could to be like his older brother.

"Next year the fighting will be over," his father interrupted firmly.

"Please, God," Mrs. Connally mumbled. "This may be the only time that I wish I had daughters instead."

"You're lucky you're going to college," Liam pointed out. Charlie had been accepted at Georgetown on the full football scholarship, just like he'd hoped. I'd been helping Mrs. Connally plant her victory plot last April when he'd come home with the news. Mrs. Connally had always made the tiny garden into an oasis, roses climbing trellises stubbornly looking for sun in the shaded patch of green, honeysuckle giving off a fragrant smell. When the war had come, she had reluctantly dug out some of her prized flowers to plant vegetables.

Charlie had run down the sidewalk, whooping. "I got into Georgetown."

"But how do you know?" his mother had asked. "There hasn't been a letter."

"There will be. Coach found out." He'd lifted me and spun me around. Then he'd set me down to hug his mother and I stood motionless, emotions cascading over me. His dream had come true, and he was going to school, not war. But I was still losing him. Charlie had talked about going away since the day we met. The neighborhood simply could not hold him.

But his excitement about college had not staved off the fact that part of him—a big part—felt duty-bound to go and fight. "Maybe you can get a part-time job in Washington with the War Department when you're at Georgetown," I offered now, trying to ease his frustration.

His face relaxed and he smiled slightly. "That's an idea." But I couldn't tell if he meant it or was just humoring me.

"Thanks, Addie," Mrs. Connally said in a low voice as Charlie walked from the room.

When we finished eating, Jack, Liam and Robbie spilled outside with their football, tossing it in the grass yard between the two houses. The boys were outpacing me now, I noticed. The twins were as tall as Charlie had been the day we met. Even Robbie's shoulders now nearly matched my own. And Charlie . . . I looked back at the Connally house. Why hadn't he come out yet?

From our rooms above, I heard the scrape of a window screen and saw a curtain move. Aunt Bess had been watching me with the Connallys, her expression undoubtedly one of disapproval. Though I had been friends with the Connallys for over a year, it seemed to bother her and Uncle Meyer now more than ever. They were forever trying to push me toward Jewish kids back in the city. "There's a dance at the Y," Aunt Bess had said tentatively at dinner about a month before we'd come down the shore. "I thought that maybe you would like to go." I had not answered. It wasn't that I disliked the Jewish kids, but even if they would have accepted me, I didn't want to go. I had the Connallys. I didn't need anyone else.

"You're almost eighteen now," Aunt Bess had pressed. "You need to meet some nice boys."

"And the Connallys aren't?" I demanded. Uncle Meyer blinked in surprise at the forcefulness of my voice.

"It's not that. But being Jewish matters. After everything that you've seen, I would have thought that you would appreciate that."

I pushed aside my aunt's disapproval and watched the boys play as they had done dozens of evenings this summer. But this time was different: it was the last time. Tomorrow it would all be gone. Swatting back a tear, I ran up the stairs to my room and grabbed the camera that Uncle Meyer had given to me as a birthday present. "I noticed you admiring it," he'd confessed. It was smaller than the one Papa had let me use and not as new. But I didn't mind; I took it everywhere, capturing bits of the city, like the shopkeepers beneath the sagging awnings at the Italian market and the old men who fed pigeons in Mifflin Park. I saved a bit of my allowance each week to buy film and had gotten permission to use the darkroom at school, rinsing the images until the contrast was just right.

I stood on the stairs, snapping shots of the boys as they tackled one another, their hair and skin golden in the late-day sun.

"Hey!" Liam scowled at the clicking sound. "No pictures."

I lowered the camera and walked down the steps. "Why not?" I challenged.

"You gotta be careful with that. Someone might think you're an Axis spy."

"Liam!" Jack cautioned.

"I didn't mean anything by it." His face flushed. But there was some truth to what he'd said: people looked at me differently since the war began. Even though I was an American citizen now and my accent had faded with time, my past meant I would never truly be one of them. I was an outsider, foreign once more.

"I doubt the Germans would want a photo of you anyway," Jack chided his twin, trying to break the tension. Liam did not answer but stormed off around the side of the house.

"But, Liam, we're going to the boardwalk!" Robbie could not imagine anyone passing up on that. His voice was drowned out by the choky rev of Liam's dirt-bike engine, then tires squealing. Seeing Robbie's face fall, I walked over and squeezed his hand, which was still a bit slick with bacon grease. Jack looked at me helplessly. Liam was so much moodier and more distant than a year ago. We had hoped that the summer away from the city, where trouble was so easy to find, would have done something to calm Liam's wild ways. There were moments when he seemed his old self, playing with his brothers in the surf. But his darkness always returned.

Mrs. Connally stepped from the house, shielding

her eyes as she scanned the side yard. "Where's Liam?"

"Gone—on his bike. He said something earlier about meeting some friends at the beach."

Mrs. Connally's face fell. "I hate that thing," she said bluntly. The bike had been a reward—Liam was allowed to buy it with the allowance he'd saved in exchange for finishing the semester with no Fs. But it had backfired, allowing him to roam farther and longer than ever before. "He's having such a hard time." She seemed to be pleading with me to do something, though what I did not know.

Before I could ask, Jack came to my side with Robbie in tow. "Ready?"

"What about the others?" I asked, purposefully vague.

But the point of my question could not have been more obvious. "Charlie's got plans."

"A date," Robbie piped up cheerfully.

"Robbie, don't." Jack shifted uncomfortably. He had been trying to spare my feelings. A foot seemed to kick me in the stomach. I had seen Charlie talking to the girl who worked the concession stand by the beach a couple of times, a strawberry blonde a year or two older than me. But I had not actually thought he would go out with her tonight of all nights. It was our last night at the shore, for goodness' sake. How could he waste it with someone he hardly knew?

A few minutes later, the jitney came and we paid a nickel each to board. Our nights had changed since last summer when the whole Connally family had made the trek to the boardwalk on Saturday nights to ride the Ferris wheel and watch the lights twinkle along the hazy coastline below. On the Fourth of July, we'd crowded together on a blanket, sharing caramel corn as fireworks exploded above and an orchestra played on the pier.

Now everything was different. Liam was off getting into trouble and Charlie was with that red-haired girl. My mind was flooded with images. Where was he taking her tonight? So those moments I'd glimpsed between me and Charlie had just been my imagination. How foolish of me! I had no right to stop him from dating, but it still felt like a betrayal—and it hurt worse than I could have imagined.

"We're here." Robbie tugged at my arm and we climbed off, then walked the last few steps to the wide promenade of the boardwalk. The shops and arcades stood in a row beneath brightly colored awnings. The heady aroma of taffy and funnel cake and caramel corn, which I normally savored, seemed stifling now. Roller coasters and other amusements rose on the massive piers that jutted out like freighters into the sea. Across the boardwalk, a serviceman who had not yet shipped out yet stole a kiss from the girl on his arm.

We walked passed the Warner Theater, its

marquee alight touting a Gary Cooper film. Once the boardwalk would have come alive with twinkling lights even before dusk, but now they were dimmed out, lights covered with a special blue film in a precaution to make the coast less visible in case of an attack. "The Miss America pageant is coming," Robbie announced as they passed a poster of a striking woman in a swim costume.

"She sure is a dish," Jack chimed in, but the words sounded forced and silly.

"Hey!" Normally I didn't mind the boys' rough banter. "That's rude to say in front of me."

"Sorry, Ad," Jack said, chastened.

But his apology did no good. My frustration, with Charlie and Liam and all of it, suddenly boiled over. The lights and merriment only seemed to amplify my sadness. I could stand it no longer. "I'm a girl, too, you know. Maybe it's time you remembered that!"

I turned away blindly. Ignoring the boys' calls, I dodged through children licking ice-cream cones and the wicker rickshaws pushed by colored men. I ran south, my sandals flapping against the boards until the sound and lights faded behind me.

Finally, I slowed a bit, breathing heavily. The sun was setting in great layers of pink, like wide swaths of strawberry frosting on a cake I'd once admired through a bakery window. The board-walk grew quiet except for the cry of a few gulls and the rhythmic thunder of the waves. When I reached Chelsea Avenue, I saw a cluster of kids sitting around a fire down on the beach and Liam's dirt bike propped against the side of the board-walk. Before I knew it, I was going after him.

I took off my sandals and then stepped onto the beach. The sand, still warm, grew damp and harder beneath my feet as I neared the water. About fifteen feet away from the group, I stopped. Seven or eight kids sat in the surf smoking and drinking out of glass soda bottles that I guessed contained something stronger. Liam was not among them, and for a moment I was grateful I had been wrong. Then a familiar whoop came across the water. Liam was almost fifty feet out paddling on a surfboard, scarcely visible at dusk. It wasn't accurate anymore to say that Liam had no hobbies. He had the dirt bike and surfing, which he had picked up earlier this summer. He was drawn, it seemed, to anything dangerous. He rose up and the water seemed to dance beneath him. I momentarily forgot my fear of the water and stood transfixed.

As Liam played to his audience, he scanned the coastline. Seeing me, he lurched in surprise. The board few out from under him and his legs went flying through the air. "Liam!" I called, panic surging through me. Seconds passed and I watched the surface, willing him to appear.

A minute later he emerged in shallow water, his

hair dark and slicked with water. As he saw me, a light came to his eyes and for a moment he almost smiled. Then his face seemed to close again and he turned from me, starting toward the group by the fire. "Liam, wait." As he neared, I noticed an odd smell mingling with the salt water, and his eyes were glassy.

"Hey, Ad." He reached into his bag and held out a flask to me. His look was daring, sure that I would say no. "I didn't think so," he sneered when I hesitated. I took the flask from him and as I raised it, the acidic smell took me back to the glass of vodka Nonna always had before supper. Wanting him to trust me but knowing better than to sip, I took a swig, cringing at the burn.

The others kids were packing up now and I feared Liam would follow, leaving me behind. I shivered. He pulled out a shirt and passed it to me, and I could smell the sweat and smoke and beer it had seen as I rolled up the too-long sleeves. He dropped to the sand and I followed, leaning back. There was a great white streak of cloud across the night sky, seeming to light it, as if someone had taken a piece of chalk and brushed it sideways. One of Robbie's ceiling sketches come to life.

I stared up at the sea of stars. "So much darkness," Liam said. I turned in amazement. Was that really what he saw? "What are you doing here?" he asked.

Running away, I thought. *Just like you.* I drew

116

my knees close under the sweatshirt and wrapped my arms around them. There were moments when Liam and I seemed to get each other, like last February when snow had blanketed Second Street in fresh white. The boys had built forts out of shoveled snow on either side of the street and it had been Liam and I on one side of the snowball fight, just the two of us against the world. "I was thinking about school this fall," I said instead, trying to find a topic easier than admitting the real reason I had come.

"School is really more Jack's turf. Anyway, what's the point? We could have had this conversation at home."

"Except you're never there!" I accused. "Or when you are, you're so busy trying to cover up the fact that you are drunk or whatever that you ignore everyone."

He raised an eyebrow. "Wow. That may be the first time I've ever seen you lose your cool."

My irritation rose. "Don't mock me. I'm serious."

"I'm serious, too. You're always so composed. I may be screwed up, but at least I know I'm alive."

"This isn't about me, Liam."

"The hell it isn't. You want to talk, fine, but it's got to cut both ways. You can't just sit there like some kind of shrink and look inside me."

"Fine." I decided to try another approach. "Truth or dare?"

117

"What?"

"You heard me." I hoped he wouldn't pick dare because there was no challenge I could think of that he wouldn't do.

"Dare." He smirked.

"I dare you to tell me what's eating you. I dare you to tell me why you've changed."

"That's a truth, not a dare," Liam protested but then he answered. "Nothing. This is my life. What else is there to do besides drink and surf and sleep? My turn. Truth or dare?"

"Truth."

"I knew it. You would never pick dare."

"Well, it's my choice," I said defensively.

"Have you ever gone all the way?"

I reared backward, shocked. "Liam!"

"It's a fair question."

"No, of course not." I hoped he couldn't see my face turn crimson in the dim light.

"Why not?"

"That's a second question. I wouldn't right now. Not with anyone."

"Not even with Charlie?"

"That's your third question. Now, it's my turn to ask."

Ignoring me, he pressed on. "You love him, don't you?"

My breath caught. Was it really so obvious? "That's your fourth. Truth or dare?"

"Addie, this is stupid. You'll keep choosing

truth and I'll keep choosing dare, because that's who we are. There's nothing left to say."

"One more," I pleaded.

"Okay, I choose dare."

"I dare you to succeed, Liam Connally. You can rebel all you want, but you don't have to go to hell in a handbasket while doing it. Hang in there, do your homework. Just get by and for goodness' sake don't get yourself killed."

"Now you sound like my mother." A quiet moment passed between us. "Truth or dare."

I took a deep breath, desperate to reach him and pull him from the corner into which he had withdrawn. "Dare."

"Really?" Surprised, he thought for a moment. "Come swimming with me."

Behind him the ocean at dusk roiled, darker and more menacing than ever. "I can't, Liam. You know that."

"Please," he pleaded in a voice that tugged at my heart. For a moment, I considered trying. It might be my only chance to reach him.

But fear clamped down anew. "I'm sorry, I can't."

He held out his hand, as though inviting me to accompany him on a journey, and I wanted— really wanted to take it. "C'mon, Addie. Live a little." I shook my head. "I thought so." His voice was guarded once more. "You're telling me to change, but you won't."

"I'm sorry."

"Me, too. I thought you trusted me."

"I do—"

He picked up his bag. "This is a joke. I've got to go."

"Don't walk away like this." Now it was my turn to plead.

"What else is there to say? You've done your good deed for the day trying to reform me. But you can't turn me into a cause, or return me to my family like some kind of trophy."

"What about your family?"

He stiffened defensively. "What about them?"

"You're hurting them."

"They'll be fine no matter what I do."

"And Robbie?" I countered. "He looks up to you."

"He's got no shortage of big brothers. Jack and Charlie are the better role models by far."

"Do you really believe that?" He did not answer but looked away, eyes distant. When had Liam slipped away from us? In the middle of a noisy Connally kitchen or in a quiet moment when no one was looking? He seemed gone down a path now too far to reach.

"This has got to stop, Liam, before someone gets hurt." But he turned and walked up the beach. I watched helplessly as he slipped back into the destructive lifestyle that seemed to be claiming him for its own.

Seven

I reached Sunset Avenue forty minutes later, feet aching from the long walk back. The brackish smell of low tide rose from the bay waters, unseen in the darkness. I eyed the Connally house, my disappointment rising anew. Liam was still at the beach or God only knew where, Charlie on his date. Nothing was the same anymore. I started for our house, then stopped with surprise. My aunt and uncle were waiting for me on the front porch. It was nearly ten o'clock. Were they mad at me for going out without asking, or coming home late, or simply for spending more time with the Connallys?

But there was no anger in their eyes. "Addie, come, sit," Aunt Bess said as they led me to the stairs up to our rooms. Aunt Bess sat down beside me on the daybed in the sunroom. "It's about your parents." She looked at Uncle Meyer uncertainly and then back to me. "They've gone missing."

All the air seemed to leave my lungs as all of the worries I'd had about the Connallys vanished. "Papa was arrested before." I willed myself to breathe against the tightness in my chest. "But he came back." My parents had remained in my thoughts of course, though fuzzier and more remote with time. Now their faces appeared sharply before me and my guilt rose. How had I let go of worrying about them, even for a single second?

Uncle Meyer brushed at his eyes. "It's not like that. I'm afraid they're both gone." In his hand he clutched a small bundle of worn envelopes. I reached out and took them, trembling as I recognized the letters I'd written to my parents, one each week since coming here. I'd described my life with great care, focusing on the best parts in hopes that it would make them stop what they were doing and come to America. It had hurt that other than once at the beginning they had not written back, even for my birthday and the holidays. My uncle's explanations about the inconsistency of wartime post had been of little comfort. Now my letters had been returned, each one stamped undeliverable.

"How long have you known?"

My aunt and uncle exchanged uneasy looks. "We knew the letters were coming back, but we didn't know why until just now," Uncle Meyer answered. Why hadn't they told me? He passed me a torn piece of paper containing a scrawl in Italian: *Montfortes no longer at this address. No forwarding address given.*

"They could be in hiding," I said, clinging desperately to hope.

Uncle Meyer's eyes flickered and there seemed to be something more he wanted to say. My parents would not have gone without sending me a way to reach them—unless they were taken unexpectedly, not given a choice.

"We don't know if they were arrested," Aunt Bess offered, as though this might make things better. She had never been there—how could she possibly know?

I turned and ran down the steps of the duplex and across the yard. I knocked, then opened the door without waiting. Mrs. Connally sat alone reading on the sofa. Seeing me, her face crinkled with concern. "Addie, what is it?"

"My parents." I told her what I had just learned. She enveloped me softly, letting me sob into the softness of her skirt.

A few minutes later, I straightened. "If I hadn't left, they might be safe." Of course, it had not been my choice. Mamma had not even told me I was leaving Trieste until we reached the ship, knowing I would refuse. But I could have fought it and even run away and gone back.

"If you hadn't left, you would have been taken as well," Mrs. Connally said softly. "Your mother did what all good mothers do, fight for their children's survival. I would have done the same."

"No, you would have gone with your boys." I was not talking back, just being honest. Anger rose up in me then. Why couldn't my parents have put caring for me first?

Robbie padded into the room then, rubbing

his eyes. "Addie, what are you doing here?"

"Just talking," Mrs. Connally said quickly, as I wiped the tears from my cheek, trying to shield her youngest from bad news. "You can stay here tonight if you want," Mrs. Connally offered.

"Like a slumber party?" Robbie asked, brightening.

His mother chuckled. "Something like that. I'll let your aunt know." I nodded gratefully and Mrs. Connally walked from the room. Robbie dropped down beside me and slipped his hand into mine, sensing my sadness. Mrs. Connally returned with a pillow and blanket, which she arranged on the couch.

"Off to bed." She shooed Robbie. He stood, but lingered by the doorway.

"Where are the others?" I asked.

"Jack's sleeping. And Liam . . ." Mrs. Connally gestured helplessly, not wanting to say more in front of Robbie. So Liam had not come back after I had seen him at the beach. Our talk, it seemed, had done no good at all. And Charlie was not back from his date either. Jealousy wormed its way into the worry about my parents and nagged at my stomach once more.

"Can Addie stay for breakfast in the morning?" Robbie asked.

"Of course, if she likes. Now go." After Robbie disappeared up the steps, Mrs. Connally hung back. "I would never try to replace your mother."

The word twisted in my stomach like a knife. "And I know that you have your aunt. But I'm here for you—we all are. And with all of these boys," she added, gesturing upward. "Well, I'm glad you're with us." As she started up the stairs, I exhaled quietly. Though I so often wanted to be a Connally, I was glad for once she had not said I was like a daughter. Tonight I could not have stood it.

I lay in the darkness, the news about my parents pressing down on me. I burrowed into the covers, trying to remember the feel of my mother's dress as I hugged her, and her smell so much like a field of lavender in early spring. There were a thousand other details that had already begun to fade with time. My eyes grew heavy. I drifted off and the ocean loomed, churning darkly before me.

A wave rose, but before it could crash down, a cracking noise startled me awake. I reached for the pocketknife that I kept under my pillow, the one Aunt Bess and the others did not know about. But it was not there. I sat bolt upright. "Easy," a familiar voice said. Charlie. His hands were on my shoulders, firm and soothing. "What are you doing here, Addie?" I sat up, recalling that I was on the Connallys' couch, not in my bed.

My grief swelled thinking about my parents, threatening to drown me and for a moment I wanted to throw myself into Charlie's arms. Then I remembered he'd been on a date. I stood, the blanket from my makeshift bed falling to the floor. "I was just headed home. Don't turn on the light," I added, hearing the hoarseness in my own voice. I didn't want him to see my tears.

"Wait. Want to go for a walk?"

I turned back, surprised. "Isn't it late?"

"Does that matter? Last night here—no sense wasting it sleeping." No, he had wasted it on a date with someone else. But I didn't have the strength to argue. I slipped on my sandals and followed him outside. The street was still except for our footsteps as we walked toward the inlet, following the curve of the bay.

"How was your date?" I could not keep the note of recrimination from my voice.

But he ignored or did not hear it. "Okay, I guess. We just didn't have much to talk about."

We reached the jetty by the bay and lowered ourselves to the rocks. I averted my eyes from the dark water below. "Hard to believe I'm leaving for school tomorrow," he remarked.

I swallowed over the protest that rose in my throat. This was it. We would no longer all be together. "Hey, what's the matter?" he asked, as I burst into tears.

"My parents," I said, because somehow it was easier than admitting I was crying over him. I told him Aunt Bess's news. "They're gone, Charlie, really gone." He drew me close and I cried into his T-shirt, dampening and then soaking the

126

material. He did not speak or try to make it better by offering false hope, but simply held me in the way that was exactly what I needed, even though I had not myself known it.

"And the worst part is that I'm angry. Angry at them for choosing their work over me. Isn't that awful?"

"Our family isn't perfect either, Addie," he said, a gravelly undercurrent to his voice. "Things got bad during the Depression," he continued, and it was as if he was opening a door to reveal things about their family. "Dad's business shut down and he couldn't find work. We would have lost the house in the city and the one here, too, if they weren't already paid for. Dad was drinking a lot and some days he wouldn't even get out of bed. I was just a little kid, but I could tell. Then one day . . ." Charlie broke off. "He tried to hurt himself." My stomach dropped as I tried to reconcile the story I was hearing with the sunny loving father I'd come to know. "Anyway, he got help and he's better now, but that's why he isn't eligible for the draft."

"Oh, Charlie," I sighed, momentarily forgetting my own grief. Scars ran deep, even in a family as close as the Connallys. I touched his arm, the skin warm beneath my fingertips. "I'm so sorry."

"It's fine. It isn't anywhere near what you've lost. We're here for you, Addie. I'm here for you."

I leaned my head on his shoulder. There was a

peaceful silence between us, only broken by the gentle lapping of the water against the bottom of the dock. A minute later I straightened, lifting my head. Our eyes locked.

Charlie lowered his head and before I knew what was happening his lips met mine, sending waves of electricity through me. A moment later, he drew back. "I shouldn't have done that."

"I love you," I blurted out. A chasm seemed to open between us, threatening to swallow me. Should I take it back? No, I would not hide from the truth. "I love you," I repeated, raising my chin and meeting his eyes squarely.

In that moment I was falling from the sky, nothing to catch me if Charlie did not respond. The entire world hung in the balance. "I do, too," he said and the declaration, just short of mine, was somehow enough. I landed in his arms, saved. He kissed me and it was the moment of purest joy, tasting and touching the very thing I had wanted for all of this time. "I've been trying to keep my distance," he said when we broke apart. So that explained why he had been avoiding me.

Before I could respond his lips were on mine again, this time more intense, a freight train neither of us could—or wanted—to stop. Then he pulled back. "We shouldn't," he repeated, more firmly this time. Was he having second thoughts? Perhaps I had done something wrong. Heat crept up from my neck. I could see the struggle within him, wanting more. If I pressed, would he stop resisting? But he straightened, intent on doing the right thing, as he always had.

"I'm not a child," I protested.

"It's not that. I mean, I held off for so long because you're like family and I didn't want to screw it up. But there's something else." I tilted my head, unsure what more could be said on this night. "College . . ."

"You're leaving tomorrow," I interjected, not wanting to disrupt the moment with unpleasant thoughts. "I'm not expecting to go steady." I moved closer to him.

But he held me off. "That's just it. Addie . . . I'm not going."

"To Georgetown? What do you mean? Of course you are."

He shook his head. "I've deferred it. I'm still leaving tomorrow, only not for college—for boot camp. That is, I've enlisted." He paused, waiting for my reaction.

A cold chill raced up my spine. "So college and your scholarship, you're just letting that go?"

He shrugged. "I'll go someday. But this is about something bigger than football and classes now. It's a chance to make a difference in the world." His face glowed with the very idealism I had fallen in love with in the first place—the same thing that was driving him to do this now. "There's a whole world to explore and I want to be a part of it." Then his expression turned grave. "You can't tell Mom and Dad."

"But how can you possibly do this without them knowing?"

"I'm eighteen. They can't stop me."

"So you're going off to war without ever telling them?" I could not keep the rebuke from my voice. "What if something happens? Charlie, they have to know."

"Telling them would only worry them. Let them think I've gone to school. I'll come back at Thanksgiving when I've finished basic training and I'm about to deploy." I sat silently, stunned by the audacity of his plan. "By then they will see it is for the best." Remembering Mrs. Connally's fear that the war would take her boys, I knew it would never be true. "It will give them something to be proud of."

"They're already proud of you." Cold terror enveloped me then. I wanted to ask, no, beg, him not to go. But it would do no good.

"I've arranged to be inducted in Baltimore, not Philadelphia," he continued. "And I'm slated for boot camp at an army base just outside Washington. So if I write and call like every-thing is normal, they won't notice." He stopped, seeing my face. "It's the best thing, don't you see?" I did not answer, unable to acknowledge the twisted logic in what he was saying. "Promise me, you won't tell."

"I promise." The words came out before I could think about what they meant, the gravity of keeping Charlie's enlistment secret from his family. "Do you mind that college will be delayed?"

"Nah, they said that they'll hold my football scholarship. I'm sorry to put this all on you, Addie, but now that there's this between us." I wanted to ask what "this" was exactly, but he took my hand. "And I was hoping—" he paused, swallowing "—that you might wait for me."

"Wait for you," I repeated, trying to get my mind around the words. Of course I would wait, the same as his parents and siblings. Wait and hope and pray. But there was a deeper note to his voice, more deliberate. He was talking about something bigger.

"Wait, and be my girl," he clarified, erasing any doubt. "I know it's hardly fair of me to ask."

"I want to. I've always wanted to."

"Then I guess that it's settled." An awkward moment passed between us and he kissed me, his embrace purposeful and strong, because now it all was real.

I pulled back, struggling to catch my breath. "Should we tell them?" Charlie whispered, his breath warm against my ear.

For a moment, I was puzzled: he had just insisted on not telling his parents about the army. But he was talking now about the two of us being together, not his enlistment. I considered the question. I wanted to savor the newness of whatever this was between us. I wasn't ready to face the scrutiny of our families.

"We have to tell them, don't we?" he continued, not waiting for an answer. "Dad will be thrilled. Mom, too, I think, though she'll be more worried about you than anything. And the boys should be okay with it, as long as I'll still share you." It was thrilling and terrifying, the notion of saying this aloud and acknowledging it in the light of day. Surely it would change everything. But things were already changing, weren't they?

I raised my hand. "Let's wait a bit. We'll tell them at Thanksgiving when you come back," I added before he could protest. "When we are all together."

"We'll get engaged as soon as you graduate." His words came out in a tumble as though he had thought about them for years. "Or maybe we should get married now," he offered, an uncharacteristic sheepishness to his voice. Couples were doing it all over, making it official before the men shipped out. There were lines in front of the courthouses, weddings thrown together quickly in the churches and shuls and parents' living rooms. But me and Charlie—it was all moving so quickly. We had barely yet kissed and I wasn't even eighteen yet, for goodness' sake. A few hours ago I had not been sure Charlie even liked me and now he was planning our wedding. He had always moved at a hundred miles an hour, a freight train plunging headlong into the future. Taking charge.

"It was a silly idea," he added quickly, retreating.

"Not at all," I replied quickly, placing my hand on his. "It's just all so fast." There was part of me that still could not believe he would want me.

"I just meant in case anything happens to me."

"Don't even say it." I cut him off too late. The war, all that stood between this moment now and our happily-ever-after, the dangers looming large. "You'll be fine." It could not possibly be other-wise.

He kissed me again and I responded instinctively, matching his passion as though we had been doing this for years and not minutes. His arms tightened around me and as the heat rose between us, I wondered if he might go further. I wanted him to. But a moment later he broke away and drew me close to his chest. I pressed my cheek against the rapid-fire beat of his heart, trying to catch my breath.

A gull called out then and I turned to see the dawn pinkening the sky behind us over the ocean. "We'd better head back." Wordlessly, we stood and started walking back, and as we reached our houses, there was a moment of awkward hesitation. I could go back to the Connallys and the sofa bed that awaited me. But something told me that if we were under the same roof, things might go too far. "You'll tell your mother I went home?"

He nodded. "I wish you didn't have to."

"You have to be up in a few hours—you need your rest." His train was at just past seven. I had seen his suitcase, packed and waiting, intended to look as though he was going to school. He would have to change it for a rucksack at some point like the ones I'd seen enlistees carrying back in the city. The deception seemed to grow larger and I was enveloped by sadness.

"What is it?"

I shook my head. I did not want to burden him when he was enlisting. "It's hard to leave you when we just found each other like this," he said, trying to read my thoughts. "But in some ways it's going to make things easier, knowing you're waiting for me. And I'll be back in three months." That sounded like an eternity. But when he did return, we could tell everyone and our life together could begin in earnest. We were together now, just like I had always dreamed. It almost seemed too good to be true. He kissed me once more, then stepped quickly back.

I raised my hand to the chain that hung around my neck holding the mizpah half heart, and unfastened the clasp. Then I slipped it from my neck and handed it to Charlie. "To keep you safe."

"But this belonged to your mother." Conflict

washed over his face. "I couldn't possibly take it, especially now."

I closed his hand around it. "You must."

"Just don't forget about me, okay? Me and us and the morning we watched the sun come up." I realized then he was scared. I wanted to tell him it was going to be fine and that he was destined for greatness wherever he stood. But I could not find the words.

"Look behind us." The sun had burst through the horizon, spreading its wings and talons through the dark clouds like a golden eagle. "It's beautiful."

"Beautiful," I echoed, seeing him silhouetted against the sunrise.

I sighed as I watched Charlie disappear into the beach house. And in that moment, I knew he was already gone.

Eight

I put on my overcoat and stepped out onto Porter Street. A late-autumn breeze blew sharply and the sky above was a medium gray. Though it was still afternoon, lights burned yellow behind blackout curtains not yet closed for the night. A bit of foil that had escaped one of the collection bins for the war effort blew along the gutter. I started north-east toward Pennsport, a tingling anticipation rising in me. Tonight was Thanksgiving—Charlie was finally coming home.

The actual moment he left was unemotional, an awkward kiss on the cheek in front of our families. Then he was gone. For me, the real goodbye had taken place at sunrise hours earlier. But it was still unbearable to watch him go, every step taking him farther from me and what we had just found between us. *Take me,* I had wanted to shout, as Charlie and his father drove away, headed for the city and the train at 30th Street Station. Of course I did not. Instead I stood silently with the rest of his family, understanding so much more than they did what this goodbye really meant.

The three months since Charlie's departure and our return to the city had passed slowly. Southern High, which had a year earlier seemed vast and terrifying, seemed to have shrunk in size, the high school halls now narrow and confining. A kind of darkness settled over me that fall: my parents were gone, Charlie too. Even visiting the Connally house had at first seemed unbearable. For weeks I avoided going there altogether.

"Are you mad at us?" Jack stopped at my locker one day in early September, clearly having noticed my absence at their house.

I averted my eyes. "Not at all. I've just been busy." It was not just that I didn't want to be in the Connally house without Charlie. Surely something, my voice, or my expression or something I said, would give away the truth—that Charlie had not gone to college, but had enlisted in the army and was training for war.

But by late September, when school had settled into its routine and the smells of summer were replaced by a tinge of crispness, I found myself heading toward Second Street, passing factory workers, now women as well as men, coming and going from round-the-clock shifts at the Navy Yard. I walked up the Connallys' porch steps and hesitated: Would they still welcome me after I'd stayed away so long? But Mrs. Connally had spied me through the glass. "Addie! Come in!" She was baking cookies while Robbie and Jack tussled over who got to lick the bowl. The smell of warm vanilla enveloped me, nearly making me swoon.

"Hey, Addie," Robbie called, not looking up from his struggle.

"Here." Jack smiled good-naturedly at his little brother and ceded the bowl. Mrs. Connally handed him the batter-covered spoon, a consolation prize. Jack held it out to me. The taste was a little less sweet, and the lack of eggs which were scarce due to rationing made the texture grittier. But it was still delicious.

There were no questions that day about my unexplained absence. I was back, and despite my fears of awkwardness, I found instant comfort being among those who spoke Charlie's name with affection. Mrs. Connally read his weekly letters aloud. He always asked about each family member and me. His references to his own life were vague, mentions of bad food and interesting people that could have been at college—or the army. He was walking a line, keeping the secret of where he really was, while trying not to lie to them.

And now in a few hours, Charlie would be back. I shivered in anticipation at the thought, scarcely able to believe it. I reached the Connally house and stared up the steps, envisioning Charlie striding toward me with that same smile that seemed to lift the world. I would manage somehow not to run and throw myself into his arms, to keep the secret just a bit longer until the right time. Worry pushed in then, nagging at the edges of my excitement. My love had not changed during the months we had been apart; if anything, it was stronger. But did he still feel the same? He had written to me directly a few times, his letters brief and vague. I wanted to believe he had kept them general on purpose, so as not to give anything away if my aunt and uncle happened to read them. I couldn't send him V-mail like the posters told us to, not without giving the secret away. We'd managed a phone call once, me in the booth in the back of Schaum's soda fountain behind the penny candy wall. But he'd been rushed and the call had cut off before either of us had the chance to say much.

I walked inside. "Hello?" The Connallys' house was filled with warm, savory smells.

"Hi, Addie." In the kitchen, Mrs. Connally was peering into a steaming pot and did not look up. She drained off the excess oil, storing it as we'd all been instructed. Nothing was to be wasted now. She leaned sideways to kiss my cheek. "Oh, you're cold." She was wearing pants, her hair tied up in a red-checkered kerchief. About a month ago, Mrs. Connally had taken a job at the steel plant. "It will be fun to do my bit," she'd explained gamely. Remembering what Charlie had told me about his dad, I suspected there was more to it than wanting to help the war effort: the Connallys needed the money.

Footsteps came pounding from the floor above, then down the stairs. Robbie, swathed in a tangle of glittery tinsel, skidded into the kitchen. "Here," he said breathlessly, offering me one end of the tinsel. "Jack wouldn't let me carry anything else," he explained, as he spun around like a top to unravel himself.

"I told you we aren't getting the tree until after Thanksgiving," Mrs. Connally said. I exhaled silently, relieved that the tree would not be up tonight. Mrs. Connally had invited Aunt Bess and Uncle Meyer to Thanksgiving dinner a few weeks earlier.

"We can't," Aunt Bess had replied quickly, when I had extended the Connallys' invitation.

"Why not?"

"Well, for one thing, they aren't kosher." Aunt Bess sounded flustered.

"You eat at Woolworth's," I reminded her. "You could make an exception, just this once. Please." I, too, had been hesitant when Mrs. Connally had first mentioned it to me; it was hard to imagine Aunt Bess and Uncle Meyer socializing with the Connallys. But it was suddenly important to me that we all be in one place when Charlie and I broke the news of our relationship. Aunt Bess had conferred with my uncle that night and hesitantly, they agreed.

"I thought having the boys pull down the decorations would keep them out from underfoot," Mrs. Connally confided to me now in a low voice. She smiled ruefully. "I was wrong."

Robbie paused midspin to look at me and his eyes widened. "Wow, you look like a girl!" The pale pink velvet dress, with its matching soft wool cardigan, was an early Hanukkah present from Aunt Bess that I'd felt obliged to wear. She had bought it a size too small and the stiff bodice and skirt above the knee gave it a sophisticated look I was quite sure she had not intended.

"Thank you, I think." Mrs. Connally and I laughed.

"What?" Robbie demanded. "I meant it in a good way."

"I'm sure you did," Mrs. Connally said and she

held the end of the tinsel to her youngest son's mouth like a gag. The war had taken a toll on her, adding faint lines around her eyes, a few gray hairs sprouting. But her smile for her boys was as bright as ever.

"Where's Liam?" I tried to sound casual.

Watching her smile fade, I regretted the question. "Out somewhere. I haven't seen him since I finished my shift." With her working, the boys were left on their own more than ever—which for Liam was the worst possible thing.

"Mr. Connally's gone to the station to get Charlie," she added now. "It will be so nice to have him home again." Her eyes searched my face. Had she guessed? "I finished work at ten, so I'm a little behind." She turned to Jack. "Your math teacher called. You've missed some home-work and you failed a quiz." Her mouth pulled downward. "I expect that from your brother, but you?"

"Sorry, Mom. I'll do better."

"How can I help?" I asked now, eager to change the subject.

"You can set the table with the good dishes from the breakfront."

I escaped the kitchen, grateful for the task to keep me busy as the minutes until Charlie's return seemed to stretch to hours. The dining room had been transformed, all of the clutter gone and a fresh flowered cloth on the table. Candles flickered on the mantelpiece. I set out the plates, ten of them pressed close.

I had just finished folding the napkins when Jack came in and began helping me with the silver.

"What happened with that quiz, Jack?" I asked. "You've always been aces in math."

"I picked up an extra route after school for the *Inquirer*." Jack had long had a paper route delivering the *Bulletin* but now with the war he had picked up a second and was working harder than ever, which explained why he didn't have the time to study. "I thought maybe Mom wouldn't have to work so much at the plant."

That was Jack, always trying to fix things for everyone. "But won't she want to know where you got the extra money?"

"I'll tell her they gave me a raise." He was willing to lie to protect the people around him. But his shoulders slumped. "It's just . . . with Charlie away and everything with Liam, you know, I want to help out, make Mom happy."

I walked over and squeezed his hand. "I know." It couldn't have been easy for him, sandwiched between Liam's dark and Charlie's golden light.

"I almost forgot." I went back to the foyer and pulled out the Green Lantern comic book I'd bought him earlier at the drugstore. I was going to save it and give it to him as a Christmas present, but he looked as if he needed it now. I walked back to the dining room. "Here."

"What's this for?"

"Just to say thanks for all the homework help this semester. It's a new one. I didn't think you had it yet."

"I don't." His cheeks rose in a wide smile behind his glasses. He was used to thinking of others and not the other way around. "Thanks, Ad."

Jack and I worked together to set the table in a familiar rhythm, neither speaking further. In some ways he was the most like a brother to me. Would he mind that Charlie and I were together now?

"What are you gonna do after graduation?" he asked unexpectedly.

I considered the question uncertainly. I'd been so wrapped up in Charlie's return that I had not given it much thought. But we were seniors now, the future looming uncertain before us. My aunt and uncle did not have the money for college. "I don't know. It's only November. You?"

"I dunno. Maybe Mom and Dad will change their minds and let me and Charlie enlist." Jack felt duty-bound to go into the army. But it was impossible imagining the gentlest of the brothers actually fighting. "Or get a job at one of the plants and take some night classes. You could do that, too, y'know."

I did not respond, as I took out the porcelain cups with the rose pattern that I loved. Most women were working now like Mrs. Connally. I saw them trudging off mornings with their lunch pails, returning twelve hours later aged a decade, the dust lingering in their hair, steps slow. Nice, patriotic girls were supposed to work dutifully in the factories. But the notion of hunching over an assembly line all day made me nauseous. I couldn't bear the thought. I did not have pretensions: I knew the place where I came from did not lead to a fancy college, or indeed college at all. But there had to be something in between.

"Get a job maybe. I've been doing well in typing class." One of the cups on the stack I carried started to teeter and as I tried to right it, it slipped and shattered on the hardwood floor. Hearing the sound, Mrs. Connally rushed into the room. "I'm so sorry."

She moved me aside gently and began to sweep up the mess. "It's all right, dear. They're only things."

But I still felt awful. She had trusted me with one of her treasured possessions and I'd broken it. You couldn't fix that.

Outside, tires screeched. Charlie! I raced to the front window. But it was not him. An unfamiliar car, long and dark, had pulled up at the curb. Two men in uniforms got out. My heart stopped. Were they bringing bad news about Charlie? "Stay here," Mrs. Connally ordered more firmly than I'd ever heard her speak. I started after her, not listening. I breathed a sigh of relief when the men walked to the house next door. Mrs. Connally hurried outside, climbing over the low railing that separated the houses to grab her neighbor Mrs. Dennison before her knees buckled and she fell to the porch.

Jack looked at me helplessly. Until now, the war had been abstract here. But suddenly it had truly reached us. Watching Mrs. Connally care for the other woman, I felt light-headed. She did not know that her own son might soon be in the very same kind of danger.

Mrs. Connally came back into the house, face ashen. "Her son Todd was killed in the Pacific."

Before we could react, the front door opened once more and we all turned toward it with anticipation. But Mr. Connally was alone. My heart jumped. "Where's Charlie?"

"His train was delayed two hours."

"He should have been here by now," Mrs. Connally fretted, shaken by her neighbor's experience. Two more hours seemed unbearable. I walked outside to get some fresh air, staring at the house next door with its service flag hanging limply. Though I did not know the Dennison boy who had graduated before I came to Southern, I could not begin to imagine his family's grief. An icy rain, almost sleet, began to fall. I shivered and drew my cardigan more tightly around me.

I looked up to see Liam walking toward the house, his gait a bit unsteady. I started forward. "Hey!"

A confused look crossed his face as I neared, as though he was surprised to see me. "Addie." For a second there was a light in his eyes like I'd seen that evening on the beach. Then it disappeared. "You look swell." He jammed his hands in the pockets of his black leather biker jacket, which reeked of stale cigarettes.

I flushed, unsure if he was sincere or mocking me. "It's for Thanksgiving dinner." The lines on this brow deepened. The holiday was everywhere, from the bulletin boards at school to the shop windows. How could he have forgotten?

He eyed the house warily, then started to turn away. "I gotta go."

"But, Liam . . ."

"What do you want?"

I want you to come back to us. But telling him would not do any good. "Your brother's enlisted," I blurted out. I had not meant to break Charlie's confidence, but some part of me thought if I shared the secret with Liam he might open up to me. It's not as if he talked to the rest of the family enough to tell them anyway.

Liam flinched almost imperceptibly, a slap to the face I might have missed, before straightening and recovering once more. "Great, so he gets to be the hero—again." He couldn't admit that he was worried about Charlie—doing so would let down the exterior he had worked to harden.

"So where are you going?" I asked, changing the subject.

"To McGinley's to hear a band." Was that a lie? A minute earlier, he had been walking home. But now he was trying to escape the family Thanks-giving dinner. "You can come with me," Liam said, his voice challenging and just a bit hopeful. I realized with surprise that part of me wanted to say yes—and not just to make him happy. I was nervous about dinner and all that was to come with it.

But Charlie would be home soon and I had to be here when he arrived. "Your mom's made a big dinner, and my aunt and uncle are coming."

"Fine." He struggled to make his voice indifferent.

"You could stay." Liam did not answer, but turned and pulled his dirt bike from where it had been chained against the gate. He wheeled it to the street, then climbed aboard and revved the engine. "Liam, wait."

I wanted to tell him that I knew what it was to feel like an outsider, to be different than the rest. But he was already speeding away, accelerating too quickly as he neared the corner. I looked back over my shoulder, wondering if I should go after him. From the other direction, my aunt and uncle were coming down the street from where they had parked, huddled together under an umbrella, tentatively navigating the strange block as though it was a war zone. Uncle Meyer wore his best suit and Aunt Bess had put on her good brooch, the one that seemed to choke the folds of her neck. She clutched a bouquet of store-bought flowers close to her breast. I saw the Irish neighborhood, which I'd long grown accustomed to, through their eyes then. The Christmas decorations were already starting to go up, amplifying the differences between where we lived and here. I went to meet them, grateful that they were trying despite how difficult it was for them.

Together, we entered the Connallys'. Uncle Meyer hung back but Aunt Bess stepped forward. "Thank you for having us."

Mrs. Connally, who had changed into her holiday dress, took the flowers Aunt Bess held out. "How lovely!" she said warmly. "Please, come have a seat."

Aunt Bess and Uncle Meyer perched on the edge of the sofa, and Mr. and Mrs. Connally flanked them in the armchairs on either side. Though neighbors at the beach for several years, this was the first time my aunt and uncle had socialized with the Connallys. "So the Eagles are having a good year," Mr. Connally ventured gamely. Uncle Meyer stared at him with a blank expression. He did not follow football.

There came a sudden clattering from the foyer. "There he is!" Mr. Connally bellowed. Charlie filled the doorway then, his hair damp and sleet-covered. The candlelight illuminated his soft skin and cheekbones, the perfect features that I had wanted for so long, that were now finally mine. I started to stand and go to him, then forced myself to remain seated. "They said you'd been delayed two hours . . . I would have come back to the station for you," his father added.

"The train made up time. I caught a cab." Charlie's eyes met mine and a spark of excitement danced between us, sharing the secret that was ours alone for a bit longer. Doubt flushed through me. Maybe we shouldn't tell anyone just yet, nurture the tiny flame a bit longer before subjecting it to the cold wind of family and friends, with all of their opinions and reactions.

Charlie's mother was hugging him tightly now, his father clapping him proudly on the back. "The football star! I wish you would have let us come to a game."

"They don't let you play that much when you're a freshman," he said mildly. I could see how much he hated lying to them. "I spend a lot of time on the bench."

Robbie flew down the stairs and threw himself around his older brother's legs. Beau followed, wriggling excitedly. "Hey, champ!" Charlie scooped Robbie up, then groaned. "You're getting heavy." But over his head, Charlie's expression grew serious. "I saw one of the Dennison cousins out front. He told me about Todd."

"It's awful, isn't it?" his mother said in a low voice. "You see now why we didn't want you to enlist, and why that was for the best." Charlie did not answer but his jaw stiffened with resolve. If anything, Todd Dennison's death would make him more determined to fight. "Your hair is so short," Mrs. Connally added. But it went beyond the hair. Charlie had an air of confidence about him—older for all he had seen. Had he changed in other ways as well?

"I guess that's the style now, with the war and all," offered Jack, who had come into the room and now stood at Charlie's side, grinning widely.

"And you look so thin," his mother fretted. "Is the dorm food that bad?" Charlie smiled weakly. How could they not see?

Charlie set Robbie down and greeted Aunt Bess and shook Uncle Meyer's hand. He looked around the room, his brow furrowing. "Liam's not here." It was more a statement than a question.

A moment of silence passed between his parents, not wanting to discuss the matter in front of my aunt and uncle. Should I say anything about the fact that I had seen Liam a bit earlier? "He's probably with his friends," Jack said.

"Kids who aren't with their families on Thanksgiving." Mr. Connally sniffed, the thought of little comfort.

"I'm sure he'll be here anytime now," Mrs. Connally said with forced brightness. "Why don't we sit for dinner?"

We shuffled to the dining room and found seats. Charlie squeezed in next to me. I looked down, trying to contain my excitement.

"Gee, what's to eat, Mom?" Jack joked, as he eyed the huge spread she had put out on the table.

We were all seated, an empty place remaining for Liam. The Connallys started to bow their heads to say grace and Uncle Meyer and Aunt Bess's expressions turned confused. They sat quietly until the prayer was over. "It's delicious," Aunt Bess said when the first course, a squash soup, was served.

"It's so hard now, with the rationing," Mrs. Connally lamented as she passed a basket of warm rolls.

"I know," Aunt Bess replied, seemingly energized by having found common ground. "I found a wonderful cookbook put out by Hadassah, the recipes are all about making do."

Underneath the table, Charlie's fingers found mine. I wished my hands were not so clammy. "Excuse me," I said, suddenly warm. Not waiting for a response, I stood as if starting for the bathroom, then made my way through the kitchen to the back porch and sunk down, just shielded from the icy rain that fell beyond it. Why was I so nervous? It was just Charlie. Except it wasn't—because everything had changed now.

The door opened behind me and Charlie's hand was warm around my shoulder. "What's wrong, Ad?" he asked, dropping to the step beside me. Our breath formed white puffs, like captions in a comic book that might hold their thoughts or words.

"My aunt and uncle," I fibbed. "It's awkward having them here."

"It's not so bad, is it? They're trying."

"And Liam's not here." I hated bringing it up. Why did I always find the dark spaces between light, even in the happiest moments? "I saw him earlier, before you got home. It was not even dinner and he was already in pretty bad shape." I spoke in a low voice, even though it was just the two of us.

"Liam will be fine, and he'll be home later." He sounded as if he really believed it. With Charlie here, the picture seemed to right itself and become whole once more. Then he wrapped his arms tightly around me. "I missed you so much, Ad," he said, pushing away the darkness, as he always had. I sank back against him, enveloped by the warmth I had barely tasted before he left, and that I had missed so terribly all of these months. Joy surged through me and air seemed to shimmer. Would I ever get used to his? "I'm just so happy," he murmured against the top of my head. "And now we can tell everyone."

Hesitation crowded in, nipping at my happiness. Though we had planned this moment for months, there was so much we hadn't thought through. "So you're still going to tell them about the army, too?" He nodded. "Which will you tell them first?"

He shrugged. "Does it matter?"

It was a fair point. His secret enlistment and our being together would both be equally shocking. I tried to imagine my aunt and uncle's reaction. Being friends with the Connally boys was one thing, but Charlie was not Jewish. I fretted that I should have told them at home and weathered the storm in private. "When?"

"After dinner. The timing is awful after what happened to Todd Dennison, but I don't feel right keeping it from them any longer."

"Are you sure we should tell them about us tonight as well? Two surprises together might be too much."

"Absolutely sure." He nodded, smiling brightly, unable to see a possible downside. He wanted to share the news with everyone, like a new toy or good grade in school.

"Charlie?" his mother's voice called from inside the house. We pulled quickly apart and stood up.

"I'm coming," he called back. "Wait," he said to me, catching my arm as I started inside the

153

house. I turned to him. "I've got something for you." He reached in his pocket.

"What? I wasn't expecting anything. Christmas isn't for weeks."

"It's not that kind of gift." My breath caught as he held out a small jewelry box to me. We had been dating—and not even really that—such a short time, he couldn't possibly think about proposing. But when I opened the box it was his class ring from Southern, nested in a bed of white satin. "I thought you might want to wear it," he offered. "Just to make things official. I should have given it to you last summer, but everything happened so quickly." Relief and a tiny bit of disappointment mixed with my joy as I undid the clasp on the gold chain I wore around my neck, which had been bare since I gave him the mizpah last summer, and added the ring. A part of me had wanted him to propose, even as the notion terrified me. But I was so happy to have this. Then I turned away and lifted my hair so he could refasten it, shivering as his fingers grazed the nape of my neck. The ring pulled the chain beneath the neckline of my dress, hanging heavy between my small breasts, a hidden treasure only the two of us knew.

"I love it." I tilted my head upward, yearning for him to finally kiss me. But before our lips could meet, there was a clattering in the doorway and Robbie appeared. "What are you guys doing out here? It's freezing." We separated hurriedly and I noticed then how cold it had gotten.

Back inside everyone seemed to be finishing seconds of turkey and mashed potatoes. As I sat before my untouched plate, Charlie passed behind me. His hand brushed my shoulder and though it had done so dozens of times before, the gesture was somehow more purposeful this time, more possessive. Mrs. Connally noticed and a look of . . . something flickered across her face. Not approval. I was suddenly anxious. Mrs. Connally loved me like a daughter; surely she would not mind me and her eldest son being together. Or would she?

"Addie, are you okay? You were gone so long." Aunt Bess looked concerned.

"I'm fine, I just needed some air." Charlie sat down beside me once more and took my hand, squeezing my fingers as if to say everything will be fine. I relaxed slightly, looking around the table, contented to all be together, one of the happiest moments I had known.

All, that was, except for Liam. "I would have thought Liam would have at least come home for dessert," Mrs. Connally said. "I even found pecans for the pumpkin pie, just the way he likes." But she was seeing a younger boy, one who still cared about his mother's desserts, fresh and warm. Across from her, Jack's jaw clenched.

Robbie pushed back from the table. "This is

bullshit," he declared, trying to sound older than twelve.

"Language!" his father barked.

Uncle Meyer started to rise from his chair. "Perhaps we should go."

"Nonsense. I insist you stay for dessert," Mrs. Connally replied. My uncle sat once more, staring hard at his plate. I felt a moment's guilt for having snared them into this. But Aunt Bess seemed to watch with interest, as though following one of her soap operas on the radio. Mrs. Connally reached for her youngest son's hand, trying to soothe him. "Robbie, darling, sit down."

But Robbie slipped through her grasp. "I'm not going to let Liam ruin Thanksgiving."

I gestured toward his hideaway beneath the steps. "How about a game of chess while we wait for dessert?" I suggested. Robbie had an amazing aptitude for the game and we would sneak in a few minutes whenever we could. But he shook his head. Even our special hiding place could not console him now.

"What are you going to do?" Jack demanded, rising, as Robbie walked toward the door and put on his coat. "What can you possibly do that the rest of us haven't tried?"

"I can try not giving up on him," Robbie said resolutely. "I can try bringing him home." He ran out, letting the door slam behind him.

Charlie stood. "I'll go get him."

But I put my arm on his. "Robbie feels he has to try, just like the rest of us." I pushed my own anxiety down. Robbie knew the neighborhood as well as the older boys. "If he doesn't find Liam soon, he'll hurry back for dessert." I stood to help Mrs. Connally clear the plates, grateful to have something to keep me busy. But my hands shook. Would Robbie be able to find Liam and actually persuade him to come home? It was odd with Liam gone, but having him here, drunk and maybe hostile, could be worse. I hated the thought. Tonight, though, I wanted everything to be perfect.

We were halfway through dessert when the first concerns were voiced aloud. "They should be back by now," Mrs. Connally fretted. "Robbie would have found Liam or come back by now."

"It's fine, Mom," Charlie said. But his voice sounded forced.

"Yeah," Jack chimed in. "Just like that time Charlie was late at football and you worried and worried."

"Thanks, pal." Charlie's tone was sarcastic.

"Don't mention it."

"The weather was bad then, too," Charlie pointed out.

His mother shook her head. "This is different." She served coffee and we drank it quietly, all of the small talk gone. Another half an hour passed.

"Let's tell stories," Charlie suggested. "I want

to hear the one about when the twins tried to come early."

"Well," Mrs. Connally began, "your father was at work when it all started." As she began to recount the blizzard and the fire truck that had rushed her to the hospital, her husband chimed in adding parts she had forgotten. "And the doctor was so surprised when there were two!"

"If you think he was surprised, imagine how I felt," Mrs. Connally added. My aunt and uncle laughed appreciatively.

"Folks, there's something I, that is we, want to tell you," Charlie began when the laughter had subsided. So he meant to tell them about us first. All eyes turned toward him. Though we had wanted everyone to be together when we shared the news, I knew he could not wait any longer. He cleared his throat. Mr. Connally looked curious, his wife pleasantly expectant, as though she might have already guessed.

I looked away. Through the window I noticed a man standing at the front door. We had been laughing so hard we must not have heard the first knock. He was wearing a uniform and for a minute, I thought it was one of the army officials who had come to the Dennison house earlier in the afternoon. But his jacket was dark blue, a police badge on the breast pocket. A chill ran up my spine. "Charlie, there's someone at the door . . ."

I was interrupted by the bell ringing and the sound of a fist knocking hard and fast against the wood of the door frame.

"What on earth?" Mr. Connally said as he rose to answer it. Everyone else stood, too. Instinctively Jack moved closer to his mother. I felt Charlie come up behind me.

As Mr. Connally opened the door, the red lights of the police car flashed on the living room wall. "Mr. Connally?" the policeman asked. "There's been an accident. You need to come with us." As if from a great distance I heard Mrs. Connally gasp.

"Is it Liam?" Aunt Bess put a hand on her shoulder.

"Stay with Mom," Charlie ordered Jack, following his father and the policeman out the door. He did not object as I came with him. Mrs. Connally's wail followed us out the door.

Seconds later, I found myself wedged between Mr. Connally and Charlie in the backseat of a musty police car. We lurched forward. A loud buzz in my ears nearly drowned out the police officer's words. "Accident . . . unconscious." I understood then that Liam had crashed his dirt bike. Bile rose in my throat. I knew he had been drinking. Why hadn't I stopped him from riding off? Charlie's hand found mine, gripped it until my fingers numbed. The policeman kept talking to fill the space and I made out that he was the father of one of our classmates and had recognized Liam, which was how he had gotten to us so quickly.

"How bad is it?" Mr. Connally croaked.

"I don't know. They're still treating him at the scene." That meant he was alive. I exhaled slightly. He would come through this. He had to. The police car turned onto Front Street, which ran parallel along the Delaware River, and then slowed by the wide expanse of water. Lights gleamed high on the Ben Franklin Bridge to the north, but on the far banks the warehouses and factories of New Jersey were shrouded in darkness.

We ran from the car. The twisted wreckage of Liam's dirt bike lay by the edge of the choppy river. Stale, brackish air filled my lungs. Several feet away stood an ambulance, its rear doors open as a stretcher was loaded in. Charlie raced to it and I struggled to keep up. Liam thrashed wildly as the medics tried to treat him, his soaked hair plastered to his forehead. There was a deep gash on his head.

"Liam, are you okay? " Charlie demanded.

Liam's eyes darted wildly from side to side. He did not seem to know we were there. "Robbie? Robbie?" Then he grasped Charlie's arm. "Save him, man." He groaned, then fell back, semiconscious.

I froze, the ground seeming to slide from

beneath me. Charlie spun away then, scanning the river. He ran toward the water and jumped in.

"Charlie!" his father cried.

"What the hell?" the policeman exclaimed behind me.

But I understood: the policeman had only mentioned Liam. He hadn't known about Robbie, who had gone looking for Liam—and undoubtedly found him. "His little brother." I recovered, turning to the policeman desperately. "He must've been on the bike, too!"

"Christ," the policeman swore. He ran back to the car and picked up his radio. "Get the search-and-rescue boat out here, stat."

I swung back to the water, lunging forward. "Charlie!" I searched the choppy surface. I made out his head for a second, before he dove back under, searching, heedless of the rough, icy water. I started forward, then stopped again, powerless to help.

"Go with Liam to the hospital," Mr. Connally said hoarsely. "We need you there."

"Please, I want to stay," I started to protest. I could not possibly leave until I knew Charlie and Robbie were safe. But hands pulled me toward the ambulance. I climbed in and sat down beside the stretcher. Liam's face was calm now, eyes closed. He looked like the boy I had met two summers ago. Pity and anger washed over me. Beside me the medic was working to start an intravenous line in Liam's arm. I shrunk back against the cold wall of the ambulance, trying to stay out of the way.

The ambulance sped through the streets, sirens blaring. A few minutes later, we reached Pennsylvania Hospital and the doors opened to garish light. After they had lifted the stretcher and wheeled Liam in, I stood helplessly in the entrance bay to the emergency room. "Dear God," I began, trying to summon the prayers I had not uttered since the day my parents went missing. The words stuck in my throat.

With a futile attempt to compose myself, I went to face what was waiting inside. Mrs. Connally and Jack had been brought straight to the hospital. They stood inside the doors locked in the same embracing position in which I had left them at the house, as though they had been magically transported there. Should I tell them about Robbie? But their faces, frozen in horror, told me they already knew. My aunt and uncle were there, too, hovering in the background, now part of this strange tableau as they waited for me. Aunt Bess stepped forward and draped my coat around my shoulders, then led me to a chair.

Minutes passed like hours. A doctor appeared. "Liam's going to be fine," he said, unaware how little those ordinarily joyous words could do to quell their terror. "Just a concussion and a cut to the head. He's a very lucky fellow."

The outside doors to the hospital opened then. Charlie limped in gray-faced, wearing a soaking wet blanket someone had placed around his shoulder. I ran toward him. "Charlie—" But he continued past, not seeing. His arms were half-extended before him, still etched in the shape of the object he had been carrying, the body that was now gone.

Years later, witnesses would still tell the story of how the oldest Connally boy had jumped into those dark, stormy waters, diving repeatedly to find his youngest brother. He had at last pulled Robbie to the surface but, unable to reach the shore, he had remained afloat treading water and cradling his brother for twenty minutes. When the rescuers finally reached them, Charlie would not release his brother and so they were pulled gently to land together, Charlie whispering softly to the lifeless body he held.

Nine

Washington, DC
November 1943

I blinked and my vision cleared, the memories of love and pain pulling me back to the present like the tide. I was still standing on the corner of 15th and H Streets, letting the crowds swirl around me as they had on the dock the day I arrived in America, and so many times in the halls of Southern. The rain was heavier now, flattening my bangs against my eyes. Usually, I loved the way it lifted the smells from the pavement, as if giving new life to the city. But now the stench of dirt and ash caused my stomach to turn.

I started walking quickly, past two policemen on wide motorcycles, desperate to get as far away as I could from the site of our encounter. Not that it would help; Charlie was here. All of the time and distance I had put between myself and the ache of what had happened evaporated like mist when I saw him standing before me. I hurried past Woodward and Lothrop, the early Christmas decorations in its windows, more austere than they might have been in peacetime, a kind of forced merriment. Workers passed one another, eyes straight ahead, not seeing. For all of the excitement of the holiday in the bustling city, Washington had a bland, antiseptic feel, so unlike Philadelphia's messy patchwork of ethnic neighborhoods. No one, it seemed, was actually from here, or expected to stay very long.

At the corner stop, I boarded the streetcar. I gazed up through the smudged window at the dome of the Capitol, its lights blackened now in case of an air raid attack. But an eerie glow seemed to cast faint gray around it, silhouetting it against the twilight sky. As we wove through the rain-slicked streets, Charlie appeared once more in my mind. I had thought of him constantly these many months, wondering if he was still off in training somewhere or had already been deployed. And I worried about him, in a way that I had no right to, really, now that he was no longer mine. But I had never expected to see him here, even though Washington had been his place first when he'd been accepted to Georgetown (and might still have been if he had not enlisted). Yet here he was in front of me and he wanted to see me again. What could he possibly want?

A single tear rolled down my cheek, hot and unfamiliar. I brushed it away before any of the other passengers could see. I had not cried the night Robbie died, nor any of the days after. I had functioned mechanically, taking on the jobs that everyone else was unable or unwilling to manage, such as getting Robbie's clothing for the funeral home. I had stood in the empty foyer of the deserted Connally house, flooded with images, my grief threatening to burst forth from its tight wrappings. I had remained dry-eyed, but I almost broke down as I looked at Robbie's secret hiding spot beneath the stairs. It was almost as if, if I walked slowly toward it, Robbie would be there waiting for me in our hideaway. Our last chess game lay unfinished on the other side of the door.

I had walked upstairs and ran my hand over the duvet, lumpy with stuffed animals Robbie had not quite outgrown, toys strewn across the floor. I laid out his navy suit, threadbare and worn at the knees and elbows from being worn by at least two brothers before him, then looked around his room for the white sneakers he insisted on wearing all the time. But those were gone now, one missing when Charlie carried him from the water, the other God-only-knew-where, most likely at the bottom of the river. Choking back a sob, I had grabbed the clothes and run from the bedroom.

The funeral had taken place two days later on a gray morning, with a coating of snow that had come too early in the season, covering the sidewalks and cars for a few hours. At the church, I'd hung at the back, overwhelmed by the dark chapel and the sea of people. Among the other kids from school and families from the Pennsport neighborhood, there were faces strangely resembling the Connallys, out-of-town relatives I hadn't known existed from New York and other places. My aunt and uncle sat on either side of me. I had not been sure they would come, but they had been waiting for me in the living room that morning, dressed in black.

The doors at the back of the church swung open. Aunt Bess cried softly into her hand at the sight of the small casket, borne by men I did not recognize.

The Connallys followed. Charlie and Jack each held their parents' arms to keep them upright. I thought I caught Charlie's eye, but he looked away. We had not spoken since that night at the hospital, but I was sure he would find me after the funeral. When we were seated, a priest began to chant the Mass. I craned my neck to see the front row. The Connallys had sat reflexively in their usual order, leaving spaces for Robbie and also for Liam, alone in the hospital with his guilt and grief. I looked to the back, half expecting to see Robbie bound in and interrupt the service noisily. He could not be in that tiny box.

As the priest went on, my thoughts turned improbably to the Connallys' next-door neighbors who had also lost a son. The blue star in the Dennison window was gone, a gold one hung crookedly in its place. There would be no stars for a boy like Robbie who had died in an ordinary, if tragic, way. The Connallys had tried to do all the right things to keep their family safe. They had worried about the war being fought thousands of miles away, all the while never guessing that danger and death might be lurking right around the corner on a street they had walked or ridden down hundreds of times.

And now Robbie was dead. I clasped at the shell bracelet he had given me at the beach last summer. Icy water seemed to swirl up around me now, as if I was there with him. He must have been so afraid. Had he called for his mother or one of the boys? Or perhaps he had blacked out and not known anything at all. He could not have possibly survived more than a few minutes.

There were more prayers in Latin and English and then it was over and we all rose as the casket was carried from the church. Someone should have spoken about the wonderful twelve-year-old who loved blocks and chess and his dog, Beau. But the family was in no shape to do it and they had not asked me. In other times the Irish would have had a wake where everyone came back after to drink and reminisce. Here there was only pain, and this quiet funeral where words failed.

By the time I reached the door of the church, the Connallys had already gotten into the long, black car that would take them to the cemetery close to the shore for a private burial. No one had asked me to go. I watched Charlie through the window of the limousine, remembering the hospital after the medics had taken Robbie from his arms and raced away in a last futile attempt to save him, even though we knew it was too late. Charlie had stood, soaked and shivering, apart from the rest of us. I had rushed to his side. "Charlie . . ." I waited for him to tell me it would be all right, to take charge as he always did. But he remained silent, arms still limply outstretched, wings broken. Nothing, not that night on the dock at Trieste or any since, had terrified me more.

Anger rose in me as I watched him seated in the limousine, remembering. He was supposed to be able to make things okay, but he had failed, even when I had tried to warn him about Liam. But I had failed, too, and so had Jack, who always tried to fix everything, and their parents—and now Robbie was dead. We were all a little bit to blame, except for that sweet, innocent boy lying in the cedar box.

I stepped forward toward the limousine to go to Charlie. But Aunt Bess was holding my arm and guiding me away. "Give them time." I was too numb to argue, so I stood watching as the car door closed.

The window opened and Charlie looked up at me with hollow eyes I hardly knew. For a second, my heart lifted, hopeful despite it all. I took a step forward. "Wait for me," he mouthed. And then he was gone.

The next morning I rose early, the awfulness of what had happened knocking into me anew. Outside the air was icy, hinting at more snow to come. As I crossed through the neighborhoods, chin tucked against the wind, I tried to figure out exactly what to say, the words that could make things if not right then just a bit better. I reached Second Street and steeled myself as I neared the Connally house. Then I stopped. Though it was after eight o'clock, the front curtains were still drawn. They must have been exhausted after the drive back from the cemetery. For a minute, I considered going home and coming back later.

But maybe I could make them breakfast. I walked up the steps to let myself in as I often did and tried to open the door, but it was locked. I reached under the flowerpot for the spare key. The door did not budge. The second lock, the one they'd never used, was bolted. I peered through a crack in the curtains. The house was dark and still, as it had been that first night Charlie brought me here to surprise me for my birthday.

"They've gone," an unfamiliar voice said from behind, causing me to jump. I turned and recognized Mrs. Dennison, whose eyes were still hollow from her own loss.

"Gone?" My mind raced. Perhaps they'd taken a room by the cemetery, or even stayed at the beach house.

"The boys packed a lot of bags and left first thing this morning. Asked me to tell the milkman they won't be coming back." A hard lump formed in my throat. There had to be some mistake. Charlie would not have just left. "They've gone," Mrs. Dennison repeated flatly, before turning and walking back into her own house.

I had returned home and, with Aunt Bess's help, called the hospital and learned that Liam had been discharged the previous night. Neither he nor Jack returned to school after that and the guidance counselor would tell me nothing. Rumors swirled about where they had gone. I went by the house every day after school, hoping that I would see Beau in the front window, Mrs. Connally at the door waiting for me. But the house remained dark and a few weeks later, I gave up. There was simply nowhere else to look.

"They couldn't have just disappeared," I burst out one night at dinner in frustration.

My aunt and uncle exchanged knowing looks and Uncle Meyer patted my hand. "I think," he said gently, "they just don't want to be found."

The rest of the school year was a blur, the halls and streets filled unbearably with ghosts. As I sat in class, it played over and over again in my head: the moments before the police had come, so filled with joy and anticipation, and then everything that happened after. Even images I had not actually seen, like Robbie laid out motionless on the gurney after they had pulled him from Charlie's arms, his face crooked and faintly blue, had gone through my mind so many times it had grown fuzzy, a record warped from being played too many times on a phonograph. What if Robbie had never gone after his brother? Liam would have come home, late and maybe drunk to be sure. Charlie and I would have shared our news, seeing the surprise and (hopefully) happiness on their faces. But that moment would now never be.

And in the darkness, the nightmares always returned. Most nights, I sat bolt upright, trying to clear the nonexistent water from my lungs, gasping for breath. Sometimes there was a moment in the haze of awakening I could forget. Then the reality would wash over me like ice. Robbie wasn't back home, playing in the yard with Beau. He was in that box I'd seen at the church, now buried underground.

I went to graduation because Aunt Bess insisted on it. She and Uncle Meyer sat somberly, clapping as hard as they could when my name was called. They'd brought me a too-large bouquet of carnations and planned a fancy dinner at Stouffer's, trying to fill the empty space left by the Connallys. There would be no great whooping crowd as there would have been if the Connallys had been there to cheer on me and the twins. Were Jack and Liam graduating somewhere else? A few weeks earlier when we had gotten our yearbooks, I'd opened to the page where their photos should have been, half-expecting to see Jack's gentle smile beside Liam's taunting grin, or at least a blank space where their images might have been. But the spots had been filled in by the pictures of other class-mates, as though they had never existed.

"I should start packing," Aunt Bess said, the day after graduation.

I looked at her blankly. "For what?" The days ahead stretched before me like a blank canvas. I would have to do something: take some classes (though I had not formally applied to college, there were night classes in which I could still enroll) and find a job, hopefully somewhere other than the plants.

"The shore," she replied. "We can get into the house tomorrow. I thought it would do you some good to get away."

I had noticed the warm weather, of course, but I had not actually considered that we would return to the shore after all that had happened. Something lifted at the corners of my heart. "Perhaps the Connallys will be coming?" I scarcely dared to hope that our other world still existed.

Aunt Bess shook her head. "I'm sorry, honey. I asked the landlord. The house next door is closed up and she doesn't think anyone will be there this year."

I ran upstairs and threw myself across the bed, sobbing. The city without them was bad enough, but how could I face the shore without the Connallys?

I looked across at the corner of my dresser where, under a paperweight, I'd kept all things Charlie—the ticket from the movie we'd seen, a scrap of paper on which he'd written me a note. It all seemed so silly now. He'd never think things were special just because they were from me.

My hand grazed something under the bed. I pulled out the box that I had nearly forgotten putting there, shortly after arriving nearly two years earlier. Neatly folded inside were a change of clothes and a pair of shoes, and foodstuffs that would not spoil, like a can of milk. How I would open it exactly I had not figured out. Things that, as a scared little girl just off the boat, I had thought I might need just in case. I had learned well that night Mamma had plucked me from our apartment to always be ready to go.

I lifted up the old shoes. There had not been a suitcase the night I left Trieste. Mamma had rushed me from the house, and it was not until we neared the docks and she set me down to catch my breath that I noticed I was not wearing shoes.

"Mamma . . ." I looked down. Desperately she had taken her own shoes, two sizes larger, from her feet, and put them on mine. Then she'd led me to the ship, heedless of the stones that cut into her own bare feet, causing them to leave a thin trail of blood.

I slipped the shoes onto my feet and felt the cracked leather, remembering. They fit almost perfectly now. Aunt Bess had bought me new shoes shortly after my arrival and other times since, dress Mary Janes and sneakers and sandals. But I kept Mamma's shoes. It was one of the only pieces of my parents that I had. I slid the box back under the bed and left the room.

I slipped from the house without calling to Aunt Bess, who was in the kitchen. Outside I found myself headed north. At the turnoff for Pennsport, I stopped. I always walked slowly past that spot, because if I closed my eyes and imagined very hard, Charlie might just be there, waiting for me.

But he was gone, and all that was left were the dark memories, looming large. *As long as I stay here, I'll never be free,* a voice seemed to say. I turned and raced west, then north of 9th Street, skirting the edge of the Italian market where the smells of meat and cheese and garlic wafting from the open stalls were heady, even with wartime rationing. But I did not stop. Grief chased me, nipping at my heels. I pressed on, not quite sure where I was going, just wanting to get away from the neighborhood and all of its memories.

Almost an hour later, I neared Center City, the streets thick with the midday crowds. I crossed Market Street, enjoying the bustle of the city street and the feeling that nobody knew me. Flags flapped in the breeze above the display windows at Lit Brothers department store and a placard on a light post bore a woman sewing, exhorting passersby to support the war and "Make do or mend." I looked west past the shop awnings toward the clock tower above city hall. A few blocks farther, the bus station loomed. I knew then that I was going. Somewhere. Away. From. Here.

I crossed the street. At the bus station, I navigated around the crowded benches and two soldiers sitting on their rucksacks, playing cards. I walked up to the ticket window. "Where to?" I peered uncertainly over my shoulder at the fronts of the Greyhound buses which sat idling, belching exhaust fumes. For a second I thought fleetingly of trying to find the Connallys, but I had no idea where they had gone. And, as Uncle Meyer had said, they did not want to be found. One bus was headed to Washington. Charlie had spoken so glowingly of the capital when he was applying to Georgetown, a city of new beginnings, "where the ground just seems to shake under your feet!" Impulsively, I opened my purse and counted the twenty-three dollars and fifty cents, all the money I had in this world. I hoped it would be enough.

"Addie?" I looked up. Uncle Meyer sat in his car by the curb. He must have seen me go and followed me to the station. Guilt washed over me. My aunt and uncle had given me everything and been so kind, and here I was about to go without so much as a goodbye or thank-you.

He stepped from the car and I walked toward him. "You're leaving." I remained silent, unable to deny it. Would he try to stop me? "Take this." Uncle Meyer reached in his pocket and handed me a thick, neatly folded stack of bills.

"I can't take that."

"Think of it as a graduation present. I know we haven't been a substitute for your folks and, well, I'm sorry."

"You've both been very kind to me." The fact that he cared was somehow enough.

"You forgot this." He held out the camera, which I had left behind in my haste. I would not have felt right taking it from him without asking. "Where will you go?"

It filled my hands, the sureness giving me courage. "I'm going to Washington," I said. My voice grew more certain with each word.

"Let us know when you get settled, and that you're all right."

"I will." I kissed his cheek, touched. He and Aunt Bess had tried when I had nothing else and that was something. "Thank you." I thought he might stay until the bus had left, but he turned and got back into his car.

I bought my ticket (which thankfully only cost eight dollars and forty cents) and climbed on the bus, then realized that once again I was going without a suitcase. The graduation money Uncle Meyer had given me and the camera were all that I had. That would have to be enough.

The streetcar screeched to a stop and I pushed my memories of home aside and climbed off. The neighborhood east of Capitol Hill, with its tony federalist brick-front houses, would have been too expensive for me before the war. But now living quarters were at a premium and the once-grand residences had been subdivided to let. I walked to the rooming house and unlocked the door to the room too tiny to be shared, with space for no more than the bed, chair and dresser wedged in. I couldn't control the radiator that gave off an endless hiss, and the air was uncomfortably hot, cracking my lips and skin. There was a shared kitchenette and bathroom that was too crowded for all six rooms. But it was a place of my own and I loved it. The other girls were friendly enough and I joined them sometimes for a movie, or in the parlor downstairs where we would listen to the radio and play cards, some writing to the boys that had gone overseas or their families back home. We'd planned to go ice-skating on the Reflecting Pool when it froze. I had built a life here, created a place where I was not just the Connallys' girl, not quite part of a now-broken family.

Only now Charlie was here, looking at me in that way again that seemed to reach right inside. I might have missed him. If Mr. Steeves had not asked me to accompany him to the meeting, or if I had not walked out to get air, or if I had turned right instead of left. So many ifs.

I started to peel off my wet clothing. As I reached in the dresser for fresh nylons, I remembered Charlie's class ring. It had hung around my neck in the murky days that followed Robbie's death. At some point that spring, I had taken it off. I pulled it out of my drawer now and held it aloft, considering. I had not had the chance to give it back—nor had I really wanted to part with it. It had seemed wrong, though, to wear it still when everything between us had been blown to bits. Charlie had said he loved me. I had thought that what I had with him, with all of them, had been permanent and real. But he had walked away without so much as a backward glance, leaving me alone. I tucked the ring in my bag. Then I fixed my hair and changed into a dry dress, trying not to think as I applied my powder and lipstick with a bit more care that it was for Charlie.

Forty minutes later I stood before the Old Ebbitt Grill, a historic beaux arts oyster bar I had passed a dozen times but never dared to enter. In the reflection behind me the crowds had thinned and a few straggling commuters made their way home for the night. I peered through the wide front window, taking in the velvet-and-mahogany parlor of cigar-smoking men. I had never understood bars, groups of people standing among perfect strangers, all for the purpose of having a drink. My breath formed a cloud on the window-pane.

On the other side of the glass I saw Charlie and my pulse quickened. For everything that had happened, my feelings were there, stronger than ever. But my excitement quickly faded. A glass of clear liquor sat before him on the bar, nearly empty. Charlie had not drank back then, ever. His face had storm clouds where once there had only been light.

Charlie was talking to himself in that way he did when he was intensely concentrating.

Rehearsing what he was going to say to me. Would he tell me that nothing had changed? I couldn't bear it if he did not love me anymore. There had been something in his eyes, which I could still read even now, that said he still wanted me, just the same as he had that night and the ones before it. My heart lifted. Why couldn't we go back? I could run to him right now and throw myself into his arms.

I reached out as if touching him through the window, stroking his hair and his cheek. All that I ever wanted was on the other side of that glass, waiting for me. A hand seemed to stop me, making it impossible to breathe. My scars had healed over the months away, forming a kind of protective armor, and I could not fathom reliving the pain if I ripped that off again. I stood frozen in place, Charlie just beyond reach. We weren't the same people anymore. We were different now, broken. Anger rose in me then. He had left that night. He might have stayed and clung to me, but he had gone. And now he was here just expecting me to take him back, if that's what this was all about. How could we be together, as if none of it had ever happened? Happiness seemed wrong, a betrayal of Robbie.

I could not go in there and face him.

"I've got to get out of here," I said aloud to no one. "This is everything I didn't want back home. This is why I left." I turned and ran, shoes smacking against the still-damp pavement. One of my heels broke but I kept running as well as I could, not quite sure where I was headed until I had reached the newspaper bureau. Though it was well after seven, a light still burned behind the blackout curtain in the second-story window above.

I climbed the stairs awkwardly on my broken shoe and knocked at the door to the editor's office. "Mr. Steeves," I began, waving away a cloud of smoke. As his eyes lifted, I faltered. How could I dare approach him, much less make this request?

"What do you want, Montforte?" His tone was brusque, but not unkind. "I'm on deadline."

"I'll make it quick. I understand you're building up the London bureau." I'd heard some of the other typists talking about it a few days ago during a break; with the war intensifying and America's invasion of the continent a growing certainty, London was becoming an even more critical base of operations for the press.

He nodded. "We had to pull men out of Berlin and Paris. And with thousands of GIs headed overseas each month, we need the coverage in Britain."

"I'd like to go." The words came out in a wobbly voice that did not sound like my own.

"Go?"

I nodded. "You'll need secretarial staff, surely."

My voice grew more certain. I'd come here impulsively, the notion of what I actually wanted vague and uncertain. But as the words formed, they felt right and I suddenly wanted more than anything to go, as far and fast as possible.

"We were planning on just staffing that locally."

"But someone with some experience with the paper. And I speak other languages—Italian, Spanish, even a bit of French." I made the case I had not known I wanted to win. Why London? Because it was not here.

"Better than the translators, it's true. It would be good to have someone who knows the home bureau," he conceded. "But wait, didn't you come from Europe?"

"Italy as a girl, yes."

"And you want to get out of here that badly?" I did not answer. "You've seen the stories, haven't you?" It seemed like a silly question, given that I worked for the *Post*. But lots of the girls out in typing never read the very newspaper they worked for, or if they did, only the entertainment and style bits. "It's a war zone, a ton of bombings, even after the Blitz."

I nodded, my stare unblinking. "I know."

"You want to leave me," he remarked, making it sound personal. "Is it about that fella at State today?" He peered at me keenly, sensing a story.

"Not at all." I had not realized Mr. Steeves had seen me talking to Charlie, or noticed the effect the conversation had on me. It was too close and personal to speak about with anyone, especially my boss.

"I never should have taken you with me," he added ruefully and I braced, sure he would refuse my request. "You need to get a passport."

I exhaled silently. "I have one." I squeezed my purse, which held the passport Aunt Bess and Uncle Meyer had helped me get shortly after I had become an American citizen.

"When did you want to go?"

"Tonight, if possible."

"Tonight? There's no way. You need a work visa. Hell, Montforte, I'm not even sure I can get you credentialed at all. They aren't letting many people in now. The Brits want folks out of the city, not in."

"I know. But you can manage it." I was surprised by my own audacity and hoped he would not find me rude. "I'll board the train for New York and you can have my papers wired."

"You've thought of everything, haven't you?" His shoulders slumped with resignation. "Fine. I'm sorry to lose you." He scribbled something on a business card and held it out to me. "Ask for Teddy White. He's a rising-star hotshot correspondent, a Brit and kind of an ass, but you'll get the best work with him. I'll wire ahead to say you're coming and I'll have your train and boat tickets ready for the morning."

"Thank you, sir." I'd been too embarrassed to ask about covering the travel, but I couldn't have afforded it myself.

"Don't mention it." I stood and started for the door, not wanting to take more of his time. "But, kid . . ." I turned back. "Whatever it is you're running from, you're going to have to face it sooner or later."

I stared at him, dumbfounded. How much did he know? "Sir?"

"Just a newsman's hunch." Then he chuckled and turned away. "Safe travels, kid." He turned back to his work, not one for long goodbyes.

Dismissed, I walked through the outer office. I had done it—I was going to London. I gazed through the window at the Washington Monument, which seemed to stare back remorsefully. Could I really leave, just like that? There was nothing keeping me. The life I created was transient, the city never really mine. And I'd done it before, leaving Philadelphia and the only life I had really known. The second time would not be nearly as hard.

I gazed out the window towards the Old Ebbitt Grill. Charlie would be wondering where I was, perhaps realizing even that I was not going to show. Should I somehow send a message? No, there was no way to explain why I had not come. And he had not given me a phone number or other way to contact him—perhaps because he did not want to give me a chance to say no.

I looked around the office, knowing I would not pass this way again. Once my life had seemed a great circle of gathered holidays and returning seasons and school-year rituals. Now it seemed to go straight, a great linear journey to a point unknown. I picked up my purse and walked from the office, closing the door behind me.

PART TWO

PART TWO

Ten

England
November 1943

I stared out into the fog-shrouded horizon, closing my overcoat where it gapped a bit beneath my scarf, then burying my hands in my muffler. Southampton, chalky and white, was a slip thickening in the distance. My shoulders slumped with weariness at the end of nearly a week of travel. We had been scheduled to arrive the previous day, but the threat of an air raid had kept us bobbling in the choppy waters just west of the Channel for hours until the all clear came. Now the morning sky was an ominous slate gray. The sea winds rose up, whipping my hair wildly. Gulls cried out sharply overhead.

I'd left Washington in an orderly fashion, not fleeing as I had done Philadelphia, but rather returning to the boardinghouse to pack and notify the landlady. I'd even bought a second-hand suitcase and packed before taking the train to New York the next morning. As we neared Philadelphia and the railway tracks wound through the gritty neighborhoods by the Navy Yard, I had pressed my fingers to the glass, feeling for the places I'd once known. The train stopped at 30th Street Station to take on passengers and for a minute I had considered hopping off and seeing my aunt and uncle. But I had closed that door months earlier and could not go back. I'd exhaled, breathing easier, as the train continued on. I would write to let them know that I'd gone instead.

After I boarded the ship in New York, I stayed on the deck, heedless of the icy rain that fell lightly, needing to see. As we pulled from the harbor and the Statue of Liberty slid from view, I was flooded with doubt: thousands of refugees were trying desperately to get to America, as I had done when I was a girl. And yet here I was leaving. London had been an impulse in my haste to avoid facing Charlie again. But England was at war, and I was going there—alone.

The second-class cabin Mr. Steeves had arranged was tiny, even smaller than my bedroom in Washington. It was all mine, though, and opulent compared to my earlier voyage to America. I was one of just a handful of civilians on the ship—so few had a reason to cross in this direction now. I did not mingle with the soldiers and nurses that danced and laughed on the decks at night. Instead I read, trying not to think of the dark, rough waters below.

But the rocking ship taunted me: going back, going back. At night I tossed feverishly. I dreamed of Thanksgiving night, Charlie striding up the porch steps of the Connally house toward me. "Now we can be together," he said, his smile as broad as it had ever been. I reached out for him, but as he neared a wave of water rose from nowhere, throwing me to the ground. When I stood up again, he was gone. I'd awakened with a start, staring around the cabin, trying to see and breathe through the darkness that surrounded me. Other times I lay awake, seeing Charlie seated at the bar in Washington as he realized I was not going to show. I was flooded with remorse: How could I have given up the one meeting I had hoped for months to have again?

A bump pulled me from my thoughts and I held the railing not to be jostled as the ship came into a harbor, guided by a tugboat. A low fog swirled, obscuring the tops of the vessels around us. "We'll be disembarking soon," someone said. I nodded and slipped through the crowd and along the deck, suitcase already in hand. The air was a thick mixture of smoke and salt.

Some twenty minutes later, we anchored and the gangplank lowered. "Quickly, please." The purser's voice sounded harried as he cast an eye warily upward. Taking in the area, I understood: Southampton, a key port city, had been a major target of the Luftwaffe. Buildings were flattened as far as I could see in either direction, as though a giant had come through, crushing the entire town under its feet. It was a thousand times worse than anything I'd seen on the newsreels back home.

I joined the orderly queue that snaked forward from the ship, passing a military vessel unloading wounded soldiers on stretchers into ambulances. My lower stomach churned and I wondered if it was nerves or something I had eaten, or whether I was getting my period and would need to find a drugstore.

We shuffled toward the arrivals hall, seemingly the only building that still stood whole. Inside, the immigration officer studied my passport for what seemed like ages before peering at me in disbelief. "You're coming to London now?"

I squirmed, suddenly sixteen again and afraid he would turn me away. "For work, yes." I met his gaze squarely and my heart thumped. "At the *Washington Post*." He looked so unimpressed I wondered if he had heard of it.

"You've got a place to stay?"

"The newspaper arranged it," I lied. In fact, Mr. Steeves had made no reference to accommodation. The officer scribbled something on the ship's log. Would he send me back? But he stamped my passport and handed it back to me. "Make sure you get to the city quickly and mind the curfew."

I exchanged some money at a kiosk and stepped from the terminal. Travelers with their luggage navigated between cars and taxis through an intersection where the traffic light listed to one side, broken. On the far side of the road, the wreckage of what had once been a pub smoldered, sending up smoke that made my throat burn. I walked toward an old man selling matches and other odd bits on top of a wooden crate. "The bus station?" I asked, wishing I could spare the money to buy something from him. I had just over sixty dollars on me, most of that from the hundred Uncle Meyer had given me for graduation, the rest from what I had earned in Washington. I needed to hold on to every penny until I was settled into my job here and figured out what things would cost.

He shook his head. "Gone. Buses pick up from the corner."

Twenty minutes later I boarded a bus bound for London and paid the driver my fare. We pulled away from the devastation of the coast. Sheep grazed the withered hills, the landscape nearly untouched. But as we neared the city, I could understand why the immigration officer had been incredulous at my coming here. At home the war had been big posters in the train stations exhorting people to buy war bonds, grainy news-reels at the cinema. Aside from Todd Dennison getting killed, it had been almost unreal.

But here the war was everywhere, inescapable. In London's outer boroughs like Richmond and Twickenham, the devastation was more sporadic, a house crushed here or there, as though perhaps a tree had fallen on it. Amidst the wreckage, people were doing strangely ordinary things, going to work and putting out the garbage and hanging wash on the lines. Closer to the city center, the scope of the damage unfurled. Entire blocks lay smashed. Traffic slowed and the bus inched forward, following the taxis and other buses through a detour where debris had made the road ahead impassible. Then came another street like that and another, until I had lost count. Though I had read the reports of the Blitz, I had imagined London, all of England really, as one step removed from the chaos of the Continent. But this was a city at war, as surely as if the German tanks were rolling down Westminster.

The bus pulled to a complete stop at an intersection and I studied the passersby on the street below. In front of a corner butcher shop women queued for whatever there was to be bought with the ration coupons. Though their expressions were calm, there was a weariness about them, shoulders stooped, the months of bombings having taken their toll. There was something odd about them, too, and it took me more than a minute to realize: none of them had any children, not babies in prams or toddlers shifted from hip to hip. They had all been shipped out of the city to safety with families in the countryside ahead of the Blitz, and even now that the bombing had stilled most remained in exile in case it should resume.

As the bus moved forward, I looked back, shivering. What would it take for a mother to put her child on a train and send them away, not knowing if or when she'd ever see them again? Mamma had done just that, putting my safety ahead of her own pain. Mrs. Connally surely would have done the same to keep Robbie safe if she could have. I swallowed back the lump that had formed in my throat.

It was nearly noon when I reached Fleet Street, having decided to use a bit of my money to take a taxi from Victoria station, rather than attempt the underground. Through the window, storied London, with its charming Victorian houses, had looked exactly as I'd expected, and at the same time not at all: coarse sandbags abutted most of the buildings and the windows that were not broken were blackened with tape or paint. "Can't go no further," the cabdriver said as we reached a police blockade hastily erected in the middle of the busy street. "Closed for security reasons." Were the newspaper offices that lined the famed block some sort of target?

I paid the driver and stepped from the cab, then paused to get my bearings. I started up Fleet Street, navigating the pavement carefully to avoid the sea of craters and debris. As I walked, my stride grew lighter. Despite the wreckage, I savored the freedom of a place I did not know at all—and where no one knew me.

A few minutes later, I set down my small suitcase by my feet and gazed up at the massive dome of St. Paul's silhouetted against the slate-gray sky, its dome guarding defiantly over streets and streets of buildings blown to rubble. Over the river behind the cathedral, barrage balloons floated like slow whales.

Something bumped into me from behind, nearly sending me sprawling. It was a man who had been walking with his head drawn low beneath the wide brim of his hat, focused on the papers he held. I waited for him to apologize. "Watch where you are going," he admonished instead, his blue eyes flashing icily.

"Hey!" I stopped, shocked by his rudeness. He had bumped into me. But I bit my tongue; the last thing I needed now was trouble. Besides, the man was already out of earshot.

Recovering, I inhaled deeply—the air was different here, coal-tinged and mixed with exhaust. I studied the numbers of the buildings: Number 19 Fleet Street, which housed the *Post*'s London office, should be just ahead.

The ground rumbled unexpectedly beneath my feet. Panicking, I threw myself into a doorway, then eyed the sky. I'd read the news articles of the sudden bomb attacks that had come out of nowhere, destroying homes and taking lives by the dozens. But around me pedestrians carried on, unperturbed. The noise came again and listening closely, I realized it was not an air raid, but an underground train traveling below.

Embarrassed, I straightened, catching a glimpse of my disheveled hair in the glass window of a stationer's shop. I could not turn up at the news bureau looking like this. I turned and walked back to a café I had passed a minute earlier. Inside, a group of men clustered at the counter, smoking and arguing over lunch about something Churchill had said. I slipped past them and found the toilet and freshened up.

When I stepped out again, the argument had reached a fever pitch. "If Chamberlain hadn't stepped in to help Poland, we wouldn't be in this mess," one of the men at the counter said.

I couldn't help myself. "That's exactly the kind of thinking that got Britain into trouble in the first place," I blurted. Then men turned and looked at me, mouths agape. I desperately wished I could fade into the walls. But it was too far gone for that. "Appeasement was a failed policy," I added.

"Oh?" A head rose above the others. I stared in surprise at the familiar blue eyes—it was the man who had bumped into me on the street minutes earlier. Hat removed, his hair was blond and neatly styled beneath.

"Yes." I squared my shoulders, as annoyed by his rudeness as his politics. "If Britain had not

197

declared war, we'd be right where we are now, only Hitler would be stronger."

"I agree. If you'd heard the first part of my statement you'd have known that." He smiled, self-satisfied. "And that is why," the man continued, "the American army needs to go across the Channel immediately." He turned away dismissively. I walked from the coffee shop, cheeks burning.

As freshened up as I could manage, I proceeded to Number 19. Inside, the reception area for the *Post* was small and crowded, a far cry from the stately lobby of the Washington bureau. I waited for the woman behind the desk to set down the phone. "Is Mr. Theodore White available? I'm Adelia Montforte from the Washington office."

The receptionist turned toward me impatiently, penciled eyebrows arched in reaction to my accent, bright red lips pursed. She wore a metal bracelet bearing her name and personal details. An identity bracelet, I realized, in case she fell victim to a bombing. "He's out."

My stomach sank a bit. I had come here depending upon the job Mr. Steeves had referenced. I did not have a backup plan—or even a place to stay.

I tried again. "I'm here about a secretarial position."

"So are they." The receptionist gestured toward the waiting area of filled chairs. She eyed me skeptically, then looked down over the desk toward my feet. Most people who came for interviews did not bring a suitcase. "You have an appointment?"

"I was sent from the Washington bureau," I repeated. I held out Mr. Steeves's card and the secretary's eyes widened slightly.

"Follow me." I avoided the resentful stares of the girls who had been waiting as the receptionist led me up a flight of narrow, uneven stairs and into a long room. It was crowded with typists like the bureau had been back in Washington. Cigarette smoke, a universal perfume, hung high in the air above. The clattering of fingers against keys was welcoming and familiar. She ushered me to an empty typewriter. "I'll give you a few minutes to get acclimated, then come back to administer the typing test."

I studied the machine in front of me, which was a different style from the typewriters back in Washington. "Hello again," a voice behind me said. I jumped. The man who had bumped into me on the street, and with whom I had quarreled in the coffee shop, loomed now over the desk. "We didn't get off on the right foot, did we?" His face was pleasant now, his voice a rich baritone.

I fumbled to find a response. Had he followed me? "I'm sorry, but if you'll excuse me, I'm about to have an interview."

"With me," he finished. I blinked in surprise.

"I'm Theodore White." He said this as though I should have already known. So this was the awful man to whom Mr. Steeves had sent me. I could feel the curious stares of the other women around me as they stopped typing to watch and listen. Clearly, Theodore White did not normally talk to the typists, much less the applicants.

The receptionist reappeared. "Mr. White, she hasn't tested yet. I was just about to administer the typing exam."

"Never mind that." He waved his hand, then turned to me. "Come." I hesitated. He cut through the typing pool self-assuredly, taking in the room as though he owned everything—and everyone —in it. Inwardly, I blanched. Was it too late to back out? The last thing I wanted to do was work with this dreadful man. But I had come all this way and had no choice but to follow him.

His office was cluttered, with a smeary window looking out at the fog-wreathed dome of St. Paul's. He cleared a stack of papers so hurriedly from a chair that they spilled to the ground. Not bothering to pick them up, he gestured that I should sit.

"So what can I do for you, beside almost knocking you over and correcting your misconceptions about the war?" I thought he was joking, though he did not smile. He was a few years older than me, with porcelain eyes. He was good-looking, too good-looking really, in that should-be-in-movies-not-standing-here kind of way. But there was a coldness about him that made me squirm.

I cleared my throat. Though I did not at all like him, I needed him to like me. "I'm Adelia Montforte. I work, that is, I worked, for the *Post* in Washington. Mr. Steeves recommended me. He said he would send word." He wore a puzzled expression. Perhaps Mr. Steeves had not sent the telegraph, or it had not arrived.

"He sent a secretary all the way across the pond." Theodore White harrumphed. "Here to keep an eye on me, most likely."

"Not at all." His eyes widened. Clearly, he was not used to being contradicted, at least not by a typist. "I requested the transfer." I hoped he would not ask why.

"Well, the work here is pretty straightforward. Typing, and some proofreading."

"In Washington, I was doing the copyedits too." I had only done copyedits a handful of times for Mr. Steeves. But I stretched the truth a bit, wanting to sound more useful than the average typist and hopeful that he could not tell the difference.

He raised an eyebrow. "Oh? Let's see how you do with this piece." He passed me a paper and pencil. His fingers were long with flat nails that said he might have been an artist. They reminded me of my father's. I tried to recall my mother's hands, but found that I could not. The little things faded with time, no matter how hard I tried to hold on to them.

I scanned the article about the displacement of the residents of a village in north France, making notes in the margins. "Well?" I handed it back to him and he scanned my corrections. "What else?"

I hesitated, smelling the minty pomade in his hair as I leaned in to point. "It's not just the grammar, see? It's about the voice. You need to put the reader in the shoes of the people, the families and children. Make them care." I was going beyond the copyedits, I knew, and into the substance of the piece. Overstepping my place. But he had asked and I needed this job. "There's a reference here to this family Reimbaud—what about the children, how this affected them? How long have they lived there and where will they go? I'm not trying to tell you how to do your job, but you should talk to the writer."

"You already are."

"Oh!" I felt my cheeks go crimson. Without realizing it, I had been criticizing his work.

But he waved his hand, not seeming to take offense. "Not at all. You've found exactly what the piece was missing. I'll take another shot at it and show it to you again."

"Are there photographs?"

He nodded, then handed me an envelope. "I didn't take these. They're from a stringer."

I studied the images, which were a bit stiff and generic, capturing the scene the way a child might have drawn it. "I'm afraid the photos are all wrong, too. They've focused on the line, but look at the mother holding her child back from the police." I traced it with my finger. "I would have centered here."

"You're a photographer, too?"

The word seemed somehow too big. "Just for fun. I like taking pictures."

"We have a darkroom here at the paper. You're welcome to use it in the off hours, though supplies are scarce so you'd have to find your own." Though he had not formally made me a job offer, it sounded then as though he wanted me to come to work.

"Does that mean I can keep copyediting?"

"Yes, you've got the job. Steeves would kill me if I sent you back. You'll be working for me." He pointed to a tiny desk in the corner of his office. "You can start tomorrow and sit there." I had imagined myself sitting with the typists like I had been in Washington, not working in such close quarters with him.

"I did some translating for Mr. Steeves also," I added. "Some French, but mostly Italian."

"You're from Trieste," he said, surprising me. I noticed then the telegram that sat open on his desk. So Mr. Steeves had written after all. Why couldn't White have just said so, instead of playing games and leaving me to dangle? My annoyance at him grew.

"Yes. My parents sent me to America as a child."

"Are they still in Italy?"

I shifted uncomfortably at the question, too intrusive for someone I had only just met, and now my boss. "I don't know. They disappeared over a year ago and there's been no word."

"And you're a Jew." His bluntness surprised me. There was anti-Semitism here like back home, I was sure. I hadn't mentioned my religion at the *Post* in Washington—my Italian surname had made it easy to avoid the subject. Mr. Steeves must have known, though, and told him. Would it would keep me from getting the job? Maybe I should deny it.

"Does that matter?"

"Not at all. My mum is Jewish," Teddy said. "But I keep it quiet." I nodded. "I'm not a bigot. I'm just surprised you'd return to Europe." I held my breath, again waiting for him to ask why I had left Washington. He could not possibly know that, too. "It's brave of you, coming here. Brave or stupid—the jury's out on that one." I looked for the smile that did not come.

I shrugged. "It's just London."

He eyed me levelly. "You think the city is safe?"

I hadn't thought about it before leaving. But after all I'd seen since arriving that morning, I knew that it was not. "As much as anywhere else," I lied. Nowhere would ever feel safe to me.

"There's no halfway in with this war, Adelia. Here you're in the thick of it. I was supposed to go," he added quickly. Though we had only just met, he seemed to need to explain why he was not off fighting. "With the army, I mean. But on the third day of basic training, I broke my shoulder trying to climb a wall. It was a bad fracture and never quite healed properly." His shoulders slumped with resignation. "Right, well, we'll give it a try," he said, jumping abruptly back to the topic of my employment. Then he stood up and began pacing the floor. There was a restlessness to him, a constant moving and tapping of the feet, as though there was music playing, even when there wasn't. "So our work here is out in the street," he began. A loud explosion cut him off, rattling the windows. He grabbed me and pulled me down under his desk. The sound came again, raining bits of plaster on top of my feet, which stuck out beyond the desk, exposed. This was not the train rumble I'd felt earlier on the street; it shook my insides like nothing I had ever experienced.

"All clear," he said a minute later when the noise had stopped. He straightened and returned the teacup which had fallen to his desk. Then he walked to the window and scanned up and down the street. "Must have been that unexploded shell that hit on Whitefriars a few nights back."

"But I thought the Blitz was over."

"It is. But the war rages on. The raids come at any time. Still keen to stay?" he asked, testing me.

I thought back to my journey into the city, the rooftops which had been sheared off, their jagged wooden beams that pushed upward to the sky. Then I squared my shoulders. Danger came where one least expected it, on city streets lit for the holidays just blocks from home. I would not be daunted. I straightened. "Yes. More so than ever."

"Well, that's all sorted." His eyes crinkled a bit at the edges and a dimple appeared in his left cheek. Then his expression grew somber once more. "It's been a bloody awful year." He did not apologize for swearing. "The people here, well, they wear a stiff upper lip but inside they're knackered." I cocked my head at the unfamiliar term. "Shattered. Exhausted. You have a place yet?" He switched topics without warming. "There's a boardinghouse in Maida Vale where some of the girls live." He scribbled an address down on a piece of paper. "And there's a reception tonight at the American ambassador's residence. Early, you know, because of the curfew. But we should be there." We. I started to protest that I was only a secretary, then thought better of it. "I'll pick you up at seven."

I had not even said yes. "Mr. White . . ."

"Call me Teddy."

"Like the bear," I blurted, instantly regretting it. He chuckled. "I suppose. Or the president.

No one has ever put it quite that way before."

"I've only just arrived and I'm a bit weary for a party."

"Early dinner, then." He smiled gamely, eyes dancing, cajoling me to say yes. I stared at him, incredulous. Even after everything with Charlie, I was still that gawky girl off the boat, unwilling to believe that a man might find me attractive.

"But you just said you've got to be at the reception." He waved his hand, dismissing the event that just seconds ago was so important. "And we've only just met," I added.

"Not quite. We met in the coffee shop earlier and I was terribly rude. I'd like to correct that." But the intent of his words as he looked at me with sparkly blue eyes was undoubtedly something more.

"All right," I said, feeling my cheeks warm. I had not gone out with anyone since Charlie. In Washington, there had been dances and parties and invitations aplenty through the other girls at the paper. Despite the grimness of the war—or perhaps because of it—the thousands of workers who had come to the capital to help seemed to need the gaiety to shake off the long hours of toil. I went along when I could no longer refuse and even danced a few times. But it all felt wrong.

I wondered again if the job was a mistake. I had come here to get away from things like this and it seemed important to set the boundaries from the start. "I'm just, as you said, knackered." We both laughed. "Another time, okay?"

"Another time, then," he repeated. He reached out and shook my hand solemnly, his fingers warm around my own. Then he handed the refugee article back to me. "There's still a story to be rewritten though."

"Me?" Even Mr. Steeves had not given me the chance to do substantive editing.

"Yes, deadline is six if you think you can manage it."

"I can." For that, I would muster the energy.

"Then it's all sorted." An unexpected twinge of disappointment tugged at me as he released my hand and turned back to his desk. "Let's get to work."

Eleven

I sat alone at my small desk in the corner of Teddy's office, wading through correspondence that he had let accumulate and sorting it into piles: matters that needed his attention, those that could be filed and those that could be discarded (or reused, if they were not confidential, for scrap paper; nothing was to be wasted). I set down the pencil I'd been chewing on and pulled back the blackout curtains to reveal the curving edge of the dome of St. Paul's, set against the azure late morning sky, rows of broken chimneys beneath it. Smoke rose above the coal-dipped rooftops, mixing with fog and soot.

I took a sip of the Earl Grey tea before me, now too cool. Then I leaned back, my eyes drifting downward to a photo of Teddy with former Prime Minister Chamberlain that sat on the windowsill. Teddy had been gone for two days on a trip, though he wouldn't say where, just that he was following up with a lead. The office was quiet without him. I had grown accustomed to his dry humor and quick laugh, his constant movement these past several months, the way he chewed on his lip when he was concentrating, or paced back and forth when trying to get his head around an idea.

Thankfully, my initial impressions of him had not borne out; though he was impatient and stubborn, Teddy was not a jerk. But he was the subject of endless speculation among the typists, I'd quickly learned after coming to work here.

"They say he flew into occupied Poland just to get a story."

"They say he's related to the Rockefellers."

"He's never been seen with the same girl twice." That last one irked me, though why I was not quite sure.

I eyed the photo of Teddy with Chamberlain once more. It was the only picture in the office and I wondered as I had before about his family and the home in Kent where he had grown up. "I went to Eton, then uni at Oxford, read English at

Magdalen College," he'd explained once when I asked, reciting facts that I already knew from the diplomas that lined the walls. "I was meant to go into banking or law. My family is aghast at what I do. To them being a correspondent is dreadfully working-class. But I love it." Teddy was something of an odd duck at the *Post*, the lone British correspondent at the American press. He'd been with the *Times* before that, but had left under circumstances that no one seemed to know—or was willing to discuss. "They pay better here," he'd offered airily once, but there was no force behind the explanation.

The cathedral bell chimed twelve and I set down the correspondence and put on my overcoat and scarf. I wove my way through the steno pool where the handful of typists clattered away on their machines, the BBC radio droning news of the war continuously in the background. A half dozen or so other offices lined the perimeter of the room, their lights off as the correspondents chased stories out in the field. I did not stop at the tea room where some of the other girls had surely clustered, gossiping over thin cheese sandwiches wrapped in wax paper. They'd treated me coldly in the months since I'd come. For a while I thought it was because I was the only American among the typists and other clerical staff. But they didn't seem to hold that against the American correspondents whom they admired from a distance, or the GIs who took them dancing on the weekends. More likely they resented me for coming over and being immediately put a step above them working for Teddy. I tried not to mind. They reminded me of the girls back home who went all silly over boys, in a way that I could never be after growing up in a big pile of Connallys.

I walked downstairs and stepped out onto Fleet Street, eyeing the gray late-April sky warily. The unsettled weather blew through so quickly here, clouds forming and starting a downpour seemingly from nowhere at all, then clearing again just as quickly.

Three American GIs walked shoulder to shoulder down the pavement and I stepped sideways in order to avoid bumping into one of them. London was, even more so than Washington had been, a city under occupation—by the thousands of American soldiers who were stationed here, filling the pubs and prowling the seedy nightlife at Piccadilly Circus. "Excuse me," the soldier nearest to me said, giving me a long sideways look. I averted my eyes, not answering. I had come to London to escape Charlie, but the boys in uniform were a constant reminder. Once as I transferred from one double-decker bus to another in Trafalgar Square, I'd imagined that I'd seen him, an image so real I had disembarked, frantically searching the crowd. But it had been an illusion; Charlie, of course, was not here.

I began to walk as I did each day at lunchtime, slipping into the crowd and moving with it. I loved winding through the back streets of the city, enjoying the freedom of life here, where no one knew me or my past.

"I wish you wouldn't," Teddy had said more than once, his mouth pulling downward. "It's dangerous."

"I'm just as likely to get hit by a bomb here as outside," I'd protested. But in truth I walked because of the devastation, not in spite of it. It had started one day as I made my way home from the bureau to my flat, which was just north of Hyde Park. As I reached the northern edge of the park, I'd been stunned to see a giant crater in the middle of the street, an empty bus dangling precipitously from it. Had there been passengers? It seemed unlikely, or I would have heard about it at the paper. Bombings were so commonplace that only those with large-scale casualties seemed to be making the news these days. I pulled out Uncle Meyer's camera from my bag and began snapping photos. After that, I walked every day, at lunch and on the weekends, too, wanting to capture it all in pictures. Most of all, I was struck by the ordinary life that persisted, like women queuing at the shops and the group of children (among the few that begun to return to the city) I'd seen playing soccer by a gaping patch in Notting Hill where a house once stood, so much like the games of our childhood.

It was a childhood that despite my best efforts I could not forget. It had been months since I left Washington and nearly a year since I left Philadelphia, but the assaults of the past were nonstop on my mind, despite my best attempts to block them out. The memories, when I allowed myself to have them, were always bathed in a kind of gold—sunshine soaking the yard where we'd played, lifting the flecks of Charlie's hair and magnifying them. Other times I imagined myself back on the Connallys' worn sofa in the city, wedged into the corner where I always sat beside Jack, Robbie sprawled across the three of us despite his mother's admonition to keep his feet down.

Liam popped improbably into my mind now. Though I thought often of the others—Charlie, of course, and Jack and sweet, sweet Robbie—I missed Liam, too, in a way that I probably shouldn't. It was the good Liam I saw, with his irreverent humor, before he had become so dark and troubled. He would know exactly how I felt among the other typists, as though I did not fit in at all.

I walked east, stepping over the edge of a curb that had been painted a striped black and white to make it visible during the blackouts. Then I skirted around St. Paul's churchyard, feeling my way south to the river. The street ended and I stepped into the full, cutting wind of the Thames. The air was sharply cool, winter not ready to cede to spring. I sat down on a bench to pull out my gloves. A couple walked down the pavement, holding hands. An unexpected pang of longing ran through me. Charlie appeared in my mind, large and unbidden, images cascading upon me like books falling from a shelf. I saw him now as I had at the State Department that day, tall and lovely in his uniform. Had he shipped out yet or was he still in training?

I opened my purse and pulled out a letter. It had been waiting for me when I returned home from work the previous evening, addressed in Aunt Bess's flowery script. Inside was another envelope, my name printed in what looked like Charlie's blocky writing. My breath had caught. The postmark was weeks old, though whether Aunt Bess had delayed in sending it or it had been slowed by the wartime post, I did not know. I'd held up the still-sealed envelope with trembling hands. Was Charlie begging me to come back or cursing me for having left? Dangerous thoughts, the kind I had kept at bay for so long, leapt up at me, a flicker becoming a flame. If I opened the letter, I would know the truth and be forced to respond. No, better to leave the past alone. I'd dangled the letter over the fire in the grate. Then thinking better of it, I tucked it in my bag.

I held it aloft now, edges flapping with the

breeze. A bell rang out, signaling that my lunch hour was half over and so I returned the letter to my bag and began to make my way back to the bureau. Inside I scanned the office to see if Teddy had returned, and felt a mild pang of disappointment that he had not. I unwrapped the leftover toast and beans I had brought for lunch. I found English food bland, lots of breaded whitefish and shepherd's pie filled with potatoes and little else; it reminded me of my aunt's cooking back home. But thanks to Teddy, I had an extra book full of ration coupons and was able to get plenty of whatever there was to be purchased; I had no business complaining.

I walked through the typing pool, where the air now hummed with chatter. But the conversation stopped abruptly as I entered, signaling something I was not meant to hear. "Is there any post?" I asked the secretary Joan, trying to act as though nothing was amiss.

"I'm sure you can check for yourself." She turned away.

"Is that any way to treat a coworker?" a voice behind me rebuked sharply. I turned. Teddy was back. At the sight of him, I was filled with warmth. I had grown to appreciate his flaxen blond hair and eyes that crinkled when he laughed.

But now his normally cheerful face was stormy. "No, of course not, Mr. White." Joan turned and passed me the mail.

"You're welcome," he said, when I had followed him into his office. He closed the door behind us. There was a heavy stubble across his cheeks and rings around his usually bright eyes. Teddy had always been a constant worker, but now the news flowed so fast even he couldn't keep up.

"I wish you wouldn't say anything," I fretted. "Your sticking up for me just makes them hate me more."

"Why should you care about that?"

Because in some ways I would always be that new girl at Southern, looking for a friend. But I couldn't tell him that. "You should have me sit out there with the others."

"I need you here." I knew from the way his mouth set stubbornly that I would not win on the point. "It's not personal to you, how the girls act," he added. "Those girls have just been through a lot. Most of them are from the East End." I nodded. The devastation had been so much worse in Stepney and Bethnal Green. "Midge, for example, lost almost her whole family in the Blitz." The girls did not just resent me for my closeness to Teddy. I had not been here through the worst of the bombings, was not one of them. "And Edie's husband is missing in North Africa." I was surprised that Teddy, who scarcely seemed to speak to the other typists, knew so much about their personal hardships.

No, simply changing the location of my desk

would not make things better. But perhaps, understanding what all the other women had been through, I could try a bit harder to be friendly. I noticed then the fine coating of soot and ash on his jacket, which he had tried without success to brush off. "You've been over there, haven't you?" As he poured two glasses of water from the pitcher on the windowsill, my concern grew. I'd suspected for months that Teddy had been making secret trips across the Channel to France, trying to learn what was coming.

"Only as far as Guernsey this time. That's still Britain."

"But it's occupied. You could have been arrested by the Germans. What were you thinking?" But I already knew: Teddy's doggedness went beyond good journalism; he was trying to prove himself. Part of him felt less than enough because he was not a soldier fighting.

He waved his hand, brushing away my concerns. "There's something coming, Adelia. I saw it, a build-up at the coast. The Americans are really going over."

Hope rose in me that someone might finally be able to stop the Germans. "How soon?"

His brow wrinkled. "I couldn't tell. Weeks or months maybe. I need to do some more digging."

"I wish you wouldn't." How much farther into danger would he go next time?

"Worried about me now, aren't you?" His tone

was more than a little pleased. I turned slightly away, warmth creeping up from my neck. My affection for Teddy had grown these past few months, in spite of my determination to remain unattached. "Adelia, going to the story—that's my job. I like you worrying about me, though." His lone dimple appeared.

"I'm serious."

"So am I. I do wish the photos were a bit better." He had to rely on stock images from the Associated Press pool photographers.

"I could show you how to take the photos," I offered. *Or go with you myself,* I thought, though that was out of the question.

But he shook his head. "I need my eyes on the story to digest it all and take notes. Anyway, there's no time to worry about all that now. I need you to come with me."

"Where?"

"Eden's called an urgent press conference without saying why. I want photos." The correspondents usually worked alone, and Teddy did not have a colleague to ask for help—except for me. He started for the door. I hesitated. Teddy had never asked me to help him with a story before. "Come on!"

I gestured to his clothing. "You can't go like that."

He looked down blankly. "Oh, right. Meet you there, then."

Twenty minutes later I stood uneasily outside the massive Foreign Office, waiting for one of the guards to decide I did not belong and ask me to leave. Teddy soon arrived in a freshly pressed jacket and polished Oxfords, the aroma of steam and sandalwood soap rising from his collar. As I followed him through the stale marble corridor, I was reminded of the day Mr. Steeves had brought me along to the meeting at State, where I had run into Charlie. "What is it you want me to do?"

"Just take down what they say. We'll see if they're allowing photos—or if there's anything worth shooting."

The pressroom was full of men, correspondents like Teddy smoking and talking and jostling for space. I was suddenly separated from him and he looked back helplessly. "You go on," I called. "I'll circle around."

"And bring us some coffee while you're at it, love," a man overhearing us joked. Ignoring him, I slid to the back of the room, trying to peer over the sea of tall shoulders. Through the crowd, I could see Teddy striding to the front, his style sure and easy among the room of stiff, suited men. Impulsively, I reached in my bag and pulled out my camera, then took a snapshot of the scene.

A hand clamped down on my shoulder. A red-coated guard towered over me, glaring. Without speaking, he led me from the room, then ripped the camera unceremoniously from my hands. "No photos," he said, ushering me toward the security desk. Was he going to arrest me or simply kick me out? I searched over my shoulder, hoping to signal to Teddy for help. But he had vanished from sight.

"I'm sorry, I didn't know," I stammered. The guard still held my camera as he led me to the front door of the building and opened it.

"My camera. May I have it back please?"

He pulled it out of reach. "I'll have to keep it. Security reasons."

"But it's mine." My cheeks began to burn.

"Say now," a voice interjected behind the guard. We both turned. A sturdy woman in a wide-shouldered pinstriped navy blue suit stood behind me. "There's no need for that. Just take the film and give the girl her camera back."

The voice of the strange woman was surprisingly firm and the guard complied. "She still has to go." Reluctantly, I walked from the Foreign Office building, grasping the camera in both hands. Teddy had given me a chance to do something more and I had failed. I started down the street, past two man in dark suits and caps who leaned against a low wall.

"Wait!" The woman in navy had followed me out the door.

"Thank you." I raised the camera slightly.

"I'm Claire." She extended her hand. She stood a good six inches taller than me with posture that Aunt Bess would have loved.

"Adelia."

Her grip was firm, just shy of masculine. "You're a correspondent, aren't you?"

"I'm helping one out. Or was," I added, gesturing toward the door that had slammed behind me. "I kind of messed it up."

"Not at all. Those blokes are missing the real story anyway." I cocked my head, curious. "The prime minister is going to tell them about the Polish émigré who has come to England with stories of what Hitler has done to the Jews. Where's the man himself, though? Come." She led me around the corner and through a door on the side of the building. I held my breath, wondering if I might be stopped again. But a different guard nodded and let us pass. Was the woman some sort of government worker? I looked over my shoulder uncertainly, past one of the suited men I'd seen outside. Teddy would not know where I had gone. But Claire was moving swiftly and I had no choice other than to follow or be left behind.

We crossed a corridor and entered a small study. A man, pale and slight, sat alone in a chair, smoking. "This is Jan Tomaszewicz from Poland." I understood then that this man, who might have been a schoolteacher or an accountant, was the refugee who had made such a brave journey to tell the world about the Jews.

"Mr. Tomaszewicz, can we get you anything?"

221

Claire asked. The man shook his head, just barely understanding. "He's too nervous to speak to the press himself," Claire explained in a low voice. "The Foreign Minister is just going to introduce him and tell the press generally what they've learned from him. But if someone could speak with him first, it might put his mind at ease."

I looked up at Claire, surprised. "Me?" She nodded and I sat down beside him. "You came from Poland?" I asked tentatively in Yiddish.

"You're a Jew?" he asked. A light seemed to dawn in Tomaszewicz's eyes as I nodded slightly. "I'm not," he said, his voice almost apologetic. "But the language, it's close enough to German."

"Can you tell me about your trip?"

He dipped his chin. "I'm not supposed to talk about the information I brought."

"I'm not interested in the information. I'm interested in you."

The man seemed to relax slightly. "I was raised in the town of Lodz. My wife and daughter—she's nine—are still there." A shadow passed his face. "I really shouldn't say more."

"I understand. My parents put me on a boat to America when I was sixteen. They stayed behind in Italy." I could hear Teddy admonishing that I should not make myself part of the story.

But doing so seemed to gain Tomaszewicz's trust. "One day when making deliveries I came upon a horrible sight in the woods," he began.

"They were forcing Jews in a truck, a regular delivery truck, you know, one that might deliver boxes to the store." He was talking fast now, telling me more than he should in the rush of emotion. "They were putting them—men, women and children—in the back and connecting something to the exhaust pipe." My pulse thudded in dreadful anticipation. "There were screams and then there were none."

I gripped the side of the table. I'd heard back home, of course, of Hitler's hatred for the Jews, how schools and businesses had been closed. I knew that some had been arrested, though I'd assumed that they were mostly political activists like my father. But murdering innocents, in civilized Europe. They had automobiles, for goodness' sake, movie theaters. I thought of my parents and felt sick. Could such things be happening in Italy, too?

"I knew I had to tell someone." I forced myself to concentrate on his words, which poured forth now. To get the story. His eyes grew moist as he told of the family he had left behind. "I tried to bring them with me, but my wife's mother was too sick to travel and she would not leave her." Though not a Jew himself, he had risked everything to help people he did not know.

From the other room came a din of voices, growing louder as the door opened at a suited man whom I presumed was a diplomat stuck his head in the room. "Prosze." He gestured for Mr. Tomaszewicz to follow him.

"Wait!" I blurted. "Mr. Tomaszewicz, may I take your photo?" He nodded. When the man who had come for him did not protest, I put in the spare film I always carried, then snapped hurriedly.

The man gestured again for Mr. Tomaszewicz, more impatiently this time. As Mr. Tomaszewicz passed me, I put my hand on his shoulder. "God bless you and your family."

"Thank you," I said to Claire when they had gone. We stepped into the hall.

"I met Tomaszewicz earlier and I sensed he needed to talk. But the translator was nowhere to be found. I thought of you."

"Me?" So the meeting had not been incidental.

"I knew you spoke some other languages and hoped there might be one in common."

I blinked, puzzled. "I'm sorry, but have we met?"

"You're Teddy's girl, and everyone knows Teddy."

"I work for Teddy but I'm not his girl." The words came out harsher than I had intended, bordering on rude.

One of the suited men who I had seen earlier outside and also in the corridor was also in the hallway, watching us with interest. My skin prickled. "I know this may sound silly," I whispered, "but I think that man may be following us."

Claire chuckled. "He is following us. Security and all that."

"I don't understand."

"When I'm working, MI-5, and my uncle, insist upon it."

"Your uncle?"

A man in military uniform came up to them then. "Excuse me, Miss Churchill? The prime minister is looking for you."

"Sorry, my dear, I must go. Good afternoon." As Claire walked off, I stood speechless, my jaw hanging in disbelief. The woman who had gotten me the interview was none other than the prime minister's niece.

After she'd gone, I waited, uncertain whether to head back to the office. I went outside and lingered by the main door where the guard had ushered me from the building. Several minutes later, Teddy came rushing out. "A dissident from Poland with proof of the awful things Hitler is doing. They introduced him at the press conference, but he didn't take questions. There's a story here, more to tell, if we can just get to him."

"I know. I met him." I could not keep the pride from my voice. "Got the interview."

"Met him? That's brilliant! How on earth did you manage it?"

"I'll explain later. Right now let's get back so you can write up the story before I forget everything he said."

225

"Me? Adelia, it's your story. You'll write it up and you'll get the byline." That would never happen, of course. At best, the story would go out under Teddy's name with a credit to me.

At the bureau, we went straight to the darkroom, where I began to develop the film. "Tell me everything and I'll write it down." As I gently bathed the film in chemicals, I recounted Tomaszewicz's tale.

"It's unbelievable," he said when I finished. "We knew that the Germans were arresting Jews and that there had been some isolated killings, but this is a whole other level of barbarity."

Suddenly, overwhelmed by everything Mr. Tomaszewicz had told me about the Jews, I could not take it anymore. "Oh!" I dropped the film into the liquid and brought my hand, which smelled of chemicals, to my mouth.

Teddy was at my side them. "I'm sorry." He was standing close to me in the dim light now, his arm touching mine. He put his hand on my shoulder.

"It's fine. It just reminds me of my own parents. Is that what happened to them?" I had told Teddy before about their political activism and the way they had disappeared.

He put his hand on my shoulder. "Would you want to know? If it were possible, I mean."

I hesitated, feeling the unfamiliar warmth through the fabric of my blouse. Something inside me stirred. "I don't know." I had been born with the need to know the truth, to peel back the lid and see what was inside. But there was a fantasy I'd allowed myself that somewhere my parents were still out there. Finding out could destroy all that. Would it be better to no longer have hope? "I suppose," I replied finally. "In some ways I'm still a child, waiting for them. I'd give anything for that to be true. Finding out what really happened might help to explain why they disappeared. It doesn't matter, does it? We just don't know." *And probably never would,* I finished silently.

He looked at the photo I was hanging to dry. "These are phenomenal, Adelia." They were good, I conceded inwardly, secretly pleased. I'd caught the light so that every line of Tomaszewicz's face was etched, a map of bravery and grief.

"Dinner tonight to celebrate. That's the wrong word, of course, for such a sad story," he hastened to add. "But you've done really good work here."

I hesitated as I cleaned up the darkroom, searching for the right answer. Teddy had made clear his interest in me ever since I arrived. I'd held him at arm's length, the idea of being with anyone but Charlie unthinkable. I opened the door, letting in harsh light. "I'm sorry, I can't."

"You would almost think there was someone back home," he baited as he followed.

I flushed slightly. "It's nothing like that." And it wasn't a lie—because there really wasn't some-one anymore, was there?

"Then what is it?"

"I can hardly date the boss," I replied, keeping my voice light.

"I'll fire you." Was he serious? But his eyes crinkled and that dimple appeared.

"Don't tease. I can't." He was watching me still, looking for a greater explanation of the things I could never put in words. I understood his confusion: I'm sure Teddy was used to women falling all over him, not refusing him. "I'm just not going out these days," I offered lamely.

"At least let me see you home. That's not out, it's in."

"I'm planning to walk."

"All the way to Bayswater?" I nodded. I walked home often in good weather, though it took more than an hour. "I'll join you. The exercise will do me good."

"All right," I relented.

"Don't sound so excited," he chided.

"I'm sorry, I was still thinking about the story," I lied, then forced a smile. "That would be swell." We started from the office and down Fleet Street, winding west past the shops closing early because there was nothing left to sell. But as we neared Covent Garden, the stalls were lively with shoppers, and the cafes packed thick with people enjoying a quick drink before heading home for curfew. I wondered if Teddy might suggest stopping for a cocktail.

"It's nearly seven o'clock," I said, surprised at how the time had passed.

"And still light out," he added. "It's lovely isn't it, these long evenings?" He took my hand impulsively. I stopped, caught off guard by the smooth skin on my own, so unlike Charlie's. But I didn't pull away. We continued on. "At our house in Kent you can sit on the patio in the evenings and watch the swans on the lake. You would love it." There was a suggestion of something more in this last bit. I stepped away, taking my hand from his.

We strolled down Oxford Circus, eyeing the shop windows at Marks & Spencer, which bore the latest fashions as though anyone had the money to wear them anymore. My own coat was darned in places that no one could see, but I'd improved it with a scarf bought secondhand at the Portobello Road market. The money I made at the paper was just enough to cover my room and meals. I had the remaining bit of what Uncle Meyer had given me tucked away beneath my mattress, but I wouldn't touch that unless I absolutely had to.

At the end of Oxford Street, the windows to a pub were smashed, jagged glass hanging from torn blackout strips. "Some American lads had a brawl," Teddy explained, a note of disapproval to his voice. I cringed, as though personally responsible. American GIs had crowded into

London, packs of young men with too much time and energy on their hands, filling (and sometimes fighting in) the bars and clubs, talking and laughing loudly on the streets. They had taxed the restrained city to the brink with their boisterous ways, seeming to fill every stereotype Brits might have had about us Yanks.

We reached the edge of Hyde Park and passed a victory garden, now withered to brush. "I miss vegetables," I said, "Fresh ones from the garden. When I go home I'm going to eat tomatoes and peppers by the bucket." Home. I didn't even know where that was anymore.

"There were oranges last week," he pointed out. I laughed, recalling the sudden shipment in the markets, the rinds that littered the gutters everywhere. I must have eaten six, sucking out the juice and eating every bit of the delicious orange flesh. Then they were gone again just as quickly, as though it had all been a dream. "You know we'll have those things in England again after the war." His voice was once again pointed: you could stay.

"The war has to end somehow first."

"It will. We're going to win, now that the Americans are coming. It won't be soon or easy, but it will happen." I admired his confidence. Most people, including me, didn't quite believe it yet. The Germans had rolled so easily over half of Europe, destroying boundaries and swallowing nations that had been for centuries. Would the Americans really be able to stop them? I could see it in the eyes of the Londoners as I walked the streets: beneath the stoic resolve, this was still very much a city under siege.

We reached Porchester Terrace. Despite Teddy's recommendation, I'd found my own place in Bayswater, a room atop a yellowed four-story town house with white shutters far from where the other typists lived. It was owned by an Indian woman whose husband was off fighting. I loved the neighborhood with its winding backstreets and tiny, eclectic shops. There was a used bookseller at the corner where I could trade in the ones I had read and then get a new one from the overflowing shelves for just a tuppence.

We passed the bookshop, its shades now shuttered for the night, stopping just after the red mailbox at Number 59. Teddy lingered awkwardly by the porch steps as I opened the low gate. "Would you like to come up for tea?" I wasn't sure of the propriety of the situation and hoped he would not take it for more than what it was. "I don't want to keep you," I hastened to add. "You must be exhausted from your trip."

"Not at all." Teddy seemed to run on pure adrenaline, always chasing the next story. "But it is a bit late, and I want to make sure our story has been filed properly." *Ours.* I stood a bit straighter at the word. "Perhaps just some water before I start back."

We climbed the long flights of stairs, which smelled faintly of curry. I opened the door to my single-room flat, glad I had straightened up that morning. I braced myself, though, self-conscious about how small it must look. He did not seem to notice. Instead he whistled, taking in the photographs I'd framed around the room of the city, the lives of the people at war. "Adelia, these are fabulous. Photography isn't just your hobby. You're really talented."

I blushed. "Thank you."

He glanced out the window then which looked down on an alley where a man was picking through the garbage cans. His brow wrinkled. "But you're here all by yourself." He was concerned about me, I realized, touched. Impulsively I reached up and kissed his cheek.

His eyes widened and he turned, bringing his lips to mine. I froze. Only Charlie had kissed me before and there was something about these strange, soft lips that was both exciting and, well, wrong. I put my hand on his chest, pushing him away. "Oh, God, sorry," he stammered, jumping back, face flushed. "I didn't mean for that to happen." Except that he had—ever since the first day we met.

"It's all right." In other circumstances, I might have been offended by him taking such liberties without so much as a date. Everything moved faster with the war, though. I saw couples intertwined in the corners of Green Park at dusk, lined up to marry at the churches on Sunday. It would have been fine if I was any other girl.

But I wasn't—and my heart was still somewhere else. "I'm sorry, Teddy. I'm just not up for that right now—with anyone."

Teddy raised his palms plaintively. "There's been no one since I met you, Adelia. Not that you asked me to be exclusive. Heck, you haven't even agreed to go out with me. But ever since I met you, I'm ruined for the rest." He smiled bashfully. "My whole life I've felt as though I was writing the story. With you for the first time I feel a part of it."

I took his hand. "I know, and I'm grateful."

"That's the last thing a fella wants," he groaned. "We're perfect together," he added. Behind him the sun had dipped low to the buildings.

"The sirens are going to go soon," I pointed out. Being caught out after curfew would result in a fine.

"I don't care," he said, still staring at me, his longing unabashed now.

"Good night," I said firmly, my head swimming with confusion. I closed the door to the flat, shaken. For a moment, I might have liked him back.

But I couldn't. The memories of home, and of

Charlie, loomed large again. I remembered the envelope in my purse, still unopened. I pulled it out, too curious to resist any longer. As I opened it, a photograph fell out to the ground and I picked it up, choking back a cry. It was an image of myself and all four Connally boys set against the backdrop of Steel Pier that last summer. Usually I was on the other side of the camera, obscured from view. Who had taken it? I tried to remember. Jack was lifting Robbie playfully, as if about to toss him over the railing to the water below. Liam stood to the side, pretending to be disinterested, but even he smiled a bit around the eyes, his anger momentarily gone. Charlie hovered behind us, protective even in his mirth, arms spread above us like giant wings. His hand was brushing my shoulder casually and I could almost feel it there now, how that touch had sent shivers through me.

I ran my fingers over Robbie's face. Though I could not remember the photo being snapped, I could feel the moment as if it was now. There was no return address on the envelope. I dropped the picture into the fire, watching as the edges curled and burned to dust.

Twelve

"Your go." Claire's long tapered fingers, short nails filed round and painted the color of pomegranates, splayed coolly against the backs of the playing cards. Her nostrils flared with concentration.

I discarded a seven of clubs in favor of a jack of hearts. Now I just needed the queen to complete the suit.

But Claire picked up a card and then revealed her hand before her. "Gin." She totaled the points. "Another round?" She was already gathering the cards to shuffle.

I had been surprised when a note arrived at my flat more than a month earlier inviting me around for tea. "A cuppa," she called it when I'd turned up. Though I had liked Claire instantly, I had not expected to see her again. Surely the prime minister's niece had lots of friends. "I do," Claire had replied candidly when I asked on my first visit. "That is, lots of people who want to be around me and go to parties and such. But no one quite so . . . real." I was not sure if that was a compliment. But I had gone again every Sunday afternoon since that first time I had been invited. We would sit playing cards for hours, sometimes chatting but sometimes not saying anything at all. Claire's Kensington flat was warm and tastefully decorated in muted shades of mauve and beige; its three spacious rooms on DeVere Gardens were grand in comparison to my own tiny flat. Schmaltzy, I could almost hear Aunt Bess call it.

"I prefer to be on my own," Claire explained once, when I remarked about it. She was at best a handsome woman, makeup skillfully applied, the flowing skirt designed to soften her large-boned frame. "Uncle Winnie wanted me safe out in the country but I wouldn't hear of it—I would have died of boredom." I smiled at her familiar reference to the prime minister. Claire had lost her own parents in a car accident at a young age and had been raised alongside Churchill's own children—a history not so very different from my own.

"It's nice to have one's own space," I agreed, nibbling one of the hard biscuits she'd put on the saucer. I couldn't imagine inviting Claire to my flat on Porchester Terrace. I didn't even have a second chair for her to sit down.

"I saw Teddy at the Berkley last week," Claire offered, pouring more tea. She had a dizzying social calendar, out most nights at the concerts and dances that had persisted in London in defiance of the Blitz and the bombings that continued afterward.

"Oh?" I struggled to keep my tone neutral as I envisioned Teddy at the popular dance hall. I had not been there myself, but had heard stories from the other girls of dancing with RAF pilots until the gin ran out or an air raid siren sounded, whichever came first. But Teddy always seemed so hard at work; it was hard to picture him at a dance. Whom had he gone with? I knew I had no right to be jealous—I was the one who had pushed him away. He had not formally asked me out again since our kiss at my flat. But it was always there—the casual mention of a show I might like at a West End theater, the bit of chocolate he'd managed to get his hands on and save for me. Teddy was still hopeful—but he didn't seem to be waiting around any longer while I held him off.

"He didn't dance at all," Claire added. "Just sat there a bit broodish. Not at all like him." Her comments were subtle but persistent, questions hidden in them.

"That's interesting." I tried not to sound too pleased.

"Something's got him wrapped up in knots." Claire lifted her head from her cards. "It's you, I suspect."

"Me?" I set down my cards and picked up the teacup, willing myself not to flush. "Teddy's my boss. We only work together." He'd been gone these past few days, chasing another story without saying where.

"Someone better tell him that. He fancies you a good deal."

"I very much doubt that. I mean, he asked me out once, a long time ago. But I hardly think he's stuck on me." I tried to keep my voice even as I waved my hand. "Teddy likes all the girls."

"I disagree. He's really smitten. Teddy's used to women fawning all over him. Telling him no is quite a game."

"I'm not playing a game," I protested. I gazed out the window at the treetops of Hyde Park, just visible above the gray brick chimneys.

"What is it, then?" Claire pressed. "Because if men aren't your thing, I know some lovely girls."

"Claire, no!" I cut her off, shocked. "It isn't that at all."

"Then what? You don't have to tell me." Claire raised a hand. "In fact, I rather prefer the mystery." But she continued to stare at me intently.

I bit my lip. Finally, I could hold it no longer. "Charlie." The whole story began to spill out of how I had met the Connallys at the beach.

"A summer boy." Claire smiled. "How lovely."

"But it was more than that." I continued, explaining the awful events that had led up to Robbie's death.

"I might have guessed. There's something about you, a bit dark and mysterious that says you've known heartbreak. How long were you together?" Claire asked.

I wasn't sure how to answer. In reality it had

just been that one night and the months of correspondence in between. "A bit. Forever. I don't know. So then Charlie went off to enlist and he decided that we should tell everyone that we were together at Thanksgiving."

"Charlie decided . . ." Claire's eyebrows lifted. "Did you agree?"

"Yes, of course," I replied quickly. In reality, I had been unsure, maybe even wanting to hold off. "And after Robbie died." I swallowed, the words hurting my throat. "Afterward, everyone just scattered. Then after a year apart I saw Charlie in Washington last November . . ."

"And you ran." There was an unmistakable note of disapproval in her voice. "Because you didn't want to be with him."

"It's not that simple."

"You can't be with Charlie, but you're not giving Teddy a chance either. You are using grief as an excuse not to move on," Claire pronounced, her voice pointed but not unkind.

I opened my mouth, ready to deny it. But that was the thing: I didn't want to stop hurting. Because letting go of the pain meant accepting what had happened to Robbie, moving just a step farther away from him. Letting go. "I'm just not ready to start up with anyone new, even a fellow as swell as Teddy." Despite Claire's bluntness, it was a relief to finally talk to her about what had happened. Chatting with Claire about boys seemed so normal, a life I might have imagined but never really thought I would have.

"So you ran away to London. Are you happy here?"

I paused, the card I had just picked up midair. Happiness was not something I thought much about. I had been happy that one night with Charlie before it had all fallen apart. But sometimes I wished I had not known such joy in light of the unbearable sorrow that was to follow—having had it once made knowing it would not come again all the worse. "You could be happy, you know," Claire said, answering her own question. "Be Teddy's girl and enjoy life for a while." I bit my lip, not answering. If only it was that simple. "Teddy and I knew each other as children," she added.

"Did you? I had no idea." I had assumed they were friends from the London social scene—I had not imagined them to have such a long history.

"Yes, when we were younger our parents thought we might wind up together." There was a note of longing in Claire's voice. Discomfort nagged at me—did Claire think I had stolen Teddy from her? "It never was on the table, though."

"Do you mind at all?"

"Goodness, no! I'm having too much fun to settle down. Teddy isn't for me," she said. "And I'd like him to be happy. Plus a correspondent, how common." Her protests came too quickly on top of one another, each seeming to contradict the last. "Anyway, there is someone else, but he's married."

"Claire!" I blurted, unable to hide my surprise.

"So you see, I know how it is to be stuck on someone."

I wanted to protest that I was not stuck on Charlie, but it was the truth. "Who is he?" I could not help but ask. "Where did you meet him?"

She hesitated momentarily. "Lord Raddingley. He's a member of Parliament." Her voice was atypically breathy. But surely someone of Claire's background would not have been impressed just by the title. "We met at a reception a few months back, and manage some time away whenever we can. Of course nothing can come of it," she added quickly, checking herself. But the hope that lingered in her eyes made my heart ache for her. "You must think I'm dreadful."

"Not at all," I replied, too quickly. I was not one to judge, but I did not want to see her get hurt. "I was thinking of going to the Tate Wednesday after work, if you'd like to join me," I offered, changing the subject.

"I can't. That is, I would have loved to, but my unit has been called down to Portsmouth." I tried not to let the rejection sting. Claire was a member of the Auxiliary Territorial Services, part of the women's unit of the army. Last week as we finished playing cards, Claire had been going to a shift manning an anti-aircraft gun near Tower Bridge. She had looked so smart in her uniform, something altogether different than the society girl I had taken her for. She was fearless, intense and ready to fight. I envied her sense of purpose.

My shoulders slumped. "I'm of so little use. They won't let the American girls join the corps."

"You just keep reporting the news, doll. That's you, doing your bit." There was a hint of unintended condescension to her words. "Anyway, that's Wednesday. I was able to put it off until then because the Spring Fete is tomorrow night. You're going, of course?" I nodded reluctantly. Claire had pinned me down the first week I'd visited to attend the fete, a benefit the auxiliary had organized at the Savoy to raise money for the Red Cross. "And tonight we're going out dancing." Claire's London circle was one of parties, too-late nights almost every day of the week with people who didn't seem to like each other very much and fizzy drinks that left her with headaches the next day. "You're coming with us."

"Tonight?" I'd managed to demur the few other times Claire had invited me along. "I couldn't possibly. I'm not even dressed."

"One of my cousins is tiny like you. I'm sure she's left something in the wardrobe that will fit."

"But I can't." I searched for a good excuse not

to go. Until now, I had been content to spend evenings curled up in my room with a book and some cheese on toast.

"But nothing. You can't just sit here and mope. You're here, so make the most of it. Come on," Claire cajoled.

"All right," I relented. "But I need to ring my landlady." Mrs. Dashani knew that I spent the evenings in my flat and on Sundays she would sometimes bring up a bit of whatever she had made for dinner. I didn't want to worry her if she knocked and found me gone.

Two hours later I found myself standing at the entrance to the Swan, a private club on a back-street near Charring Cross. The dress that Claire's cousin had "left behind" was nicer than anything I had ever owned, maroon silk and snugly fitted through the bodice, with a flared skirt that swished around my knees when I walked. The fascinator, which Claire insisted I wear, perched uneasily on my head like a bird's nest. Inside, the club was noisy from the chatter of too many people crowded around small tables and a band that played unseen behind a floor full of couples dancing a jitterbug to a lively rendition of "In the Mood." I swatted at the cloud of cigarette smoke in front of me, taking in the revelry that seemed a world apart from the rubble-strewn streets outside.

Claire passed me a glass of champagne and we

angled to a table in the corner. Her own dress was black and tightly fitted with fur at the cuffs. She took in the room with a dismissive sweep. "It's not the same since they bombed the Paris," she sniffed. For a second, I thought she was talking about the city. But she meant the Café de Paris, a popular nightclub that had been hit by a German airstrike a few months earlier, killing scores of patrons just like us, who were simply out for a dance and a drink. I looked around the packed room warily.

"Perhaps we shouldn't be here."

"Now, now, if you start thinking like that, then Jerry has already won. That's him," she said, jumping topics with uncharacteristic abruptness. I followed her gaze across the room with confusion, half expecting to see a German soldier. But she had pointed out an older British man. "Lord Alastair Raddingley. The bloke I told you about." Her voice was pinched.

The married one. I studied Lord Raddingley, trying to understand the attraction. He was bespectacled and paunchy, with hair more gray than black. With his expensive dinner jacket and cuffs, he was indistinguishable from a dozen other men in the room. But Claire stared at him, transfixed. "We love who we love," Mrs. Connally had said once, not knowing that the boy I was pining over was one of her own sons. Lord Raddingley seemed benign enough. But taking him in, I was troubled: How far had things gone between him and Claire? Was it just a crush or something more?

The song ended and as the crowd on the dance floor broke, I spotted Teddy. He had not been at the bureau for the past two days and I'd assumed he was still away on a story, but there he was, looking fresh and relaxed in his dinner jacket. I started toward him, torn between feeling relieved and wanting to chastise him for chasing what was surely a dangerous lead. Then I stopped—he was speaking to a willowy blond-haired woman I did not recognize.

"Amelia Hartwell," Claire observed mildly from behind me. "Her father is a viscount."

I had no right to mind Teddy talking to another woman, I reminded myself. It was me that had told him no. I started to turn away. But he noticed me then and excused himself from Amelia Hartwell and made his way across the room.

As he neared, my heart lifted—I was genuinely glad to see him, more so than usual. "Ladies." He kissed Claire's cheek, then quickly turned to me.

"You're back," I greeted him.

He leaned forward, as though he wanted to kiss me, too, his hair giving off a hint of Brylcreem. Instead, he took my hand awkwardly. "Only just this afternoon." His face was somber. Why wasn't he happier to see me?

He dropped my hand. "I thought you said you don't go out."

He was hurt that I had come here after turning him down for so long. "I don't. But Claire insisted." My explanation sounded flimsy. Perhaps Claire pressed me to come knowing that Teddy would be here. "You look busy anyway." I gestured toward Amelia Hartwell, who stood watching us.

The orchestra struck up again, this time a slower song, "People Will Say We're in Love." "Shh, enough quibbling. Let's dance." His hand was shaking as he reached out to me, and it was the first time I'd ever seen him nervous. I hesitated, sensing that even more so than the kiss at my flat, the dance might be the start of a path I was not ready to go down.

"Go on," Claire urged with a chuckle. "Give the bloke a break."

Not waiting for an answer, Teddy took my arm and led me to the dance floor. For a moment, I considered pulling away. But his face looked so hopeful. He wrapped an arm around my waist, surer than I might have expected. Warmth swept over me as our bodies neared, giving in to every-thing I had fought these past months. My muscles relaxed and I leaned into him, leaning my head lightly against his shoulder. His breath was warm and smelled faintly of spearmint.

I wrapped my arms around his neck and tilted

my face to his. "Now tell me where you've been."

"No work talk. Can't we just dance?"

I stopped swaying. "You can't treat me like a partner on some stories, then shut me out entirely on others." I pulled back, my frustration rising. "Don't you trust me?"

"It isn't that." He faltered. "I went for you."

I pulled back. "For me. Went where?"

"To Italy." The ground seemed to wobble beneath me. "I tried to find out for you, about your family."

I was suddenly angry. How dare he go traipsing into my past without asking me first? "I never asked you to do that."

"I know, but I thought that you would want to know." Because who wouldn't, really? Part of me wanted to leave my parents where they had been, living my childhood in Trieste. But if that were true they would have come for me, would have written. No, they had disappeared.

"And?" I asked, fearing the answer.

"I failed, Adelia." His face collapsed. "Trieste is occupied by the Germans now, you know." Of course I did—I kept a map of Europe on my wall, updated the colored pins with every news story. "I couldn't even get close. I'm sorry."

Gratitude rose up in me then. He had tried, really tried, to help. I put my hand on his arm. "Thank you."

"Anyway, you were right. Probably best to

leave it alone." There was a darkness around his eyes that had not been there before.

"What was it?" I pressed, but he would say no more.

He drew me close as another slow song began to play. I melted into him. Teddy was a good man, and he cared about me a lot. Claire was right: things really could be good between us, if I would just let them. I rested my head on his shoulder and let the song carry me away from my memories.

He pulled back to look deep into my eyes. "How do you do it, Adelia? Disarm me like this?" I saw then the depth of his feelings.

"Oh, Teddy," I said, wrapping my arms around him. He whirled me around the dance floor until the lights became a blur and the past seemed to spin off me like dust. Everything else faded and just for this one moment it was all enough.

The song ended, and I stepped away from him reluctantly, not quite ready for it to end. "Thank you."

"Another dance?"

But the room had grown warm, and the champagne caused my temples to throb. "I'm afraid I'm a bit weary. I should probably head out."

He touched my arm, unwilling to let go of the moment. "Then I'll see you home."

I started to say no, that I could manage by

myself. But looking in his eyes, I did not want to turn away anymore. "I should let Claire know. I'll meet you at the door."

I found Claire at the edge of the bar. "I'm going. Teddy's taking me." I waited for her reaction, but she seemed distracted. "Do you want to come?"

Claire shook her head. "I have plans." Her voice was low and conspiratorial. Across the room, Lord Raddingley had disappeared. Claire must be going somewhere to meet him. I wanted to tell her not to do it, that she deserved so much better than this. But her eyes were aglow as she started for the coat check.

I debated going after her, then turned back to the gathering. Perhaps it had been a mistake to take Teddy up on his offer to see me home after all. There was something about the way he held me that suggested more between us—much more— and I was not at all sure that I was ready. But he had already started for the exit and lingered there, waiting for me expectantly.

I took a step toward the door, then froze. A roaring came in my ears, so loudly it seemed for a second as if there might be bombs. But the room around me continued unaffected. I stared at the door, unable to move or speak.

Standing behind Teddy, in the entrance to the club, was Charlie.

Thirteen

Charlie?

I blinked twice. Surely it was my imagination, like that afternoon by the buses on Trafalgar Square, or the dream that I had so many times. But he was still standing before me in that crisp olive green that seemed to have painted all of London. He was real. The uniform fit as though made for him, smooth across his broad shoulders. Over the months we had been apart, I'd seen his face in my mind a thousand times, his luminous brown eyes making me swoon just thinking about them. I'd wondered sometimes if it was my memory that had made him seem more beautiful than he was, but now I knew without question: he was the best-looking soldier—and man—in the room.

But what was he doing here, thousands of miles from where I had left him? Looking for someone, came the answer as I watched his head swivel, gaze predatory and intent. He scanned the room, assessing it, and for a minute he was back on the football field, in command and planning the next play. He had not seen me yet. I could duck into the crowd and slip out the side door, run away—again.

My feet remained planted, though, legs concrete. A moment later, Charlie's head turned in my direction and his face lifted with recognition. It was Washington all over again. He did not look surprised, though, as he had then—this time he was looking for me, and his finding me here was planned and deliberate. Our eyes met. Several emotions seemed to cross his face at once: joy and relief (and yes, even a bit of anger) collided with one another, then exploded like fireworks in the air between us as he started toward me.

He crossed the room in three steps, seeming to slice through the crowd. "Addie." His voice was guttural and hoarse with relief. He removed his hat and folded it, fiddling with the gold insignia pin. His hair had been shorn even shorter than in Washington, leaving a fuzz that reminded me of a baby chick. I wanted to reach out and run my hand over its softness. Once it had reminded me of the ocean on a breezy day, dipping and rising once more. But most of it, including the curly bits that had once brushed against his collar, was gone.

As he leaned in to kiss my cheek, a familiar whiff of aftershave tickled my nose. I fought the urge to turn my lips to meet his. He straightened and I stared at him. "You're in London." I still could not believe that he was actually here, standing before me. I reached out and touched his sleeve to be sure. "Are you following me?"

He laughed, a loud chuckle that unsettled me. "Hardly. You and I just have a way of always winding up in the same place." Was that true?

"I am sure as heck glad to see you, though."

"It's just so odd how we both keep turning up. First Washington, now here."

"A kind of kismet," he replied, taking it a step further. I didn't believe in fate anymore, not since that night by the Delaware River. Because fate meant accepting that it was all part of a bigger plan, and that sweet-faced, twelve-year-old Robbie was meant to die. "My unit was transferred here," he explained.

My eyes traveled to the winged pin on the front of his uniform. "You're flying?"

He nodded. "We're based out of the airfield at Duxford, East Anglia."

But something did not make sense. "I thought you were infantry."

"I was." I had been almost relieved when he told me that back home. I remember thinking that it would take months, maybe a year, to get all of the soldiers over there by foot and perhaps the war would be over then. But now he would have to fly planes, presumably into enemy territory, because Charlie the Great always had to do something larger than life. My anger rose. Why couldn't ordinary ever be enough? "It's a long story," he added. "Anyway, that's what brought me to England." He had not come looking for me.

But something about his explanation still didn't make sense. "If you're stationed at Duxford, then what are you doing in London?"

He looked uncomfortably around the room. "I'd rather not discuss it here. Maybe if we went somewhere else."

"Okay." Over his shoulder, I glimpsed Teddy. He was still standing by the door holding our coats, his face puzzled. "That is, I can't. I'm sorry."

Charlie followed my gaze. "Theodore White?"

"You know him?"

He grimaced. "I know of him. What does he have to do with anything?"

Before I could answer, Teddy walked over. "Adelia, I thought you were ready to go." He put his hand on my back, and I squirmed at the sense of ownership the gesture seemed to convey. His face was still bright and hopeful from our earlier dance. But my affection for him a few minutes earlier was dwarfed by my ocean of feelings at seeing Charlie standing before me.

"Teddy, this is Charlie Connally. Charlie, may I introduce Theodore White?"

"Not necessary. I've read your work." The two men shook hands. Charlie's eyes dropped to Teddy's left hand, which lingered at my elbow, and a storm cloud formed on his face. "Addie and I are . . ."

"Childhood friends," I finished for him. The phrase echoed hollowly, so far short of what it should have been. But I certainly couldn't explain what existed between us then, or now. I held my breath, waiting for Charlie to contradict me and tell Teddy it was something more.

"Addie?" Teddy repeated the nickname, a bemused smile about his lips. "How charming." I watched helplessly as the divide between the past and the life I had created here seemed to evaporate.

"Teddy," a man called from one of the tables. Turning, I recognized Ed Reyes, the senior editor from the *Guardian*.

Conflict washed over Teddy's face. "Ed . . . I've been trying to corner him for ages. Do you mind?" he asked me.

"Not at all. I'll wait." As he walked away, I exhaled silently.

"You're with him?" Charlie said when Teddy was barely out of earshot. His voice was full of disbelief. My annoyance rose. Couldn't Charlie imagine Teddy liking me? But it wasn't that, I realized. He simply could not fathom me being with someone else.

I struggled for the answer. "What difference does it make?"

"Because when you left Washington I thought you were on your own." Charlie had assumed that if I couldn't be with him, I wouldn't be with anyone, which until tonight had been true. I had done the same. In my mind, Charlie was frozen in time, alone with his sadness when I stood him up at the bar in Washington. Had he dated others in the time since I had gone? I had no right to be mad about it—even less right than he, since it was I who had done the leaving this time. But the notion still stung.

Around us the festivities seemed to intensify. The band swept into a raucous "Boogie Woogie Bugle Boy." From the bar came the popping of a champagne cork, followed by a cheer. "You still haven't said what you're doing in London," I pressed, even though Charlie had already said he didn't want to talk about it here.

"I might have come into the city to make sure you were all right," he confessed. "I can see you are." His voice was unmistakably jealous as he gestured stiffly with his head toward Teddy. "I'll just leave you two." He started to turn away.

"Charlie, wait." I reached for his arm and he seemed to wince slightly at my touch.

But he did not pull away. "You don't owe me any explanations."

"How did you know I was in London?"

"I went to the bureau in Washington and asked." I tried to imagine Charlie confronting Mr. Steeves. "He gave me your address. I couldn't come looking for you, of course, until I was transferred here. I got leave as soon as I could to come down to London. Your landlady told me where to find you. You left for England without saying a word." His tone was accusing.

Like you did after Robbie died, I wanted to

counter. He was the one who had first broken the silent pact I'd thought I had with the Connally boys to always be there for one another. But I was not ready to rip open that scar, which ran so deep.

"You didn't come to meet me at the bar that night," he said. I stepped back as sharp thorns seemed to form a barrier in the space between us.

"I never said I would," I countered lamely. "I just couldn't bear it after everything that happened." I searched for an explanation that would somehow make what I had done better and found none. "I'm so sorry."

"It's okay," he said, his anger ebbing. "I'm just glad to see you. But I don't want to crash the party." He tilted his head in the direction of Teddy, who was still talking to Ed Reyes but trying not to stare at us. "I should go."

"Wait!" My voice rose, swallowed into the din of the gathering. Was he really going to leave, just like that, after we had only found each other again? In Washington, I had not been ready to talk. Now I was hungry for his company, his presence a dream I did not want to end. "I mean, we haven't even had the chance to catch up."

"No." His face brightened a shade. "We haven't."

"Perhaps tea tomorrow?"

"No good, Ad. We tried that once, remember, planning a meeting? You stood me up." I wanted to tell him that would not happen again. But he was right. "Let's get out of here right now."

"I can't." My eyes traveled to Teddy, who was still watching me. I could not simply walk out with another man right in front of him. But I desperately wanted to talk to Charlie.

"Meet me outside," I said in a low voice and suddenly we were back home, our fledgling relationship a secret in the shadows of the beach houses.

"Good evening," Charlie said loudly enough for others to hear. He put on his hat, then started for the door.

I walked over to Teddy, who rose as I approached. "Sorry to interrupt. I just wanted to say good-night, Teddy, I'm going home now. I've got a bit of a headache."

His brow furrowed as he handed me my coat. "Are you ill?"

Hearing his genuine concern, I felt instantly guilty. "Just the champagne, I suspect. But I'm going to call it a night."

"I can go with you."

"Goodness, no. You stay and talk. I'll just take a cab and see you first thing." I kissed his cheek and then sailed away before he could argue. Though I did not turn back, I could feel his sadness and confusion at losing what had almost, but not quite, been.

Outside the air had chilled and the streetlights and theater marquees of Shaftesbury Avenue were blackened. I scanned the block, straining to see through the low fog that had rolled in. Charlie was not there. My heart sank. Had he given up on me or had I misunderstood?

I started for the taxi stand at the corner. Charlie appeared suddenly from the shadows of a shop doorway. I looked over my shoulder. We needed to go before Teddy came after me. "Come on, let's walk," he whispered.

I paused uncertainly. We had walked often back home during summers at the shore, on the beach while the surf crashed in the darkness or by the calmness of the bay. He had walked me home in the city. But it seemed odd to take to the night streets for no reason. "It's past curfew, and there could be an air raid."

He waved his hand, seemingly unconcerned as one who had already touched death too closely. "This way." He pulled me down a narrow lane, away from the main thoroughfare. I followed him and we traveled wordlessly across the slick pavement, past the backs of shuttered shops, silent except for some rustling around the garbage cans. Even in this city thousands of miles from home, he led me, sure in his path.

The passageway ended at a wide street. Charlie started around the corner, then jumped back, drawing me close against a building. "What is it?" He put a hand over my mouth, skin warm against my lips, as the yellow of a bobby's flashlight flickered into view. Then he pulled me in the other direction and back down the alley, turning off in a different direction. We ran swiftly and silently, children not wanting to get caught at a game of hide-and-seek.

A few minutes later, the street opened up at Embankment, the panorama of the Thames unfurling before us. Barges glided silently in both directions, skaters on dark ice. I tried to catch my breath as we slowed.

We paused, staring across at the far bank in silence for several minutes, taking in the full scope of the destruction in the cool moonlight, some buildings half-standing or destroyed, still others untouched. I could not help but marvel at the randomness of it all, strikes as happenstance and unfair as Robbie being snatched from us.

Charlie looked back over his right shoulder, where Big Ben and Parliament loomed, standing sentinel. "It's funny, isn't it, just a couple of kids from South Philly here in the middle of all this?"

I nodded. "Sometimes I think I stepped into the wrong story." But right now it was the two of us, just the same as on the dock or in the city back home.

"You shouldn't be here," he said, a note of protectiveness rising in his voice. "It's too dangerous, with the bombings."

I wasn't sure whether to laugh or take offense. "You're here."

"And I kinda like it," he admitted. "There's a realness to it all."

"I know," I replied, understanding. Here, the danger was apparent, not hidden as it had been back home. We should not be out though, I thought, casting one eye uneasily to the sky as I had begun to do since coming here.

"Come." Seeming to read my thoughts, Charlie led me down the Strand, stopping before a pub called The Dog in the Woods. Though the windows had been blacked out and it was well after closing time, boisterous laughter seeped through the cracks. I hesitated. I wanted to be alone with Charlie, not in a place packed with others. But it was too dangerous to stay outside, and I didn't dare to invite him to my flat.

Charlie opened the door and smoke and noise poured out. "We can go somewhere else," he offered over the din of male voices, as the smell of stale beer assaulted my nose. "Not much of a place for a girl."

"Woman," I corrected. My spine stiffened. "Let's go in."

He led me through a mix of GIs and locals to a small table beneath a Boddington's sign, then left me and squeezed through to the bar. I sat down—the low-key pub was a welcome respite from the club and nightlife where I never quite felt comfortable. Beneath the hum of voices, Glenn Miller played from an unseen photograph.

Charlie returned a few minutes later with a half pint of cider for me and scotch for himself. So the hard drink I'd seen in front of him at the bar in Washington had not been an aberration. I studied his hair again as he sat down, again missing the way it used to roll and dip. But the trim cut gave new definition to his jawbone and cheeks.

He leaned in, one hand beneath his chin. Closer I could see that there were circles around his eyes and his mouth was grimly set in a way that I did not remember. "Tell me everything." Charlie always had a way of drawing a person out, making him or her feel like the only one in the room.

Looking into his eyes, it would be easy to fall back into the old ways. But there was so much embedded in his request, I did not know where to begin. "I was working for the *Post* and there was a chance to come over here."

"Right about when I saw you in Washington." His eyes were challenging.

"Yes, just then." I swallowed, glossing over the bit about how I'd asked for the transfer after seeing him. His hand was on the table and I had to force myself not to reach out and take it. How could I not, when all that I ever wanted was right here in this very room? The ache was excruciating.

"It's still mostly secretarial, but Teddy lets me do some copyediting." I hated mentioning his name to Charlie.

Charlie's eyebrows rose. "You work for him?"

"Yes." My eyes met his.

"I mean, I knew he was with the *Post*. I guess I just hadn't put two and two together." He frowned, not bothering to hide his displeasure. "You two must spend a lot of time together."

"It's not just me. There are about a half dozen or so British girls. They're not fond of me."

"That's hard to imagine."

"The American and all that." I could not, of course, tell him that their resentment had as much to do with the fact that I shared office quarters with Teddy as with my nationality.

"Do you mind?"

I shrugged. "Not really." The lack of company wasn't so bad. I enjoyed my lunches strolling the streets and peaceful Sundays in my flat, not really speaking to anyone. And I had Claire as a friend now. But the feeling of being disliked took me back to my early days in Philadelphia, trying to fit in with the other kids. "It wouldn't change anything if I did. Thank you, by the way, for the photograph you sent."

His brow creased. "I didn't send anything."

"Oh." There was an awkward silence, embarrassment warming my cheeks. His denial and the confusion that accompanied it seemed genuine. But if he hadn't sent me the photo of the boys, then who had?

"Cheers." He raised his glass to mine, then downed about half the scotch without grimacing.

"You still haven't said if you and Teddy are together."

I took a sip of cider. "Not in any real way." Charlie's shoulders dropped slightly with relief. "Does it matter?"

"It doesn't, I suppose." He stared hard at his nearly empty glass, fingers tapping against it. He was jealous. I was pleased and at the same time annoyed.

Had he dated? I suspected again that I did not want to know the answer. "Tell me more about your family. You said Jack's taking classes?"

"Jack has a friend," he said bluntly, pronouncing the last word with emphasis. I cocked my head, not understanding. Jack always had friends. "You see, it turns out Jackie doesn't like women."

"Oh!" I brought my hand to my mouth. I had heard jokes about gay people—*faegele*, the women on Porter Street called it, referring to odd Saul Scheerson the haberdasher who lived alone in the apartment above his butcher shop.

I wanted to protest that it wasn't true. Suddenly, though, it all made sense, the way Jack seemed different and a bit uncomfortable and the way he couldn't really join in the banter about girls with the others. There had been a dance once at school and as I had hung back by the wall, trying not to stare at Charlie and his friends, Jack had come across the gymnasium in an act of mercy and asked me to dance. His hands on my hips had been stiff and formal, in the places they were supposed to be, but immense discomfort which I had chalked up to him thinking of me as a sister.

"I don't think Mom and Dad have figured it out quite yet. I don't understand it myself." He swirled the bit of remaining liquor at the bottom of his glass. To Charlie, Jack's strange choices were just another part of life that had not turned out the way he had planned.

"You still haven't told me about your work."

"Just army stuff." He shifted. "I was picked for flight school down in Georgia and I did well enough. Now we're all just waiting for orders. We'll all be shipping out soon." The planned American invasion and the opening of the second front was the worst-kept secret in Britain—it had been debated hotly in pubs and cafes for months, the question not if, but when. The conversations had become more hushed lately, though—it was as if everyone knew the moment was drawing near and didn't want to give anything away.

He gestured toward my cider glass, still half-full. "Another? That has to be getting warm."

I shook my head. "It's late. We should go." Last orders had been called a few minutes earlier and around us the crowd had thinned. The barman was wiping down tables now and sweeping up, gently signaling they were about to close. Charlie helped me on with my coat.

Outside the air had cooled. As I started across

the pavement, my foot slipped on a broken pavement stone and I lurched forward. Charlie's hand shot out as though lunging for a pass at one of the games and he caught me. For all of these months, I had tried to stand on my own. Yet here he was, rescuing me again. His hand lingered on my arm. It felt good—so good—and I hated myself for that.

I pulled my arm away. "What time is the last train back to Duxford?"

"I've got a room at one of the soldiers' hotels, just off Grosvenor Square." So he was staying. The neighborhood around the American embassy had come to be called Little America because of the thousands of troops billeted there. GIs swarmed the streets, walking in groups of three or four. But Charlie had come to find me alone. "I'll see you home," he offered.

"No need. I'll just find a cab."

"It's well after curfew."

"The Tube, then. I'll find my own way."

We stood motionless, staring at one another. "So what happens now?" I could not help but ask. For a few minutes, it had been almost like the old days, or close enough to still feel right. But he was headed his way and me mine, two balls bumping into one another before spinning unstoppably in opposite directions.

"I don't know. I didn't think about it. I just knew you were in London and came looking as soon as I could." So unlike Charlie, who had always seemed to live his life by some grand plan. "I had to see you." There was an odd finality to his words.

"Charlie, what's going on?" He'd never been any good at keeping secrets from me, but he was tense and strange in a way I had never seen. "Is it your family? Did something happen?"

"No," he replied quickly.

"Then what?" He did not answer. My voice rose an octave. "What is this all about?"

"My work."

"Yes, of course. I know the troops are just awaiting orders to go over. It must be so nerve-racking."

"It's more than that." His voice turned low and gruff with new urgency. "I'm part of a special unit that is doing reconnaissance work."

"I thought you were waiting to fly out of Duxford."

He shook his head. "I am. That is, I'm not. I can't say more."

My frustration rose. He must have had reasons —good reason—for not talking about his work. But my fears grew as I imagined the unknown danger he faced. "Please, I just want to know you are going to be all right." My words sounded foolish; how could any of us promise that now?

But his jaw set stubbornly. "I should never have told you. You work for the paper, for Christ's sake. For Theodore White."

"Charlie, I would never say anything."

"I just had to see and touch it all again one more time. You. Us." Though he would say no more, he was going soon, this time for real.

Panic shot through me like lightning. "You don't have to do this," I said, almost pleading. By taking on these missions, maybe Charlie was trying to rewrite the past, or to get some control of his life. Once he had taken all the right steps, following the script that had been written for him: a football scholarship, college. The night he'd pulled Robbie from the water had changed all that, and I could sense a destructive streak in him now that reminded me of Liam. "Is this about Robbie?" Charlie recoiled as if he'd been slapped. "What happened to him wasn't your fault."

"I dream about him all the time," he replied after a minute. "That he's falling from that dune like the day we met you." He still could not bring himself to say his brother's name.

"You caught him that day."

"Right. Only in my dream I can't. And I couldn't when it really mattered." There was a wild, desperate look to his eyes. "He should be here now, playing sports and starting to like girls, not lying in a box in the ground."

"Getting yourself killed isn't going to change that. You're chasing a memory," I said, my tone pleading.

"At least I'm not running away. Isn't that what

you did by coming here?" His voice rose. We stared at each other for several seconds, the truth laid bare between us. "When did this get hard?" he asked, softly now. "Barely back in the same place and fighting. I don't want to part badly, Ad. Matter of fact, I don't want to part at all." He stepped closer.

"Me neither."

His lips were upon mine then, and his arms circling me, in the same way and the same places they had been that one night. But it was nothing like the kiss, tentative and innocent, that we had shared on the dock. His movements were rough, hardened by time and fueled by the liquor I could taste and smell. His eyes were closed and he was somewhere else, trying to erase all that had been. Everything was different.

"Stop." I put my hand on his chest.

But he was demanding now, pressing me back against the cold stone of the building, trying to persuade me. His hands cupped my face to keep me close. "It isn't wrong," he murmured. "It's exactly as it always should have been."

I pushed him away. "I can't. We shouldn't, not like this."

"But, Addie, before everything happened . . . I thought we were just starting out."

My head spun with confusion. I wanted him, more than anything in my life. But not like this. "Don't you see? Too much has happened. We can't pick up as though it hasn't." He left me once; how could I ever trust him again?

He stepped back. "I'll go." The words punched at my heart. If only we had more time to figure it out. "You don't have to run again," he added softly, looking at me with those puppy-dog eyes so reminiscent of his youngest brother. "Good night, Addie." He tipped his hat and started to turn.

I wanted to cry out as deep regret thudded down upon me. I had only just found Charlie. Though I needed him to go, I fought not to call out and stop him. I could scarcely bear to have him walk away from me again.

Fourteen

As Charlie disappeared around the corner, I turned, lost in the darkness and fog that suddenly swirled all around me. Regret loomed and I started forward, wanting to run after him and throw myself into his arms, to tell him that I had been wrong. But then I stopped, remembering all of the reasons I'd held him off in the first place. I stood, immobilized. Coming to London had seemed the answer, a way to escape the past. It had not removed my pain, though, just dulled it for a time. Now it was back, throbbing a thousand times worse for having been denied.

Suddenly a siren cut through the air. This was not the familiar signal of curfew that had rung out hours earlier, but something louder and more intense. A buzzing came from overhead, growing rapidly. At the corner, people streamed down the stairs of buildings with none of the usual weariness, running for the shelter at the corner. An air raid—and this time it was for real.

As I started for the shelter, an explosion rocked the street below me, sending me sprawling forward. Not daring to get up, I crawled to the base of the nearest row house, shards of glass and rubble cutting into my hands. I cowered in the corner by a staircase, covering my head from the hot dust and debris. The sky above lit up like fireworks over the boardwalk on the Fourth of July. I'd heard tales of the Blitz, and even felt a distant rumble from a V-1 on occasion as I lay in my flat at night. A few times I'd been roused from bed by Mrs. Dashani's knocking and we'd made our way to the corner shelter, only to return after the all clear. But this was my first real air raid and as the explosions came, closer and relentless, I grasped frantically at the pavement, willing myself to become part of it.

There was a moment's lull between detonations. I peered up, choking against the smoke and dust that filled the air. On the sidewalk where I'd stood moments earlier, a boy, no more than five or six, stood motionless amidst the people that rushed past him to shelter. I started to go toward him. But there was another explosion, shattering the window above my head and sending glass raining down upon me as I ducked for cover once more. When I looked up again, the boy was gone. Had I imagined him to be there? It seemed impossible that a child could be out in this alone. I started once more in the direction where I had seen the boy, but someone grabbed me from behind.

"Bloody fool!" a cockney voice exclaimed harshly. Hands pulled me into a cellar shelter closer than the other one I had seen. "Get inside!" Where was Charlie? He could not have gotten far before the air raid began. I prayed that he had made it to safety.

I scanned the street again. Not seeing the child, I climbed the rest of the way down the ladder to the shelter. It was crowded, with a dozen or so people squeezed awkwardly into the tiny, closet-like space that should have held half as many. The air was thick with the smell of sweat and smoke. I blinked, trying to adjust my eyes to the dim light. Across the shelter, I saw a familiar figure, seated on a crate, half facing away from me. It was Lord Raddingley. What was he doing here, in this run-down basement? A woman sat close on his lap, torso pressed against his. Claire. I started toward them, squeezing in between people and trying not to step on anyone. They must have been caught on the street, too. Closer,

I stopped. The woman on his lap was not Claire, but another woman, yellow-haired and heavily made up. Her body was pressed close to his in a way that left no mistake about their intimacy. I stifled a gasp.

A minute later the sirens stopped and the air outside grew still. People began to unfold themselves from the crowded space. I climbed up the ladder and stepped out onto the street. At the curb, something sat hunched in a ball, teetering dangerously close to the road and threatening to fall into it. As I neared, the ball straightened. The child I had seen during the bombing raid had not been an apparition after all.

"Are you okay?" There was no response. The child stared straight ahead, not meeting my eyes. He wore secondhand clothes that had been darned at the cuffs and his face was blackened with soot. But beyond that, he did not appear to be injured. "Hello? Are you hurt?" He looked at me blankly through a too-long fringe of blond hair. Perhaps he was in shock, or did not speak English. I tried again in Italian, then switched to French, then Yiddish. Nothing worked.

People were hurrying now from the shelters back to their homes. Sirens wailed, from emergency vehicles racing to the sites with the most damage. A charred smell filled the air, burning my nose and throat. "Come." I took the boy's hand and walked to a bobby at the corner, who seemed to have lost his trademark blue cap in the chaos. "I found a child."

The policeman covered his mouth and coughed. "No one's come looking for him. One of the street lads by the looks of him." Where were his parents? "Nearest orphanage is south of here across the bridge. I can't leave my post, but I can have someone take him to the stationhouse and send him there in the morning."

I shuddered at the thought of the child locked up for the evening, taken by the police as I might have been the day I arrived in America because there was no one to claim me at immigration. "I'll take him myself."

"Theed Street, just over the footbridge. But you won't get a cab and I can't let you walk. There's the curfew and likely more raids before this night is over. You'll have to leave the boy with me."

I braced myself for an argument. I would take the child to my flat if I had to before I would turn him over to the police. But before I could make my case, there came a crashing noise from the corner as the roof of a building that had been hit by a shell began to cave in. "Bloody hell!" the policeman swore, running in the direction of the collapse.

I turned to the boy and held out my hand. He hung back uncertainly. What would I do if he refused to come with me? I couldn't force him.

Then he slipped his hand in mine and the soft, warm fingers felt so much like Robbie's, I might have cried. But there was no time. I looked around for a taxi and found none. "Come," I said softly and began to walk quickly through the streets, relieved that the boy kept up without complaint.

A few minutes later, we reached the river, not far from where I had stood with Charlie just hours earlier. I stared at the Hungerford Bridge spanning the Thames, long and bare and exposed. Searchlights licked the sky, looking for the next wave of bomber planes.

I started forward toward the footpath, but the child pulled back. "Don't be afraid," I urged, not sure why he should believe me. But then I noticed he was missing a shoe and the cracked sole of his foot was seeping blood into the pavement, just as Mamma's had the night she put me on the boat. It must have hurt him terribly for blocks, and yet the strong little boy had said nothing.

I peered desperately across the bridge once more. Then I knelt, gesturing for the child to climb on my back. He was denser than his slight frame suggested and I struggled under the weight. I started across the bridge, trying to stay low.

We reached the other side and I straightened, breathing easier. Theed Street was, as the policeman had said, not far beyond the base of the bridge. As we turned onto the unlit street, the door to one of the houses flew open and a woman dressed in black-and-white nun's garb rushed out. "Leo!" I set him down and he ran toward her. Kneeling, she grabbed the child and began speaking close to his face scolding him in German, though whether to the boy or herself I was not quite sure. I was caught off guard by the language, which no one spoke openly in London these days.

"I'm Jayne Highsmith," she offered in English. "Sister Jayne, they call me here."

"Adelia." The woman wrapped her arms around the child, then looked up expectantly at me. I must look so odd in the party dress I'd borrowed from Claire, now wrinkled and filthy. "I found him on the street over by St. Paul's."

"Leo's always running off," the woman explained apologetically. "He's one of about two dozen children that we were able to bring over from a refugee camp near Lille. We managed to get sponsors to bring them here before the German occupation. It's a bit cramped and they'd be better off outside the city, but we've had no choice since a bomb damaged the abbey in Surrey last month. They're the lucky ones—we still have another thirty little ones awaiting their papers in the north of France." Lucky. Someone had called me that once, and in retrospect they had been right. Appreciation welled in me for my aunt and uncle, who had been willing to take me in.

"Are they orphans?"

"Some have parents back in Europe who sent them ahead for safety. Leo's had it worse than most. His parents were killed on Kristallnacht." I'd heard of the rampage in Germany and Austria, Jews beaten, their homes and shops destroyed. "And no one here can communicate with him." She stopped, seeing my puzzled look. "Leo's deaf."

So that explained why he had not responded to my questions. I looked down at the boy, who must feel so isolated and confused. "He's all alone."

"He has a sister among the children still waiting for paperwork in France."

"Couldn't all of the children be brought out at once?" I asked, curiosity making me more direct.

"We only had papers for so many—and we got the most urgent cases out first. Leo, without his hearing, was most vulnerable." I nodded. There was no telling what would happen to someone like him if he had stayed. "His sister will be here soon enough." There came a faint rumbling and the woman looked upward uneasily. "We should be inside. You're welcome to stay until it's light out."

"No, thank you, I should be getting back." I patted Leo's shoulder and he looked up with an almost-smile. Watching as he followed the woman back into the house, a part of me wished I was going with him.

I started back toward the bridge. The sky was

beginning to pinken now, illuminating the street before me. The devastation of South London was beyond anything I had seen since my arrival, entire blocks decimated, not just from this night but the past months of bombing. At the entrance to the underground at Waterloo, which had been hooded with aluminum to keep its lights from planes overhead, people climbed the stairs to the street with rolled blankets in hand. The tube stations had become places to sleep during the Blitz and many still went there, either for safety or because their homes had been destroyed and there was simply nowhere else for them to go. Their faces were haggard from lack of sleep but they moved forward, jaws set grimly. A mother leaned against a light post, holding two infants and looking as though she might collapse at any second. I reached in my pocket and fished out whatever coins I had, then handed them to the woman, wishing that I had more to give.

I recrossed the footbridge into the city. The streets were calm now as Londoners began their morning, stepping around the broken boards and rubble as they made their way to work. At the corner, the fire brigade hosed down the charred rubble of a building and a policeman guided traffic around the wreckage, which protruded into the roadway. At the base of St. Paul's, I found a cab and gave the driver my address. As I slumped in the backseat watching the shops of Piccadilly

Circus scroll past, I tried to make sense of what had happened with Charlie. The very deepest part of me had wanted to see him and to run into his arms. But something had stopped me from getting too close again.

I asked the driver to stop short of my address on Porchester Terrace, and paid him. Then I hurried up the steps, past Mrs. Dashani's door before the landlady could see me in the previous evening's clothes. In my room, I took my dressing gown from the hook, then walked to the toilet down the hall to run a bath. Ten minutes later, I sank into the steaming tub, guiltily avoiding the line where the hot water was supposed to stop for rationing. Baths were one of the things I loved best here—the steep porcelain tub on brass-footed legs. I poured in some of the bath salts I'd splurged on at Boots.

As the water enveloped me, my thoughts returned to Charlie. Even as I had wanted to be with him, part of me wanted to flee again as I had in Washington. Resentment seeped in that he had come and complicated things just as I found a new start. My life here was nothing grand—a tiny flat, a job which, for all of the extras, was still just a typing job. But I was my own person here—not just an extension of the Connallys. I would not leave again. More to the point, I didn't have anywhere to go.

I sank deeper in the water. I shouldn't linger, I

knew; I needed to get dressed for work. But my muscles relaxed in the warm water and my eyes grew heavy.

I was standing on the beach at Ohio Avenue, watching Liam surf in the distance. The waves grew larger and I tried to shout to him over the breaking surf to come in. But he could not hear me. A wave loomed large, swallowing the beach and crashing down upon me. The current was fiercer than it had ever been before, threatening not just to sweep me away but to tear me apart, pull my limbs from one another. Through the water a hand felt for me and even though I could not see, I knew that it was Charlie. I reached for him but then he was gone.

Loud knocking jarred me awake. I sat up in the tub. How long had I been asleep? The water had grown lukewarm, and I was chilled. The sound came again from down the hall. Hurriedly I dried and put on my dressing gown. "One moment." Had Charlie come to find me?

But it was Teddy who stood in front of my door, his face tight with concern. "Addie, are you all right?" He averted his eyes from the neck of my gown. "When you didn't turn up for work, I was so worried that something had happened." Ten past ten, read the clock on the nightstand. More than an hour after I should have been there—and it wasn't like me to be late. "The landlady buzzed me in. I should have called first." But, panicked, he had not. "Are you ill?"

I brushed a piece of damp hair from my eyes. "No, I'm perfectly fine. I'm so sorry to have worried you. Just give me a minute." I slipped into my room and closed the door, then dressed quickly in a fresh blouse and skirt before opening it again. "Come in."

But his forehead remained creased. "I rang to check on you last night after you left, to make sure you were feeling all right and had made it home safely. Mrs. Dashani said you had not come home yet." So his dark look was not only due to my failing to turn up to work. I held my breath, waiting for him to ask where I had been or demand some sort of an explanation. But Teddy was too much of a gentleman for that. And perhaps, since he had seen Charlie at the party, he already knew.

"I decided to walk back," I offered lamely. My explanation sounded implausible in light of the curfew and the headache that had caused me to leave the club in the first place. "I found a child lost on the street and I had to get him back to the orphanage."

"By yourself? That was terribly risky. Did you hear about that awful raid by the river?" he asked.

"Yes." I had not mentioned getting stuck on the street during the bombing raid, since that would make clear I was still out hours after I'd left him.

"The little boy—Leo—he's deaf and his sister is still stuck in France." Tears sprang to my eyes.

"Now, now." Teddy patted my shoulder.

"I'm sorry I alarmed you," I said, wiping my eyes. My apology sounded as though it was about something much larger.

"It's no worries. I'm just glad you're safe." Teddy dipped his hat in front of him. It was filled with flowers, still damp from where he had picked them. "For you."

"They're beautiful," I said, touched by the sweet gesture. If only they were from Charlie. I turned away, swallowed by guilt.

He waved his hand at the hat. "Keep it. You can give it back at the office."

"All right, then." I lifted the sweetness to my nose. "The morning briefing," I remembered suddenly the press conference at the War Office. "I'll finish getting ready and meet you there. Don't wait for me or you'll be late."

But Teddy remained in place, feet planted. "That Charlie . . . It's quite a coincidence, your old friend from home turning up." He tried to sound offhand but his voice was pinched.

"It certainly is."

"What's he doing here?"

I faltered. "He's based out of Duxford."

"And he just popped down to London to see you?"

"I suppose."

We stared at each other uneasily for several seconds. "I should go."

I watched him walk down the stairs, remembering with more than a bit of sadness our dance the previous night. That one moment with Teddy had been simple and joyous, a glimpse of what a normal life might have been like. I had almost been able to forget about the Connallys. But then Charlie appeared, calling me back—as if he had known I was going and somehow had to stop me.

I put the flowers in water and finished dressing. I opened the door to leave, then yelped with surprise. Charlie stood on the other side, hand aloft, just about to knock.

"You!" I exclaimed.

"You were expecting someone else?" He wore a thick brown bomber jacket that gapped just a bit at the neck and I fought the urge to bury my nose there. Charlie's eyes flickered as they drifted to the flowers on the nightstand.

I studied his face, any remaining anger from the previous night disappearing in the soft pools of his eyes. "I know I said I wouldn't bother you again. It's just that bombing raid started so soon after I walked away. I shouldn't have left you alone." He was haggard around the eyes and faint stubble covered his chin. I could still smell the liquor from the pub the previous night. He had not showered or slept.

"You can see I'm fine."

"May I come in?"

I stepped back, mindful of Charlie in the too-close space. His body seemed everywhere at once. He glimpsed around the room uncertainly. "Top floor, narrow stairs . . . something of a firetrap." He scowled. His tone proprietary, the concerned big brother once more. I bristled. He did not have the right to worry about me now. But the old habits died hard, and at the same time, I was secretly a bit pleased.

He went on, "And even more dangerous with the bombing raids. What was White thinking?"

My anger rose at his criticizing the flat of which I was so proud. "Teddy had nothing to do with it. I found this place on my own. I love it here," I persisted. But I suddenly saw the space through his eyes, small and not enough.

"So you were okay last night during the bombing?"

"Yes. You?"

"I had just made it to the underground station, thankfully. It was the worst one since I've been here. I'm glad you're all right," he added.

"I was—and then the most unusual thing happened." I told him about Leo and the other children. "The war is bad enough, but surviving it as an orphan would be horrible."

"They aren't all orphans," he pointed out.

"Leo is," I retorted. My mother and father had still been alive when I'd come to America but I remember feeling completely alone, parentless.

Outside, a clock chimed half past ten. "I have to get to work."

"I'll walk with you." I opened my mouth to argue, then decided against it.

It was a brisk spring morning as we made our way along the northern edge of Hyde Park, the grass and bushes damp as though it had rained the previous evening. The fences had been torn down, melted for the war effort and patches had been cleared and tilled for victory gardens.

We passed a line of couples outside a church, women dressed a bit too smartly for the weekday morning, men mostly in uniforms. "A lot of people getting married," Charlie mused. We might have had a wedding, nothing fancy, just a justice of the peace and perhaps a small party in the Connally living room. I watched, feeling the lost promise of what might have been ours if things had turned out differently.

Then he stopped and turned to me. "I'm sorry." It was the first time I had ever heard Charlie apologize. "I got it all so very wrong last night. I couldn't bear to leave things that way between us."

"It's all right. We've been through worse." I tried without success to make this last bit sound light.

His face remained troubled, suggesting something more. "What is it?" He bit his lip.

He looked over his shoulder, then lowered his voice, unable to hold back any longer. "Like I started to say last night, I've been doing some reconnaissance missions and that sort of thing, over northern France." A chill ran through me. He had already been over to the fighting and I hadn't even known. "Being with the boys up at Duxford is cover. This is top secret stuff. None of the Brits—and only a few Americans—even know. We can't risk leaks, especially now. I'm not supposed to talk about it—I already said too much." But the words spilled out and he was trusting me now, as he once had. "I'll be leaving soon and I probably won't be coming back to London. I had to see you again before I go." He faltered, unable to say more. But his face betrayed the danger of the mission that lay before him. It all clicked into place: his meetings in Washington, and turning up in London just now.

"Oh, Charlie!" The magnitude of what he was doing finally hit me. Why couldn't he just enlist like everyone else? Because once Charlie had a plan, a way that his whole life was going to be. But that was gone now, blown to shreds.

"I'm sorry I couldn't tell you the whole of it earlier," he said, as we neared Whitehall.

I understood then that the darkness I'd sensed in him last night had not just been about Robbie but the mission that stood before him. I wanted to tell him that he could save a thousand boys and that still wouldn't bring back his brother. But he needed to do this. I embraced him and drew his head to my shoulder, feeling his breath warm through the fabric against my skin.

In the distance a clock chimed eleven. "I've got to go." It would not be fair to leave Teddy waiting and worrying again. But I looked desperately over my shoulder, not wanting to abandon Charlie. "There's a charity fete tonight at the Savoy," I offered. "I know you hate those sorts of things."

"I do, but I'm willing to suffer through it just this once. For you." He smiled, causing my stomach to flip just as it had when I was sixteen.

I stopped short of the entrance to the War Office. Though Teddy was surely inside, it felt as though he was peering out one of the many windows, watching me with Charlie. "Until tonight, then."

The briefing was breaking up as I entered. "I didn't think you were going to make it," Teddy said, the mildness in his voice forced.

"I couldn't get a taxicab." I followed him out onto the street, waiting for him to press my explanation.

"You didn't miss much, but there's a story I want to get filed before the fete tonight."

"Yes, I wanted to speak with you about that."

He stopped and turned to me expectantly. "Don't tell me you're going to try and get out of going again."

"No, I'm still going . . . but I've invited Charlie."

"Well, there will be plenty of American soldiers there, I should expect. Good to make him feel welcome." He sounded as though he was trying to convince himself.

We reached the office, and I followed Teddy through reception and up the stairs. When we reached his office, he closed the door behind me. "There's something else. I did some checking with one of the girls over at the American embassy." Teddy had an endless network of contacts across London among the women who worked in the government agencies and elsewhere, whom he'd either charmed or dated and somehow left on stunningly good terms. "She said there's been loads of activity around the old airstrip at Wellford, lots of supplies headed that way. I wonder if Charlie's being here has anything to do with that."

"I told you, he's with his unit." I wished I did not know so much.

He eyed me levelly. "He hasn't been to Duxford in a week."

"You were checking on him?" How had Teddy managed that so quickly?

"No, of course not." Teddy looked away. "I just think that Charlie's being here could be about something much bigger." He stood and began pacing as he did when he was excited, running his hand through his hair. "I'm going to head out to Wellford today and see what I can find out."

He stopped midsentence, seeing my face. "What is it, Ad?" I hesitated. If Teddy followed up on the story, he could jeopardize Charlie's mission —or Charlie himself, but I couldn't admit that without letting him know he was on to something.

"Maybe we should hold off." He looked up, staring at me with disbelief. "I just think that with the launch coming, we might compromise something important."

"And Charlie?" Teddy asked sharply. I braced myself for the confrontation that I had been dreading. "What does he think?" He blinked and conflict registered on his face, the journalist trained to ask the hard questions, but who could not bear to know the truth. "Charlie . . . he's more than just an old friend, isn't he?"

"No. That is, we dated briefly. But that was all over a long time ago." I shifted, unable to lie to him. "Yes, we were together." But it was so much more complicated than that. I told him everything then about Robbie and that fateful night.

"Last night when we were dancing, I thought that maybe things were finally starting to happen between us," Teddy ventured. He looked at me hopefully, wanting to hear that Charlie's reappearance changed nothing. He cleared his throat. "I'm sorry about his brother. It's tragic. But it's in the past. This is personal, and it's clouding your judgment."

"I'm not asking you to leave this alone for Charlie, but for the good of operations. You know that, don't you?" He did not reply, tacitly admitting the truth of what I'd said. "Please." Sensing a crack in his resolve I put my hand over his. "Do this one thing for me." I watched him wrestle with his instinct to follow the story and how it clashed with his feelings for me. "So you'll hold off?" I exhaled slightly. "Thank you, Teddy." I kissed him short and full on the lips, in a way that should have been so much more. I tried not to think about how much of it was gratitude, and whether or not I was using him.

"Don't ever ask me again," he said, and stormed away.

Fifteen

Charlie was waiting for me out front of the Savoy that evening, breathtaking in his crisp dress uniform and freshly combed hair, framed against the eggshell-blue early-evening sky. He watched me somberly as I neared. "You look like you did the day I came home from training." I smiled. In fact, the dress I wore now was reminiscent of the one I'd worn that Thanksgiving night in color only, the light fabric of this one so unlike the heavy velvet of the first. I'd put that one away for good, the memories it bore too painful to wear again.

We walked into the club and stood awkwardly by the bar as a sea of partygoers swam around us on all sides. The evening dresses were a step up from what they'd been at the Swan the previous evening, lots of last season's Schiaparelli and Chanel. Close beneath the festive atmosphere, though, there was an air of weariness. The festivities must go on—to stop would be to admit defeat. But the war had taken its toll and people with no reason to celebrate in their hearts were simply here because they were supposed to be. There were fewer soldiers than I might have imagined, their numbers thinned, and most of the men were civilians, tuxedo-clad.

Charlie gestured toward the wide ballroom floor and the orchestra which played on the far side. "Would you like to dance?" Our brief relationship had been one of solitude, preciously few stolen moments and quiet nights alone on the bay. It felt strange to be out together in public, a harsh and unfamiliar light shined on us. We had, in fact, never danced.

But as his arm circled my waist and his other hand took mine, we fell into an easy rhythm. We might have been anywhere, just the two of us. "I had the craziest dream last night," the singer, a colored woman, crooned smoothly. "Yes, I did, I never dreamed it could be. Yet there you were in love with me." I rested my head on his shoulder.

As the song ended, Claire came up and cut

between us. "Darling!" I stepped back reluctantly. She kissed me on both cheeks, European style. She looked impeccably chic in a maroon silk dress with cascading lace that suited her large frame.

"May I introduce Claire Churchill." I watched Charlie's face as he processed the name.

"You must be Charlie," Claire said, as he took her hand. I had called around to Claire's flat after work that afternoon to tell her about Charlie's reappearance. "The one who broke Addie's heart." He dropped her hand abruptly as though it scalded him. "Do it again and I'll kill you." She laughed, as if to take a bit of the edge, but none of the meaning, off her words.

Charlie's mouth fell open. "Excuse me, I'll go get us drinks," he said, recovering a moment later before escaping.

"He's a handsome one!" Claire exclaimed when Charlie was barely out of earshot. She was a bit unsteady, I noticed then. It was not like Claire to drink to excess. I scanned the room, looking for Lord Raddingley, but did not see him. "Does this mean you're together now?"

"It's not that simple, Claire."

"So you're going to just keep running?" I did not answer. "If you want to be with him, then be with him. Poor Teddy," Claire mused. Her face hardened unexpectedly. "What is it about you, Adelia?" She cocked her head. "You're not so terribly good-looking." There was a forthright-ness to her words that made them blunt, but not unkind. "Yet every man seems ready to fall on his knees for you."

"It's not like that," I protested. Though I'd pined for Charlie for what seemed like a lifetime, I hadn't asked Teddy to like me as well.

"Don't you know I'd give anything to have a man feel about me like either of those two do about you?" She had almost everything—money and purpose and connections, but not love.

"I don't see Lord Raddingley," I offered, changing the subject.

Claire's expression fell. "Alastair has an early morning tomorrow so we said good-night." Was that just another lie? My anger burned white-hot as I recalled Lord Raddingley and the girl in the bomb shelter the other night. Claire should know the truth about him. But I could not bear to tell her that her married lover was in fact cheating on her as well.

I cleared my throat, changing the subject. "I'm going to go check on that boy I found tomorrow or the next day." I had told Claire earlier about the Leo and the other children. "See what he and the others need. Maybe I can find them some secondhand clothes. You should come with me when you get back."

"Me?" Claire tossed her head. "I'm awful with children. I may actually be allergic." She chuckled at her own joke. Then her face grew serious. "But I'm glad that you've found something useful to do. I just wouldn't want you to become too attached."

"It's just so sad, all of these children with no place to go."

"They have to have sponsors to come here," she replied, with the distance of one who had become callous to the harsh realities brought on by war. "At least some have made it here. The Americans haven't taken any."

Charlie was returning now, balancing three glasses of champagne. "Enjoy your evening," Claire said before he could hand her one. She sailed off.

Across the room, I glimpsed Teddy speaking with two women and trying hard not to stare at me. Was he still mad about not running the story? There was no anger on his face, just sadness. I did care for him, but my feelings were dwarfed by what could not be denied between Charlie and me. Having felt the difference, I could not be with Teddy now—but I didn't have to be with another man in front of him. "Do you mind terribly if we go?"

Charlie looked from me to the untouched drinks in his hand and then back again. We'd scarcely arrived. Surprise, then relief, crossed his face. "Of course. I only thought that you would want to, you know, do the ordinary things." He handed me one of the glasses of champagne, then downed both of the other two. "No sense wasting it." I took a sip, then set mine down on a table.

We slipped from the club, walking as we had the previous night in the direction of the river. In the distance, a clock chimed nine. A group of young women in snug-fitting dresses rushed past in the opposite direction, giggling excitedly, leaving a cloud of perfume in their wake. As we neared Embankment, the cool night air washed over my face like fresh water. I lifted my chin to study the fog-shrouded sky above the smokestacks of a factory on the far bank. Quiet, at least for now. The fog had cleared to reveal a blanket of stars.

"Claire Churchill, huh? How did you meet her?"

"It's a long story."

"She's quite something."

"She's swell." Despite Claire's cutting words a few minutes earlier, I was suddenly defensive of her. First my flat, then my friend: Who was Charlie to come in here and judge my life? "I'm worried about her, though. Last night, when the raid started and I had to go to the shelter, I saw the man Claire is involved with, only he was with someone else. It will hurt her terribly."

"Then don't tell her."

"How can I not? She would be living a lie."

"Maybe she would prefer it that way." There was a deeper note to his voice. "We can't always help who we love, even if it's the wrong person."

His words seemed a refrain of his mother's so long ago.

Was I that person to Charlie? I didn't ask, fearing the answer. We walked in silence for several minutes in the fragrant spring evening air, our destination unclear. "Do you miss home?" I asked.

"The old home, sure. I miss my family, even after everything. But it's easier sometimes being away, you know?"

I understood: here it was almost possible to imagine that none of it had happened. "Because of Robbie, you mean."

"Because of everything. I've never moved on or gotten over you," he confessed, reaching for my hand. I hesitated, just for a fleeting second but long enough for him to notice. What were we doing here anyway? He stepped back. "I'm sorry. Old habits and all that. I know this isn't what you want anymore. I won't try to make it happen again. I understand you keeping your distance. You must blame me terribly." His words came out staccato.

"Blame you?"

"For what happened with Liam."

"Not at all. We were just children ourselves. We couldn't have known." In truth, I blamed both of us, Charlie for not listening to me, myself for not trying harder to make him hear. But it wasn't that simple: the night it all happened, I was the one who stopped Charlie from going after Robbie as he ran from the house to find Liam. No, none of us were innocent, but I wasn't going to tell Charlie that now, as he raced off headstrong on a suicide mission to redeem himself. I reached for him.

But he stepped back, leaving my arm floundering. "You tried to warn me."

"Yes, but even I had no idea how wrong it would all go."

"You told me Liam was in trouble. I was so caught up in my own world, college and then the army. If I'd slowed down even a little bit, things might have been different. But I didn't—I never saw him." Laid bare before me was the depth of the guilt to which he clung. "I could have done more to help him," he continued. "But I was too wrapped up in my own life to do anything about it. It's my fault."

"No." I turned and took his hands. "You couldn't have stopped him." But the question nagged at me: What might have happened if Charlie had tried to help his brother? My mind reeled back to the night it all happened. "He asked me to go with him that night," I confessed aloud. I saw Liam standing on the porch of the Connally house. In retrospect, it seemed more like a plea. My guilt rose. Surely it all would have turned out differently if I had agreed.

"Liam?"

"To the bar or wherever he was going. If I had, I could have brought him home." I saw the night then as a movie with a different ending, coaxing Liam back to the family gathering, all of them together and safe. But I hadn't gone—because I was waiting for Charlie.

"You couldn't have possibly known. Don't blame yourself."

"Isn't that what you are doing?"

He pulled away. "It's different. I'm his older brother."

"He's my brother, too. You know that." Even now.

"I was older, I was supposed to keep him safe. And God help me, part of me didn't want him to come home that night drunk and angry," he said, his voice hoarse with guilt. "I wanted everything to be perfect and I didn't want him to mess it up."

"I know." I had felt exactly the same. "Are we really going to spend tonight fighting over who can take the blame?" I asked, cutting off the refrain before it could begin anew. "It won't change anything."

"No, but I'm trying to understand. If you aren't angry at me about Liam, then what's keeping us apart?"

"You left," I blurted, fully realizing the reason myself for the first time. "In Philadelphia, I mean." There it was, out on the table between us.

"I didn't."

"The day after the funeral I came to the house and you were gone. All of you."

"No, Addie. It wasn't like that. Mom was so devastated she couldn't go back to the house. I helped Dad take her away, because he wasn't much better off himself. I got them settled with my aunt down in Florida. But by then my leave was up and I had to report back to the base. I wrote to you and tried to tell you. Letters and letters." I could tell from his expression that he was telling the truth. "You never got them?"

"Not a one." It might have been the war and the mail, of course. But had someone intercepted them, hoping to keep us apart? I found it hard to believe my aunt and uncle had intercepted them.

"I assumed you never answered because you were angry. I came back in June on my next leave to make things right. But you were gone, and your aunt and uncle wouldn't say where. I figured you didn't want me to find you."

So he had come for me—too late. The realization threatened to overwhelm me. All of this time, I had told myself that he had not cared enough. But some part of me had never believed it. And now I knew the truth. "I had no idea." I scuffed my foot against the pavement.

"Now you do. There hasn't been anyone else," he added. "In case you were curious. Not for a single second."

Floodgates of relief opened within me. He held

his arm out. I hesitated and then took it, burying my fingers against his side for warmth. Walking this way we might have been any couple, happy and unscarred. "Did you ever wonder what it might have been like if that night had never happened?" I asked.

"All of the time. You and me together somewhere, living a normal life."

"Or maybe it wouldn't have worked."

He squeezed my hand tighter. "Nah, it was always going to be the two of us."

Charlie stopped again, turning to me. "How long are we going to keep trying to do this, Addie, trying to outrun each other? Maybe for once we could run in the same direction."

"Being together again won't change the past." It had not just been Charlie, but his whole world I had fallen in love with. Could we still work together now that that world no longer existed? "I don't want to be loved for a memory."

He touched my cheek. "Not a memory. It has always been you."

I raised my hands, a kind of surrender. I had fled halfway around the world to escape him and yet here he was standing in front of me with that same smile I'd known since the day we'd met. I simply couldn't run anymore.

I reached up and cupped his face in my hands, bringing his lips down to mine. There were no more protests inside me, or reasons it could not be. He kissed me and I stepped closer, allowing myself to feel the full force of his embrace. A moment later he pulled back, holding me close and breathing hard. "So what happens now?" I asked.

A siren went off before he could answer. I looked around helplessly; we were by the wharf, exposed and far from any shelter. Charlie took my hand and we ran, him pulling me so hard I thought I would either fly or fall. The ground thundered beneath my feet, threatening to throw me down. Abandoning any hope of finding a shelter, he pulled me into a doorway as something exploded overhead. He buried me in his arms, protecting me from the shower of hot rock and debris that pelted down on us. *We are going to die right now,* I thought, as we fell, his weight crushing me. Had it been like this for Robbie those final moments in the water?

"In here!" a civil defense warden across the street called to us, holding open a door to a shelter we had not seen. But it was across the wide street. Taking my hand, Charlie decided for me and pulled me low across the road. We dove into the shelter, already packed to the door. He pressed close against me, opening his jacket to keep me safe. I wrapped my arms around his warm midsection. His heart beat hard against the side of my head.

The bombs were dropping closer now, rattling

the walls. Plaster fell from the ceiling above, choking my throat and nostrils. Reaching the shelter was no guarantee of safety—one had been hit not five blocks from here last week, killing all twenty-six people in it. The bombing was not directly overhead now but concentrated to the south. I thought of Leo and the other children on the other side of the river and prayed that they were safe.

Time passed, forty minutes, maybe more. Finally the bombs grew fewer and fainter, like a distant thunderstorm waning on a summer evening. "All clear," the warden said. Reluctantly I pulled away from Charlie, the air chilling between us unpleasantly. I straightened, my back aching and stiff.

"Look," Charlie said as we reached the street. A piece of shrapnel had embedded itself in the collar of his military jacket.

I shivered, grasping the magnitude of what had just happened. "You could have died." Of course we were all going to die; I'd understood that harsh truth since losing Robbie. But that didn't make the imminent prospect any less terrifying.

"Not me," he said. "I'm lucky." For all that had happened, some part of him seemed to believe fortune would keep him safe. "Anyway, I was with you, so I would have died happy." Our eyes met. He brought his lips to mine, seeming to forget that we were in the middle of the city street with dozens of passersby climbing from the shelters, emergency crews running to fires the bombs had set off. I should have stopped him, but warmth and memory rushed over me, extinguishing any sense of propriety. I reached up and grasped his shoulders. His lips were a salty mix of the sea and the tears that had once been.

He broke away and took my hand and began walking toward the taxi stand at the corner. We were almost running now, the past nipping at our heels. We climbed into the lone cab with its headlights half blacked out and bumper painted white. Inside, we did not speak, as if afraid to break the spell that somehow made this moment possible and all right. He gave the driver an address I could not quite hear over the buzzing in my ears. Then he slid closer. I was nearly in his lap now as he kissed me once more. His hand was at the hem of my skirt.

The cab detoured around some burning wreckage, then slowed in the blackened street at Tottenham Court Road to pick up another passenger. But Charlie flung a bill into the front seat. "Keep driving." We sped up again, the bewildered face of the man on the street disappearing from the window.

"Stop here," Charlie requested at the edge of Grosvenor Square. The American embassy loomed large on the far side.

"One quid," the driver said, as though the

money Charlie had handed him a moment earlier didn't count. Charlie did not balk, but handed the driver the extra fare. Rain began to fall as we climbed from the cab, pelting the leaves above and falling heavy on my hair. He led me toward a hotel that had been converted to house the soldiers. At the curbside a gutter had gotten stopped and a puddle several feet across had formed, blocking our way. Without asking, Charlie lifted me up, and as he carried me over, it was as if he was saving me from the water once more. He did not set me down, but instead carried me around the side of the hotel and up a set of back stairs, navigating the wet, metal steps carefully. Tinny piano music tinkled above loud voices in the lobby.

On the top floor, he unlocked and pressed open the door to a small room no bigger than a broom closet. There were two narrow beds, one made up, one bare. Charlie's rucksack stood in the corner packed neatly as though he had just arrived. The air had a dank smell, like laundry not quite dry.

He set me down and we stared at each other. Wet clothes clung to our bodies. "Charlie . . ." I should not be here. But it was too late—I could not walk away from him again. His fingers reached the top button of my dress and it fell open, followed by the others, one by one. I pulled his wet shirt over his head to reveal the torso I had seen a thousand times in my dreams since we had last walked the beach together. Clothes seemed to slide from us and I was pressed up against him, the one body I had always wanted, with nothing in between.

He laid me down on the sheeted bed, cradling my head, then squeezed in beside me as well as he could in the narrow space. His hands ran along the silhouette of my body, as I had dreamed a thousand times, only better. I rose beneath his touch, the strange feelings I had known all of these years suddenly making sense. It was like getting the birthday present I'd wanted for years, only to find that it was even better than I'd imagined. He murmured my name against my ear as he entered me. It hurt for a moment and then it didn't, and it all faded until there was nothing left.

Afterward he lay beside me, not speaking, holding on tight. I wanted to ask what now. We could not possibly go back. But the questions were too many and too hard so I burrowed deeper into his arms. "Do you mind that it happened?" he asked.

"Not at all," I replied truthfully. I had always expected to wait for marriage. But the rules were all different now, jumbled.

"I'm glad." He reached behind me for a towel and dried my hair carefully, as though I was a child.

"I'm sorry I left without telling you, in

Washington, I mean." Though he had already forgiven me, I felt the need to explain. "I just wasn't ready to face you."

"And now?"

"Now, yes, I think so." I was clearer, in a way that I had not been before. Lying here in Charlie's arms in this odd, smelly little room, I felt as if I was home for the first time since Robbie had died. And I never wanted to leave again.

His face broke into a wide smile and I kissed him, owning what had always been between us. "When did you know?"

"About us? The first day we stepped out of the car at the beach house. I saw you upstairs through the screen, even before the others did. Then you stepped outside." A light dawned in his eyes as he relived the moment. "Your hair was all blown from the bay breeze." I stared at him, so surprised. So he had known from the first as well. "You were just a kid," he said with a rueful laugh. "Scrawny as a stray cat, with those dark, dark eyes." He cleared his throat. "And then that day I came into our parlor and you were sitting at the piano, wearing that peach dress, playing so beautifully I thought my heart would break." How had he remembered that? "And it all changed." Changed indeed. Was I glad? I had pined after Charlie, craved his attention for years. But it had been simpler somehow when it was just a crush, the feelings unrequited.

All that time I thought he had not seen me and considered me just a child, he had loved me back. "But you always talked to my brothers," he added. "So I thought it was just me."

"I was nervous around you."

"Nervous? Ha! That's a trick. Not nervous now, are you?" He grabbed me and drew me close for another kiss. Then his face grew serious. "I have to leave soon, you know that."

"How soon?"

He shrugged. "I don't know." And even if he did, he might not be able to say. "The work we do, you see, is going to be even more important with the invasion coming." His eyes had a wild, desperate look. "Scouting out pockets of German troops, rescuing our own men who are trapped behind enemy lines. We could save hundreds, no, thousands of lives." And it was going to get him killed.

"Charlie, no, that's madness. Why you?"

"Because I'm good at it. Because it's my duty. And it has to be someone, doesn't it? You think it's irresponsible," he added when I did not answer.

I hesitated. I did not want to quarrel with him now. But I had never been any good at holding back. "I think your family has lost enough." The Connallys had lost one son—how could they possibly bear to go through that again?

"I'm coming back," he said, acknowledging the truth in what I had said.

"I know that you are."

"And not just for them." His head had turned toward me ever so slightly and he was looking at me with the faintest twinkle in his eye, the light that I had not seen in so long, so reminiscent of the boy he had once been. "I'm going to come back from this, Addie," he repeated, pressing against my unspoken doubts. For everything that had happened, he still believed he could control his own destiny. "I'll be back to make things right between us. You mark my words. And then we can get married." I swallowed. To me this had been a night, a chance to have what had once been taken from us. But suddenly we were back together as if nothing had ever happened. Except that it had. "Of course if that's not what you want, I under-stand." Apprehension crept into his voice.

"No, it's not that."

"I mean, we'll get married just as soon as I can get leave. I always imagined having our families at the wedding, but with everything that has happened and the war, I think we ought to do it as soon as possible, don't you?"

Suddenly his embrace was suffocating me. I sat up. "What are you doing?" he asked.

"I should go."

"No, stay. It's past curfew and there could be more bombs. I'll sneak you out and see you home before first light." He put his arm around my shoulders and drew me down, then rested a heavy arm across my chest. "You don't really want to go, do you?"

"No." In point of fact, I did not. I burrowed deeper into the warmth of his chest.

"Would you go back to the States for me, Addie?" he asked. "Things here are just so dangerous. I couldn't bear it if something happened to you."

"I can't." Though touched by his concern, I could not help but be annoyed. "How can you ask that of me?"

"I'm worried."

"I feel the same way about you. Are you going to turn and run?"

"But I have my mission, it's different."

"And I have my work. Should that matter any less?" He did not answer and the disagreement hung odd and unpleasant between us. "You come back safely and then we'll go home together."

He rolled onto his back, clasping his arms behind his head. "I'm not sure where home is anymore. Everyone is so scattered."

"Washington, maybe, or somewhere else. We'll figure it out." I rested my head against his chest.

"Let's get married now," he said, weaving his fingers through my hair.

I pulled away. "What?"

"Not now exactly, but first thing tomorrow. Let's find the chaplain and get married."

"But . . ." I was too stunned to form a response. It was not that outrageous an idea—there were couples marrying quickly all over Britain and America now, many of them knowing one another a far shorter time than Charlie and I. And it was not a new idea—we'd planned to marry more than a year ago.

"Why not? Is it your family?" It had always there beneath the surface, the fact that I was Jewish and the Connallys Catholic. But in the rush, I had not even thought about my aunt and uncle, who would never, ever be okay with this. "Because I'll convert if it's important to you."

"No," I interjected. "Becoming Jewish is not something you do for another person. It would have to be because you believed it."

"I would," he insisted, revealing the intensity with which he wanted this, his determination to make it happen. I leaned against him, loving him more than ever. "Or if not, maybe if we just agree that the kids could be Jewish."

Kids. My head swam. I had not even decided if I wanted children. This was all moving so quickly and at the same time it had taken forever to get here. Two days ago, I could not have fathomed that we might be together again. Now he was here. But who knew what might come next? If I had learned anything, it was to take the moment, because it might not come again. "Okay—I mean yes."

"Really?" His eyes were wide and disbelieving.

"Yes."

A smile, the widest of his I'd seen in years, spread across his face. "There's a chapel on the far edge of Grosvenor Square that a lot of the fellas are using now. We can do it there. Let's meet at ten."

"Okay, but I should go now."

"Not yet." He reached for me again. His kisses were everything I had imagined a thousand times in my dreams, fueled by the years of wanting. Then it was over and I clung to him, falling into a kind of blackness where I felt everything and nothing.

Later, I awakened, feeling the familiar yet strangely intimate warmth against my side. I had not planned to fall asleep. I rolled over, bits of sunlight streaming through the blackout curtains. Warmth enveloped me as I studied him. I had seen Charlie sleep before, napping on the Connallys' couch as the breeze blew the curtains through the open window. Then his face had been peaceful. But now he wrestled in his sleep, fighting an enemy unseen. I reached for his shoulder and he calmed beneath my touch. Perhaps it was a battle I could help him win.

I rummaged in my purse for a scrap of paper and something to write with. *Going to my flat to freshen up. Meet you at the chapel at ten.* I set the note on the nightstand, then took one last look at Charlie, fighting the urge to lie down beside him once more. I had to go now, but in just a few hours we would be married. I blew him a kiss.

In his sleep, he smiled.

Sixteen

I slipped from the soldiers' hotel and started to make my way west toward Hyde Park and my flat, conscious of my evening dress that stood out among the morning commuters. Excitement surged through me, quickening my step. Today was my wedding day. I would take Charlie's last name, really become one of them. I tried it on for size: Adelia Connally. Meet him at the chapel at ten, he had said. Darker thoughts intruded then: I would have to send word to Teddy that I would be late to work again. I would not tell him why, of course, until after. He would be crushed. Would he even go so far as to fire me?

Brushing away my worries, I walked onward. The air was fresh and warmed by the spring sun and a few faint buds had begun to sprout on the bushes that lined the park. I paused at the news-stand at the corner to pick up a copy of the *Times*. Teddy and I wired our stories to be filed in Washington thousands of miles away; we seldom saw the finished product and only then weeks or months later. AIR RAID WORST SINCE

BLITZ read the headline. It was hard to believe that just hours earlier, we'd been caught in the bombing. The raid, the story said, had been worst south of the river. My breath caught, thinking of the orphanage. How had Leo and the other children at the orphanage fared? I had to know. The clock over the hotel at the corner read 7:10. Still more than two hours to get back to Charlie. Impulsively, I walked to the taxi stand at the corner and gave the address of the orphanage.

The cab wound through the streets of Belgravia, past the still-posh shops and Georgian houses that were well-tended even amidst the wreckage. Sitting alone on the wide taxi seat, I could not help but remember Charlie and the ride we had shared the previous evening. I grew warm, thinking of his hands all the places they should not have been. I had let things go further than they should have—much further. But it would not matter now that we were getting married.

As we neared the river, the memories vanished. The morning sky over South London was dark gray, streaked with pink. A thick cloud of smoke from the previous night's raid seemed to smolder, as if something was still burning. The cab made its way painstakingly across the bridge in thick traffic, then drove east along the river. At the corner a woman sat upon the tall heap of rubble that had once been her house, not seeming to notice the blood that ran down her cheek. Beside her on the ground lay two bodies covered with blankets, one unmistakably small. My throat tightened.

We stopped once more, blocked by a snarl of buses ahead. "I'll get out here," I said, unable to stand it any longer. I paid the driver and leapt from the cab, running in the direction of the orphanage.

I reached Theed Street and exhaled with relief. Though there was a giant crater in the street and a lorry turned on its side, the house where the children lived stood intact. I paused to catch my breath in front of a bakery that was just opening despite its shattered front window. Then I went inside and used two of my ration cards to buy two loaves still warm from the oven.

Sister Jayne answered when I knocked at the orphanage. "Oh, hello," she said, looking surprised.

"I hope it's not too early."

She wiped her hands on her apron, then gave an airy wave. "Nonsense. With this many children, we never close." But I could see her eyeing my wrinkled evening dress questioningly. "Come in."

I handed her the bread and followed her inside. The wide house with its high, cracked plaster ceilings was chilly, even in late spring. "Too expensive to heat in winter," I could hear Aunt Bess say. The boys and girls were seated around two long, worn wooden tables, somberly eating bowls of porridge. Leo was at the far end of one.

I raised my hand. He didn't smile, though I thought his eyes showed recognition. The children watched with anticipation as Sister Jayne cut and handed out slices of bread thin enough to go around. She did not keep any for herself. I waved off the piece she offered me, then immediately regretted not taking it to slip to Leo. What these children really needed was not just bread, but a rasher of bacon or bit of sausage to bring some color back to their cheeks and put a bit of meat on their bones.

"We do what we can for food," Sister Jayne said, sensing my thoughts. "But we don't have an icebox so it needs to be nonperishable, or eaten quickly."

I followed her to the sink where she resumed rinsing dishes. "I worried about how you'd fared with the bombings last night."

"We were fine. It's difficult calming so many terrified little ones. But we were spared any real damage." She gestured for me to follow her away from the children and up the stairs. She opened a door to a room, giving me a tour though I had not asked.

"They sleep here." There were no beds, just thin straw mattresses on the floor, ten to a room where there should have been four or less, blankets not more than pieces of burlap. "Or in the cellar when there's a raid."

"That can't be easy. Is it just you?"

"There's another sister who comes down weekends when she's able. We're managing. Keeping them in a routine, that's the most important part."

But as she closed the door and started back down the stairs, Sister Jayne's face remained creased, without any sign of relief. "I'm afraid there are other problems, though."

"Oh?"

"We received word yesterday that the government has denied our request for additional visas for the children."

"That's awful." My heart sunk as I pictured a girl version of Leo, stranded somewhere dark and ominous. "How can they do such a thing?"

"They don't want more homeless children in London. They say there aren't enough resources to care for the ones we've got without an individual sponsor for each."

I stopped at the entranceway to the kitchen. "Is there any sort of appeal process?"

"No. The policy isn't likely to change any time soon. And we don't have time. The children that were left behind are in a dreadful spot close to the coast. If they aren't relocated soon, they'll be taken by the Germans, or caught in the fighting." Her eyes filled with tears. She brushed them back. "We've saved this lot and that's something."

Not to him, it isn't, I thought, looking at Leo who finished his bread, unaware. He had lost his whole family, except for the sister that could still be saved.

"I've contacted colleagues of mine in Canada to see if they can take some children," Sister Jayne said. But even if they could save the others that way, Leo and his sister would be an ocean apart. "I'm sure something will work out," she added without conviction.

The children were finishing their breakfast now and clearing their dishes. "Well, thank you for showing me around. I must be going," I said, remembering Charlie.

"Thank you for the bread—and for checking on us." I started back toward the river, my footsteps heavy. Dark clouds had formed, blanketing the sky that had just been so bright. I'd found the children safe from the bombing, but was more worried than ever about those who had been left behind, especially Leo's sister. There had to be a way to help.

I ducked into the red phone booth at the corner, pulled some coins from my purse and dialed Claire, one of the few people I knew who actually had a phone in her flat. But there was no answer. Perhaps she had found Lord Raddingley at the fete after all. I should have said something about seeing him with another woman. Bile rose in my throat at the thought of the jerk who didn't deserve her.

Pushing it down, I dialed again, this time the

news bureau. "Hallo," Teddy's familiar voice greeted, answering his own line because he was the only one in yet. "White speaking." He was always in the office at dawn, not needing more than a few hours' sleep.

"Teddy, it's me."

"Adelia, is everything all right?" His voice was alert, filled with concern. It was not like me to ring.

"I'm fine." I swallowed. It seemed unfair, asking him for help right as I was about to marry Charlie. But I wasn't asking for me. "But remember the group of orphans I told you about?"

"Of course, that little chap you rescued, Leo." Teddy had a great head for names.

"Some of them, including Leo's sister, are stuck in northern France, and can't get papers. Their visas have been denied."

"Dreadful."

I licked my lips. "Do you think there's anything to be done?"

There was silence on the other end of the line. I held my breath, waiting for him to tell me it was impossible. "I've got an old classmate from Magdalen who heads Immigration." I exhaled slightly. Teddy knew everyone. "No promises, but I'll try." It was no small thing I was asking, but he did not want to let me down.

"Thank you."

There was a moment's silence and I could hear

him wondering about the previous evening, where I had gone after leaving the Savoy. "You'll be in?"

I knew I should tell him that I would be late, but I could not bear to tell him why—not until it was done. "Yes. See you soon." I set down the receiver. Teddy would try, and that was better than nothing.

Rain had begun to fall heavily, a sudden morning shower. I hesitated, looking uncertainly in the direction of the river. I needed to get back home quickly and change, but did not have enough money for another cab. I ran to the corner and ducked into the underground station. I hurried down the escalator onto the platform, which was three deep with passengers, crowded even for the morning commute. There was an impatience in the air that suggested travelers had been waiting for a while.

But after only a minute, a train rumbled into the station and we jostled aboard. I stood, pressed closer than was comfortable between an older suited man and a woman holding a miniature poodle. As the train began to move, Charlie appeared in my mind. Today was my wedding day. Was this really happening? I was suddenly light-headed. A quick trip back to my flat to change, then off to meet him. I mentally inventoried my few dresses, none of which seemed quite right, even for standing up in front of a chaplain. It should have been so much different. Somewhere familiar, the Connallys' shore house perhaps, with both of our families present. But that world no longer existed. I wrapped my arms around myself. At least we were both here and together.

The train slammed suddenly to a halt, wheels grinding with an awful screech. I grabbed the pole to stop myself from falling. Women cried out and the poodle scrambled in its owner's arms, paws scratching me as it tumbled to the ground. The lights in the car went out, pitching us into total darkness. Around me there were groans and whispered swearing, the failings of London transport all too familiar.

Several minutes passed, the smell of perspiration and cheap perfume seeming to intensify by the second. I drummed my fingers against the pole impatiently. I wanted time to wash and dress, to make myself look as pretty as possible for this most special of days. I seldom took the underground and it had not occurred to me that I might get stuck. I exhaled, willed myself to be calm. Surely we would move soon.

But we did not. Though I could not see a clock I could feel the passage of time, twenty minutes, then thirty, like water dropping slowly from a leaky cup. People suggested theories to one another in low voices or into the air in front of them: mechanical trouble, a broken track ahead.

I leaned against the pole. Others, weary of standing, dropped to the floor of the train car. There came a distant rumbling. The poodle whimpered from below. Voices grew louder and more frantic: what was happening? I tensed, fear mingling with my urgency. Daytime air raids were rare, but they had happened. My skin grew moist in the too-warm air. I had left just enough time to get to the orphanage and back to change and meet Charlie. But it had to be at least nine o'clock now.

Finally the lights came back on and the train started moving again. There was a smattering of applause. I relaxed slightly. I could still make it. Then the train stopped once more. Though the lights remained on, we did not move. The minutes ticked on endlessly. A man produced a screwdriver and tried to pry open one of the doors, to no avail. Someone else suggested breaking a window. But even if we could free ourselves from the stuck car, the tunnel around us was dark and close, nowhere near a station. We were trapped.

"A breakdown ahead," came a whisper, passed down through the car, though whether it was from an authoritative source, I could not tell. The thought, even if true, was of little consolation. I had no idea how long something like this might last. I had to get to Charlie. *Please,* I prayed silently, *not today of all days.* He would be waiting for me at the chapel.

And I was going to miss him.

But still we sat, not moving. I imagined Charlie in his freshly pressed uniform, wearing a curiously twisted expression as he told himself that I would not stand him up a second time. This could not be happening. I willed him to somehow know that I would be coming, and that nothing would keep me from him this time.

Finally the train began to roll slowly forward. I held my breath, this time too afraid to hope. We rolled into Green Park station and I pushed my way to the door. There was no time to go home and change. I needed to meet Charlie right away. I took the underground steps two at a time to the street where rain no longer fell and ran through the puddled streets toward the chapel near Grosvenor Square. The clock above the embassy read ten forty-five.

A soldier waited anxiously in front of the chapel, clutching a handful of gardenias. But he was shorter, with red hair and freckles. "I'm looking for Sergeant Charles Connally."

"Don't know him," the soldier replied distractedly.

I ran inside the chapel and repeated the question to the minister. "There was a young man waiting here for about an hour in his dress uniform." My heart wrenched as I pictured Charlie, thinking I had stood him up again. I started in the direction of the soldiers' hotel. I would explain everything.

The hotel looked smaller and more run-down

in the light of day, rotting apples fallen from trees covering the broken cobblestones. Inside, the lobby was deserted except for a maid sweeping the hardwood floors. The smell of stale beer and cigarette smoke hung heavy in the air. The cleaner eyed me and I sensed that the sight of a woman in the previous night's clothes was not an unfamiliar one here.

"I left something upstairs." Not waiting for an answer, I ran up the stairs to Charlie's room. The door was unlocked and the bed stripped. None of his belongings remained. It was as if he had never been here at all. I ran my hand over the mattress, remembering the previous night and half wondering if it had been a dream.

I noticed then a scrap of paper on the nightstand. *Shipping out,* the hastily scrawled note read. I could see the bit of his thumb growing inky as he wrote it from that way he always held the pen too close. *Wait for me.* He'd left it here, hoping I'd come back, or perhaps because there hadn't been time to send it. There was a damp spot on the paper. A raindrop, perhaps, or something else?

Clutching the paper, I hurried to the window. If he had not gotten far, I could run after him and explain. But the street was empty. With tears in my eyes, I took one last look around the room where we had shared everything, then slipped out into the cold gray morning.

Seventeen

An hour later, as I stepped freshly washed from my flat on Porchester Terrace, I was still in a daze: Charlie was gone. I thought back to the hotel where we had been so happy just hours earlier. He must have known the previous night that he was being deployed soon. I recognized now the finality in his words, the reason for his urgent push to marry me. But he hadn't wanted to pressure me or use his leaving as an excuse. If I'd known the truth, I would have hurried to the chapel, instead of risking the detour to the orphanage. And we would be married.

I started east along the pockmarked pavement which had begun to dry under the rising sun, headed in the direction of the news bureau. It was late morning now and commuters should have been at their offices but as I reached Oxford Street, I realized that something was different. People clustered at the shop windows, huddling close to listen to the radios. Outside a music shop, someone had set up a speaker. I moved closer. "What is it?"

"Haven't you heard?" a man asked. "The Americans have gone across. The invasion of Europe has begun." So that's why Charlie had left. Though his reconnaissance work would not likely have made him part of the initial invasion, he would be needed to fly more than ever now. Panic seized me as I pictured the dangers that he would face. I pictured him lying beside me just hours earlier, everything we had always wanted finally ours for the taking. And now he was gone—perhaps this time for good. If only I had made it to the chaplain's on time! He still would have left, I knew, but we would have been man and wife. Now he was gone to face terrifying danger, not understanding why I had failed to meet him yet again, perhaps believing I didn't love him.

Tears began to gather in my eyes as I ran, trying to block out the drone of the broadcast that spoke of anti-aircraft fire and tanks and casualties. The Americans entering the war in Europe was something I'd wanted for so long. But now all I could see was the peril Charlie faced.

A few minutes later, I stopped, breathless. I knew I should go to the bureau as planned. Stories of the invasion would be bursting, Teddy trying to cover all of them at once. But I was on the edge of Hyde Park, not far from Claire's flat. I headed in that direction, eager to confide in her about Charlie and have her help me make sense of it all. Then I stopped, remembering Claire's unkind words the previous night, the resentment I'd glimpsed for the first time about the attention I received from Teddy and Charlie. It was just the liquor, I told myself. She was still the closest thing I had to a friend.

Claire answered the door looking fresh in her auxiliary uniform, no sign of weariness from the previous night's revelry. Of course, with the invasion on she would be deploying herself, and have more important things to do than chat with me. "I'm so sorry to show up unannounced." I searched her face for any sign of the anger she'd shown last night.

But she smiled warmly, then stepped aside and let me in. "Not at all. I've got to report in an hour, but there's time for a quick cup of tea. Is something wrong?"

I followed her upstairs to her flat. "Charlie."

Claire's face tightened to a storm cloud. "What has he done now?"

"It's nothing like that. It's just that . . ." I faltered, wanting to confess everything but somehow unable.

Then she smiled devilishly. "You've done it, haven't you?"

I stepped back, mortified. "You can tell?"

"Only me, yes. No one else will see it, not even Teddy, I promise." Teddy. He would have been so hurt to know about me and Charlie if we had gotten married. "There's a glow about you. Was it wonderful?"

"Better than that," I confessed with a flutter of excitement as I remembered the feel of Charlie pressed close. "Only now he's gone." My tears came then in spite of myself. I swiped at my eyes, ashamed to be moping about such things when there were so many bigger problems of war and suffering to worry about.

"There, there." Claire handed me a tissue. "You can't cry now with all of the soldiers going and whatnot. Very un-British, stiff upper lip and all that. Don't be glum. You had your moment, that's the most any of us can hope for right now. More, even." I waited for Claire to reassure me that Charlie would be all right, that he would come back. But after everything she had seen, she would not make false promises. "Wait here," she instructed instead, then disappeared into the kitchen.

As I looked out the window across the treetops, my shoulders slumped with exhaustion. Maybe I should go home. Charlie wanted me to, and Teddy would surely understand.

Claire returned a minute later with some toast and tea. I hadn't eaten since the previous day. "Better?" I swallowed and nodded, not really sure if that was true. "Good. No sense moping about."

"I suppose."

"Poor Teddy," Claire mused. "I suppose he doesn't have a chance now."

No. "How could he?" Even gone, Charlie had all of my heart. "I'll have to tell him."

"Why? Charlie is gone and things with Teddy are just for fun. Don't be so stiff about it all. Just take it as it comes." I wished that I could be as light as Claire. But an image of Charlie pulling farther away into the darkness shrouded my mind.

"Anyway, it wasn't just fun with Charlie. He asked me to marry him."

"Oh?" Claire's eyebrows rose. "You hadn't mentioned."

"No." Was that because I feared she might disapprove? "We'd originally planned to wait until he came back, but then Charlie decided we should do it sooner."

Claire cut me off. "He decided."

"Yes."

"Again." It was not a question. I could see where Claire was going with this, the way it seemed to reaffirm her perception that Charlie called the shots. I wanted to take issue with how Claire was interpreting the facts. But now seeing it laid before me, she was right—Charlie had made the decision for both of us, had presumed I'd want what he did.

"He rang looking for you, by the way. Teddy, that is." Her point about Charlie having been made, she seemed content to change the subject.

"Did he?"

"Last night. Said you weren't at your flat." So Teddy had come looking for me after the fete. "I nearly forgot to mention." But had she really, or had the omission been planned?

I gazed out the window at a woman sitting on the ground by the park's edge, holding a swaddled baby in one hand. A hat lay upturned in front of her in hopeful anticipation of a few coins. How silly my problems seemed by comparison to the suffering and struggles of others! Leo and the orphans popped suddenly into my head.

"There's something else. Remember the orphanage I told you about? There's a small group of children left stranded in France and they can't get papers to come over."

"And you want me to ask my uncle." I nodded, relieved she had guessed what I did not have the nerve to raise. "Oh, Addie, how can I possibly right now? I'll try but the immigration laws are passed by Parliament, and now everyone is completely tied up with the invasion . . ." She stopped, seeing the pleading in my eyes. "I'll try, but don't get your hopes up."

"Thank you, Claire, I know it's a lot to ask."

"I'll have to do it when I get back."

I started to protest that it wouldn't be soon enough, then stopped, her words sinking in. "Back? Where from?" Until now, Claire's assignments had been day trips or overnight at most. But there was a rucksack, smaller and smarter than Charlie's, leaning on the wall by the door.

"We're going over," Claire said, with a tilt of

her head south, implying the coastline. She said this so casually that she might have been speaking about a day at the seaside. It took me a minute to realize that she meant crossing the Channel into war-torn Europe.

"You can't be serious."

"A group from the Auxiliary is organizing at Portsmouth. We won't deploy right away, of course, but once the Americans have pushed inland, we'll be headed to France to bring supplies to the medics. I've gotten special clearance to join them."

"That's so dangerous." My admiration for her rose.

"We aren't actually going to the front, just to a field hospital." Still, she would be risking everything to save lives, in a way that I could only imagine. "But I'm leaving today to help with the organizing effort."

Charlie was gone and now Claire—and I was being left behind once more. At the full realization, my heart sank.

"There, there. You'll be fine here and you'll have Teddy to look after you."

But that wasn't enough—no matter how much I wanted it to be. I finished my toast and coffee, then gestured to Claire's uniform. "You're busy. I should go."

"Let me get my things and I'll walk you out." She started for the bedroom.

As I stood, something by the edge of the area rug caught my eye. A lone cuff link. I picked it up. "Lord Raddingley was here?" I called through the open bedroom door.

"Yes." She appeared from the bedroom. I cringed inwardly as her face lit up. "He's growing fonder, I think." I thought back to two nights ago in the bomb shelter, my awful secret about Lord Raddingley and the girl. I could not tell Claire and devastate her just as she was about to undertake a dangerous assignment. I tucked the cuff link in my pocket.

Claire picked up her rucksack and we walked down to the street. She paused at the newsstand, scanning the headlines though it was of course too soon for news of the invasion to have been printed. I pointed to a black-and-white map of the French coast on the front page of the *Times*. "The fighting is mostly here, so as long as Charlie is flying east of it . . ." My voice trailed off.

The woman behind the kiosk eyed me sympathetically. "You poor dear," she clucked, assuming the worst from my eyes, which must have still been red. "Your husband?" the woman asked. "Boyfriend?" There was a hierarchy, it seemed, of worry and grief and those who were entitled to them.

Before I could answer, Claire slipped her hand into mine. "Father of her bastard child," she quipped wickedly. The woman's jaw dropped and before she could respond, Claire had whisked me down the street.

We parted at the corner. "Promise me you'll be careful," I pleaded. I was suddenly aware of the danger that seemed to lurk at every turn.

"Back in a few weeks." Claire gave me a firm hug instead of her usual airy kiss. As I watched her walk purposefully toward South Kensington station, my shoulders slumped: I had been strong like that once, too. I remembered the girl who had come to America alone, who had fought her way in and made a place for herself. Then I had thought myself small and helpless. But I realized now what it had taken to make my way. That girl, the strong one, I hardly knew anymore.

From a church tower above, a bell began to chime. I looked up. It was past lunch time and I still hadn't made it to the bureau. Hurriedly I walked back down the stairs to the red phone box at the corner.

"The *Post*, Mr. White's desk," Joan answered.

"It's Adelia. May I speak with him?"

"Adelia, he's terribly busy." There was a clattering, the phone being grabbed from her hands.

"You still aren't here. What the hell happened to you?" Teddy's voice burst through. "Are you all right?"

"I'm fine."

"Are you with Charlie?" He did not bother to hide his jealousy anymore.

331

"No, Teddy. He shipped out this morning.

"I'm sorry I'm not there yet," I continued before he could ask anything else. "I was on an underground car that was delayed." The explanation, a half-truth, seemed the most appropriate. "I'm on my way."

"Good. I can't manage without you." Did he mean in the office or was he talking about something bigger? "But I wanted to tell you also, I spoke to my friend over at Immigration. I'm afraid it's a no-go. Helping those children before today would have been hard enough. But now with the invasion . . . Well, it's impossible." I knew Claire would not be able to help either. "Parliament has shut down all of the visas by legislation. There's nothing to be done." His voice was sympathetic.

"Thank you anyway," I said, knowing that he had really tried. But I was flooded with disappointment. Charlie was gone, Claire too, and now I couldn't help the children. I felt so useless. I reached in my pocket and my hand touched the cuff link I'd inadvertently taken from Claire's flat. An idea began to form in my mind. "If you can spare me a bit longer, I'll be there shortly."

"But you said you were on your way. Adelia, what are you up to?" I hated keeping secrets from Teddy, but he was a journalist and his job was to expose the very things I was trying to protect.

"I'll be there soon," I said, replacing the phone in the cradle.

Big Ben was chiming half past one as I crossed the park in front of Westminster. I paused, steeling myself, then walked up the grand entrance of Parliament and through the gilded foyer to the front desk. "Adelia Montforte." The guard tilted his head at my accent (mostly American with a bit of Italian, and not at all British) and his face hardened as he prepared to turn me away. "I'm here to see Lord Raddingley." I raised my badge from the *Post*, hoping that it looked official.

But the guard remained unimpressed. "You have an appointment?"

"Yes," I lied.

He rang the office and gave my name, then listened for several seconds. "The minister is busy." My heart sank.

I squared my shoulders, trying again. "Tell him that I'm a friend of Miss Churchill's."

I held my breath and counted: one, two . . . Exactly ninety seconds later, Lord Raddingley appeared on the marble stairwell. He looked at me blankly, trying to place where we might have met. People like him did not notice ordinary folks like me. "Let's walk," he said, anxious to get out of the lobby and away from the curious eyes of his peers. I followed him out of the building into the park across the street where pigeons fed by the garbage cans.

He stopped by a bench but did not sit. "How can I be of service? I'm sure I don't have to tell you that today of all days, Parliamentary business is more than a bit frantic."

"I'll be brief. I'm a friend of Claire's."

Something flickered across his face. "I've met her socially." Socially at her flat last night, I thought. But I did not want to overplay my hand. "A lovely young woman."

I considered challenging his lie directly, then decided to take a different tack. "I need your help. There's a small group of refugees in northern France. Jewish children, about thirty of them, who have been stranded by the fighting. I want you to arrange their papers."

"That's quite impossible," he said in the practiced voice of those used to denying requests. "The government isn't issuing any more visas right now for anyone who does not have an individual sponsor."

I bit my lip. "You dropped something in her flat, I think." I opened my palm to reveal the cuff link, holding it back far enough so he could not grab it.

He flinched for a minute and recovered. "There's no telling where I lost it."

"You know, I'm with the *Post*," I said, holding up my badge and upping the ante.

"Surely the paper has better things to worry

about than gossip mongering. Especially today."

"I suppose." I feigned defeat.

He pressed his lips together in a faint, smug smile, confident that he had won. "If you'll excuse me, I must be getting back."

"Terrible bombing raid the other night, wasn't it?" This was the last weapon in my arsenal, the one I'd hoped not to have to use. "The shelter over on Savoy was very accommodating, though." Lord Raddingley's eyebrows lifted as I emphasized these last words, letting him know that I had seen everything. "I'm sure Claire was terribly worried about you." The cuff link was of limited use, especially with no one to corroborate my story. But Claire, if told about the woman in the shelter, could choose to destroy him. He could not afford her wrath—or that of the Prime Minister.

He considered my words for a long moment, then cleared his throat. "I suppose someone really should help those poor children," he conceded. I exhaled slightly, a tiny bit of air from a too-full balloon. "Give me a few days to get it in place and the visas will be waiting for you at the front desk. And, Miss Montforte?" I turned back. "Don't bother me again."

I wanted to push and tell him to leave Claire alone. But right now, I needed his help. I looked at him levelly. "Lord Raddingley—don't give me a reason." Not waiting for an answer, I turned and strode across the park.

Eighteen

"Addie, this is brilliant!"

We were sitting in Teddy's office at the *Post* bureau a week after my confrontation with Lord Raddingley. Teddy fingered the slim packet of transit visas I'd handed him, wide-eyed. I hadn't told him about my visit to Parliament when I'd finally made it to the office late that afternoon, nor the next, not sure that Lord Raddingley was going to keep his word.

Indeed, when I'd gone back to Parliament for the passes two days later, the guard at reception had looked at me blankly. "Nothing, miss."

"But if you ring Lord Raddingley surely he will know about it." My voice had risen.

"He's been called away on business," he'd said, dismissing me. I'd walked hurriedly by Westminster Abbey, past the pigeons that splashed in puddles at its base. My cheeks burned. I'd been duped. I fingered the cuff link in my pocket, which I kept close, even at night. Did I dare to make good on my threat? I could hardly do it now, while Claire was away on assignment with the auxiliary. And humiliating Lord Raddingley, while perhaps an effective bluff, would not help the orphans at all if I acted upon it. I'd checked back at Parliament the following day and after the weekend, my rage growing.

Finally this morning, a week after I'd confronted Lord Raddingley, I'd arrived at the bureau to find a brown paper package with no return address waiting for me. "It was on the mat when I arrived," Teddy said. I ripped it open and pulled out the passes inside. My heart soared.

"How did you manage it?" Teddy asked now.

I took the passes back from him. "A good journalist doesn't reveal her sources," I quipped, giddy with triumph. I could not tell him the awful secret about Lord Raddingley—or how I had leveraged it. Teddy would surely be angry, too, that I had used my position at the paper to get what I had wanted. But I had gotten the visas.

I put on my coat. "I'm going to tell Sister Jayne the good news."

"Addie, wait." Teddy reached for my arm, a look of longing rolling over his face, as it always did when we touched. But conflict quickly replaced it. "Maybe you should hold off a bit."

My heart grew somber, hopes doused. Having the passes was one thing, but the children were not out yet. "We still need to get these visas to the children in France."

Teddy frowned, his dimple pulling downward. "Yes, that's the trick. Normally I'd take these on the next ship that was allowing correspondents and make sure they got to the orphanage. But now that the Americans have gone over, there's no telling when that will be." I nodded. Correspondents did not have the kind of free access to the continent they'd enjoyed before the invasion. Only a small group of AP reporters had gone over with the troops and sent back dispatches. At least one of them had been killed alongside the soldiers in the initial wave on Omaha Beach.

"We'll manage it," I said firmly. We had come too far to fail now.

"Perhaps in a few weeks, when the fighting pushes inland, we'll have better luck." There was no conviction in his voice.

I'd already mentioned the possibility to Jayne, though. I'd gone to the orphanage over the weekend, as much to keep busy as out of concern for the children. With Charlie gone and Claire on her deployment, I was lonely and I couldn't face the long hours in my flat, staring at the map of Europe and fretting over where they both were now.

Sister Jayne had been washing laundry in great tubs, each of the children helping in some way. I reached over to Leo, who was trying to fold a sheet twice his size. Then I rolled up my sleeves to rinse. "You'll soak your dress," Jayne protested, as I wrung out the first garment.

Ignoring her caution, I took the clothes and began to soap them in the warm water. I had not washed bedding by hand since leaving Italy and the lavender scent took me back. My hands soon grew red and chafed but the ache in my arms was a good one. I looked over at Leo, wanting to tell him: *Leo, we're going to bring your sister.* I knew that I should not. He looked up and smiled, as though reading my mind.

"I may be able to help the children," I said in a low voice to Jayne instead. Her face lifted with so much hope I instantly regretted it. Lord Raddingley had not yet come through at that point. "It's still just a chance, but I'm working on a connection for some visas."

"Bless you, Adelia. That's wonderful." Then her eyes clouded again, too afraid to hope. "Of course, even with visas, it's going to be so hard to get them out." Her face creased with the experience of one who had taken care of many. "It's no easy thing, moving a group of children that large, especially now with all of the fighting. But we're grateful to you. You've done so much." She tilted her head in the direction of the kitchen.

"You got a new icebox." I was not sure what that had to do with me.

"A man brought it for us. Blond chap. Said he was a friend of yours." Teddy. I'd mentioned to him in passing the fact that they didn't have one. How had he managed to get it so quickly? It would not have been easy, even for him. He cared because I did.

I looked over at Teddy now. He had not said anything about the icebox and I didn't know if I should ask him. He was just that way, helping people quietly without seeking credit. I'd seen him on the street, walking along a line of women queuing for soup before a charity kitchen, pressing coins into their cracked hands and giving candy to the children until his pockets were empty. Despite his admonishment not to become part of the story, he cared and was doing what he could in his own small way to help. He was such a good man. I wanted to hug him and tell him how grateful I was for what he had done. But the one thank-you he wanted was the one I couldn't give—because my heart was still with Charlie.

"You're right, of course, about not getting their hopes up. Perhaps you could see if one of the correspondents from *Le Monde* might have a connection?" He did not answer, but looked over my shoulder with a puzzled expression. I turned. Claire was standing in the door of Teddy's office. "Claire!" She had never come to the bureau, even before her deployment. Her normally crisp uniform was soiled and wrinkled, and hair completely out of its usual order.

I rose and rushed to her. "What are you doing here? Are you hurt?" But she remained silent, her face a blank mask. I had seen that look twice before in my life, the night that Aunt Bess had told me that my parents were missing and the night that the policeman came to the house about Robbie. A buzzing started in my ears, growing to a roar.

Claire crossed the room, her face uncharacteristically grave. "It's Charlie," she said. The ground seemed to drop out beneath me and I lurched forward, stumbling into her arms. "Darling, his plane has gone down."

I'm not sure whether I fell or fainted. When I looked up, I was lying on the floor, Claire and Teddy hovering above me. I vaguely recalled Teddy's arms catching me as I fell and pulling me sideways so I didn't crack my head on the edge of his desk.

"Drink," Claire said, producing a glass of whiskey, from where I had no idea. I did not take it, but let her raise the glass to my lips, scarcely tasting the fiery liquid.

Then I pushed it aside. "Tell me," I croaked. "Tell me everything."

"We were in transit when I overheard a radio dispatch that a plane had gone down deep in Germany, close to the Czech border. The Addie Rose, it was called."

I looked up at her in disbelief. "He named his plane after me." He had not told me. But Claire said he had been over Germany. Charlie should not have been that far south. Had he kept that from me so I would not worry more? Or perhaps he had not known.

I looked up at Teddy, who was watching me, and I braced for his questions about Charlie's mission and how much I had known. But he simply cleared his throat. "Let me make some calls and see what I can find out." Teddy left the office to find another line, not wanting, I suspected, to speak in front of me.

"Charlie . . ."

"There, there," Claire soothed as she cradled me, feeding me sips of whiskey. "Look at you—you've even got men rescuing your other men." I did not respond to her feeble attempt at a joke, but lay back limply, staring out the window at the deceptively blue sky. Charlie was missing. It could not possibly be true. The Addie Rose, he'd called his plane. Because some part of him, despite it all, still believed I was good luck. Couldn't he see that I destroyed almost everyone I touched?

Once upon a time I would have prayed. "Please," I would say each night as I lay in the darkness, willing God to bring my parents safely to America. At some point I'd wondered if it would it do any good to say it more than once. So I had added more *please*s beneath the flannel sheets that smelled of rose water, a hundred and as many as a thousand, repeating the word late into the night. Then news had come about my mother and father and I had not prayed again. Could I now? It wasn't just that I had forgotten the words—I had simply stopped believing.

The door to Teddy's office opened and he reappeared, jaw set grimly. "What did you find out?" I said, trying to sit up even though the room was wobbly.

"Let's get you home," he said.

"I want to know," I insisted. I would not go until I had answers.

But he shook his head. "Not here." As he looked down the hall furtively I understood his hesitation was about something more than protecting me: German spies were thought to be everywhere and he would not speak in a public place, even the bureau, for fear of jeopardizing operations—and perhaps Charlie himself. He and Claire helped me past the curious secretaries downstairs into a cab.

"I should get back to my duties," Claire fretted, standing at the open door of the taxi.

"I've got her," Teddy said, sliding in beside me. I leaned my head against his shoulder for comfort. Neither of us spoke. My mind reeled back to the cab ride I'd taken with Charlie to the hotel and everything that had happened afterward in his room. But the heat that usually came when I thought about such things was extinguished by sorrow.

The cab stopped on Porchester Terrace and

Teddy helped me out. But I was able to manage the steps on my own. "He was flying over Munich," Teddy said in a low voice when we were inside my flat. Without asking, he put on the kettle, then turned back to me. His brow furrowed. "I thought Charlie was part of the unit flying sorties out of Duxford. He should have been over northern France or Belgium."

"That was a cover," I confessed. There was no point in hiding the truth anymore. "He was flying reconnaissance missions on his own." I waited for Teddy's anger that I had not told him the truth about Charlie or the real reason I had asked him to kill the story. But his expression remained calm. "Has there been any word of him?"

"None."

"The embassy." My voice cracked with desperation. "Surely they can help."

"I put in a call but so far nothing. Claire said she would check with her uncle as well. We're working with all of our contacts." Gratitude rose in me. Teddy had not liked the fact of Charlie, but he was doing everything he could to help. "But crashing over Germany . . ."

Changed everything, I finished silently. He continued, "They're going to fly over the site to try and check, when they can do it without jeopardizing operations. Of course, we must consider the Germans could have captured him."

Which would be worse. My stomach turned as the full weight of the situation crashed down on me. "Oh, no."

"We don't know that, Addie," he said earnestly, taking my hand. He used the Connally boys' nickname for me now, the one he had always eschewed. Teddy might have been conflicted: Charlie had been his biggest rival for my attention. But his voice was filled with genuine sadness, which scared me more than perhaps anything else. "He could be hiding in the woods. But that's very dangerous territory. I'm afraid you must prepare yourself for the worst." I buried my head in his chest and wept.

Nineteen

I set down the book I'd been reading carefully so as not to get it wet, then sank deeper into the bath, closing my eyes. It was Sunday night, the murmur of a BBC program and the faint smell of coriander coming through the floorboards from the Dashani kitchen below. For a moment I could almost imagine I had just arrived in London and life was like it was back before I'd met Claire, when I used to spend all of my nights like this, alone. Back before everything had happened.

But it wasn't. It had been more than six weeks since Charlie's plane went down. My stomach churned as it did every morning when I woke up and remembered. There had been no further word of him. "At this point," Claire had said on one of her brief visits back from duty, "we have to assume that he is gone." She spoke kindly but firmly, not wanting to hurt me needlessly but unwilling to give me false promise.

"But we don't know. He could be arrested, or injured somewhere, or in hiding." It was the last of these, the most hopeful thought, that I kept anchored firmly in my mind. Charlie had crashed in a wooded area and was simply staying out of sight until he could make his way back safely. I could not bear to think of anything worse.

Claire had not pressed further to wipe away the last of my hope. She came back as often as she could between her own missions, keeping me busy with dinner and films, quieter fun more suitable than the clubs and parties she otherwise might have frequented. Teddy helped when Claire was away, offering his company in an unassuming way when I was amenable, and retreating graciously when I was not.

Of course, I hadn't given up on Charlie. I'd done my own digging, visiting the War Office and other government agencies that might have information, using my press credentials and Teddy's connections to gain access. But when the bureaucrats in their dusty offices would finally see me, they would offer me weak tea, then tell me that they had no information about Charlie's mission or whereabouts. Really, their raised eyebrows and barely veiled exasperated tones implied, the British government had better things to do than find a lone American.

Finally, I'd gotten an appointment with the military attaché at the US embassy, Colonel Miller, a man with salt-and-pepper hair and a deeply lined face. "I understand that you're trying to find out about Sergeant Charles Connally." He pulled out a file. "We don't even have his mission listed officially. He was supposed to be flying out of Duxford."

"He was working on some confidential matters," I said.

Colonel Miller's eyebrows rose. Clearly he knew about Charlie's work, though I was not supposed to. "Miss Montforte, we have hundreds of thousands of men in combat, and official channels for sending news of their well-being. I cannot simply hand a file to anyone who walks through the door."

"Please." I cut him off before he could refuse me. "I've known him my whole life." That wasn't exactly a lie; in reality I'd only met the Connallys a few years earlier, but some part of me felt as though I had known them forever. "We were supposed to be married. I just need to find out what happened."

"Very well." He thumbed through a file, then

pulled out a sheet and handed it to me. "I'm terribly sorry." The paper gave Charlie's date of birth and aircraft identification, as well as the date and location from which it had taken off. My blood turned to ice. *Missing,* it read. *Presumed deceased.*

That had been four days ago. I dropped the paper and staggered numbly from the embassy, not bothering to thank Colonel Miller. The report had told me nothing conclusive, I reminded myself as I hurried down the cool granite steps of the embassy, which occupied one side of Grosvenor Square. I averted my eyes from the soldiers' hotel opposite it. Of course Charlie was missing; the rest was just a guess. But I wondered why they presumed him dead, the facts and information not contained on the paper that had led to that conclusion.

I had not yet told Claire or Teddy what I had learned. Saying it would only make it more real. With no further inquiries to be made, Charlie missing was the painful status quo. I stepped from the tub now and dried, then put on my gown. Charlie's image had grown clouded in my mind. I still thought of him constantly. But I had stopped dreaming about him, just like my parents and Robbie. That—even more so than the information I had seen at the embassy—was the surest sign that he was gone.

And yet still I could not accept it. It was easy

enough to pretend he was simply off fighting. Hope of his recovery had faded like a dying ember but some part of me wasn't ready to acknowledge that he was gone in the same way that Robbie was, to begin grieving for him. I thought about what might have been between us. We had come so close. Our night at the hotel played over and over in my mind. We had not known it was the last time.

I put on my nightgown, then walked to my desk, eyeing the stationery box. What did the Connallys know? Though I knew how news of those killed in the fighting was conveyed from my time in Washington and the Dennison boy, I was unsure if the War Department sent letters when one was only presumed missing. I should have been the one to write and tell them. But anything I'd said would have been guessing, and that would only make things worse.

Beside the stationery box sat the package containing the visas Lord Raddingley had gotten for me. I'd waited for weeks, hopeful that Teddy would be able to make a connection to get the visas to the children. He'd tried as tirelessly to do that as he had to help me get word of Charlie. But though the Allies had pushed inland, the children were in an area that was surrounded by fighting and the Allies weren't authorizing anyone to go in there now. My optimism grew fainter as time passed and promising leads did not pan out. Even

Sister Jayne had stopped asking when I visited.

Looking at the passes now, my frustration grew. Every day that passed meant heightened danger for the children. They might already be gone. This wasn't like Charlie, missing and beyond reach. We knew where the children were, or had anyway. If they were still there, we could help them. Impulsively, I changed into my dress and shoes, then started from the flat. I walked downstairs and phoned the bureau but Teddy's line rang and rang.

Forty-five minutes later, I stepped from a taxi at Hampstead and started up the fashionable High Street, its darkened shops shuttered and sandbagged, pavement deserted. Mindful of the curfew I was breaking, I hurried in the direction of Teddy's flat. It was three blocks north, the ground floor of a single Georgian house, set back from a quiet street by well-tended gardens.

I rang the bell. As he opened the door, his eyes widened. "Addie, what is it? Is something wrong?"

Everything, I wanted to say. But I forced a smile. "Not at all. May I come in?"

He stepped back, the correspondent too caught off guard to ask further questions. I had been here once before, dropping off papers. His two rooms were elegant, with dark oak trim and high windows, and overstuffed red leather couches that suited his bachelor lifestyle. His walls were as bare as those at the bureau, no photos or personal mementoes. Unlike his office, his flat was neat, tabletops clear of papers and cups. It wasn't just that he had a housekeeper come in and clean—between long hours at the office and chasing stories, he simply spent no time here. It was as if he could not bear to be alone.

Except now. He was wearing a smoking jacket and a bottle of brandy sat on the table before him. Duke Ellington played from the record player on the bookshelf.

"I'm sorry I didn't ring first," I said, suddenly a tinge nervous. "I just wanted some company."

"Would you like a drink? I've got a chardonnay that's almost passable. Or there's some Ribena, if you'd prefer."

"That would be lovely." He poured a bit of the black-currant syrup into a glass and added water before passing it to me.

I followed him into the sitting room. "I tried the bureau. I thought I might find you."

"Yes, well, now you have." His normally bright eyes were dark.

"It's about the children." A disappointed look crossed his face, as he realized I'd come for more than just company. Then his expression turned guarded. "I know we've had no luck with the correspondents. But someone else, the church maybe, or the medics, surely someone can help." My voice rose pleadingly.

351

"Addie, come sit down." I started to protest, then lowered myself to the leather sofa he indicated. "There's something else." His face bore that bearer-of-bad-news look I had come to know only too well. But I was nearly immune to pain, like a wound that had not healed properly but had grown callused and scarred. "You know I reached out to a Red Cross contact."

"Yes." He had told me the plan a few days earlier. Though so many leads had fallen through before, I could not help but hope.

"They can't manage it. The area where the children are has been cut off by the Germans as they've fallen back. Not even food or other basic aid can get through."

My heart sank. Leo's sister and the others were not only trapped, but hungry. I cleared my throat. "So what's next?"

His shoulders slumped and he looked away. "There is no next." His voice was scratchy. He was more upset than I had ever seen him at the idea of disappointing me. "We can't chance putting the visas in the mail, and none of our couriers are going now."

"What about taking them yourself?"

"What are you talking about? One can't just go sailing across the Channel these days."

"It's possible. You've been over dozens of times." I looked him squarely in the eyes, challenging him to deny it.

He shook his head. "That was before the invasion."

"But you could manage it now. You have enough clout to get a pass. If we come up with a story about why we're traveling together . . ."

"We? You want to come with me?" He stared at me disbelievingly. Perhaps this time I had gone too far. "You can't be serious."

"You said yourself the photos are awful. I can take better ones for you."

But he refused to take the bait. "It's nearly impossible to get accredited. Especially if you're a woman."

This last bit rankled me. How many times had I heard that as a reason why I could not do something? "But just think of the stories we could get. The photographs alone could win a Pulitzer." He blanched, offended by the notion that a prize was what he was after. "I mean, think of all the people we could help by telling their stories to the world."

"You're not a correspondent, goddammit! You're a secretary." His words cut through me like a knife. Ever since the Tomaszewicz interview, Teddy had treated me like an equal partner. But his words were not intended to hurt—he was just trying to stop me from going.

"Addie," he said, more softly now. "This isn't about your being a woman."

"Then what?"

"You're Jewish." He blinked hard. "And with the things they're doing to Jews . . ." I turned away, not wanting to hear what was coming next. "You heard Tomaszewicz, interviewed him yourself."

The story of the Jews being gassed was never far from my thoughts. "That was just one village." But my voice was hollow and I knew even as I said it that it was not true.

He shook his head sadly. "Only it isn't. There have been reports just like it of killings all over Europe like the one he described. Jews. Gypsies and homosexuals and clergy, too, but mostly Jews. In trucks and factories and camps—by the thousands." My stomach turned. There were stories in the papers of Jews being relocated and detained in camps, but if what he was saying was true, then why was no one writing or screaming about it?

He raised his hand, cutting me off. "It's out of the question. I'm not taking you. It's too dangerous. And I'm not going myself," he added before I could jump in again. He took both my hands in his.

Teddy was forever chasing stories. So why was he refusing the challenge now? "I thought you wanted to make a difference."

"By reporting the news. Not becoming part of the story. Addie, this is daft. You know I'd do anything for you. But I'd be jeopardizing my credentials and risking all the important work we are trying to do. Surely you see the big picture."

I sniffed. "I suppose." His point was a fair one, but all I could see was Leo's sister and the other children left behind. A few years earlier and one of them could have been me. "But we have to help the children—"

"We don't even know if they would still be there when we arrived." His words were like a slap. With the Germans killing Jews and the children behind German lines it was only a matter of time. "Addie, I don't mean to be hard-hearted. But children are suffering everywhere, even in Britain. Eighty died in a bombing at a school north of here months back. And that bloody awful bombing at the underground station."

I nodded. But he seemed to suggest that these things made saving the orphans somehow less important. For me, it meant more now than ever. "If there's a chance to save them, we must try," I pressed.

"Is this about Charlie?" he asked abruptly, and I saw he was unable to hide the depths of his feelings for me. I still hadn't told him what I'd learned about Charlie at the embassy. "Saving those children won't bring back Charlie—or his brother," he added gently. I wanted to snap back at him: How dare he presume? But looking into his eyes, I realized that Teddy had come to know—

really know—me. He was right: I was trying to rewrite the past.

This was about more than the Connallys, though. And I wasn't about to give up on these kids. "No, these children really need our help."

"I'm sorry. I can't." His eyes darted back and forth, searching for my reaction. "Addie, I want to help. You know that. Helping a few dozen children isn't going to change what they're doing to all of those people—your people." But it would be something. "And I'll be goddamned if I'll let you go, knowing now what they would do to you if you were caught. Don't be a hero," he added. "Do you know what they do to heroes? What they did to Tomaszewicz's family?"

"No," I breathed. Though I had only met Jan Tomaszewicz once, his family and especially his nine-year-old daughter had become real to me. I often wondered how they were doing.

"They were hung in the town square."

"Stop!" I cried, covering my ears although it was too late.

"And that is why I won't help you with this. Even if you hate me for it."

I opened my mouth to respond, then closed it again. "Okay," I said simply. I would get no further with him and neither of us needed a fight right now.

"I really am sorry about them—and about Charlie, too." I pulled back, the unexpected mention of his name stinging. "I know how hard this is for you. He was a brave chap, and well, I'm sorry."

"Thank you." In that moment, I was drawn to Teddy and his straightforward views of the world. He liked me and wanted me safe; it was as simple as that. I moved closer and let him put his arm around me, draw me close. When I looked up, our lips were just inches apart. For a second I was tempted: Charlie was gone and Teddy was here, wanting to protect me. Why not accept the comfort he was still so eager to give?

Because Teddy was not Charlie. I could never feel anything close to what I had felt. And it wouldn't be fair. Instead, I leaned my head against his shoulder and we both sat in silence. The record reached the end and the needle began to skip. Teddy's weight grew heavier above me. I pulled away and he did not protest, so I knew even before looking that he was asleep.

I watched Teddy, with his head tilted back on the sofa. He breathed lightly, giving off the faint smell of sour liquor. His face was clear. There were none of the demons I'd seen as I lay beside Charlie. Even at his darkest, Teddy was placid, removed from the tragedy and despair that surrounded him. I reached for the throw blanket at the bottom of the sofa and covered him with it. I looked around. What now? I'd come to try once more to persuade him to help me, but that had failed. My eyes traveled to his coat, hung over the edge of one of the chairs. His press pass dangled from it. If I had one of those—actual correspondent's credentials, not a secretary's—for myself, I could find a way to have the visas delivered—or at least I could try.

But I did not. Standing quietly so he would not wake, I walked over to his desk. Teddy had said he'd learned that the orphans were unreachable by the Red Cross, but how? Perhaps there was some information, something he had missed, that might provide a clue to their whereabouts. I scanned his desk. I should not be looking through his things, I knew. But, my curiosity piqued, I opened the top drawer. It creaked loudly. I froze, then looked in the direction of the sofa, but he slept undisturbed. Inside was a folder thick with papers. I was surprised; I assumed Teddy did all of his work at the office. What did he have here? There were news clippings of his own stories and at first I thought it was simply a collection of everything he had written. But the typeset was strange, certain letters dropped ever so slightly. To the untrained eye, it would not have been apparent. But having spent months working with the close typeset of the newspaper, I could discern the pattern immediately: it was some sort of code. Teddy was not just writing articles for the *Post*; he was sending encrypted messages in the stories. He had refused to help with the orphans not just because he was worried about his career, but in order to protect some sort of operation.

Why hadn't he told me? I wanted to run over and wake him and demand answers. But if hadn't confided in me before, then there was no reason to think he would now. I rifled deeper in the desk. There was something else, a thin yellowed paper, a mimeo of some sort of report. I lifted it up and as I saw the familiar language, my heart skipped: Italian. I recalled then how Teddy had gone checking for my family. But he had found nothing and said that it was best to leave it alone. He had not mentioned this.

I scanned the paper, translating the language that always came back to me like a forgotten prayer: Gustavo and Ilena Montforte—arrested for helping Jews escape. I paused, puzzled. My parents had been political activists; they had not been in the business of helping refugees. The report was dated July 10, 1941—less than a month after I had left Trieste. The horrible truth hit me then: the police must have come to check registration cards and I was missing. My parents were arrested—and likely killed—because they had helped me flee.

A sob rose in my throat. It was my fault that my parents were gone. Grief tore through me anew, sharp as the day I'd learned they'd been taken. I stood helplessly in the middle of the room. I was completely alone. I hadn't been able to help my parents any more than I could help Charlie. But the children might still be there waiting.

I walked numbly to the chair where Teddy's coat hung. I picked it up and unclipped his press pass, which bore a blurry nondescript photo of Teddy plus stamps in several languages. He had a ticket to get into France and he wouldn't even use it. A pass like this, if I had one, could get me into Europe. My anger grew, not so much toward Teddy but at a system that made me dependent on men like him, unable to help on my own. If only I could use his. I picked at the plastic which covered his photo with the nail of my index finger. But I could not get off the coating without tearing it and making obvious I'd tampered with it. I caught a glimpse of my reflection in the mirror above the fireplace. If my hair was lighter and shorter, or covered with a hat, I might be able to pass.

I stopped, taken aback by the audacity of my own idea. The pass clattered to the floor. I picked it up hurriedly, glancing at Teddy, who had slept through the noise. I'd come here to persuade Teddy, not betray him. But he would not help and this might be the orphans' last hope. I would not get all the way to France on this, of course—my passport and credentials would not match. But I could at least get into the staging area at Portsmouth and perhaps find someone who was going over and might be able to help. I could go tonight and be back before he even awoke in the morning. Hurriedly I rolled my hair up tightly and put the hat atop it. I could just about pass for a man. I went to his wardrobe and hurriedly dressed in his clothes. Then I took his hat and coat and slipped from the flat.

Twenty

I stepped out of a taxi onto a darkened country road near Portsmouth. "Here?" the driver asked in disbelief, after I asked him to stop a good half mile outside the naval base. "It's the middle of nowhere." That was the idea. I didn't want to attract attention by having him drive any closer. He eyed me warily, as though I might be a German spy, and I hoped he wouldn't call the Home Guard to report me. I paid him the fare up front, plus a tip in hopes of showing my goodwill, trying not to wince at the exorbitant total, nearly twenty pounds and a good chunk of my savings. There hadn't been a choice; buses didn't run at this hour and I didn't want to risk waiting and having Teddy wake and come after me. I'd lucked out finding the lone cab sitting with its lights dimmed at the third taxi stand I'd tried.

As the city had faded behind us and we'd bumped along the winding roads of rural Hampshire, I'd stared off into the darkness. My mind reeled from the truth about my parents' disappearance. I was to blame, just as surely as Liam had been for Robbie's death. Teddy hadn't told me what he'd learned, of course, to spare me the pain of knowing. But he hadn't told me about his other work either. So many lies.

I buttoned the top of Teddy's coat and drew his hat low over my eyes, then hurried along the road in the chilled night air. It dead-ended at a high fence topped with barbed wire, the naval base on the other side. Steeling myself, I started for the gate. It was hard to see how the invasion had been a surprise to anyone. Even at night, the naval station at Portsmouth was a hub of activity. Large battleships lined the harbor. Planes roared low overhead as though they might crash upon us at any second, leaving a heavy petrol scent in the air. Uniformed men scurried between trucks loading on pallets of supplies in the semidarkness.

At the pedestrian gate, I lifted my pass to show the military police officer, praying he would not ask to see it more closely. I held my breath as the guard scrutinized me. "Press staging is that way," he said finally, jerking his head to the right. "Down that road, turn at the corner. Second tent." I exhaled silently. "But better be quick about it." Before I could ask why, he had turned away. "Oy! You can't park your lorry there," he yelled to someone else. I hurried in the direction he'd indicated, past a soldier at an anti-aircraft gun who did not look at me, but kept eyes fixed on the muted sky above.

I neared the press tent, then paused. I'd grabbed Teddy's pass impulsively, and in the cab I'd tried to come up with some sort of plan. I could not, of course, go all the way to France and deliver the visas myself. If I could find someone, though, a reporter or medic perhaps, who was going across and then bribe him with what little money I had left after the taxi, perhaps I could persuade him to deliver the visas. But now, the problems with my already-flimsy plan became more apparent: How would I find the right person, someone good who would deliver the passes and not simply take the money, or have me kicked off the base because I did not belong there? I contemplated my next move.

I entered the tent. Inside, a dozen or so men sat around talking and playing cards. The air was thick with cigarette smoke and sweat. I pulled my hat and coat closer to avoid detection. "Just arrived?" a man asked. I nodded. I could not risk talking to anyone. "You're lucky. They've been promising to get us on a ship for two days. We might actually get out tonight."

Across the room I spied a lone female correspondent talking to an officer. Despite Teddy's denial, there were a few women among the press corps. I started in the other direction—I might be able to fool the men, but a woman would see through my disguise. She turned toward me. At the familiar profile, I gasped. "Claire!" I blurted, in spite of myself.

Her expression changed from panic to confusion and surprise. She was not wearing her auxiliary uniform, though, but rough pants and shirt made of camouflage. I sensed that she was doing some other kind of work; delivering medical supplies had just been a cover. Her expression turned angry and for a fleeting second I panicked that she herself might turn me in. She shook her head faintly, signaling I should not come over. Then she glanced to the right, subtly guiding me toward the exit.

I slipped from the tent. A minute later, Claire joined me. "Hello," I managed to say.

We eyed each other warily. For all of our friendship, this was war and secrets abounded between us. "What in bloody hell are you doing here?" she demanded.

I considered asking her the same thing, but didn't want to agitate her further. "I need to get the visas to the orphans."

"Does Teddy know?" Her eyes traveled to his pass which hung around my neck. "You're going to get yourself killed, not to mention ruin Teddy's career. You could even jeopardize operations." Did she know, I wondered, about the other work Teddy was doing through the paper?

I crossed my arms. "I was just—"

"Not thinking." Her tone was accusing.

"Trying to get someone to deliver the visas," I corrected.

"I could ring Teddy right now. Or have the pass revoked."

"Or you could help me."

"All correspondents," a military police officer was calling inside the tent. They were leaving and I hadn't even found someone to take the papers.

"But you won't. Because you know that I'm finally standing for something—just like you."

Something in her face softened. "Come on, then." She led me to the queue of correspondents that were shuffling forward. "There's a small group of journalists cleared to go. But their transit has been held up by fighting—until now."

"I thought it was impossible to cross."

"It was. But a few towns have been liberated, Caen, Cherbourg, and there's a small area of coast under Allied control. They've found space on a supply ship headed for LeHavre. It's still terribly dangerous. Come along. We must hurry if we are to get you on that boat."

"Claire, wait." I grabbed her arm. "I wasn't actually planning to go myself. I just wanted to find someone to take the visas."

"You are the only one that you can trust," she replied firmly. "I would do it for you, but I'm not going in that direction."

"But there's no way I can manage it," I said, hating the weakness in my own voice.

"It's probably impossible," she agreed. "And dangerous to boot."

But it was the children's only chance. "I have to try."

"Come on, then." At the front of the line, a military police guard was checking names against a list. Mine—or Teddy's rather—wouldn't be on it. I would be stopped. But Claire led me to the front of the line. "Don't say a word," she whispered. "This is Theodore White from the *Washington Post*," she told the guard.

"He's not on the list."

"Surely there's room. I'm Claire Churchill, by the way." She held up her pass.

The guard's eyes widened. "I do have one who got sick." Before the guard could speak further, Claire dragged me past him and onto the ship. Beyond the harbor was shrouded in darkness.

"Stay here," Claire instructed in a low voice as she pushed me into a corner. She started from the ship.

"Claire, wait." They were about to close the gate of the ship. Now was not the time. But I could not go with more secrets still between us. "About Lord Raddingley." At the mention of his name, her face lifted. "He's not what he seems to be. I'm sorry . . . There are others." A helicopter droning noisily overhead nearly swallowed my words.

For a moment, Claire looked as though I had struck her. "I know." Her voice was resigned, but with an unmistakable note of hurt.

"Then how can you possibly still want him?" Even if she loved him, strong principled Claire could not stand for that.

"The work," she said with a jerk of her head toward the spot where she'd stood speaking with the officer minutes earlier. "There was a leak and we had to see if . . . Well, I really can't say anything else." Her voice trailed off, the space between us growing once more. "Alastair wasn't the traitor. He's a bastard, but at least he's loyal to the Crown." She smiled sadly. I understood then that she was close to Lord Raddingley because she had to be. But it wasn't that black-and-white—she had feelings for him. Knowing about his betrayal and staying close to him anyway must have been so painful. "It wasn't like that in the beginning. I'm fond of him and I wished that had been under other circumstances." Her eyes held a mix of anger and sadness that belied her feelings for him. It was never that simple.

"I didn't want to hurt you, but I thought you should know."

The ship's horn blasted. Claire looked over her shoulder. "I wish I could go with you. When you dock, head south from Le Havre. There's a Carmelite convent about forty miles from the coast and they should be able to help you get the visas through." She squeezed my arm, unable to do more without attracting attention. "There's no special protection for correspondents, you know. Don't get yourself killed." Then she disappeared through the crowd.

A sailor herded us toward an enclosed, too-warm area at the stern of the ship. "Stay inside," he ordered. The ship jolted, pushing off from the dock and as the deck beneath my feet began to sway, the full magnitude of what I had just done began to set in. Even with Claire's instructions, I had little idea where I was going, how to get there—or back.

The supply ship lurched precipitously in the rough Channel surf. Around me correspondents sat on benches or on the floors propped up against walls. Some dozed, eyes half-closed, passing the hours still until we reached land. Those were the ones who had covered the war previously, approaching the danger with a certain resignation. Across from me, a young reporter checked his equipment as earnestly as if he were going into combat. I squeezed onto an empty space on a bench, tilted my head back. Despite the danger and my nerves, there was nothing to do but wait. The rocking of the boat took me back to my flight from Trieste. Mamma and Papa appeared in my mind, more real than they had been in years, so vivid I might reach out to touch them. The cable in Teddy's desk had confirmed what I'd long known: that my parents were gone. Even as a child, some part of me had always known that it would end badly. But I thought it was the danger of their work that put them in jeopardy. I never imagined it might be me.

A rumbling noise, louder than any we'd heard previously, jarred me from my half sleep. "This isn't right," someone murmured beside me. My nerves tingled. "The fighting must have shifted. Another cock-up." A barrage of machine-gun fire rattled too close, shaking the ship beneath us, like the air raids but quicker and more relentless. I rose to my tiptoes, trying without success to see out a small round window through the blackness on the other side.

"You're from the *Post*," a man asked, eyeing my pass. He took a swig from a flask, his breath giving off an astringent smell. Cringing, I nodded. I braced myself now for the man to ask questions or say that he knew Teddy and I was not him. "I don't know if they're going to get us across."

As if on cue, the boat lurched sharply to the left. Were we turning around? For a second I was relieved. I didn't belong here and I wanted to get back to the relative safety of England. But it was too late—and this was my only hope of helping the children.

But the ship straightened and carried on. The water grew unexpectedly rougher, churned not only by the surf but the fighting. We rolled left, then back again. A wave caught the boat then, sending us pitching to the right and I sat hurriedly, grabbing the bench so as not to fall, fighting my nausea.

The explosions and gunfire gradually slowed, a storm fading. When it had stopped altogether, I slipped from the cabin and onto the deck, looking around for a sailor who might stop me because it was too dangerous. I focused out at the horizon as I'd been taught as a girl, taking small breaths to calm my stomach. To the east, the sky was pink and smoky with unseen fighting. How had I gotten so far from home? Was this what it had looked like the night Charlie came over? My heart longed for him and I realized suddenly that he was not off fighting somewhere. He was dead. I forced down the bile that rose in my throat. I could not let sadness sweep me away now.

Instead, I tried to focus on formulating a plan. When we arrived, I would try to find the Order of Carmelites that Claire had told me about. I had not thought about what I would do afterward, though—or how I would get back.

The correspondent who had spoken to me inside was behind me again, having followed me from the cabin. Had I not been dressed as a man, I might have thought that he was interested in me. "After we dock, they're planning to shuttle us to

Cherbourg because of some unexpected fighting near Le Havre," he offered. My heart sank. Cherbourg was nearly forty miles east of where we were supposed to land. It would take days to get back by foot—if I could do it at all.

We were nearing the coast now. The other correspondents jostled forward onto the deck, slippery from the faint rain that had begun to fall. It was daylight now, and the murky water stretched to where it met muted gray sky. Teddy would be awake and he would have realized what I had done. On either side of us in the Channel large warships loomed like sentries, protecting the thin strip of water around the beaches that the Allies had liberated just weeks earlier.

A few minutes later the bottom of the boat scraped. There was no dock, just a small inlet by some rocks. Someone pushed me from the boat and water seeped into my boots and ankles. The sky lit up suddenly and the ground shook, sending us sprawling onto wet sand. Smoke and gunpowder filled my lungs. This was war, what my mother had fought so hard to save me from. I had gone halfway around the world only to find myself back in the thick of it.

I straightened, taking in the wide swath of sandy beach rising to German combat positions, now abandoned. This landing spot had weeks earlier been a battlefield. The bodies had thankfully been removed but equipment, broken weapons and abandoned packs were still strewn like driftwood across the beach. A smell, burning and something more, hung in the air. "Off quickly," a sailor ordered. "Stay together." There were open trucks waiting for us, but as the others boarded, I hesitated. Going with them would take me far away from where I needed to go. If I got on the truck, I would never reach the children.

Desperately, I scanned the beach. It was wide-open and there was no way for me to walk away without someone seeing. But there was a dune about fifteen feet away, no bigger than the one Robbie had fallen from when we were children. I started toward it.

"You!" the sailor called after me. I turned back. "Where do you think you're going?"

Still not wanting to speak I made a gesture indicating I needed to relieve myself, then pointed toward the dune. "Be quick about it," he said. I hurried over and ducked behind the dune. Should I wait until the truck pulled away? But the guard would surely remember I was there. Crouching low, I began to move away from the trucks, in the direction where the rumbling grew louder. Twenty feet ahead stood what had once been a building of some sort, flattened by shelling days earlier. Beyond lay a road, my only chance. I ran toward it as quickly as I could.

"Stop!" The sailor's voice came, louder and angry. But I was far from him now and close to the brush. I kept running, heedless in the direction of the trees. "You can't . . ."

There was a sudden explosion, deafening boom and white light. And then I knew no more.

Twenty-One

I was in the water, deep this time, head completely submerged. I struggled to reach the surface, but I could not break through. Above me I saw a shadowy figure. Charlie! I raised my arms, reaching for him. But when I looked up again he was gone. Instead there was a light, blindingly bright. I kicked my legs and tried to swim toward it.

I struggled to focus my eyes. In the blurriness, a shadow moved. "Charlie?" I called, more certain than I'd ever been in a dream that he was here.

I blinked and my vision cleared, revealing an unfamiliar white wall in front of me. I was in a narrow bed with crisp sheets. Out of the corner of my eye, something shifted and I turned, yelping as pain shot through my side. But it wasn't Charlie: Claire sat half-asleep in a chair beside the bed. I inhaled a metallic smell and I realized I was in a hospital of some sort. I raised my hand to find my cheek swathed in bandages. An intravenous line ran to my wrist.

"Thank goodness you're awake," Claire said, sitting up, relieved. "I'll ring for the doctor."

"Wait." My throat was dry and scratchy. I gestured toward the pitcher on the table beside me and she poured me a glass of water, then helped me take a sip. "What happened? Where am I?"

"You're in hospital in Surrey. You set off an unexploded ordnance on the beach in Cherbourg when you tried to go your own way." The images rushed back to me of sneaking away from the boat, hearing the sailor yell. "You're lucky to be alive," Claire added.

There was that word again. My stomach sank as I remembered the explosion just before I was knocked out. I looked around the hospital room frantically for my bag. "Where are the visas?"

"Gone, I'm afraid. Your clothes, or Teddy's rather, were ripped right from you by the blast." Panic rose in me. The visas could not be gone. I would get to Lord Raddingley, beg or threaten him if I had to, in order to have them reissued. I started to sit up, but pain sliced through me. I lay back down weakly. "Where's Teddy?"

"Just getting coffee. He hasn't left the hospital since you were admitted."

A mustached man in a white coat appeared in the doorway. "Miss Montforte, I'm Dr. Talley." Without speaking further, he began to examine me, shining a light in my eyes. Then he gestured to my gown. "May I?" I nodded, cringing as he cold, unfamiliar hands pressed against my midsection. "We removed a piece of metal from the exploded ordinance in your side." So that explained the pain. "It didn't hit anything vital, but we are worried about infection. It will heal, and the rest are just scratches." He picked up the chart that hung from the foot of the bed and made some notes.

"How is she?" Teddy's familiar voice, heavy with concern, called out as he strode through the door. Then, seeing me awake, he stopped. Relief broke across his face. "You're awake!" He rushed to me and touched my cheek, not bothering to mask his affection.

It occurred to me that I did not know how much time had passed. "What day is it?"

"Friday," he said. Four days since I'd set out for Portsmouth. His forehead creased. "Do you remember what happened?"

"For the most part." I swallowed.

"She'll be fine," the doctor said. "We'll want to monitor the wound for infection and she'll have to get back on her feet slowly. Plenty of rest and she can go home in about a week." He walked from the room, leaving just Teddy, Claire and me.

An awkward silence passed between the three of us. "I'm going to freshen up," Claire said, slipping from the room.

I cleared a spot on the edge of the bed for Teddy to sit. But he walked to the window, and when he turned back, the relief in his eyes had been replaced by anger. "You betrayed me," he said. "Stole my pass, my clothes. My credentials have been suspended because of you. You've threatened my reputation as a journalist."

"I'm so sorry," I said, meaning it. But some part of me remained unrepentant. Tricking him had been wrong—but even as I apologized, I knew that I would do it all over again in a heartbeat if it would help the children.

I had to ask about the clippings I'd seen. "Teddy, the newspaper stories in your drawer." Surprise and panic crossed his face as he realized I had seen them. "What's it all about?"

"You haven't told anyone, have you?"

"No, of course not. But I had no idea."

He walked to the door and closed it, then returned to me. "I'm doing some work with the Polish resistance. Even before Tomaszewicz came over I was helping where I could, carrying messages and such." I thought back to his mysterious trips, supposedly chasing stories. "Then after you met Tomaszewicz, I went back to see him and he put me in touch with some of the key partisan factions. I send their information back to Washington for them. I'm sorry I didn't tell you sooner. I didn't want to put you in danger. You understand now why I couldn't jeopardize that to help the children."

"Completely." But my mind whirled as I tried

to process everything he had told me. "I'm sorry if I risked things."

"There's no way you could have known. I'll fix it." I looked up, more in awe than ever of him. "But no more secrets between us, okay?" I nodded. I should tell him also that I had seen the truth about my parents in his file. But I was too weary to talk about it now. He dropped to the bed beside me and touched my cheek. "I'm just so bloody relieved you're okay." He took me in his arms, forgiving me in an instant.

I looked down at the white of my hospital gown. "But I failed."

"Not at all. It worked."

"What do you mean? I couldn't get to the children."

"No, but your going raised the alert for the Red Cross. They've pressured the Germans and have moved in to take control of the children." I was flooded with relief. They still were not safe, but they were closer now. "They'll be brought to London. Claire spoke to Lord Raddingley and he has agreed to have the visas reissued." I could not imagine what that conversation had been like. Had the charade between them persisted?

I lay back, exhausted but relieved. The children, including Leo's sister, I prayed, would be safe. Then my spirits sank. It was a drop really in an ocean of despair, compared to the thousands I could not save. But it was something.

Teddy ran his hand across my forehead, brushing the hair away from the bandage beneath. I winced. "Does it hurt?"

"No, but I must look a sight."

"You look perfect." He leaned closer, eyes aglow, and I wondered if he might kiss me.

But just then Claire came back into the room. "It's all arranged."

"What is?"

"We're having you discharged from this dreadful hospital and you'll come and convalesce at our house in Brighton. We can't keep you here in this germy hospital. The food is awful and you're just as likely to catch something."

"The doctor agreed?" Teddy asked.

"He wasn't keen at first but I promised him full-time nursing. So it's settled. You're coming with me."

I walked into the guesthouse and sank wearily into the seat by the window. I'd been here for almost three weeks. At first, Claire had not allowed me to do anything but stay in bed. But then she'd been called off for assignment, leaving me with the nurse, whom I persuaded to help me walk, first around the gardens and later the fog-bathed apple orchards.

By the time Claire had returned three days later, I was up and about and it was too late for her to stop me. "Fine, but don't go walking on the beach. It's mined and you've already been through that once." I shuddered.

So I walked along the edge of the estate that faced away from the coast, going a bit farther each day, watching lambs play in the rolling green fields that showed no signs of war. Today I'd overdone it a bit in the warm August air. Breathing heavily, I poured a glass of water, willing the pain in my side to ease. The nurse had left my dinner, soup and thick brown bread on a tray and I ate, more hungry than I had been in some time. The guesthouse was a lovely cottage with a bedroom and kitchenette and bright yellow curtains. Claire had some of my things sent down from London and buying everything else I lacked. Outside, a summer breeze blew the scent of cut grass upward through the open window. But the bucolic air seemed like a taunt. I needed to be back in London, working at the paper, not sitting here uselessly. I would ask Teddy again to take me back with him.

My eyes drifted gratefully to the basket of fresh fruit on the table. Teddy had brought it a few days earlier, having scoured at least three markets to find the bounty of oranges and apples that had begun to trickle back into the city. "I've got to get back," he said reluctantly after helping Claire to bring me here. I nodded—there were stories that would not wait to be written. He had come every weekend since then to bring me food and share stories from the office. "Midge has been filling in for you," he had told me on the previous visit. "Her typing is good enough, but she's not much for conversation." I'd smiled, imagining Teddy trying to make conversation with the dour older woman.

After I finished eating, I washed and changed into my nightgown, then slipped into the freshly made bed. The cottage sat on a bluff high above the sea and through the open window I could smell the water. I stared out at the horizon. Light flickered over the continent, though whether it was fighting or a storm, I could not tell. My eyes grew heavy.

A knock at the door pulled me from my thoughts. "Coming!" Claire was away on a mission. I imagined for a second that it might be Charlie, magically reappeared. More likely the nurse, who usually came to check me once before bedtime and make sure I had not over-exerted myself, per Claire's orders.

"Addie? It's me." Teddy's voice came through the door, and the vision of Charlie evaporated.

"One minute." A bit of disappointment mixed with surprise as I put on my dressing gown, then opened the door. Teddy stood on the doorstep, perspiring faintly in the thick summer air. His tweedy travel coat and hat were covered in dust and cinders. "Teddy, what on earth? How did you get here?"

"I drove," he said simply.

Through the rain and the night and the blackout. I shivered, imagining him navigating the blind curves around high hedges in the darkness. To reach me. "But the curfew."

"I've broken worse." He smiled roguishly. "May I come in?"

I saw then how very much he cared for me, the depth of his affection. I had not misled him or promised him anything, but he came faithfully, still holding out hope. "Also, I wanted to bring you this." He held out an envelope. I took it and opened it hurriedly. Inside was a piece of yellowed typed paper bearing the Western Union heading. A telegram—from America. Aunt Bess had written a few times since I'd been here, brief descriptions of life in the neighborhood back home that seemed not to have changed at all. But this was clearly something different.

"You didn't have to come all of this way," I said as I unfolded it. He shrugged. He might have sent it by post or even courier. But he had wanted to come himself. "Thank you," I said, touched. "And as soon as I read this, I want to hear all about the story . . ." I stopped midsentence as I read: "Your uncle has suffered a heart attack and the prognosis is not good."

"Oh, no." Though she was too proud to ask, it was Aunt Bess's way of saying that she needed me. Calling me home.

Sadness washed over me then as I pictured my uncle in his horn-rimmed glasses and plaid vest that last day as he saw me off at the bus station. We had not been so very close, but he was Papa's brother, the closest link I had to my parents. And he had been good to me. I reached under the bed for my suitcase, which Teddy had brought from London when I first came from hospital. "I'll need a leave from the paper." Then I stopped again, looking around and picturing my flat back in London. For all of its messiness, I had created a life in England and I wasn't sure I was ready to leave. But after all that Aunt Bess had done for me, I had to go, at least for a few weeks.

Teddy stepped close and took my hand. "You're not well enough yet to travel to America."

"I don't have a choice."

"I'll go with you. I've always wanted to see the States," he half joked. "But we can't possibly go at this hour," he added before I could protest. "We'll leave at first light."

He was right, of course. I let him lead me to the couch. But I pictured Aunt Bess, thousands of miles away and all alone. Uncle Meyer was all that she had in this world. Looking up into Teddy's devoted eyes, I was suddenly grateful that he was here. I kissed him on the cheek. He hesitated for a minute, surprised, then wrapped his arms around me.

There was another knock at the door. Not waiting for an answer, Claire rushed in as Teddy and I broke apart. "So many visitors in one night," she said, taking us in. She looked down at my open suitcase. "What on earth?"

"I have to leave. My uncle is seriously ill. Teddy just brought the news."

"I'm going with her," Teddy said, as though it was already settled.

I started to protest, then decided against it. Instead, I turned toward Claire. "I know you'll say I'm not well enough to travel." She was staring at me oddly. "What are you doing here anyway?" In all of the commotion about Uncle Meyer, I'd nearly forgotten that Claire was supposed be off serving somewhere. No, she was not staring at me, but past me at Teddy so sadly, as if asking for his forgiveness. "Tell me," I demanded.

"It's Charlie." My stomach dropped as I waited for further confirmation that he had died, or worse yet, details about how. I thought after the last time that my heart could never break again, that nothing could ever hurt like that because the pieces would never heal. But the scream rose up from deep within me, ready to be let free.

She didn't say anything more until she reached my side. "They found him. Addie, Charlie is alive."

Twenty-two

The car Claire had arranged raced in the darkness along a winding country road flanked by high hedges. "Brought into a field hospital in Dover," Claire had explained back at the cottage, though I was scarcely able to hear her. "Apparently he's been there for weeks." So he had been close by all this time. How had I not known? And why hadn't he sent for me?

I sat now beside her in silence, my plan to rush home to America to be with Aunt Bess slipped by the wayside. Teddy sat in the front seat beside the driver, staring straight ahead and not speaking. It could be a mistake. Another soldier, not Charlie. For so long I'd conditioned myself to the pain, I was immune, it now seemed, from hope. I grimaced at my reflection, pale and disheveled, in the car window. I should have made myself look better for Charlie. But I could not wait any longer to see him, to start the life we had wanted for so long. He would still want me, of course, as he had the day he shipped out. Or would he? After all, he had left London thinking I'd stood him up at the chapel. Maybe that was why he had not let me know he was safe. How I regretted all the times I had pushed him away for reasons that seemed so important—reasons I could not even remember now. Whatever time we might have was fleeting. I would be his and we would run with this.

"How did you find him?" Teddy asked.

"I heard a story on base about a pilot who had crashed in Germany, just over the Swiss border. He was able to make it across on foot, despite a slight leg fracture. Quite remarkable, really."

"Are you sure it's really him? It could be another pilot." There was an unmistakable note of hope in Teddy's voice.

"I put two and two together and checked. It is definitely him."

We soon reached a military base reminiscent of Portsmouth with the same barbed wire-capped fence and sense of non-stop activity. At the gate, the car stopped and driver rolled down the window. Claire reached over to show her pass. We drove on past large tents and makeshift barracks, stopping in front of a two-story redbrick building with hospital markings. I started out of the car, but she stopped me, placing a hand on my shoulder. "Addie, wait. There's something you should know. Charlie took a terrible blow to the head and he has trouble remembering." So that was why he had not sent for me the second he returned. It seemed inconceivable, though, that he would not know me at all. "You must prepare yourself."

"It won't matter," I insisted. Once he saw

me, everything would be fine. I was sure of it.

Claire led me and Teddy into the hospital and we followed her in the direction an orderly pointed in response to her query about Charlie. There was just one door at the end of the hall. I pushed past Claire, running now. My footsteps pounded against the tile, echoing against the walls.

Not pausing, I burst through the door. At the sight of Charlie lying in bed, my heart stopped. It was really him. His face was marred with cuts and bruises that had begun to heal in the weeks since he crashed. But underneath his eyes were clear, his face the same one that I had known for so long and loved with every breath—and that I had thought I would never see again. He was pale and shaken but still whole. Alive. Even here in this darkest of places, stripped of all glory, he was magnificent, all I ever wanted. My heart soared.

"Charlie?" I took a step toward him, arms outstretched. But his face was blank. A pain shot through me sharper than the night I thought him dead, or the night we lost Robbie, worse than anything I'd ever felt. Charlie did not know me. His eyes were cloudy and he blinked as though just waking up.

I licked my lips, and tried again. "It's me, Addie." He did not respond, but smiled as one might to a stranger, his expression vague and pleasant. My heart sank. "We know each other from back home in America. We're neighbors at the shore and we went to the same high school and then when we met in London . . ." I faltered. It was so strange to be telling him the history between us, to have to remind him of what we once had.

I reached for his hand. "Charlie, please." Something inside him seemed to shift slightly. His eyes flickered, great thunderclouds rolling over him as he struggled to remember who he was and all that had happened. But he gulped for air, swallowed. "Addie?"

Joy rose within me. "It's me."

"You're real." He leaned his head back, overwhelmed by the strain. "All this time I thought I dreamed you." His hand pulled from mine.

"I'm really here." I fought the urge to throw myself into Charlie's arms, lest I injure him. Instead I put my hand on his chest, feeling as it rose and fell. He winced and I pulled back. Was he in pain? "Charlie, thank goodness you're all right. They said you were missing and presumed dead." Outside the door to his hospital room, I saw Claire and Teddy watching us.

"They thought that because my plane crashed and I wasn't found." A look of terror came over his face as he remembered for the first time, reliving what had happened. "But I was able to make it away from the crash site and over the border. It was all part of the plan, Addie."

"Plan? You mean you crashed on purpose?'

"Sort of. Another plane was dropping special operations troops at a site in Slovakia to rendezvous with the partisans. I was supposed to set it down hard to distract the Germans from where they had gone and then flee on foot. But I landed a bit harder than expected—crashed, really—and I was off target."

"That was a suicide mission." Perhaps because he felt he no longer had that much to lose.

"It worked."

"That was a very brave thing you did. Brave and stupid."

"I could say the same about you." He was talking, of course, about my foray across the Channel to help the orphans. But how could he possibly know? He held up a newspaper by his bedside. I took it from him, surprised to see my own image staring back. It was a story Teddy had run in the *Post* about my work with the orphans, my efforts to help them. I hadn't wanted him to write it, but he said raising awareness would help more children just like them. The *Times* must have picked it up on the wire. "I didn't realize at the time that it was you." His eyes filled with admiration, then clouded again. "You could have been killed."

"Yes, well, we're both fine now." I held my hand out to him, willing him to take it. But he did not. It was as if there was an invisible wall between us. Something flickered across his face. Why was he hesitating? Behind me came a shuffling sound. I turned to see a nurse standing behind me, tall and thin with pale blond hair wisping out from beneath a white cap, coming in to fix his blankets. I stepped back, the delay in our reunion unbearable as she tended to him. I expected the nurse to leave, but when she was finished, she lingered, fingers resting lightly on Charlie's shoulder. I exhaled silently, waiting for her to do something else to examine or help him, something to justify her presence—and that touch.

"He hit his head badly when the plane crashed," the nurse explained. "His memory loss was severe, but it's been coming back a bit at a time."

Charlie looked up at the nurse. "I remember a lot more now."

"How wonderful." Her voice was flat. I waited for her to run to fetch a doctor and share the news. But she remained planted at Charlie's side.

"They airlifted me here. I couldn't remember anything, but Grace nursed me back to health." The way he said the nurse's name made my heart twinge. He looked up at her and grimaced at the pain the movement caused.

Grace. The name ricocheted around my head as she hurried to adjust his pillows. "Is that better, darling?" she asked, the last word exploding in my ears. *Darling.* I knew then why he had pulled back from my touch.

"Yes, thank you. Addie is an old friend from home," he said. I cringed at the description, so reminiscent of the time at Southern when he'd described me as being like family. How had we gotten back there? Perhaps part of his memory was still missing and he did not remember all that we had been to one another. "Addie, I'd like you to meet Grace." He reached up and took her hand.

My ears rang. So they were together. It must have been some kind of passing infatuation while she nursed him back to health while his memory was gone—something that could be easily undone now that I had found him.

"Lovely to meet you," Grace said. Her English accent was posh, bespeaking years of governesses and boarding school. I could not answer over the dryness in my throat. "I haven't had the chance to meet any of Charlie's friends since he proposed."

My heart stopped. "You're engaged?"

Grace smiled. "Only just." My mind whirled. Charlie was mine, just months ago, before he left London. What happened to forever?

Of course he had not known that. He had lost his memory and been caught in a fog where the past and all we had shared together did not exist. But he remembered now, didn't he? I waited for him to tell her that it had all been a terrible mistake.

Silence filled the room. "I'll give the two of you a few minutes to catch up," Grace said, patting his shoulder before walking from the room.

Charlie stared at me uneasily. He understood all that had been between us, and he knew what this meant to me. "I should be going," I said. But my legs were leaden.

"When I crashed, I lost my memory. Grace cared for me and, well, she's a good woman." It would be too easy to dismiss Grace as the one who had been there by his side when it all happened, a product of timing. But the way he looked at her told me it was something more.

I was angry at him suddenly, not just for Grace, but all of it. "So was this some kind of a payback?"

"No, it was nothing like that. Addie, you didn't show up at the chapel. What was I to think?"

"I was caught on the underground on a stuck train. When I got there you were gone." Great waves of regret rose up, crashing down upon me. "So that's it, then." He did not answer. We'd had a second chance and thrown it away. There would not, it seemed, be a third. I saw it then, the life we might have had together. It was so real that if I reached out I might have touched it. But it would never be, like a land too far to reach, or a place we had missed along the way.

Charlie reached into the drawer of the nightstand beside his hospital bed. He pulled something out and extended his hand to me. The mizpah. I had nearly forgotten. Somehow through everything, he had managed to hold on to it. "You keep it," I said. He shook his head. It wasn't his to have anymore. In that one gesture I knew that he was setting me free and that it was over between us forever. I took it and started for the door.

"Wait, don't go."

"What? You don't want me for yours anymore but you don't want to let me leave. You can't have it both ways." He bit his lip, unable to disagree.

He turned away, his face haggard and inconsolable. He would leave Grace if I asked him to. If I reached out and took Charlie's hand, he would be mine again. In fact, there was a desperate, pleading look in his eyes that said that was exactly what he wanted me to do. It could all be mine, and the old Addie who had wanted nothing but him would have taken it. I wasn't that girl anymore, though, and it would make him somehow less the man that I loved. From the doorway, I caught a glimpse of Grace, holding her breath, her eyes pained and fearful.

I stepped back from Charlie, an inch and a lifetime, an ocean rising and filling between us.

Teddy came into the room. I looked over my shoulder, hoping that Claire would come in and not leave me alone with the two men. But she had disappeared from the corridor. "Good to see that you're all right," Teddy said, walking to Charlie and shaking his hand. I imagined what a blow it must have been for him, hearing the news that Charlie was alive and knowing it could not help but destroy any chance that something might develop between us. Teddy smiled, but beneath the mask, he was crumbling, certain that with Charlie now back, he had lost me. Then he turned to me. "Adelia, I've checked and there is a liner that sails from Plymouth tomorrow."

"A ship?" Charlie asked.

"Yes, my uncle's taken ill and I have to get back to Philadelphia." Charlie's face fell. He did not want me to leave.

Then something behind his eyes shifted and his shoulders went slack. "He's a good man, Addie," he whispered, nodding toward Teddy, who stood close to the door, as if I needed his permission. Letting me go. "Safe travels. And give my love to everyone at home," he added, as though nothing had changed and his family might still be there waiting.

"Goodbye, Charlie," I said. I kissed his cheek, savoring the smell of his skin for the last time.

"I've arranged for the car to take us back to Claire's to get my car and then we can go to London for our things. Are you ready to go?" There was a note of ownership in Teddy's voice as some part of him still hoped I might be his. I felt that pull again, being tugged between the two men and I knew if it went on any longer I would be ripped to bits until there was simply nothing left of me.

Frustration exploded in me then. I was caught between them, when the truth was I didn't want—or need—to belong to anyone.

Teddy and I started from the room. As we reached the hospital lobby, I stopped. "Teddy, wait. About this trip—"

"You want to do this alone," he said.

"Yes." I glimpsed Claire watching us from across the parking lot.

"Marry me, Ad," Teddy said, and as he looked up at me, his eyes were bright and hopeful as a child on Christmas morning. He stood before me, palms raised plaintively. I saw then the life that could be mine. A normal life. Not boring—Teddy would undoubtedly keep traveling and getting into the scrapes chasing stories for which he was known and I could go along with him. Or we might have a family. He would love me unconditionally. Why couldn't I take that and run with it?

I opened my mouth to tell him yes. The life he offered appeared once again, gleaming like a shiny jewel. But something stopped me, seeming to hold me back, the dream just beyond reach.

"Teddy . . ."

"You're not coming back, are you?"

"I'm not sure," I said, realizing even as I spoke that I was not.

"I've known for some time I couldn't win," he admitted.

I tried to ignore the feeling of being a prize at a fair. "Since when?"

"When you were in the hospital. You were calling out in your sleep," he said, and I could tell by the skip in his voice that it wasn't his name I had been calling.

But that had been weeks ago. Even after, he had played along and said nothing, just happy to have my company. For everything that I had done, he still loved me and wanted me to be his. Remorse filled me then. He deserved so much better than this. He deserved someone who could love him wholly.

But I could not hide in his affections either. It was time for me to know myself instead. I reached out and Teddy's eyes lifted with hope in a way that broke my heart. I bypassed his lips and kissed him firmly on the cheek. Then I stepped sideways, moving away from him and Charlie both.

"I'm sorry." And I walked from the hospital by myself, knowing it was time, finally, to go home.

PART THREE

Twenty-three

Atlantic City
August 1944

I sit at the top of the street, gazing out at the row of shore houses, still lost in memories. What am I doing back here? I should be in London, working at the paper and starting a life with Teddy. I start the engine and turn the wheel, headed back. But something steadies me. *You made the right choice,* a voice too calm and sure to be my own seems to say. I start forward.

It has been more than a week since I'd walked from the hospital in England. I had not gone alone: Claire had followed me as the guard hailed a taxi for me just outside the base. "So you're leaving?" I cringed, waiting for her to rebuke me for throwing away Teddy's love so callously and running again. But she had smiled. "I'm proud of you, lass. You're standing on your own two feet now. I don't know what you're looking for. But I hope you find it."

I'd left Claire with kisses and gratitude and promises to write, and made my way north over her insistence that I could not possibly go alone. I stopped at my flat to pack a bag, but there had not been time to visit the orphanage. As my train pulled from Waterloo Station, I looked in the direction of Theed Street. Leo's sister and the others should be arriving anytime now and I wouldn't be here to see them, or his joy at their reunion. I'd done what I could. I sent up a prayer for them and imagined it blowing north with the wind.

During those long days as we crossed the Atlantic, Charlie's face kept appearing in my mind. Though I had chosen to leave, I could not help but be angry at him. He had professed to love me, but he had fallen in with Grace so easily. And not just a fling—he had asked her to marry him.

It was late when we docked in New York, the Statue of Liberty shrouded in fog. I cleared Immigration easily this time with a wave of my US passport, so different than my arrival as a girl. I made my way into the city and found a room. The next morning I caught the first bus from the Port Authority to Philadelphia. I approached Porter Street in the still of pre-dawn and found the slanted row houses unchanged. I let myself into the house. Perhaps Aunt Bess was at the hospital. I dreaded the notion of going there and reliving that most awful of nights when we lost Robbie. But I found Aunt Bess in the living room. She sat on a low chair, wearing a dark dress. The clocks and mirrors were covered with black cloth.

"Oh, honey," Aunt Bess cried, standing up. I

was too late. Uncle Meyer had died before my aunt's telegram ever reached me. The neighbors who had come for shivah had departed, leaving now-dried-out kugel and desserts in good dishes they would collect later.

"I'm so sorry," I said, putting my arms around her. "I wish I could have gotten back from London in time." My voice was suffused with guilt.

"That's all right. It wouldn't have changed anything." Aunt Bess's face was pale and drawn, eyes ringed from days without sleep. She looked older and fragile. I had never before stopped to think about my aunt and uncle's relationship. But in her grief, I saw the richness of their marriage that had played out alongside me while I had been oblivious, caught up in my own life. I remembered Uncle Meyer as he followed me to the bus stop the day I left. How I wished I might have the chance to thank him once more for the camera and letting me go.

It was too late for my relationship with him, but not for Aunt Bess, who suddenly looked so small. "I love you." I put my arms around her. "We're the only family we've got."

I helped Aunt Bess clean up the shivah dishes and persuaded her to rest while I returned the special low chair she'd sat in during the eight days of mourning to the shul. When I was done, I found myself walking the old familiar path to Pennsport, winding past the kosher deli and across the trolley tracks. The neighborhood was the same, only with new products in the old shop windows, advertisements touting cigarettes and new appliances instead of war bonds. Closer to the Irish neighborhood there were more cars, some sleeker models I did not recognize.

I pushed on, assaulted by the old smells of onions cooking in houses and too-warm garbage rising from the curb. Walking the familiar streets, I felt renewed. Whole, in a way I hadn't for years or maybe ever. But as I reached the Connallys' block, I stopped. Ghosts of the boys were everywhere, playing stickball in the street, sitting on the porch. Robbie might come bounding down the stairs as he always had, not sullen and sleepy like his brothers, but bright-eyed and hungry for breakfast and the day that lay beyond.

I had expected the Connally house to be boarded and shuttered. The porch was freshly swept, though, and fresh flowers were in the windows. My heart skipped a beat. Had the Connallys returned? I walked to the door, nearly opening it as I once might have before I caught myself. I knocked. A large, unfamiliar woman appeared in the doorway. "Yes?"

I stepped back. "I'm looking for the Connallys." I prayed silently that the woman was a maid or some relative I had never met.

But the woman shook her head. "People who

used to live here? We bought this through a broker. Owners were long gone and I can't say where."

I walked away deflated, the windows seeming to stare after me. I could not bear to look back at the house that now belonged to someone else. "They're gone," I said aloud, needing to hear the words to believe them. They had left long ago. But seeing it made it hurt more and the realness of it all seeped through me, as though I was losing them all over again.

"I tried to go to the Connallys' house," I confessed to Aunt Bess later that morning as I helped her finish cleaning up. The *Breakfast Club* program played low from the radio on the table. "It isn't theirs anymore."

She nodded, as though she already knew. "About that—Addie, there's something I have to tell you."

I raised my hand. "If it's about Charlie, I already know."

"Not Charlie, but Liam."

But my head swam, the idea of more memories too painful. "I don't want to hear it."

"Another time, perhaps." She raised her hands, retreating. "There's something else. I want to sell the house." I looked around in disbelief. Though I'd run so far, I had always taken for granted my aunt and uncle's home and the fact that it would be there. "The stairs have become difficult and without Meyer, I just can't bear to stay." She trailed off, her eyes wet.

"Where will you go?"

"They've built some senior apartments in the Northeast. My friend Trudy moved there." She was watching me, asking permission.

"Of course I'll help you. What do you need me to do?"

"I can manage the house here, straightening things to put it up for sale. But I left so much at the shore."

I tensed up at the word. "I thought you didn't go down this summer."

"We didn't. We had planned to but then Meyer started feeling poorly." I had thought his illness was sudden. Why hadn't she written to me sooner? She continued. "But we already paid, so the owner let us keep the rooms and the shed, too. Our things there need to be retrieved. I couldn't manage it myself."

Nor could I, I thought. The emptiness here was nearly unbearable—how could I stare at the memory of what had been right next door at the beach? But looking at my aunt's face, which had been hollowed out by grief, and her pleading eyes, I could not refuse. "I'll do it." I regretted the words the moment I spoke them.

"I don't need everything. You can give away the beach things. I just want the photos—and anything that was your uncle's."

"Okay."

"Take the car."

I hesitated. Uncle Meyer had taken me driving a few times during my senior year of high school in the abandoned lots down by the shipyard, but I did not have a license. It would be quicker than the train, though, and I could leave whenever I wanted.

The weatherman came on the radio then and we grew instinctively quiet, as though Uncle Meyer might be here to shush us so he could hear the forecast. We both chuckled. Then Aunt Bess's face grew somber. "What is it?" I asked.

"I know you have your own life and you'll be going back to London. But, well, I miss you."

"I'll be back," I promised, meaning it. I thought back to the letters I never received from Charlie that would have changed everything. And I wanted to ask if it was her who had kept them from me, and if so, why? But she had done what she thought was best and reopening the past would not change things now. I exhaled, letting go of the anger, and started for the car.

So I had come, driving the route to the shore that had always meant such happiness. I stopped at a five-and-dime on the way to get a couple of changes of clothes and at a gas station in Egg Harbor, grateful that the car, which Uncle Meyer used as a traveling salesman, had an A-sticker, which exempted it from much of the gas rationing.

405

Pushing down the waves that loom dark in my mind, I focus once more on the narrow strip of Sunset Avenue in front of me, the last few steps of this journey the hardest. I park in front of the house where we once rented rooms and step out of the car into the bright sunlight. Beside it, the Connally place looks as though it has been frozen in time. It has a fresh coat of blue paint the exact shade it had always been. Even the porch swing still hangs at the same angle.

I stand motionless. If I do not move then Robbie might come running out the door at any moment, zeppelin in hand zooming high above his head.

I exhale. Everything is not the same. There has been work done at the house: a pile of cut boards by the steps, the smell of wet paint. Another new family, undoubtedly, has bought the shore house like the one back in Philly, people who have no idea what the property meant, the things that had taken place there.

Forcing myself to look straight ahead, I walk to the boardinghouse where we had rented rooms. I take the key that Aunt Bess had given me and open the door to the storage shed. My nose is instantly filled with the camphor smell of mothballs. I pull a damp box from the shed and brush a cobweb from it. Then I stop uncertainly. Aunt Bess had not asked me to sort the boxes, just to bring them home. I can just put them right in the car. But perhaps I can get rid of some of the things she does not need. I am curious, too, about what's left behind after all of this time.

I lug one of the boxes to our rooms upstairs. My eyes travel through the screened window, down to the patch of grass between the houses where the boys once played. Swallowing over the lump in my throat, I force myself to look away. The smell of musty cardboard rises as I open the box. There is a framed photograph of Aunt Bess and Uncle Meyer standing in front of a car, an older model than the one I drove down here, dressed for some sort of excursion. They are smiling in a way I had never seen and even though he was wearing a hat, I can see that my uncle had a full head of hair. Younger people, with their own hopes and dreams.

I cough to clear the dust from my throat, then continue sorting. They are mostly vacation things, like the old woven blanket Aunt Bess used for the beach, the now-cracked bucket and shovel she had gotten me with the best of intentions, not realizing I was too old for such things.

Sometime later, I look up. Outside the sun has dipped low behind the houses along the bay. There are no lamps here and soon it will be impossible to see what I am doing. It is later than I thought and I should head back before dark. But I have only made it through one box and there are still four more to go. Some part of me, too, is not ready to leave yet. I could stay the night and finish up in the morning. Why not? I pull a musty blanket from one of the boxes and curl up on the empty bed on the sunporch. Through the open screen I can almost hear the boys' voices, mixed in with the crashing of the surf. The salt air fills my lungs like a lullaby and despite my closeness to the sea, I do not dream at all.

I awaken early, bright sunlight shining through curtainless windows. My body is stiff from sleeping on the thin mattress in a way it hadn't been a few years earlier. I lie motionless, assaulted by the familiar brackish smell, rolling back through the years. I am caught up in a cyclone of memories, taking me back to places I don't want to go. I sit up. I need to finish the boxes and go. There is noise below, different than the cars on the street, a low, repetitive swishing. Someone must be working on the Connally house next door. My heart aches as I think of the changes they are making, heedless of all that came before. I sit up and crane my neck out the window, but can see nothing. My soul cries out for coffee. I put on my shoes and make my way down to the street.

I start in the direction of the coffee shop at the corner of Winchester Avenue. The counter looks unchanged and I half expect to see the boys at the counter, ordering milk shakes. I buy coffee, then go to the phone booth in the back, put in some coins and dial.

"Addie, thank goodness." Aunt Bess's voice floods the line with relief.

"I'm sorry I worried you. I got caught up sorting and decided to stay. I should finish up later today."

We talk for a few more minutes before ringing off. I finish my coffee, then start back toward the house. As I near the Connally house, the swishing sound comes again and curious, I stop and turn back.

I follow the noises, rounding the corner to the back of the house next door. A tall, thin man stands upon a ladder, his back turned, moving boards. His wide shoulders and narrow hips are familiar. Charlie. My heart lifts. But of course this time, it cannot be; he is in England recuperating. With Grace. Pushing down the hurt, I take a step forward. Closer now I can see that the man's hair is a darker shade, his build thinner.

There, repairing the house, is Liam.

Twenty-four

I take a deep breath, finding my voice. "What's a nice boy like you doing in a place like this?"

Liam freezes, but does not turn. "I heard this is where all of the cool kids hang out," he replies slowly. He spins, his expression disbelieving. He jumps off the ladder and starts toward me.

"Liam!" I yelp, running forward. Surprise and

then delight flood his face as I fling myself at him. He catches me in his arms, warm and tight, and I draw close to him like a dry plant to water. I rest my head on his chest and he cradles it, fingers entwined in my hair.

"It's really you." He lifts me off my feet and spins me around.

Once I would have protested for him to stop. But now I just allow myself to melt in his arms. A moment later, he sets me down. I step back and an awkwardness crystalizes between us. He is leaner now, jawline carved in a way I hadn't quite remembered. But his eyes are unmistakably the same.

"I was looking for coffee," I blurt abruptly, mindful that I am still wearing yesterday's clothes. Suddenly I am sixteen again and sounding stupid. "You're here. That is, I didn't know."

"I drove back down this morning. Had to get more supplies from the city."

"I wasn't planning to stay," I confess. I might have picked up the boxes and gone last night. If I had, we would have missed each other completely. But something had kept me here.

"Your aunt isn't renting next door," he observes.

"My uncle died."

"Oh, I'm sorry." But his voice is level, the neutral response of one who has known deep suffering and almost grown immune.

"I just came to pack up some things for my aunt."

"Well, I've got coffee. Come on in and see what I'm doing."

I hesitate, starting to tell him that I've already had some. Though I had gone by the Connallys' house in Philadelphia hoping someone might have returned, I find myself now not wanting to step inside, to cross the threshold of a door I had closed forever. But he looks so hopeful, I cannot refuse.

Inside the house is a wreck in a way that would have driven Mrs. Connally mad. The furniture that remains has been pushed to one side and covered with a tarp. Thick smells of paint and turpentine fill the air. "The house had really fallen to pieces with the storms and being empty."

I am puzzled: it has been less than two years since we had summered here. Could things really have fallen to pieces so quickly? But there were cracks and damage, undetected through the years, that had been amplified during the time we were gone. Liam is trying to bring it back, restoring it and making everything just as it had been before, only fresh and new. But there are improvements, too, like the window he cut between the living and dining areas to give it a more airy, modern feel.

As he walks to the kitchen to pour coffee from his mom's old percolator, I look around, trying to grasp the scope of his undertaking. He is, quite literally, rebuilding the house from the outside in. "You're doing all of this yourself?"

He nods as he hands me a too-warm cup. "I've still got to finish most of the bedrooms and the deck. Need to get the major outside work done before the weather changes."

"It's going to be swell," I say, meaning it. I take a cautious sip. I had feared I might find the house unbearable, see ghosts everywhere. But the memories of Robbie playing and ducking under the table are merry ones, warming me.

"I thought . . ." His voice cracks. He turns away abruptly. "I've got to get this done before dark," he apologizes, starting for the back door.

Is that my cue to leave? I can go back to the boardinghouse and load up the boxes, be gone for good in an hour. But my feet remain planted. "Let me help." I follow him to the back door. He hesitates, relying on others still unfamiliar to him. "I'm not much with tools," I say, "but I can paint for you."

"Your clothes are going to get ruined."

"I don't mind."

"Wait here," he instructs. I stand alone in the house I had once known so well, the walls seeming to whisper to me. A minute later he returns with one of his old T-shirts. "Put this on." I pull it on over my clothes and the too-large fabric envelops me in his familiar scent, as it had the night I tried to talk to him on Chelsea Beach. I walk outside and pick up a brush.

We work alongside one another without

speaking. There are so many things I'd like to ask him about the time since I'd last seen him and how he had come to be here. But I fear if I press, he might pull away, as he had when we were younger. The silence broken by the humming of the saw and the gulls overhead. I look over at him as he sands the wood, fingers dexterous. Watching him work I am reminded of the boy who seemed to dance on the waves, agile and carefree in that moment, unheld back by anger and fear. How had I forgotten that part of him?

His shoulders are broad, tapering to a narrow waist and long legs. I see him for the first time as a man, fully grown into himself, reminiscent and at the same time not at all like Charlie. Warmth rises, confusing me. I force my eyes back to my work. I fall into an easy rhythm painting, the repetitive up and down motion somehow soothing. The work is simple and the ache in my shoulders satisfying in a way I had not anticipated.

From around the house comes the sound of sandals slapping against pavement. I turn toward the sound, glimpsing a flash of brown hair out of the corner of my eye. My breath catches and I half expect to see Robbie, still eleven years old, carrying a bucket of sand crabs he'd caught off one of the docks in Chelsea Harbor, water sloshing over the sides and leaving dark streaks on the street. But it is an unfamiliar boy and he walks into one of the rented houses down the row, the screen door slamming behind him. My eyes burn as I remember exactly how hard this is. Blinking, I force myself to focus on the painting once more.

"Let's take a break," Liam says a while later when the morning sun has climbed late in the sky. Gratefully, I set down my paintbrush and drop to the porch steps. He goes inside and returns with two glasses of iced tea. A fine perspiration coats his upper lip and wets the ends of his hair. We sit beside each other, not speaking, the silence growing more awkward by the second. I want to jump up and grab the paintbrush again.

"So what have you been doing these many years?" he asks.

A year and a half, I want to say. But I know that it feels like more. There are so many levels on which I could answer his question. I decide to take the simplest. "I was in Washington, then in London, working for the paper."

I wait for him to chastise me for going to a place as dangerous as London. But he is not Charlie. "Did you go all the way back to Italy?"

I shake my head. "It wasn't possible with the fighting. But I was able to confirm what had happened to my parents." A burning rises in my throat and I stop short of sharing the whole of the awful truth.

He does not press. "So you came home?"

"Just to help my aunt for a bit," I reply quickly.

"My folks are down in Florida," he offers. I start to tell him that I already know. But I am not ready to mention Charlie. "I've got a boat now, docked over at the marina." He is speaking in all directions, trying to fill the space between us. "I'm planning to start a small business. Fishing trips and that sort of thing."

The Liam I had known was not one to fish. "So you're going to stay down here year-round?"

"Yeah. There's nothing left for me back in the city. I'm more whole here. The seawater," he says. "It's in my bones, you know?"

I nod, understanding. There's a part of me that still cannot breathe deeply unless the air has salt in it. "Liam Connally, settling down," I muse, half-chiding. "A house. A business. Next thing you know you'll be getting married."

"Who would want me? I'm so broken." He tries to make his voice lighthearted, but a note of sad truth rings through.

"Not at all." My heart twists as I remember the boy he was, before all of this. I want to reach out and put my arm around him, but somehow I can't. "You've started over." The easiest thing for him to have done would have been to move far away where no one had ever heard of the Connallys or the accident at the bridge. But he had returned. The house is a second chance for Liam—a chance at redemption. "I would have imagined Jack settling down first, though," I offer, then instantly regret it.

"My brother's a queer."

"Liam, don't." For a minute I take his comment as mean-spirited, the Liam of old. But his tone is neutral, non-judging.

"I don't say that to be mean," he adds. "I say it because it is the truth. What is so wrong with the truth? He's happy actually, living with someone outside of Philadelphia." In some ways, he is more accepting of his brother than Charlie was.

I finish my iced tea and stand to carry the glass back inside. On the low table by the door there is a notebook and pencil. I pick it up. "Is this yours?"

"Yeah." He jumps up and takes it from me, a guarded look crossing his face. "When I was coming through it all, I started keeping a journal. I liked it, so now I'm working on a story."

"You're writing," I marvel. "I had no idea."

He shrugs. "It's nothing much." As he returns the notebook to the house, I wonder if he's writing about everything that happened, and whether I might be in it.

He returns a minute later, finishes his iced tea and sets down the glass. "I should get back to work. You don't have to help me. I know you've got to get through those boxes for your aunt."

"I should get those finished so I can head back," I concede reluctantly. I've enjoyed working here and I'm not ready to go.

"Well, come back over for dinner," he said, seeming to read my mind. "I caught some fresh bass and there's plenty. We'll have a good meal before you go." He ends on a downward note.

By dinnertime, I think, I should be packed up and on my way back to the city. But his face looks so hopeful, I cannot refuse.

The sun has sunk low in that late summer way, casting long shadows of the houses on the pavement, as I make my way, hours later, across the patch that separates the boardinghouse from the Connallys'. I've showered to rinse off the packing dust and put on a fresh cotton dress, pinning my hair back at the temple where my bangs have started to fall in my eyes again. I walk around the side of the Connally house. Liam is grilling fresh fish over the old grill in the backyard. I study him, noticing the way his hair curls at the collar, the lean silhouette of his cheekbones and jaw. Has he grown handsomer in the time we were apart, or had he been that way all along and I had just been so blinded by Charlie I had not noticed?

He carries over two plates and we sit on the porch, watching the last embers of the fire die, crackling upward into the darkness of night. A kind of awkwardness seems to hover above us. We never had easy conversations, even in the old days.

"There's wine, if you'd like some."

"No, thanks." I notice he does not have any for himself. That part of him, I can only hope, is gone forever. "It's quiet," I say.

He nods in agreement. "Even after all of these years, I'm not sure I can get used to it. Growing up with three brothers was rough, though. I know it seemed like a party to you, but there was always someone faster, smarter, bigger. I just didn't know how to make my way in a place like that." He'd run away because it had been too much, just like Robbie hiding under the stairs. "Sometimes I actually envied you, being alone."

"I wasn't alone. I had you all." He does not respond. "I saw Charlie," I offer, unable to keep it to myself any longer.

Something flickers across his face, though whether it is anger or pain or something else I cannot tell. "Where?"

"Washington, and then London. He was wounded."

"Yeah," he says gruffly. "Mom and Dad keep me in the loop." So the Connallys had stayed in touch with each other, but not me. I am an outsider to the family once more.

"He's okay now."

He always is, Liam's cursory nod seems to say. "You and Charlie were together, weren't you?" There is a catch to his voice. "Never mind, it's none of my business."

I don't want to answer. But his eyes are probing, needing the truth. "Yes. Before it all happened—and a bit in London, too. How did you know?"

"You notice a lot from the sidelines," he remarks wryly. "I always knew. I could tell from the day we met you. What happened?" He looks at me squarely.

"Just one bad start too many." I struggle to keep my voice nonchalant. "Maybe some part of me knew that it wasn't right, that if I was with him I could truly never be free. Anyway, he's engaged now."

"Grace."

So he knows about that, too. Of course he does—she's his brother's fiancée, after all. My stomach roils as I picture Grace: blonde, winsome. Not Jewish. Everything Charlie is supposed to have. I swallow against my pain. "Charlie and I, it was impossible. It just wasn't meant to be."

He shakes his head. "It was a choice. Look at me—after it all happened I could have gone another way, but I chose not to. We have a choice—it is up to us whether or not we take it."

I consider this. I might have claimed Charlie back from Grace and said to hell with the consequences. But there was part of me that was stifled under the weight of him, his plans and dreams, and all that had happened. No, Liam is right: I had walked away, made the choice and

419

left. I clear my throat. "It was over when he left Philly after the funeral. It just took a lot longer for us to realize it."

"I," he says stiffly, "would not have left you." I open my mouth to tell him that it had not been Charlie's fault with everything that had happened, the impulse to defend him as strong as it had been years ago. I want to say that it had been circumstances, grief, anything but Charlie's own choice to go. But Liam is right: he would not have left. Emotions too deep to describe stir in me as I remember that he was the one by my side, defending me. In a funny way, he still is.

He is staring out across the fence at the bay where the sun has dropped from view. I am seized with the urge to take his chin and turn it toward me, to kiss him. I stop, caught off guard by the notion. It had never been that way between me and Liam, had it? I was recovering from Charlie and it would not be fair to make him a substitute for his brother.

"It's late," he says, following my gaze.

"Yes." For a second it seems as though we are talking about something else. I peer over his shoulder at the clock in the kitchen, surprised to see it is almost nine.

"And there's a storm coming." I think of the clouds I'd noticed gathering to the west before sunset. I'm not a good enough driver to manage the roads in bad weather.

"Why don't you stay here?" he suggests. "Your old rooms can't be comfortable. You've got nothing there." I hesitate, looking up at the Connally house and feeling the memories that threaten to swallow me whole. Another night at the shore, when I hadn't planned to stay at all. I want to get in the car and drive, as far and fast as I can. There was a reason I left all of this behind. "It's Friday. Labor Day weekend. There's no rush." My shoulders sag and a wave of sudden exhaustion overcomes me. Staying here is exactly what I want to do, I realize. But can I really, alone with Liam and all of the awkwardness between us? I study him. His eyes are clear now and his complexion healthy. Behind the surface, though, is the hauntedness that will always remain.

"Aunt Bess will worry." The coffee shop, where I'd called her earlier, is surely closed.

"You can call her from here. I had a phone put in." His eyes are searching, not wanting me to leave.

"All right, but let me get a few of my things from next door."

I return to our rooms for my nightgown and toothbrush. When I return to the Connally house, I ring Aunt Bess. "Hello," she answers, her voice fuzzy despite the early hour. I imagine her sleeping to try and outrun her memories and grief.

"I'm sorry to have woken you. I'm going to

stay another night to finish packing up." I do not mention Liam, not ready to talk about finding him with anyone.

"Okay, just be careful." Something in her voice suggests she already knew. Had Aunt Bess sent me here on purpose, wanting me to find Liam? It seems unlikely, given how hard she and Uncle Meyer worked to keep me from Charlie and how they felt about me being with someone who was not Jewish. But perhaps she has changed, too.

Liam comes inside as I hang up. "I'll get you settled." I follow him upstairs. He leads me past several bedrooms draped in cloth, in various states of painting and repair, and up a second flight of stairs to the attic loft Charlie and Robbie once shared. My chest tightens.

"It's the only room I have ready," he says, almost apologetic. There is only one bed now, a big one that he's made up with crisp sheets. He must have been sleeping there himself.

"I can't possibly take your room," I protest.

"I like sleeping on the sunporch," he replies, and I remember that he always had. He lingers for several seconds in the doorway.

"Good night, Addie. It's great having you here." I wonder if he might kiss me goodnight. But he starts down the stairs.

After he's gone, I wash and change, then climb into bed. I lie in the semidarkness, beneath the sheets that contain a hint of Liam's aftershave. Rain begins to patter against the rooftop. It seems odd to be here, this place I had not even thought still existed. This had been Charlie's room and I see things as he once had, looking out at the boardinghouse where I used to sleep. Moonlight reflects against the whitewashed plaster, illuminating the crack where Robbie had hit the ceiling with a Frisbee. Thinking of him still hurts, but differently now. My thoughts turn to Liam. I wanted to kiss him—out on the porch and now. The impulse surprises me. Is it just being back here and trying to make sense of all of the memories, or is it something more?

I see him once and then let him go and drift off to sleep.

Twenty-five

The next morning, I awaken to the sounds of the gulls calling to one another above the bay. I sit and stretch. Light fills the high open space. It has to be at least ten. I pad barefoot downstairs through the house to the sunporch. The blankets at the foot of the divan are folded neatly and the smell of brewed coffee and eggs tickle my nose. I look up at the house that Liam is repairing with such care. What have I done to make amends for my own misdeeds?

Outside Liam is busily sanding a long plank. The sandy earth is damp from the storm that has come and gone. "There's breakfast if you're hungry." He does not look up. I notice suddenly the urgency in his work.

At the far end of the yard, freshly washed sheets hang drying on the line, more than are needed for just him and me. "Liam, you aren't doing this just to live here yourself, are you?"

"No." He stops, eyes meeting mine. "We've got to get most of this done before they arrive."

My breath catches. "They?"

"Mom and Dad and the others. I asked them to come," he says, looking away. Hope rises, then falls in my chest at the idea of seeing all of the Connallys again. Would it really be that simple to get them to come home? "It's just all so broken. Mom and Dad nearly split, the rest of us scattered to the wind. The house in the city is gone, but it was always about this place. I thought maybe if I fixed it up, they'd come." He's trying to repair the damage he had done and bring the family back together.

"Charlie should be coming, too, with his family." I tilt my head, confused. Liam and myself and the others, we are Charlie's family. But Liam is referring to Grace. She's Charlie's family now. Will I ever get used to reality as it now exists? "Do you mind?"

Even though I had left of my own accord and

really, truly set Charlie free, to have to watch him and Grace together would be torture. I swallow. "Of course not. They're family." I had just seen Charlie days ago in the hospital, but he had not mentioned coming home, even after he remembered who I was.

So Liam had invited all of the Connallys back purposefully. But my arrival had been happenstance. He had not included me. "I didn't think you'd come if I asked you directly," he adds. Would I have? Being here just with Liam was hard enough, but the whole family would be unbearable. For a minute I consider leaving before they arrive. No one expects more of me, really. I do not even belong anymore.

Liam waves his arm up at the house. "That's why I'm doing this. I'm trying to bring the family back together." I stop, stunned by the audacity of his plan—not just to fix up the house and live here. He is trying to reunite the family he had destroyed and undo the heartbreak he had caused. He looks at me hopefully. "We can do this. We just have to get them all back in one place."

We. Suddenly I'm his partner in all of this. I want to tell him that with or without me he cannot do it, that it is impossible to rewrite the past. That, above all else, is what I had learned about my own life these past months in London. There is something in his eyes, though, that says he needs this, needs to try to make things right.

He is clinging desperately to this one hope and I cannot take it from him.

But still I need to warn him. "We can't go back."

"I'm not trying to go back," he replies firmly. The past is not a place to which he wants to return. "I'm trying to build a future. If you have to go, I understand." There is a sudden guardedness to his voice, the lone, defensive Liam of old.

"We should get working," I say.

His eyes widen. "You'll help me?" He sounds too scared to hope. I nod. "Does that mean you're staying?"

"I don't know." Panic rises in me. I was supposed to be here a day, get Aunt Bess's things and go again. Yet I feel myself being drawn back in slowly. I can go, now, pile the boxes in the car and sort them back in the city. There is nothing stopping me. But Liam's face is hopeful now, more so than I've ever seen. I cannot destroy that. "I'll stay—at least through the weekend," I add hastily.

Liam looks as if he wants to argue for more than that. But he swallows, backing down. "Only if you want to."

I do want to stay, I realize. I hold out my hand. "Then I guess we'd better get started."

"Try this." It is nearly evening and we have been painting for hours, first inside the house and now out.

"Can't," I reply, distracted. I hold a dripping paintbrush in one hand and a roller in the other; my forearms are uniformly covered in white paint. But we hadn't stopped for lunch and the scent from the plate he holds under my nose is tantalizing. "Mmm, what is it?"

"Gumbo. I traveled some after everything happened, and I learned how to make it when I was down in New Orleans. Tried out the recipe the other day, but I had to substitute a few ingredients I couldn't get." He lifts a spoonful to my mouth, and the warm, spicy sauce floods my tongue with flavor, warming me on the way down.

"Delicious." I nearly miss the second mouthful which he aims at me as I speak. He holds the spoon beneath my lower lip for a second to catch the drip. "Let me wash up and we'll break for dinner."

"No time to break," he answers earnestly. "It might rain tonight and I want to get as much done as possible."

"But I'm hungry," I protest, an almost whine. "You can't tease me with something that good and not let me eat."

"I'll feed you," he offers.

"Okay." I turn back to my painting, not taking my eyes from my work as he spoons the gumbo for me. It is the oddest feeling of helplessness. I dip my head to meet the spoon and let the soft pieces slide down my throat. Small drops of brown sauce fall from the fork, grazing the edge of the paint bucket.

And all the while, I am intently aware of Liam. He feeds me slowly and with great care, not taking his eyes from me in between bites. His forearm grazes my cheek each time he brings the spoon to my mouth. I want to lean across the soppy bowl and kiss him. I stop, surprised at the thought. It is the third time I've had it in two days. Something is drawing me to him now, strong and unexpected.

"Thanks," I say, when he has scraped the bottom of the bowl. "Aren't you going to have some?"

He shakes his head. "Not hungry. It was fun watching you, though." He grins wickedly and I can feel my cheeks flush.

"Liam!" I swat at him playfully, sending drops of paint cascading through the air. Then I wait for him to retaliate, but he does not.

"It won't change things," he says, suddenly somber. I stop, brush suspended midair. "I can fix this house all I want, but unless Robbie is gonna come bounding through that door, it won't change what I did. I know that." I shift, not answering. We are getting to it now, that deep place we'd been circling since seeing one another. The attraction I'd been feeling for him these past two days seems to evaporate and I see him once again as the boy, whose selfish recklessness caused his little brother to die.

There is a moment of painful silence between us. "I should wash the dishes." He jumps up and the bucket between us on the deck tips and spills.

"Oh!" I scramble to right it and reach for a cloth. As we wipe the mess, I look down at his hands. "Dammit, Liam." This was bigger than spilled paint. I am angry at him still for all that he had done years ago. I beat at his chest and he does not try to stop me, but absorbs the blows with sharp silent, breath. A moment later I stop and crash my head against his chest sobbing. "Why?" I ask, over and over, demanding answers he does not have. Then exhausted, I lean on him silently. Forgiveness, it seems, is harder than I might have thought—perhaps because it is not mine to give.

"After I was released from the hospital, I tried to turn myself in to be arrested." His words spill out. "But the police wouldn't take me because it was an accident. I'll answer for my crimes in another way." His voice is hollow. For all of his healing, there is a place inside him that would never be whole.

"I've tried a million times to figure out who I was and how I could have done those things. I was just so lost and I never quite fit in. I went lower afterward," he confesses. "More drinking and drugs. I was on the street. Jack found me and got me into a program. He saved my life."

Neither of us speaks for several minutes. "You tried to warn me, so many times—that day on the beach and in the city. But there was nothing you could have done to make me hear."

"No." It is true. Through all of the pain and shock and pondering what might have been, I had never once hated him. "I understand in a way. You see, when I was in England, I found out the truth about my parents." I swallow. It is the first time I have told anyone. "They were arrested because I was missing. It was my fault."

He puts his arm on mine. "Addie, that's not at all the same. You didn't do anything. You didn't even have a say in leaving Italy." He leans back and I take in the lean silhouette of his torso. A shiver runs through me. Is it nostalgia? No, there is something about him, subtle and more vulnerable than Charlie, that draws me to him.

Then he smiles, and the darkness blows away like dust. "I wanted to ask you to come, too. That's why I sent the picture."

"You?" I turn in disbelief to see him nod.

"I wanted to ask you to come back. But I didn't have the nerve. So I mailed you the photo, long before I asked the others." All that time I had thought it was Charlie or even Jack who had sent the picture. I had not imagined that it was Liam who had been searching for me and calling me home. "But when that didn't work—"

"You got Aunt Bess to help." I hadn't thought TO QUESTION WHY SHE NEEDED THE THINGS SHE HAD LEFT down here.

"Yes. I contacted her when I started this a few months ago, but she said that you were in London and there was nothing she could do. I guess when you came back for the funeral . . ."

"She had a change of heart," I finished for him. How odd that after all of her years of keeping me from the Connallys, she had helped bring me back to them. But fortune had played a role, too—if I hadn't come back because of my uncle, I might have missed them again.

"I didn't think you'd say yes if the invitation came from me," he says sheepishly.

I want to tell him that it isn't true. What would I have said if Liam had asked me to come? I'm not entirely sure. I would have remembered the old, angry Liam who had caused so much pain, not the man who stands before me now. "Well, I'm here now."

"Being away, was it easier or harder?"

I shrug. "Being away just makes it easier to forget."

He nods in agreement. "When I was away I could pretend Robbie was still here, running down the street."

"I couldn't stand to be here but I couldn't separate when I was away. I was always torn."

"And now?" Liam is looking at me, green eyes expectant.

"I don't know." When I'd come home for my aunt, returning to London had seemed a foregone conclusion. But what did I have left there, really? I had turned Teddy away and could hardly go back and work closely with him at the bureau as I once had. I had helped the orphans. Charlie was gone. There was nothing left for me now.

He steps back and surveys the porch. "I think we've done all we can for tonight." It is getting dark and hard to see. He takes the paintbrushes to wash and disappears inside the house. I look up at our rooms at the house next door. Earlier, I'd rung Aunt Bess to tell her I would be staying a few more days. She didn't argue, but I worried about leaving her for so long after all she had been through.

Pushing down my guilt, I walk to the edge of the porch to peer at the house on the far side of the Connallys'.

"What are you thinking about?" Liam asks, returning with coffee.

I wrap my hands around the warmth of the mug he hands me. "Remember that time when I broke the window and you took the blame for me?" He nods. "You were trying to protect me. I only wish I had been able to do the same for you when things got tough."

"I'm not sure you ever needed protection," Liam observes. "Even as a girl you were so strong." I look at him, surprised. I had not seen myself that way, and I hadn't imagined anyone else had either. "You were tiny and quiet, and we all wanted to protect you. But for Christ's sake, you had just come halfway around the world. By yourself. No, you weren't the one who needed saving. We needed you."

The music changes to Cole Porter, and for a second we might have been in the Connallys' living room back in the city, their father dancing their mother around the frayed rug while the boys and I watched and grinned. Liam pulls back and cups my chin. For a moment, I think that he might kiss me, but he uses his thumbs to wipe away the wetness beneath my eyes. Then he holds out his arms to me expectantly. "Shall we?"

"Dance, here?"

"Why not?" We stand. As he spins me around, the record skips slightly as it rotates on the turntable, an imperfection that would never be quite right again.

He kisses me suddenly, brief but strong. So he felt it, too. I kiss him back, not hesitating, surprised at how right it feels. Then he pulls back and there is fear in his eyes. I lean forward and draw his lips to mine. A minute later we break apart, breathless. "I had no idea," I murmur.

He smiles ruefully. "Because you never saw me. All you saw standing in front of you was Charlie."

I open my mouth to tell him that it isn't true, only then I see that it exactly is. I had always been so wrapped up in Charlie I hadn't been able to see past him. "I'm sorry." I touch his cheek, marveling at its softness beneath my fingertips.

But he stiffens and pulls away. "You love who you love. I don't blame you for that. But I don't want to be a poor substitute for my brother. I don't want to be second choice. And I don't want this to be about my family." The old, angry Liam seems to surface for a moment.

"It isn't," I reply quickly, meaning it.

He takes another step back. "Good night, Addie." He walks inside, leaving me alone and shaken, unsure what had just happened between us.

I hear his footsteps on the stairs and then the floor above. Should I go after him and try to make things better? I do not want to let him just walk away again. But it will do no good—he has walked in the shadow of his brother for so long, some part of him will never believe me.

I go upstairs to the room where I am staying, still confused. Liam had wanted the kiss, too; I could feel it. Why does this have to be so complicated?

There is a knock on the door. "Come in."

Liam appears, a dark silhouette in the doorway. "Addie, I'm sorry. It's just that for so long I wanted you to see me. I thought we were the same, a couple of outsiders, different than the rest. But you were always chasing Charlie."

"It was over long ago," I say, the realization crystalizing as I speak it. "You can't let go of some parts of the past and not others. Don't I deserve a fresh start, too?" He does not answer. "It's not about Charlie. Not anymore."

I stand and walk to him, pull him into the room.

My lips are upon his now and we are drinking each other in and it is still not enough. He pushes me back, opening me in a way I have never quite felt before, without boundaries or control, different than anything before.

I groan, a guttural, foreign sound from somewhere deep. My hands reach up to curl underneath the bottom of the headboard where it meets the mattress. My back arches. My head twists from side to side, as though knocked by violent waves. Sex with Liam is different from the measured tenderness I experienced with the only other lover I had known. In bed, Charlie had been like he was when running or playing football, measured and graceful. But Liam's movements are a racehorse unharnessed, as powerful as they are urgent. His kisses are almost bites. He grabs me to keep me from falling off the bed as we roll frenetically from side to side. He lifts my skirt and enters me. I scream.

After, we lie in a breathless tangle. Our eyes meet. "Wow!"

"Yeah." The lights are on, I realize. With Charlie it had been darkness, hands fumbling. But now we are before each other, exposed. I shiver. Mistaking my nervousness for cold, he reaches for the edge of the blanket and wraps it around me. I burrow in it, grateful for the shelter, and nestle closer in his arms.

When I awaken, I'm assaulted by feelings of confusion and guilt. Is this wrong? With Charlie, we had been planning to get married. But to let so much happen with Liam so soon . . . I am not that kind of a girl. I came here to pack away boxes and move on. This is not the time for getting involved with anyone, especially Liam. Nothing between us could ever work or be simple.

I sit up to go. Feeling me pull away, his eyes snap open. Suddenly awake, he grabs me and draws me close.

"Liam . . ." I try to say between his kisses. I pull back, averting my eyes from the low bit of his stomach.

"What is it?"

"I think we made a mistake."

"Okay, so we won't do it again." But his hands travel down my body.

I pull away. "Dammit, Liam, is it always that simple for you?"

"I just don't understand why it has to be complicated. You want out, fine with me." A note of defensiveness crept into his voice.

"I'm sorry. But this is hard."

"No, losing Robbie was hard," he says stiffly. "This is just life."

"It's not that simple."

"It's exactly that simple. You've constructed this wall around yourself, Addie. It reminds me of someone I once knew," he adds, smiling ruefully. I see him as a boy, so defensive and pushing everyone away, too afraid to get close. "But I won't let you shut me out." My eyes wander toward the door. "Don't, Addie. Leaving now will just make things more awkward the next time. It's been a beautiful night." I feel my cheeks warm. "In a few hours the sun will be up and I'll make you breakfast. What do you say?"

I lean back beside him and rest my head easily against his chest. "It's just weird, you know? Like I had to go all the way around the world to find this." Suddenly it seems like one big circle.

"Maybe going away brought you home again."

"Maybe." I had always felt some sort of connection to Liam, both of us outsiders. But I had never understood it until now. I settle back in his arms. There is a kind of clarity about him now, a strength forged in the fire through which he had walked. He might have continued his downward spiral, spurred on by his grief. But he had chosen to climb back up and live.

"You believe me now, that this is just about us?"

"I do." His voice is sincere, a man calm and confident in his place. "I mean, you chose to leave Charlie, right?"

"Right." Grace had been there, but if I fought I

knew that Charlie would have been mine. I had left, though, because I could no longer live under the weight of all that had happened between us.

"You could stay," Liam says, a mumble in half sleep. My breath catches. "This will never be whole without you."

"I'll stay for now," I reply. "To help you with the house." More I cannot promise. I gaze into the darkness of the rafters. Outside, rain beats steadily against the rooftops. "We won't be able to paint tomorrow."

"We'll work on the inside." His voice is untroubled.

I nod. I never did mind the rain. "But, Liam . . ." I hesitate.

My mind reels back to hours earlier when we were working on the house. "Look." He showed me a part of the yard, set off with wooden beams, where his mother could have a garden. I saw how much he had wrapped up in his plan. Liam had tried to create everything exactly. It would take more than some paint, though. No matter how carefully he restored the house, Robbie would never come running around the corner. Memories were one thing, the future quite another. Could it ever be home again?

I want to tell him that it might not work, that even if they do come he might not be able to set things right. He seems open now and so vulnerable and I want to save him the disappointment of having his hopes crashed. But hope is all he has right now and I cannot take that away from him.

I wrap my arms more tightly around him and will his plan to work.

Twenty-six

I struggle against the tide, fighting to stay close to the shoreline. I try to grasp a large weathered log, but the piece of wood breaks free with the next wave and I am reduced to clutching at the ocean floor, the liquid sand running futilely through my fingers. With every ounce of energy, I fight to stand and bury one foot deep in the wet earth. But even when I have anchored myself, I continue to be dragged by the tide until it seems that I might be torn in two. I am beaten insistently by the wind from the waist up, while the undertow wraps around my calves like a whip. When I can withstand the pain no more, I throw my arms up with abandon and fall backward, allowing the waters to engulf me and sweep me away.

I awaken with a gasp, rather than a scream, strangely calm despite the violent images. I blink my eyes open. Sunlight blazes through the curtainless windows, bathing the room in light. My muscles ache in a strange but not unpleasant way and my cheek is raw from where Liam's stubbled face had rubbed against mine, over and over again. I stretch and turn, reaching for Liam once more. I find myself looking for Liam, needing him. Self-loathing rises in me—I cannot—will not—depend on anyone again.

But the space beside me is empty and below I can hear the dull, repetitive rhythm of Liam's saw. Memories of the previous night flood my brain. What had happened? And what did it all mean?

Pushing the questions away, I change into clothes and head outside, eager for fresh air. I bypass the back porch where Liam is working and set out for a brisk walk. I start instinctively in the direction of the beach. As I near the boardwalk, I stop, surprised. Once I would have avoided the water, but strangely now I am drawn toward it. I take off my shoes and the damp sand is cold under my feet as I walk the beach parallel to the shoreline, but staying back from it. Gulls cry out as they dip low to the water. The wind seems to change directions. The air resists me, whipping sand across my skin; it takes all of my effort just to keep moving.

I pause to rest. A warplane buzzes overhead, and I look up at the sky in that nervous way I have not quite shaken from the air raids in London. It is one of ours, of course. Taking in the wide contours of its wings, I cannot help but think of Charlie.

I tear my eyes from the sky, focus straight ahead. I think back to my earlier nightmare. My dreams have evolved, I realize. In the earlier years, I'd been nearly powerless. Lately, I had been able, albeit with great difficulty, to resist the current a bit. "I'm getting stronger," I say aloud. If my dreams could change, then maybe they aren't inevitable. Does there exist a remote chance of ending the nightmares entirely? Energized by the possibility, I start back.

I do not go to the Connallys' but back to our old rooms at the duplex where my clothes remain, to shower and change. As I dry my hair, a car door slams below. Someone is here. I'd been so caught up in my night with Liam that I'd nearly forgotten: the other Connallys are coming. Let it be their parents, I pray.

But Charlie is always early. Through the window I spy him, stepping out of the car, just as he had the day we met. He walks with a slight limp, a scar that will perhaps fade over time or maybe not heal at all. For a moment, my heart soars.

I finish dressing and then rush down the stairs. Near the bottom, I stop. Despite my shower, Liam's scent seems to linger around me, screaming the truth. This time last year Charlie and I had been planning a future together. How has it come to this?

I take a deep breath and step outside. Charlie

turns. "Addie," he says, that catch still in his voice, taking me in as though it had been years and not just days earlier in England. He stares at me with disbelief. He didn't expect to see me and he is surprised, even more so than in Washington. "What are you doing here?" His words stab at me. This was my home, too.

But before I can respond, the passenger door to his rented Oldsmobile opens and Grace's long, willowy frame appears. "Hello, Adelia." Grace steps toward me, impossibly chic with her hair in a silk scarf, eyes hidden behind dark sunglasses. As she nears Charlie's side, my heart breaks. Seeing him standing with Grace, it is like the time he had gone on that date at the shore, only a million times worse. My eyes sting. The quiet haven Liam and I have created these past few days seems fragile and overfull. I'm in the way. I should leave.

"Liam," Charlie says, looking over my shoulder. His voice seems to choke on the word and I know that this is the first time the brothers have seen one another since everything happened. Charlie recovers and starts toward his brother with long, confident strides. Liam stands frozen, his face helpless, overwhelmed by emotions and the reunion that is so much harder than he had imagined.

The brothers shake hands, unable to feign a hug. "Addie's here," Charlie remarks. How odd that this should be the first thing that they discuss. Close behind me, I feel Liam stiffen. He does not want to share me.

Liam laces his fingers in with mine. Charlie's eyes drop lower and then rise again, widened with surprise. Liam's gaze lifts defiantly to his brother's, daring him to say something. I brace for confrontation; neither Charlie nor Liam is one to back down. I pull my hand away, unwilling to be caught between two men again.

Grace walks up beside Charlie and for once I am glad she is here. "Hello."

"I'm Liam," he offers, trying to break the tension. "And this is Addie."

"We've met."

"Oh, yes, of course." Beside me Liam tenses again, uncomfortable with the history he does not know.

"Nice to see you again, Grace," I manage to say.

The brothers eye each other icily. Charlie's fists are clenched low to his side.

"Thanks for coming," Liam offers.

"I wanted," Charlie says slowly, "to be here for Mom."

Liam raises his hands, acknowledging that it will have to be enough. "Mom and Dad won't be here until tomorrow," Liam says. So for tonight it would just be the four of us, with no one else to break the awkwardness.

The boys walk to the car to get the bags. "I heard your plane crashed," Liam says, switching to the war, somehow an easier topic.

"I was in a dogfight over Munich," Charlie replies, describing it all to his brother in a way I have not heard before.

"I wanted to go, too," Liam offers, surprising me. I cannot picture him enlisting. Would it have been a shot at redemption—or suicide? "They wouldn't take me, though, after everything that had happened."

At the mention of the fighting, Charlie grimaces with frustration. "I should be over there." Some part of him was still with the soldiers he had left behind.

"He wanted to go back, or even to the Pacific," Grace says in a low voice so the boys cannot hear. A knife shoots through me as I remember the pain and fear of his going to war the first time. "But they wouldn't clear him medically." Even as I exhale with relief, I feel for Charlie. Being sidelined and unable to help is so contrary to who he is—it has to be killing him. I start after him, my first instinct to try to offer comfort in the way only I can. Then I stop. It isn't my place anymore.

The boys have come inside and Liam is showing Charlie some of his work on the house. Charlie peers out the back door critically. "You aren't rebuilding the shed."

"No, I thought it would leave more space for the garden." The tension returns between the brothers, their rift unhealed by time.

"Let's go to the beach," I blurt. Anything to break the awkwardness between them.

Both boys looked at me with simultaneous surprise. "You?" Liam asks.

I shrug. "I didn't say I was going in the water."

"Addie is afraid of the ocean," Charlie explains to Grace.

Liam chimes in. "Yeah, and there was this one time when we first met her that we threw her in."

"We?" Charlie repeats with mocking disbelief. As the boys carry the story, talking over one another, a look of curiosity crosses Grace's face. She has Charlie, but there is still a part of his past she will never share.

A wave of sympathy for Grace washes over me. "Come, I'll help you get settled." Grace smiles thankfully in return. She isn't the enemy really, I reflect as I lead her up the stairs to the guest room Liam has just finished restoring. Even if she had not come along at the field hospital, Charlie and I would not be together. It was timing and fate —if I dare to believe in that again—and who we are that had kept us apart—not another woman.

An hour later we are settled on the beach, the air a degree or two cooler with the first hint of fall. The smell of suntan lotion tickles my nose, sending me back. Charlie pulls a football from his bag. "You aren't serious." Liam groans.

"Of course."

"All right. You asked for it." Liam leaps to his feet, planting an easy kiss on my cheek that sends shivers through me.

"Your leg is too weak," Grace frets. I, too, worry that Charlie cannot manage. But he limps gamely after his brother.

I watch, marveling how the light and the way they move are unchanged after all these years. Once I would have had my camera with me to capture the moment. The photos might have been the same, save for the boys' size—and the fact that two of them are missing.

A few minutes later they return the ball to the blanket. Liam runs to the water's edge and dives in, owning the waves as he did in his surfing days. Charlie follows, leaving me alone with Grace once more.

I peer north, drinking in the familiar topography of the tall hotels and piers. The shore has the feeling that the war is over already. The beaches are crowded, the boardwalk bustling. But the scars of war remain. The Convention Center, once used to train new recruits, now houses convalescing veterans. I imagine them sitting by the door in their wheelchairs gazing sadly across the ocean at the unseen fighting that had ruined their lives forever.

"You don't like the water?" Grace asks, trying to make conversation.

"I've always been afraid of it," I say. "And then after everything happened with Robbie, I hated it even more."

"But he drowned in the river, right? Not here."

"Yes, but it's still the water." It's all jumbled together somehow in my mind. "I didn't like it, even before." For a second, I'm annoyed. It's really none of her business. But she is trying to be kind. I take a deep breath. "I'm sorry we didn't have time to get better acquainted in England." Liam is not the only one who needs to make amends. "My aunt needed me to come home. It was a difficult time."

"It still is," Grace blurts, and I know then that Charlie still lives with his ghosts.

"Time heals," I reply softly.

"I hope so."

I had been so focused on my jealousy of Grace, I never stopped to think how she might feel about me. "I didn't ask for that. It's over, Grace, and if I'm being honest it has been for a long time. We're different people now."

"I know, and I'm glad he's got his memory back." Grace's chin juts out defiantly. "I want him to choose, not win by default." Her words are an echo of Liam's as she stands and takes a step toward the ocean.

That night Liam grills again, steak this time, the charcoal briquettes sending up embers like tiny fireworks into the almost dark sky. At the table, Charlie produces a bottle of red wine. I eye the glass he holds out to me uncertainly. I desperately want it to dull the awkwardness and pain, but do I dare in front of Liam? "It's okay," Liam says calmly. "I'm fine."

When we've finished and cleared up, Liam heads back outside. "A few more hours of work. I want to get the garden just so before Mom arrives." He does not ask Charlie to help and Charlie does not offer.

Grace yawns. "Excuse me. It's been a long day with the travel and I'm exhausted." She starts for the stairs, then turns back. Doubts flicker across her face at leaving the two of us alone. But she is too proud to hover.

Charlie watches her protectively as Grace climbs the stairs. I expect him to follow, but he remains seated, dividing the rest of the bottle of wine between our two glasses. "You're looking well," I observe. "You have your memory again, too."

He nods. "All of it, thanks to you. When I saw you, it came flooding back." Was he glad? Or were there parts he would rather leave forgotten?

"What are you going to do now?"

"I'm too injured for active duty. I've been

offered a promotion, and a job in Washington if I want one. But I don't know." He, too, has been reshaped by his experiences, perhaps too much so to ever go back.

"You could go to Georgetown at night."

His face brightens. "I could, couldn't I?" School is an old dream, to dust off and try anew. If only everything else was that easy.

"I'm glad you're well."

"Thanks. The rehab was intense and Grace has been a wonder." He speaks her name a bit self-consciously and I feel the punch in my gut that might never go away. "She's a lovely woman. But this thing that has always been between us . . ." He reaches out, hand floundering midair. "I can't fight this."

My breath catches a bit at the unexpected shift back toward us. Such conversations are too dangerous—and at the same time moot. "You must. You're getting married."

"I didn't mean for it to happen like this. I'm sorry if that sounds disloyal to Grace, but it's true. She was so kind." Kind. I would never want to be described that way by a man who purported to love me. I feel a moment's sympathy for the woman who has everything she'd ever wanted. "Anyway, I wouldn't have wanted to come back to you like this." He points toward his legs. His limp is minor and almost healed, but to Charlie the imperfection makes him somehow less of a man. "I'd always wonder if you were here out of love or pity."

"You should know the answer to that." I am suddenly angry at Charlie for making decisions for all of us, just like Claire said he always had.

But I was the one who walked away, I remember then. And our dream had died before he was ever injured, so long ago we had not even realized. "Even if we could turn back the clock we'd still be standing here or somewhere pretty close."

"How can you say that? We had everything when we were together," he says. He gestures upward. "It just isn't the same."

"There's a reason that feelings like that come only once, Charlie."

"I still think we would be together."

I shake my head. "There was a time when I believed that. I thought we were some sort of star-crossed lovers and that all that kept us apart was circumstance."

"When did you stop feeling that way?"

"Today, when I saw all of us together and how we changed. I'm not that same scared kid who put you on a pedestal. You need that, Charlie, you always have. Grace gives you that adoration. I can see it in her eyes. God bless her, she'll probably be able to do it for the rest of her life." Part of me would always want him, and wonder what would have happened if I had made a life with Charlie. But that door is now closed.

"I've never been able to tell Grace the whole story about us. The whole thing feels too close, y'know?" I nod. "What holds this family together is all of the stuff we've been through. That's hard for outsiders to take."

He tilts his head toward Liam, who is working intently in the yard. "So you two are together?"

"Yes." The word comes out with more certainty than I had planned. I hadn't thought about it consciously until just now. After all, it has only been two days. But there is no hesitating or couching it, like I had done with Teddy in London. "Liam and I are together." I savor the words, owning them.

"And you're staying?"

The harder question. "I haven't thought about it."

"Don't hurt him, Addie. He's been through so much. I don't know if he could take it if you left again." The weight of others' happiness is suddenly heavy on my shoulders once more.

He stares out at the window in the direction of the ocean and I can tell he is thinking about the fighting overseas and not being a part of it.

"It's tough, isn't it? Not being there, I mean." He looks up in surprise. "I remember being in London and so desperately wanting to help. I felt powerless."

"Yeah." He smiles faintly. On this one level, at least, we can still connect.

"It's almost over," I say. Paris has been liberated in the week since I left, a sure sign that this couldn't go on forever. "And we will win."

"Maybe," he says slowly, "our own war is coming to an end, too." He kisses me on the cheek and the longing in me that will never completely disappear rises, then ebbs again as he stands and joins Grace upstairs.

Desire pulls at me as I watch him go. Not for Charlie, though. It is Liam I want. I start toward the porch, wanting to cajole him upstairs. Going to him with Charlie and Grace here feels somehow wrong, though. I turn away. As I climb the stairs to the loft, I remember the night before. Perhaps Liam will come to me again. But even after I undress and climb into bed, the hallway remains still. With Charlie and Grace here, it seems everything has changed.

Twenty-seven

It is late afternoon when I hear the crunching of tires over stones and the screech of brakes. I set down my paintbrush and follow Liam around the side of the house. The Connallys stand frozen, looking up at their house as though seeing it for the first time. Drinking in the sight of them, I am unable to speak. Mrs. Connally, in a gray pinstripe dress with white cuffs, is a different person, an elderly relative of herself. Her once-lively cap of red hair is now back in a firm knot, strands of gray beginning to creep in at her temple. The circles under her eyes which appeared the day of the accident had never gone away. Beneath his straw brimmed hat, Mr. Connally still gives off the appearance of a grizzly bear, one now worn with age. He lumbers slowly, advancing ahead of his wife.

"Addie." Mrs. Connally's voice is the same, only softer. I lean forward and kiss her cool, dry cheek. She embraces me tightly as if clinging to a life raft, oblivious to the paint that threatens to seep from my clothes to her own. "We didn't know you were coming back."

"Neither did I."

"Mom . . . Dad." Liam steps forward.

"Liam." His parents speak flatly, almost in unison. Mr. Connally stares hard at his son, taking in the changes of the time since they had seen one another. Mrs. Connally looks away, unable to mask the anger and love that mix in her eyes.

From their car comes a sudden clattering and a yellow dog squeezes out of the backseat, tail wagging slowly. "Beau!" I cry as he ambles over. He is overweight, his snout more gray than gold. But his lick on my hand is unmistakable. Through it all, the old fella is still here.

"That's about as much excitement as he manages these days," Mr. Connally offers. "Ten is pretty old for a dog."

Liam kneels, ruffling Beau's fur. "He missed me most." For a moment he is transformed to the insecure boy I met that first day, who cared so much about being taller than me. Then he straightens and gestures toward the car. "We should get your things."

Mr. Connally lifts the small suitcase he has brought with him. "These are our things." Liam slumps beside me. They could not be planning to stay more than a few days.

I turn to Mrs. Connally. "I remember another day of unpacking," I say, calling upon the memory of our first summer in an attempt to ease the tension. But Mrs. Connally simply nods, the nostalgia a painful reminder of her loss.

"You've done a fine job of reopening the house," Mr. Connally remarks as we go inside. He and Mrs. Connally walk a few feet apart from one another, not moving in unison as they once had. Separate, Charlie had told me that day in Washington, which now seemed so very long ago. Their relationship with Liam was not the only thing that needed to heal.

"Addie's helped me a lot these past few days." The Connallys look at me with surprise, as though I am still a child and incapable of being any real use at all.

Automatically we all gravitate toward the kitchen. I put water in the kettle and begin to rummage through the cupboard.

Mrs. Connally looks around anxiously. "Charlie?" She has not seen him since he's come home from Europe. I look at Liam, worried that he will be hurt by his mother's preoccupation with her eldest.

But Liam pats her arm, seeming to understand. "He's already here. He and Grace went to the beach. He looks good."

"And Jack?" Mrs. Connally asks.

Liam shakes his head. "He's got a big conference for work." Among us lies the truth that Jack was simply too tired to weather another family confrontation. He has his own life, has managed to break free.

"Our Addie," Mrs. Connally says as she plants an easy kiss on my cheek.

"How's your place in Miami?" I ask.

"Small, new. Close to the water, like here." Mrs. Connally's face drops. "Only it's nothing like here. But we couldn't go back to the city. Everything has changed. The neighborhood isn't what it was." Other families had moved in and would create their own stories on the streets where we had lived and worked.

The door clatters and Charlie and Grace walk in. I marvel at how Grace's classic beach wrap is unwrinkled and her hair pristine, not blown wildly from the ocean winds as mine would have been. "Oh!" Mrs. Connally sets down her tea so hard it splashes across the counter, then flings herself at her oldest son. "You're here." She pulls away, staring at him.

"Mom and Dad, this is Grace," Charlie says. I stand back, having never felt more like an outsider. I do not belong here.

"So nice to meet you." The warmth in Mrs. Connally's voice is genuine at meeting her future daughter-in-law. Envy rises in me.

Liam, seeming to sense this, comes up and takes my hand. "Why don't you show Mom what we've done with the yard?"

"I'm going to dress," Grace says softly to Charlie.

I lead Mrs. Connally out back. "See how Liam restored the garden." I point, driven by a need to point out all he has done to make things right. Mrs. Connally's face crumbles, the garden a reminder of a time before. I see then how far I have come in my grief. But for her, Robbie's mother, it might never change. I reach down and squeeze her fingers in mine. "I think Robbie would have loved it, don't you?" Not talking about him would not make things any easier.

Beau meanders out back and lies down on the deck in his usual spot from years ago, as though he had been there yesterday. If only it could be that easy for the rest of us.

"You try and do everything to protect them." Mrs. Connally's voice is flat and her eyes cloudy, as though elsewhere. "Swimming lessons at the Y from the time they were two. No riding in cars with friends." She drops her head to her hands. "And still it was never enough." A minute later, she looks up. "You knew, didn't you, about Charlie and the army? Back when he was keeping it from us?"

"I did," I say, unable to deny it. "I'm sorry I didn't tell you." I wait for the anger which will surely come.

But her face remains impassive. "You were doing what you thought was best. We all were." I cannot tell if her forgiveness is genuine, or if she is simply too tired to fight anymore.

"Grace seems nice," I offer.

"She does," Mrs. Connally replies, her voice carefully neutral. "I just always thought that maybe you and Charlie would wind up together." Me, too. So she had not guessed or known after all. I flash back to the Thanksgiving night it all had happened. The news of my relationship with Charlie had sat untouched like a forgotten present under the tree the day after Christmas. I consider telling her everything that happened, the reasons Charlie and I could not make it work. But none of it matters anymore. "Come." We walk back inside.

When I return from dressing for dinner, Liam has set out cold roast-beef sandwiches. The talk has turned to politics. "And now with Stalin making moves," Mr. Connally is saying. One war was not yet over, and another already beginning.

"All that planning for war, but no one has

planned for peace." As Charlie talks about politics, a light dances in his eyes that I have not seen since before it all happened. I know then that he will go to Washington.

Sitting around the kitchen table, warmth envelops me anew and my spirits soar. Home is bigger than Charlie and what had happened between us. My story may have started with him, but it didn't end there. In this most solemn of places, I am happy again in a way that I thought the war had ended for good.

My hand runs over something—the old groove in the edge of the table that Robbie had worn with his pocketknife—he'd gotten grounded for a week for making it. It is still there—but he isn't. Robbie and Jack are both missing. We are here, but not whole. Regret washes over me. My stomach turns. I had let myself depend on the Connallys once before, a trap I would not fall into again by getting too close. The room is suddenly warm and I step from the house, gulping for air.

Outside the sun has nearly set and Liam is working on the porch swing in the semidarkness. "Hey." I move toward him. "You disappeared." He had escaped, so quietly I had not seen him go. Concern pushes through me that he is feeling excluded again and might return to his old ways.

But when he looks up, his face is peaceful. "I just wanted to get this finished before tonight." No, he is not alienated as he had once been.

Rather, despite his happiness at having them all back, he just finds the quiet easier. He straightens and draws me close. I press up against him, growing warm and wishing that it was just the two of us alone at the house once more.

"It's great having everyone back, isn't it?" he asks.

"Yes." It isn't easy all being together again to be sure, but it feels right in a way things haven't in years.

"Mom and Dad seem different somehow." So he had noticed, too.

"It's hard—for everyone. A lot of people and memories in one place."

"Is that why you've been keeping your distance?"

I look up at him, surprised. "My distance?"

"When you didn't come to me last night, I thought you didn't want this anymore." He does not finish.

"I was waiting for you to come to me." We laugh, realizing the irony of our misunderstanding.

"I thought Charlie coming back had stirred up feelings."

"If anything, it is the opposite." I wrap my arms around his waist, watching first his surprise. It is quickly followed by relief as he realizes I have chosen him. That I want to be here with him, not just wound up but actually picked, like kids choosing kids for a kickball game, seems to matter to him a great deal.

"How are you doing?" I ask.

"Happy, angry, sad, relieved," he rattles off in a monotone. "I don't know what I was expecting."

"Well, they're here and that's something."

"Doesn't look like they're planning to stay very long, though."

"Well, you'll just have to change their minds."

"Do you think I can? Both of them, Mom especially, just seem so far beyond reach."

I search for an optimistic response. Finding none, I squeeze his shoulder. "First things first. Let's get this damned paint job finished already."

But he stands motionless, staring at me. "What is it?" I ask, sensing his uneasiness. He has dreamed for so long of having his family here. Is it now too much, bringing back all of the pain and memories?

"I love having them here," he whispers. "But I can't stop thinking about being alone with you." His voice is husky, sending heat searing through me. He reaches for me and we fumble in the darkness like teenagers afraid of getting caught. Hearing the voices of the others inside, I start to protest. But I am swept under by his touch. He pulls me around the side of the house and I stand paralyzed with disbelief as he lifts my skirt. He enters me against the side of the deck, moving silently in the darkness, and I bite into his forearm so I will not scream.

Twenty-eight

"Addie, I need your help with something." It is not long after breakfast and the others have gone to the beach. The Connallys have all been back a few days and life has lost its vacation-like feel, everyone falling into a kind of routine. I enjoy watching Mrs. Connally readjust to her old home, placing things this way and that, "where they belong."

I follow her up the stairs to the storeroom adjacent to the loft where I have been staying. I avert my eyes as we pass my bed, flushing as I recall Liam slipping up here the night before, as he had each night since our secret tryst on the deck. "When we left the city, I had many things sent here," she explains, ducking low under the sloped storeroom ceiling. Boxes lie untouched, with a thick coating of dust. "I can't bring myself to throw anything out."

"I don't think you should. This will be a treasure trove for your grandchildren someday."

"Or a fire hazard."

I open one of the boxes. Inside is a stack of framed photographs. The top portrait is of one of the boys, not older than two, propped up on a sofa amidst some stuffed animals. As I pick it up, Robbie's laugh leaps out at me. "Oh!" I drop the photo back in the box.

"What is it?"

"Nothing." I tuck it under some other pictures before she can see. Standing hurriedly, I bump into something hard and black. Mrs. Connally lifts it up.

"My old typewriter. I wanted to be a writer."

"I had no idea. Liam's been writing a lot."

"Charlie told me. I should have given this to Liam years ago." She rubs a bit of dust from the keys, then runs her fingers over them affectionately.

"He was too young. He wouldn't have appreciated it then."

"But he will now." She looks over at me. "He's going to be okay, isn't he?"

"More than okay." My words sound like a promise.

"I had to lose one son to save another." Her voice is close to breaking. "God help me, I'll never know why."

She goes on. "I had a child a long time ago." It takes me a minute to realize that she means before the boys . . . and not with Mr. Connally. I struggle to mask my surprise. "A little girl. I was sixteen and I gave her up." She chokes back a sob. "She would have been just about your age. So when we met you that day at the shore, I almost felt as though you were her. I know you weren't, of course, but in some ways it was like a second chance."

"That's what Liam's looking for. A second chance." I use her words, gently urging her to give him what she found in me.

She clears her throat. "You two are together now." Her tone drops a bit at the end.

"Do you mind?"

"No," replies Mrs. Connally quickly, brushing the hair from her eyes. "I guess I was a bit surprised is all." Because we did not fit? "I always thought you and Charlie would wind up together. But I'm glad. Liam's always had so much less," Mrs. Connally adds, her face brightening. "I'm just so happy that he has you."

Relief floods me. But Mrs. Connally's words echo in my mind. *Has you.* What does that mean anyway? I have only just run away from the tug-of-war between Charlie and Teddy and her words sound dangerously close to the detestable sensation of ownership I'd fled.

"Did your aunt Bess ever talk to you about . . ." Mrs. Connally falters. "Things between a man and a woman?"

I fought the urge to laugh aloud. When I was seventeen, Aunt Bess had wordlessly handed me a book that talked about baby chicks and showed a picture of Michelangelo's *David*, but that just gave me more questions than it answered. But that seemed so long ago, I think, recalling my one night with Charlie in London—and the passion that Liam and I share now. I swallow. "I under-stand a bit."

"I just want to make sure that you are careful." Was she speaking out of concern for me or her son? "Just don't lose yourself—or what you want for yourself." She is speaking of something bigger now than getting pregnant, and her voice contains a deeper note of experience.

I see the Connallys more clearly then. They are not perfect, and never have been. Their father is depressed and once drank. Mrs. Connally, with her own hidden past, had done her best to keep them together through it all without enough help or money.

"Come on." I take the typewriter gently from her hands, then lead her to the stairs. "I think Liam is waiting for this."

As we reach the second floor the phone in the kitchen rings.

I set down the typewriter. "I'll get it," I say to Mrs. Connally, not wanting her to rush. I walk downstairs and pick up the phone. "Connally house."

"Addie!" Jack's voice floods the line.

"Oh, Jack! We miss you."

"Yeah." He clears his throat. "Picturing all of you around the table without me feels a little strange."

So come home, I want to say. But he doesn't belong here anymore.

"How's everyone?"

"The same—only a little less so."

"Except Liam. He's a whole new man."

Not really, I think. The good bits of Liam had been there all along, just needing to be polished so they would shine. "I hope you give yourself some credit for that, Jack. He told me what you did for him."

I can almost hear him shrug. "Liam had to save himself. What about you, Addie? Who's saving you?"

I laugh. "I'm a lost cause."

"Is it hard being around Charlie and Grace?" His voice is solemn. Same Jack, worrying about everyone else.

"No, it's kind of normal. I don't think we're quite friends yet, but we're getting there. But enough of this—you always manage to talk about everyone except yourself. How are you?"

"I've got a life now, Addie, one I think you would like. I've got someone. He's really nice." I can hear him holding his breath, waiting for my reaction.

"I'm happy for you."

"Thanks. I'm done with the half-truths now. I've got friends who have never heard of our street. I wonder, though, if I'll ever eat a meal without tasting sand in my food or stop smelling salt in the air when I'm a hundred miles from the sea."

"Or stop hearing waves on street corners. Or stop seeing gulls," I finish for him. "I wonder the same thing. I guess it's just part of us, like our skin and our hair. I tried to outrun it for a long time, but it's part of me now. And you want to know the strangest thing? The farther I ran, the worse it seemed to get. But now that I'm home, I really don't notice at all."

"So you're staying?"

"Yes." I didn't realize it is true until I said it. There are people who went, like Jack and Charlie, and people who stayed. I went as far as I could and still came back here. I would not go again.

We talk a few more moments about nothing. "Well, I should let you go."

I clasp the receiver, not wanting to let go. "Don't be a stranger."

"I won't."

"I won't let you." Tears come to my eyes, spilling over with the click on the other end of the line.

As I set down the receiver, Grace rushes into the kitchen. "Thank goodness you're here!"

Hurriedly, I dry my eyes. "What is it?"

"Charlie and Liam are trying to kill each other."

I run out the back door just in time to see Charlie, still in his bathing suit, take a swing at his brother. Liam ducks and tackles him at the waist and they both fall to the ground. As they struggle, they roll off the deck, crashing to the muddy earth beneath.

Stop it! I want to shout. But I hold back, knowing this is what they need to do.

"This had to happen," Mr. Connally murmurs, echoing my thoughts. Liam will never truly be able to let go of his guilt until he makes his peace with each of them; Charlie, who still clings to his rage, is the last and toughest person with whom Liam needs to reconcile.

"What set them off?" I ask.

"You," Grace says stiffly. "Charlie warning Liam not to hurt you." Just as he had warned me not to hurt Liam. He was trying to protect us all, even now. "Charlie's too weak for this," she frets, but I shake my head. Even with Charlie's injury, the brothers are closely matched in strength and anger. Though the struggle seems to go on endlessly, it does not get bloodier.

"Let's go inside," Mr. Connally says. We cannot see the fight from here, but only hear the soft thuds and expletives, which at last give way to heavy breathing and hoarse words.

I can stand it no longer. I step back out onto the deck and peer over the edge. The boys still lie on the ground, entangled but no longer fighting, "I'm sorry, pal." Liam's fingers are still clenched in his brother's hair. Satisfied, I return to the house.

"What happened?" Grace demands.

"They found each other," I reply, not caring whether or not she understands. I return to the kitchen to help Mrs. Connally prepare dinner.

No one mentions the incident later when we sit down to eat. The signs are there, though. Liam and Charlie, freshly showered, sport a range of cuts and bruises they had inflicted on one another.

"I love what you've done with the upstairs," Charlie says, as he passes the rolls. "When we come back at Christmas, we could add some shelves."

"You mean you aren't staying?" Sadness washes over Liam's face as he realizes the truth. Part of him had really believed that he could bring them all back permanently, to live here together as they once had. "I thought you'd stay. Even if you don't want to live at the shore, they've put up some new places that are really nice by the Navy Yard in the city."

Charlie shakes his head gently. "My future is in Washington. Grace and I have talked about it, and we're going to get a place there. But we'll visit often now. I promise." He has gone too far to ever really come back.

"What are you going to do?" Liam asks his parents.

"What do you mean?"

"I mean that this is your house." I can hear the exasperation in Liam's voice. "You don't belong in Florida like a couple of old fogeys. You belong here."

"Excuse me," Grace says, standing and clearing some plates as a pretext to leave the room.

Mr. Connally shakes his head. "It's too hard, son."

"Why? Because I'm here? I'll leave. I never really belonged here anyway."

"Is that what you think? That we don't want to be around our children?" Mrs. Connally's voice rises. "You boys are the only thing that matter."

"Not me."

"Even you, Liam. If we learned anything from what happened it is that we don't have much time. For Christ's sake . . ." I am stunned to hear her curse. "Your father had a heart attack last year."

"What?"

"Dear," Mr. Connally protests. "That's not important now."

"Not important?" Liam's nostrils flare. "Why didn't you tell me? I'm your son!" He turns to Charlie. "Did you know?" Charlie shakes his head. He would have been off training.

"We didn't want to worry you."

"I'm fine." Mr. Connally dismisses the topic with a wave of his hand. "I've given up my pipe and I'm taking care of myself. The point is we shouldn't be throwing away the time we've got."

"Exactly," Liam persists. "So move back up here."

"I don't know." Mrs. Connally dabs at her eyes. "I keep seeing him everywhere." No one has to ask whom she means. "Being here is hard."

"Being everywhere is hard," I interject then without meaning to. "Running doesn't make the pain stop. You take it with you." I can feel Charlie's eyes on me then.

There is a long pause. "She always was the smartest of us," Charlie says at last. I am grateful that Grace isn't in the room to hear him.

"Actually, Liam told me that," I reply. He clears his throat, unused to receiving the credit.

"Mom and Dad, you would be closer to me and Grace here than you are in Florida," Charlie says. "That would mean a lot to us, especially now."

"So?" Liam turns to his parents.

"Let us talk about it," his mother says. She walks to her husband and puts her hand on his arm. He looks up and blinks, as though her touch is unfamiliar. Something softens imperceptibly between them. "I think that's fair."

Grace reenters the room and Charlie's face brightens as she nears. Once I would have hated another girl making him smile. But I am glad for him now, happy about the life he has created for himself.

But something is still not right. Finally I can longer remain silent. "Why," I demand, "is no one talking about Robbie?" There is no response. "I want to tell stories and laugh. It's the closest we can get to having him with us."

My question is only met with silence.

The next morning we walk outside to the Connallys' car. I climb into the backseat. "I feel like I'm ten years old again," I remark and Liam, who has slid in beside me from the other side, pulls my hair for effect. "Hey, quit it! Liam's bothering me," I mock whine.

"Liam," Mr. Connally tries to sound stern as pulls the car from the curb. "Don't make me turn this car around." We erupt into laughter.

We fall into heavy silence as we drive away from town, following the coast south. It is a sunny morning with the feel of early fall and we might be going hiking or for a picnic. There had been very little discussion about it. "I want to go tomorrow," Mrs. Connally had stated abruptly the night before after I had brought up Robbie. It went without saying that we would all go together. Only Grace had remained at the house, grateful, I surmised, that there was not room in the car.

Mr. Connally slows and pulls to the side of the road. As I climb from the car, I stumble and Charlie instinctively puts his hand on my arm. "Sorry," he mumbles, pulling back, a faint redness coming to his cheeks. Though certain things can no longer be between us, he will always try to protect me.

The cemetery sits on a gentle slope, just off the main road. I'd imagined it any number of times, but I had not been here when he was buried, or after. We climb over a low fence and trudge upward amidst the tombstones until we reach the spot on the hill overlooking the bay. Robert Joseph Connally. Beloved son and brother. The date of his birth and death follow.

Mrs. Connally drops to her knees and begins to sob as freshly as the day they had buried him. Mr. Connally kneels beside her. We stand in silence, allowing them the moment that they need to have. My eyes are dry, no tears left to shed. From above, the seagulls call out mournfully.

I look toward the ocean. The coastline carries on for miles in either direction, unbroken. The waves are tamer now, unobtrusive and undeserving of the hate they engender in me.

A cool breeze blows through, signaling a shift. Charlie helps his mother to her feet and she buries her head in his chest. Liam stands apart. I walk to him. It is the oddest of feelings—a relationship so new with someone I have known for so long. The regrets loom once more: if I had seen him standing before me years ago, maybe he would not have spiraled out of control. Robbie might be alive today. But no, I had to go through it all and have my heart broken by

Charlie to be ready for this place. It simply could not have been otherwise. I move closer to Liam and as my fingers interlace with his, I know the choice I made was the right one.

"You did a good job," I offer to Charlie, knowing he would have picked the location when his parents were not able. "This is a nice spot."

"Yeah," he agrees. "Robbie would have hated it, though."

"The location?" I ask, surprised.

"Nah, the cemetery. He would have thought it was a waste of a perfectly good football field." We share a smile.

But Liam remains solemn. "It's not the same without you, buddy," I hear him mumble. And then it is time to go home.

Epilogue

"Quiet again," Liam observes. He and I sit alone on the beach, listening to the sounds of the gulls and crashing surf that are inescapably a part of our lives. The Connallys had flown back to Florida two days earlier to gather their belongings and move back up here.

Charlie and Grace have left, too. Yesterday Charlie had stood by the packed car. "Grace wants to get to Washington and find a place to live." And perhaps just a little bit to escape

473

Charlie's family and the weight of memories she does not own.

Charlie and Liam had hugged, patting each other hard on the back. "Come back soon, brother."

"I will."

"Be well." I kissed Grace's cheek and it was almost, though not quite, as if we were friends.

Charlie had stood before me uncertainly. "See you again, Ad."

I threw my arms around him, not caring that Grace and Liam were watching and might mind. We would have a real goodbye, like the one we had denied ourselves so many times before.

"I don't know which I prefer, the quiet or the craziness," Liam remarks now. With the others gone, our lives have returned to the simple routine we had known before, working on the house in the mornings, strolling to the beach in the afternoon. But the nights have changed: long and languid in his bed, exploring one another until we collapse, exhausted.

Earlier we had finished a meal of steamed crab legs, which Aunt Bess had never let me eat as a child. After Liam had surprised me with a small chocolate cake. "For your birthday," he said. "Even though it isn't until tomorrow." I was touched, and while I could not help but think of that birthday three years earlier when the Connallys has made me feel one of them, some part of me was glad that this time it was just the two of us.

"A letter came for you," Liam said. I took the envelope, which had been forwarded by Aunt Bess. My heart lifted as I recognized Claire's bright scrawl. She must have written just after I'd left. "Addie, I hope you are well." Her voice crackled through the writing, as though we were in her flat, playing cards. It seemed a million years ago. So much had happened since then. "I checked in on Leo for you." I smiled, picturing her among the midst of sticky-fingered children she had once professed not to like. "Teddy and I are going to the theater on Friday." I'd been avoiding the letter I needed to write to Teddy, telling him I would not be returning to London. Perhaps he already knew. Claire's letter continued, "I guess those correspondents are not so bad after all." Would Claire and Teddy at last find each other? There was a tinge of jealousy as I imagined two of the people I love most loving each other. But I wanted—really wanted—them to be happy.

I look out at the ocean. The tide is coming in, bringing the water closer with each wave. "Everyone will be back soon," I remark. "This time for good."

"Just Mom and Dad. I'm happy about that," he adds. "But Charlie's got to get back to work. I should be heading out, too."

I turn to him, surprised. "I thought you were planning to stay."

"I was, but, well, with Mom and Dad coming back, my work is done here. I came back to bring the family home and put a period at the end of it all. This is my parents' house. I'm glad I could give it back to them. But it's time to move on."

A scream builds within me. I've only just found all of this—and him. And now he is going, too. My stomach twists. Without realizing it, I had come to count on him being here.

The sense of abandonment, that I've kept buried since my mother put me on the boat, bubbles to the surface. "Where?"

"I don't know. Take the boat and head south. Why?" His question hangs like a challenge between us.

I speak slowly. "I guess I've just gotten used to our being together." In that moment, all the loose pieces of the weeks we have spent together come together and I see clearly for the first time all of the feelings that have been developing between us.

He meets my eyes squarely. "Me, too. I was thinking we could visit the Outer Banks." So his plans include me—he means for us to go together. As my shoulders slump with relief, I realize how very vested in him—and us—I've become. "It might be nice to take a trip somewhere, see a bit of this country." I nod. I have been all over

Europe but never west of here. Perhaps with someone else, it would not feel like running. "I'm not sure it matters so much, where we go. Let's hit the water and stop when we find someplace we like."

"We've got to tell your parents. They'll think we're crazy."

"We are crazy. We'll never make it."

"We're probably going to kill each other within a month."

"Probably. I'll let you win but I'll still be right."

"That's exactly what I'm talking about!" I explode with exasperation. Then I look over and see that he is joking and we both begin to laugh.

"I have to take the boxes back to Aunt Bess and help her move first," I say a moment later. She will be disappointed that I'm going, though I don't think she ever really expected me to stay.

"Do you want me to help you?"

I shake my head. The tiny house with its sparse belongings would not take long, though I suspect hidden in the drawers and closets I will find the story of a woman I never really knew. And there are some things that I still need to do for myself.

"But you'll come back," he says and there is a note of pleading to his voice. His face holds a hidden disbelief that for everything he has done, he still might be given a chance at happiness. "Come back," he repeats plaintively, his voice cracking a bit at the end.

"Of course. I promise." I am done with running. "Another thing—I think I want to go," I say and his face crumbles. "To college, I mean." I wait for his reaction. "Not just now, but soon." I need to have that for myself.

I wait for Liam to laugh or tell me it is a silly idea. Even out of high school it had never been a serious possibility. "I think," he begins, in his slow thoughtful way, "that it's a fine idea."

"Really?" My heart lifts.

"Really."

"You could come with me. Get your degree."

"Me?" He shakes his head. "Nah. I've never been much for classroom learning." He tapped his notebook. "I have what I need. I could come with you though. Get a place close by and just be, well, close." He does not use the word *married* and for that I am grateful—it had been bandied about too readily with Charlie and I am not ready to think about it again. Now it is his turn to look hopeful. "What do you think?"

"Sounds good. Something tells me when it's all over, though, we'll come back here."

"Might be a good place to have a family someday."

"You want kids?" I ask.

"Yeah." I am surprised. It had not seemed like

Liam. But watching him now, it makes perfect sense. "You?"

I had not thought about it until just then. "I think," I begin, forming the idea as I speak, "that I would like to adopt." Leo appears in my mind.

I scan the coast. "I'm not sure I'm ready to leave again."

"Maybe that's the best time to go. I never liked staying at a party or anywhere else until it stopped being fun." Panic flashes through me as though it were years ago, Liam only living for fun. It's not all going to be a party, though. How will we last?

By not making each other any promises other than this day, comes the answer from somewhere deep inside me. With Charlie, there was too much talk of tomorrows. But Liam and I are here today because we want to be. Something tells me, though, that we will make this promise over and over again each night.

I take off my shoes and walk to the water's edge. It is after season and we are alone except for an old man, searching for coins and other bits of metal some twenty meters down the beach. The dampness seeps between my toes and the sand feels more solid than it ever has.

"Are you okay?" He comes up behind me. "I know this isn't your favorite place."

"Will you do something for me?"

"Name it." I take his hand and lead him into the shallow water. He stops, surprised. "Are you sure?"

Not at all. But I nod, taking a step deeper until the water, colder now that summer is over, is nearly up to my waist. A wave rises behind us and he bends to lift me. "No, let me do it myself." As the wave crests high above, I dive beneath it, as I have seen him do so many times. Icy darkness surrounds me, as terrible as anything I'd ever dreamed and at the same time not bad at all. I find the bottom under my feet, then push for the surface, break through.

"I'm proud of you," he whispers in my ear. I do not answer, but concentrate on staying afloat, swimming with the current I had fought all of these years. In the distance I can almost see a young boy, dancing atop the waves. But Liam stands next to me now, supporting me but letting me do it on my own, and I feel strong in a way I never quite have before.

Only then do I allow myself to be lifted into his arms.

Acknowledgments

More than twenty years ago, when I first began writing in earnest, I conceived of a story in which a lonely young girl became close to the family of four boys next door. Perhaps influenced by Louisa May Alcott's *Little Women*, I was fascinated in my own work by the young girl who would become Adelia, her relationships with each of the Connally boys and the dynamic between the brothers themselves.

In developing *The Last Summer at Chelsea Beach*, I was thrilled to be able to return after so many years to the ideas and pages I'd begun years earlier. It enabled me to explore many of my favorite themes: first crushes, unrequited love, missed connections, fateful meetings, redemption and second chances.

I quickly realized that the story belonged in America during the Second World War. This period and setting provided such a rich canvas to explore life and hardship on the home front. I was curious, too, to explore the interplay between different ethnic, religious and social groups during a time when we were supposed to be united in war, but in reality were quite stratified. Although I've written a number of books set during World War II, this was my first novel set predominantly in the United States. I enjoyed the challenge of imagining places so geographically close to my childhood a generation ago. The book also allowed me to return to one of my most beloved places on earth, England. I've endeavored to be as accurate to the time and place as possible, but the mistakes are all mine. All of the characters are fictitious (I have fictionalized Churchill's niece in her entirety), and resemblances to real-life people are purely coincidental.

There are so many people to whom I am indebted in my writing career. Over the past few years, I have come to appreciate more than ever the community of writers, bloggers and readers that all join together for the love of the book. There are too many to name individually, but I'm so grateful to my fellow authors at MIRA Books, to my sisters from the anthology *Grand Central: Original Stories of Postwar Love and Reunion*, to my fellow authors in the Tall Poppy Writers, and to myriad bestselling authors, who are so generous with their mentoring and support.

Then there are the pros, and I am so fortunate for them and the ways they make my work exponentially better. Gratitude to the brilliant Susan Swinwood and our partnership, which keeps getting better with age; to Erika Imranyi and our partnership, which is just beginning, Emer Flounders and the entire team at MIRA

Books, as well as Sammia Hamer, Sally Williamson and the entire team at MIRA UK. Deepest appreciation to Scott Hoffman and Susan Ginsburg, as well.

Finally, there is the village: my husband, Phillip, and the three muses; my mom and my brother; my colleagues at Rutgers Law; and countless other friends and family members. Without you, none of this would be possible—or worthwhile.

Questions for Discussion

1. The sense of place plays a very important role in *The Last Summer at Chelsea Beach*. Which setting did you find the most evocative?

2. Siblings often fall into distinct roles within a family. Did the relationships between the Connally brothers remind you of your own siblings, or families you've known?

3. Addie's choices altered her life very drastically. Have you ever lamented a path that you might have taken but didn't?

4. It seems at some points in the book that Charlie and Addie are fated to be together, but at others they seem star-crossed. Do you believe in destiny and meant-to-be, or is love a matter of free will?

5. Addie was rather an independent woman without many close female friendships. Why do you think that is? What was it that drew her and Claire Churchill together?

6. Did any details in the story differ from your perception of life on the home front during the Second World War? What surprised you?

7. What do you think it was that Addie really wanted out of life, and did she succeed in getting it? What did she have to sacrifice or compromise?

8. Which of the men in the book would you have chosen for Addie (or none of them)? What is it about Addie's upbringing and circumstances that influenced her romantic decisions?

9. How do you feel about who Addie ends up with at the end of the book? How do you think Addie and Liam fare after the end of the book?

Center Point Large Print
600 Brooks Road / PO Box 1
Thorndike, ME 04986-0001 USA

(207) 568-3717

US & Canada:
1 800 929-9108
www.centerpointlargeprint.com

9/15

DATE DUE

OCT 05 2015			
DEC 31 2015			
4/11/16			
MAY 03 2016			
AUG 20 2019			
JUL 01 2021			
Barrett Hous			
4-5-24			
2-10-21			
1-12-23			
7-20-23			
			PRINTED IN U.S.A.